Praise for the Novels of Connie Brockway

So Enchanting

"Exceptionally entertaining characters, a wildly original plot that cleverly spoofs the spiritualist craze of the late Victorian era, and deliciously humorous writing give *So Enchanting* its bewitchingly irresistible charm."
—*Chicago Tribune*

"Although her contemporary romances are delightful, Brockway here delivers a historical that will make her fans rejoice." —*Library Journal*

"Two perfectly matched protagonists engage in a sexy and entertaining battle of wits and wiles as RITA Award–winning Brockway triumphantly returns to historical romance. With its expertly detailed Victorian setting, deliciously clever writing, and captivating plot, this wicked romance will cast a bewitching spell."
—*Booklist*

Skinny Dipping

"Realistically quirky characters, delightfully clever writing, and a warmly nourishing story about family, friendship, and love come together brilliantly in *Skinny Dipping*, Connie Brockway's latest beguiling tale of a woman who discovers life is all about commitment."
—*Chicago Tribune*

"Spiked with her addictively acerbic wit, Brockway's latest beguiling blend of women's fiction and romance . . . unfolds into a richly nourishing tale of family, friendship, love, and laughter." —*Booklist*

"Bittersweet and touching . . . [a] most satisfying tale."
—*Romantic Times*

continued . . .

"Just right for a long winter day." —*Minnesota Monthly*

"A witty, warmhearted novel that will keep the reader laughing. This hilarious, mysterious, and romantic book is a keeper." —Romance Junkies

"An exquisitely rendered setting, an abundance of complex family dynamics, a story that explores what it means to belong, and a beautifully developed romantic relationship guarantee the appeal of this well-crafted tale for both romance and women's fiction fans alike." —*Library Journal*

Hot Dish

"Rapier wit and dazzling prose. . . . Brockway writes sheer magic." —Elizabeth Bevarly

"A dazzling contemporary debut!" —Christina Dodd

"A hilarious, bittersweet look at going home." —Eloisa James

"Wry, witty, and wonderful! This cast of unforgettable characters will tickle your funny bone and your heartstrings." —Teresa Medeiros

"This combination caper and comedy-of-errors story is just wacky enough to keep you giggling. Brava!" —*Romantic Times*

"A smart and funny page-turner." —All About Romance

"Splendidly satisfying. With its surfeit of realistically quirky characters and sharp wit, *Hot Dish* is simply superb." —*Booklist*

ALSO BY CONNIE BROCKWAY

Hot Dish
Skinny Dipping
So Enchanting

The Golden Season

CONNIE BROCKWAY

AN ONYX BOOK

ONYX
Published by New American Library, a division of
Penguin Group (USA) Inc., 375 Hudson Street,
New York, New York 10014, USA
Penguin Group (Canada), 90 Eglinton Avenue East, Suite 700, Toronto,
Ontario M4P 2Y3, Canada (a division of Pearson Penguin Canada Inc.)
Penguin Books Ltd., 80 Strand, London WC2R 0RL, England
Penguin Ireland, 25 St. Stephen's Green, Dublin 2,
Ireland (a division of Penguin Books Ltd.)
Penguin Group (Australia), 250 Camberwell Road, Camberwell, Victoria 3124,
Australia (a division of Pearson Australia Group Pty. Ltd.)
Penguin Books India Pvt. Ltd., 11 Community Centre, Panchsheel Park,
New Delhi - 110 017, India
Penguin Group (NZ), 67 Apollo Drive, Rosedale, North Shore 0632,
New Zealand (a division of Pearson New Zealand Ltd.)
Penguin Books (South Africa) (Pty.) Ltd., 24 Sturdee Avenue,
Rosebank, Johannesburg 2196, South Africa

Penguin Books Ltd., Registered Offices:
80 Strand, London WC2R 0RL, England

First published by Onyx, an imprint of New American Library,
a division of Penguin Group (USA) Inc.

First Printing, February 2010
10 9 8 7 6 5 4 3 2 1

For Lilah,
whom I loved before I met

Chapter One

March 1816

"You had best look over these papers, Lady Lydia," said Robert Terwilliger, senior partner of the Royal Bank of London, to the exquisitely beautiful woman sitting across the desk from him. The beauty reluctantly accepted the sheaf of papers he held out and began reading, allowing Terwilliger the opportunity to study her.

At twenty-four, when most young ladies would have been considered on the shelf, Lady Lydia Eastlake showed no signs of relinquishing her place not only as one of the *ton*'s most notable nonpareil but *the* nonpareil.

Even Terwilliger, no follower of fashion—his three grown daughters' attempts to educate him notwitstanding—could appreciate Lydia Eastlake's dash. Ecru-fluted silk trimmed the emerald green pelisse covering her elegant and well-curved figure, while her shimmering burnt-caramel-colored curls peeked out from beneath a spring bonnet bedecked with feathers, fronds, and flowers. The glossy locks framed a face noted for the perfect proportion of her small, angular jaw, straight nose, arched dark brows, and high cheekbones.

And then there were the eyes: long, dark lashed, and exotically tilted, they were a color so vividly, deeply blue that they appeared purple. Strong men, it was said, could lose themselves in the thrall of her eyes.

Robert Terwilliger was not a strong man. And it would take a very strong man indeed to rein in the likes of Lady Lydia Eastlake. She was a headstrong, self-indulgent voluptuary, but also absolutely captivating, utterly charming, and infectiously merry. But worse, she was completely independent.

Since she'd come of age three years ago, Lady Lydia had not been under any single man's supervision as daughter, sister, niece, wife, widow, or ward.

Terwilliger hadn't known her parents personally, having inherited the position as her personal banker, but he'd heard of them. Their affair had been for a short while notorious.

His older brother's death had left Ronald Eastlake heir to an enormous fortune that had its basis in the noble family's many ancestral land holdings and had been expanded by his brother's willingness to invest in trade—literally. The Eastlakes owned a shipping empire. It had also left his brother's widow, Julia, free to marry.

That the pair had been in love for some time was obvious, for no sooner was the mourning period ended than Eastlake convinced Julia to elope with him to France because no clergy in the country had been willing to marry them. They'd cited "affinity"—the old biblical edict against marrying one's brother's widow—as a reason.

Luckily, the French clergy was not so traditional.

Once wed, because of the enormous fortune involved,

and because anyone might bring a suit to have the marriage annulled on the grounds of affinity against them, they decided never to return to England and put their marriage at risk. Their resolve to uphold this decision was strengthened by the birth of their daughter less than a year later.

By all reports—and there were many—exile suited them very well. The Eastlakes were renowned in international circles for their glamorous, globe-trotting lifestyle, their recklessness and their laissez-faire attitudes. They'd taken Lydia with them everywhere they went. The courts of Europe had been her playgrounds, the far reaches of the English empire her backyard.

Famous, sought after, rich, and in love they might have been, but to Terwilliger's mind none of that excused their neglect of their child's future. The notion that they might not always be young and vibrant and alive apparently never occurred to them, for they'd neglected to make provisions for the care of their only child should something happen to them. Which it had, in the form of a fatal carriage accident.

Thus their deaths had left Lady Lydia at fourteen the heir to one of England's largest unentailed estates, meaning the property was hers alone to do with as she wished and did not need to be preserved to be passed on to another generation. Having no kin, she'd become a ward of the crown and the Prince Regent had named as her guardian one of his own cousins, an elderly, fiscally responsible but physically unavailable cousin of the old king, a Sir Grimley. Poor lass had gone from being the pet of a dozen European courts to being the only child in Sir Grimley's Sussex house with only paid caretakers for companions.

Then, when Lydia had turned sixteen, her godmother and mother's childhood friend, Eleanor, the widowed Duchess of Grenville, had taken the budding beauty under her wing and presented her at court. To this day the two women remained fast friends, despite the fact that as soon as Lydia reached her majority and inherited her wealth, she'd flown free of what few constraints the duchess had imposed upon her and become reliant only on her own whim. That surely was the only counsel she'd ever seen her parents heed. Still, as a sop to convention, she had engaged a Mrs. Cod as her companion.

Terwilliger glanced at the woman who was seated even now at Lady Lydia's side, a small dumpling of a female with frizzy rufous hair and a habit of popping her chin in and out that gave her an uncanny resemblance to a spruce grouse.

Soon after reaching her twenty-first birthday, Lydia had begun introducing Emily Cod as her chaperone and companion, claiming the older woman was a widowed second cousin. Rumor had it Lady Lydia had plucked Mrs. Cod out of the madhouse to fulfill the position rather than submit to a more suitable—and less lenient—chaperone.

Certainly, Emily Cod was suspiciously well suited to play doyenne to a high-spirited and independent girl. She was amiable, uncritical, and had the laudable (at least, from a debutante's viewpoint) ability to fall comfortably asleep while sitting upright. She also had an unnerving propensity for "collecting" things from the homes they visited, an open secret amongst the *ton* that had given rise to the Bedlam rumor.

"What exactly are all these numbers to tell me, Mr.

Terwilliger?" Lady Lydia abruptly asked, looking up from the papers on her lap.

"Ah, well . . ."

She noted the direction of his gaze and gave an elegant wave of her gloved hand. "There is nothing you can say to me that you cannot say in front of Emily, Mr. Terwilliger. She owns far more of my secrets than you."

"Very well, then, Lady Lydia." He took a deep breath and exhaled. "You are bankrupt."

She gave a start, then broke into charming laughter. "I just *knew* you had a sense of humor, Terwilliger. I confess, I had about given up hope of ever seeing it, but I *knew* it was there."

He stared at her, confounded. "But . . . I *have* no comedic bent, Lady Lydia," he stammered. "I am quite serious. You *are* bankrupt."

Rather than reply, Lady Lydia blithely reached over and plucked a paperweight from Emily Cod's lap. Terwilliger hadn't even noted when the older woman had picked it up. Mrs. Cod smiled apologetically.

"And this is why you insisted I cancel my luncheon appointment to meet here at your offices? Could this not have waited?" Lady Lydia asked.

He peered at her closely, trying to gauge whether she understood the full meaning of his words. She had never had a head for numbers, but she was no fool, either. Should she have wished, he had no doubt she could have understood her finances. So he could only surmise she had no wish to do so. And why should she? It had always seemed her funds would be inexhaustible.

He remembered their original meeting three years ago, when she'd come into her seemingly limitless inheritance and he'd been assigned her accounts. She had been twenty-one, a pretty, immensely wealthy orphan. From a banking perspective it had *not* been a successful union. He knew he had mismanaged her wealth. But so, too, had most bankers and stockbrokers mismanaged everything during the wretched economy of the time. No, he was not entirely to blame himself. The stock markets had been abysmal, land prices were falling and food costs rising; it was three years of inflation and recession. And she *was* profligate. Ridiculously, ruinously so.

"Let me try to explain another way, my lady. Your assets are gone. You are poor."

"Poor?" Lady Lydia repeated, tasting the word as though it were some exotic, and not altogether pleasant, flavor. "What do you mean by 'poor'?"

"Poor, as in one who has no money. As in, you *owe* more than you *own*." He tapped the thick stack of bills on the desk before him.

The celebrated violet eyes abruptly lit with amused comprehension. "Ah, I see. This is about the barouche."

Again, the heart-stopping smile appeared and Terwilliger steeled himself against her charms, knowing his will alone was an inadequate defense. His duty here was clear. She must leave his offices with no doubt about the direness of her situation. He had allowed her to sally about in blissful ignorance too long.

"I swear I could not help myself," she pouted prettily. "It has yellow wheels, Mr. Terwilliger. *Jonquil* yellow."

"It is not simply the barouche, Lady Lydia," he said. "Your funds have been completely exhausted."

She frowned, looking a bit perplexed that her pout

had not achieved the desired effect of having him recant his words. "Just how exhausted?"

"Aside from the new yacht and barouche, in the last three months you purchased six paintings and a pianoforte for some musician—"

"He's a talented composer and he needed a pianoforte."

"There is always a composer or an artist or furniture maker or someone who needs something that you are always too ready to give," Terwilliger said in exasperation.

It was one of the reasons one cared so much whether Lady Lydia's spendthrift ways led to her ruin; though madly profligate, wildly impulsive, and supremely spoiled, she was also ruinously generous and marvelously appreciative. She was the consummate bon vivant. Her delight in the most negligible flower was as great as it was for the grandest of academy paintings and just as sincere. One lived more in the company of Lady Lydia. Saw more. Felt more.

He pressed on. "In the last three years, you landscaped the Devon property, all eight hundred acres of it, made sizable contributions to various soldiers' aid societies, widows' and orphans' societies, and"—he consulted a piece of paper set apart from the others—"single-handedly funded an exploration to North Africa by the Royal Society of Atlantis." He looked up, hoping she would deny this last allegation. She didn't.

"They showed me some extremely convincing evidence that points to the site of the fabled lost continent," she said primly. "Pray, continue."

"And need I mention the full staffs kept at three

separate houses, the horses, gowns, bonnets, jewelry, the weekly salon you host, the parties and balls—"

"No," Lady Lydia cut in smoothly. "You needn't. But you misunderstand me, Terwilliger. I do not want to know how I exhausted my funds, as you so picturesquely put it, but how exhausted my funds are."

At this, Terwilliger made an exasperated sound. "They have expired."

She scrutinized him closely and seeing no wavering said, "I will sell the Derbyshire farm."

"It's already been sold."

She frowned. "It has? When?"

"Three months ago. I wrote you and asked you how you intended to fund the Atlantis expedition and you wrote back saying I should sell whatever was necessary. I did so. I sent you the contracts by messenger and you signed them."

"Oh. Yes. I recall. But surely there's something left from that sale?"

He shook his head.

"Sell one of the houses."

"They are all on the market and no one has made an offer and I doubt anyone will. There are few people these days looking to purchase properties without acreage."

"The coal mine, then," she said decisively. "I have never liked owning—"

"It is no longer producing."

"All right," she said in the tone of one capitulating to an unreasonable request. "Sell some stocks."

He shifted uncomfortably. "Since the war ended, the stock market has collapsed. I have tried to be prudent, but I have failed you here. Your stocks currently have no appreciable value."

Now, finally, he'd breached the wall that wealth and entitlement had built around her. Her smile wavered.

"Tell Honeycutt to sell my shares of Indian Trade fleet," she said, naming the man who oversaw the shipping venture that to the greatest part had financed the Eastlake empire.

Terwilliger stared at her.

"Well?"

"But . . ." he stammered, flummoxed. "There is no fleet."

She frowned. "Of course there's a fleet. At last word, they were preparing to return from India fully laden."

"Two weeks ago, all five ships were captured by pirates off the east coast of Africa."

"What?"

"I wrote you about this. Twice. I sent word seeking an interview, but you—"

"The crews!" she interrupted, blanching.

"Your shipping company had just enough available capital to pay the ransom demanded," he hastily assured her, and she drew a relieved breath. "No lives were lost. But the ships and their cargo are gone. I wish you had read my letters," he finished fretfully.

"So do I," she murmured. "I would never have purchased that barouche."

He watched her, miserable, and told himself he had done his best, that he could only offer advice, which Lady Lydia oft ignored, and while he was willing to admit that his advice had been bad of late, every one of the financiers and bankers and investors he knew had been just as culpable in their failure to predict the country's current financial predicament.

In great part, her situation was of her own making. Then why did he feel terrible? He hadn't captained the fleet, spent the money, or ruined the stock market.

He felt terrible because he sincerely liked Lady Lydia. She was a flame, a life force who burned brilliantly, fascinated, warmed and, yes, was possibly destructive, but still one would hate to see a fire such as hers extinguished.

"I see," Lady Lydia finally murmured. "What can I do?"

No good would come of equivocating. "Your property, both real and intangible, is gone. When liquidated, your personal assets may pay off those debts you have incurred and leave you enough so that, if carefully managed, you might live adequately."

"Adequately? That sounds encouraging," she said, brightening. "What exactly does that mean?"

"I estimate two hundred fifty pounds a year. Enough for a small town house, a maid, and a cook. Perhaps a butler."

"Dear God," she breathed, collapsing back in her chair. "I am destitute."

She meant it and he conceded that in her world, the only one she'd ever known, the uppermost strata of the *ton*, she might as well be. Her life as hitherto known was no more. Even in Sir Grimley's house she'd lived like a small princess, surrounded by every conceivable comfort and luxury.

"And Emily, too?"

"I'm afraid not. Perhaps she can return to wherever

you found her," Terwilliger suggested, smiling apologetically at Emily Cod.

She blinked at him, her fingers twitching in her lap.

"Good Lord, Terwilliger, you make it sound as if I overturned a rock one day and there she was. I didn't and she can't." There was finality in her voice, a hint of the iron will few would warrant as belonging to the laughing Society beauty. Beside her, Emily Cod relaxed, her fluttering fingers stilled.

"Then there will be no butler," he said.

Lady Lydia considered this edict a moment before saying, "I do not think I can live like that."

He didn't, either. Still he said, "Many people make do without a butler."

"No," she said, shaking her head. "I'm sorry. I can't be poor. Too many people depend on me. Craftsmen and merchants, artisans and wine brokers, tradesmen and such other businesses."

This was doing it a bit brown. "They *do* have other clients," he said.

She frowned, more annoyed than offended. "I do not think you properly appreciate my position, Terwilliger. I am not just another member of the *ton*. I am"—she cast about for the appropriate word—"I am an industry."

Was she twitting him? She'd always had an odd sense of humor.

"Terwilliger," she said with a touch of exasperation, "I dine at an establishment and its reputation is made. I import a certain varietal wine for a dinner party and within a week the vintner has orders for the next five years and the vineyard where the wine comes from is secure for a decade. I wear a perfume and not only is that fragrance's popularity guaranteed, but the perfumery's, too. The same can be said of the mill that produces the silk for my gowns, the musician I hire for an afternoon salon, the composer I employ to write a new sonata, the cheese makers whose products appear on my sideboard, the milliner and horse breeder and the cabinetmaker and the carpet weavers . . ." She trailed off, studying him to gauge whether he understood.

He recognized in surprise that she was right and once again was visited by the uncomfortable notion that behind all her frivolity, Lady Lydia understood very well the world in which she lived. She *was* an industry. True, the *ton* was filled with fashion makers, but no one save Beau Brummell had captivated the public imagination like Lady Lydia Eastlake. She drew crowds wherever she went. People stood in line outside the shops she frequented and lined Rotten Row each afternoon hoping to get a glimpse of her riding past in her barouche.

It wasn't just that she was pretty or witty; there were plenty of pretty, witty women in the *ton*. It wasn't just her extravagant lifestyle. It was that she was all these things *and* independent. And happily, successfully so, for all appearances. Small wonder she fascinated Society both high and low. Her like was as exotic and rare as mermaids.

"Well, Terwilliger?"

"The only counsel I can give is that you find a *very* wealthy husband."

"You mean *marry*?" She sounded as though he'd just suggested she sell flowers in Covent Garden.

He nodded. "As you should have done years ago. You should have wed your fortune to another of equal stature and yourself to a man devoted to the concept of economy. A temperate, conscientious, careful fellow with an impeccable pedigree who could have multiplied your net value while still allotting you a generous allowance."

"An allowance. Someone to portion out to me that which is already mine." She gave a delicate shudder. "But, yes, I suppose I might have to consider marrying," she finished.

"Surely things have not come to that?" Emily cried softly.

"I'm afraid so, Emily." Lady Lydia nodded. "We must face facts and the fact seems clear: I must wed," she finished in sepulchral tones.

Easier said than done, Terwilliger thought unhappily.

"What is it now, Terwilliger?" Lady Lydia demanded, seeing his glum expression. "Has the earth opened up and swallowed my town house?"

"May I speak frankly?" he asked, certain he was about to overstep himself. But he had three daughters, all of whom he'd successfully married off, and he was confident he knew something about matchmaking. Even though he did not belong to the exalted ranks to which Lady Lydia did, he surmised that when all was said and done the concerns and requirements of the *ton's* bachelors were simply amplifications of those from his own strata. But most of all he felt compelled to offer advice because he felt partially responsible for her current predicament.

"By all means."

"Lady Lydia, for years you have been turning down marriage proposals from the finest and wealthiest gentlemen of the *ton*. I do not think of an eligible bachelor who would risk humiliation by tendering a second offer."

"I am sure there exist a few men who have not yet proposed marriage to me." Her tone was dry.

"True," Terwilliger said slowly, "but given the quality of those whom you've already turned down, I doubt someone with a lesser pedigree would think he would receive a different answer than his betters. You are famously unattainable, I am afraid."

"You don't think anyone will offer for me?" The idea clearly startled her.

He cleared his throat, trying to find the line between candidness and delicacy. "I think that the men who would suit your particular requirements are just as famously proud as you. Once it is known that you are in financial straits, the reason for your accessibility will be evident."

"But everyone marries to better their situation," she said. "Either financially or socially. I may not bring wealth to the union, but I still have an ancient and honorable name."

"Very true," he said. "But the manner in which you have deported yourself these last years has given the polite world reason to believe that you consider yourself above dynastic politics. You have made a reputation as someone who need only please herself and does not concern herself with the choices of others."

"And so I am. Or rather, have been," she corrected herself.

"Exactly. *Have been*," he said. "There are those who will take malicious delight in the necessity that drives your marital ambitions. Including former suitors and rivals." He sought for some nicer way to phrase the next, but in the end, Terwilliger proved himself a banker. "They might seek to decrease your value in the eyes of potential suitors."

Such smallness not only repelled her but fascinated her. "In what way could they do this?"

"By mocking your past refusal to marry as pretentious and suggesting that you are desperate."

"I am."

"Such ruthless honesty. Few men would want their future wife to be the subject of their friends' derision or consider themselves the only choice left to a desperate woman."

She inhaled at the ugly words. "No. I can see that they would not."

"Don't misunderstand me, Lady Lydia," he hurried on. "I have no doubt you will entertain many offers once it is known you are interested in matrimony, but those gentlemen who come up to scratch might not be of the sort you could have chosen had you done the responsible thing and married years ago."

"And just what sort of gentlemen do you imagine now will be paying me court?"

"Well," he said, picking his way carefully. "I would expect them to be either men who would be happy with the name and cachet you bring to the union or men who feel the press of time in which to produce heirs."

"I see," she said. "In other words, social climbers who will not care that I am desperate or old men as desperate as I."

"In the greater part," he admitted uncomfortably.

"I'm afraid that won't do," she said.

"No. It won't do," Mrs. Cod inserted, head bobbing in agreement.

"What do you mean?" he asked.

"I refuse to marry a mushroom for the manure from which he's sprung. Nor shall I marry an old man to be his broodmare."

"I don't think things are quite so grim as that. Doubtless there are healthy young heirs to lesser fortunes who will be thrilled should you show them some encouragement."

"How much of a lesser fortune do you suggest I must consider?"

He would not lie. In the upper echelons of Lady Lydia's world, marriages were contracted to bolster foundering empires or grow them. It was a rare case for two people to wed for other reasons. "Substantially less."

"That won't do, either. If I must marry, I expect at the very least to continue on in a situation akin to the one I now enjoy."

He had no idea how to respond. She sounded as though she thought she had a choice.

"Who knows the extent to which I am in debt?" she asked.

Terwilliger lifted a hand. "It is generally assumed that everyone in Society is in debt. It isn't as if you had lost a fortune gaming in one evening. You do not have any single outstanding debt. You have dispersed your fortune over a large field, Lady Lydia. Deeply and widely."

"And enjoyed every moment of it, Terwilliger," she said with another smile. "How many are privy to the information about the fleet?"

"None as yet. Once it gets out, there will be nasty financial repercussions for all involved, including this bank. I shall, of course, remain discreet, but the rumor mill will begin to turn soon enough."

"When do you expect the crew to return?"

"Well, we have to send ships for them and then return them here. The journey around the cape is a long one. I should say three to four months."

She thought a minute. "I need this Season, Mr. Terwilliger, the entire Season without being hobbled by suggestions that I am in desperate straits."

"Why is that?"

She rose to her feet. "Because before my future husband learns of my poverty he must be so convinced that I am his perfect mate, the news will cause him nothing more than slight disappointment."

He gazed at her in bemusement. "And who is this future husband?"

"Good heavens, Terwilliger," she said, motioning for Emily Cod to rise, too. "I will only know that after I have met him."

Chapter Two

At the same time, one hundred and twenty-three miles northeast of London on the Norwich coast near the small town of Cromer, a similar meeting was taking place at Josten Hall.

Captain Ned Lockton, recently retired from His Majesty's naval service at the age of twenty-eight, sat in the library of his ancestral home facing his family: his brother, Marcus Lockton, the Earl of Josten; Nadine, the earl's wife; and his widowed sister, Mrs. Beatrice Hickston-Tubbs. Also in attendance were two eighteen-year-old, sullen-looking Pinks of the *ton* whose resemblance declared them kin: Josten and Nadine's son and heir, Harry, and Beatrice's Phillip, fondly known as Pip to the family. Though no one was feeling very fond of either young man at the moment. The rest of the children, Beatrice's twenty-year-old daughter, Mary, and Josten's fifteen-year-old twin boys, being unimplicated in the current crisis, had elected not to attend the family meeting, already showing more sense than both boys combined.

Beatrice regarded her tall, redheaded son worriedly, then glanced with similar concern at Harry, who was blond and elegant. They were such handsome, angelic-looking lads. How could simple high spirits have led to such a pass?

Because Lockton men were passionate and proud and, mayhap, a bit overly confident.

Now she glanced at her brother Ned, two decades her and Josten's junior. Luckily, he had been the family changeling, born without any of the famous Lockton passion or conceit. Lucky for them, too, for if he had any of those family traits, he would never fall in with their plans for him.

"There is nothing else for it. You shall have to find an heiress and wed her as soon as possible," Josten said to Ned in his most commanding voice, which was impressive, indeed.

Unless, that is, one happened to be Captain Ned Lockton, who did not look the least bit awed. Not, unfortunately, because Ned owned any of the cool, imperious unflappability of, say, a Beau Brummell or Lord Alvanley. No, thought Beatrice, Ned simply looked genially oblivious. His handsome face held not a whit of annoyance or affront. He seemed much more interested in the apple he was peeling than the conversation.

"Do you hear me, Ned?" the earl asked, his ruddy, equally handsome face set into the stern lines of a born patriarch.

A smile curved Ned's well-molded lips, briefly scoring his lean, tanned cheek with the dimple. It was a very nice dimple, Beatrice thought with more relief than approval, one that would soon hopefully play havoc with the ladies' hearts. Having popped off to join the navy fourteen years ago, he'd never had the opportunity to take his rightful place as one of the *ton*'s most eligible bachelors. Instead, taking his godfather Admiral Lord Nelson's advice, Ned had joined the navy rather than have purchased a commission. It still annoyed Beatrice.

If a fellow must indulge his patriotic fervor he might as well look good doing it, in a lovely red coat and scarlet sash. Naval officers didn't even get to wear their uniforms ashore. In Beatrice's opinion, a terrible mistake on the part of the admiralty. Ned would be downright dashing in uniform.

Beatrice studied her younger sibling critically. She wasn't as familiar with him as one might guess a sister should be. He'd been home only a week, and in the preceding years she'd seen him but a handful of times, on those occasions when he'd been home awaiting a new assignment. And, to be honest, at those times she hadn't paid much attention to his looks. All Lockton men were ridiculously good-looking. She took it for granted. But now she was gratified to see that a hot Barbary sun had only burnished his tousled locks to a brighter gold and rather than scalding his complexion permanently red, the sun had left him tanned. Not stylish perhaps, but better than boiled.

Thank God, Ned's face had been spared in naval battle. He would not be nearly so useful in solving the current unpleasantness without his breathtaking masculine beauty. A shadow caught in the cleft of a manly chin and a thicket of dark lashes obscured the clear blue-gray eyes lowered on the apple in his hand. His nose was Romanesque, his brow clear, and his physique that of a young Adonis.

It would have been better, of course, if his Olympian

beauty had been married to Olympian forcefulness, like Marcus's. Young ladies did so like a forceful man. How affable, accommodating Ned had ever managed to captain a ship full of ruffians was a matter of open debate. Still, Beatrice had noted the attention he'd already garnered from the ladies of Cromer. Hopefully, London ladies would be equally impressed. They had to be.

"There's no other way to do it," she muttered.

Ned glanced up. "No other way to what, Bea?"

"To restore the family fortune!" Josten roared. "What do you think we've been talking about? Did I not make clear that we are in dire financial circumstances? I should think the necessity of your finding a rich bride would be self-evident."

"Don't mean to be so thick-witted, but . . . my last visit home the family fortunes seemed secure. What happened to them?"

"Oh, what *didn't* happen to them, Neddie?" Nadine cried, waving her lace kerchief about. Her fair ringlets bobbed around a face still as pretty as it had been when she and Marcus had wed. "The investments failed, the Corn Laws are making it impossible for the farms to profit, the children stand in dire need of things—"

"What sorts of things?" Ned broke in, glancing with interest at his nephews. They slouched lower in their seats. They were under strict orders not to speak, which, as both of them were notably voluble, would normally have presented them a challenge. But under their uncle's mildly inquisitive gaze, they seemed to maintain their silence without much difficulty after all. Odd.

"Oh, you know," Nadine said, her gaze shifting away. "Things young people need."

Bright spots of color appeared on Nadine's round, soft cheeks. Ned regarded her mildly.

"Such as . . . ?" he prompted.

"Oh, for God's sake, Ned," Josten said irritably. "The essential point is that we haven't the proverbial pot to piss in. Does it really make any difference how we came to such a pass?"

"Well, since I'm the one whom you have asked to marry an heiress to recoup the lost fortune, I don't mind admitting that I should like to know."

There was nothing accusatory in Ned's voice, and his posture was as relaxed as ever. Nonetheless, Nadine blanched and her eyes welled with tears. "You are being horrid, Neddie."

"Am I?" Ned asked. "Forgive me. That wasn't my intent. I'm simply curious as to where the pot we are all used to piss in has gone."

Despite the severity of the situation, Beatrice could not suppress a chuckle. Ned could not know how droll that sounded because Ned wasn't droll. Or at least he never had been before. Lockton men were known for their beauty and forcefulness, not their *bon mots*. Josten shot her a reproachful glare. She stopped chuckling, reminding herself that these were serious matters.

"You are acting in a most self-centered fashion, Ned. War has ruined you. You used to be such a sweet boy." Nadine sniffed. "I would have thought your tenure as an officer would have invested you with a sense of duty and dedication. Your family is in dire circumstances, the earl's heirs have seen their legacy whittled down to nothing, poor Beatrice's Pip might be forced to give up his clubs." She shuddered gently. "And her Mary could well end up having to marry into trade."

"Oh, surely things aren't that bad!" Beatrice spoke up, unwilling to allow so grim a forecast for her daughter to go unchallenged.

Nadine ignored her. "And you are the only person who can put it to right and yet you refuse! Oh!" She covered her face with her hands and commenced sobbing.

"Did I refuse? I don't recall refusing." Ned frowned in an expression of intense concentration. At times like this Beatrice wondered if the leg wound that had resulted in his retirement had somehow left him dickered in the nob. Unless, and this thought was vastly more uncomfortable, he was simply gammoning them.

Could Ned have grown ironical? It seemed unlikely. Where and when would he have developed such a trait? Certainly she didn't remember him as such. He'd been a pleasant lad, so much younger than the rest of them and given to rumination. Indeed, to her memory the only impulsive thing he had ever done was hying himself off to join the navy.

Perhaps she didn't remember him all that well? She'd been married by the time he'd made his unexpected arrival in the world. Still, there had been years when they'd all lived together after their father's death had left Marcus the earl and her own husband's demise had left her an impecunious widow with two children. Marcus had insisted she and her children return to Josten Hall.

She vaguely recalled Ned as a sweet, self-contained boy—something of a changeling in a family notable for their passionate excesses. She also recalled that as a youngster it had often—perhaps always—been Ned one counted on to remain calm during innumerable family dramas. Calm but not ironical. One would think one would remember if one's brother had an ironical bent.

"You'll do it, then?" Nadine was asking, peeking at Ned through her fingers. Her eyes, Beatrice noticed, were dry. "Find a rich bride?"

"Well, there is still the matter of why it's necessary for me to do so. Not that I won't," he added hurriedly as Nadine's now fully revealed lower lip began to tremble, "but I cannot help but be overcome with curiosity."

He finished and then waited, smiling expectantly first at Nadine, then Beatrice, and finally Marcus. None of them could hold that guileless gaze for long.

"Gaming!" Josten finally burst out. "If you must know. It was lost gaming."

"Ah." Ned nodded. "I'm sorry, Marcus—"

"It weren't me," Josten denied hotly. "Not much, anyway. It was Bea's eldest, Pip, and—"

"And your Harry," Beatrice said, leaping to her son's defense.

"Good Lord," Ned murmured. "I hadn't realized gaming was a team effort."

"Don't be ridiculous," Josten said, his face red with ire and, though he would die rather than admit it, embarrassment. "They weren't playin' together. Mostly. And it weren't as though they ran us into dun territory in a night or even a fortnight without any help from other corners. It took them a good year to ruin us."

"Ah. How gratifying that the next generation has shown such self-restraint," Ned said, once more turning his attention to his nephews.

Pip, his face nearly as red as his hair, was picking at

his nail while Harry flipped determinedly the pages of *La Belle Assemblée*.

"And a good thing, too," Marcus said. "Because it will allow you time to court some rich girl before the rest of Society realizes we haven't sixpence to scratch. Harry assures me no one's added up parts to tally the whole yet or he would have been, er . . ."

"Shown the door?" Ned suggested.

"They wouldn't dare!" Josten thundered.

"And all these debts just crept up, did they?"

"Well, yes, Neddie," Nadine said. "This will be darling Mary's fourth Season and so it was essential that she have a new wardrobe to keep the shine on the bloom a mite longer."

Nadine spoke without a trace of reproach, but still Beatrice blushed for her daughter. They all agreed Mary should have accepted their neighbor Lord Borton's proposal, her one and only offer to date. But the strong-willed chit had refused on the grounds that she would not share a household with Borton's spinster sister. Beatrice, who had lived with her sister-in-law in complete harmony for fifteen years, could not imagine why.

Not that Mary's wedding Borton could have saved the current situation. He had money enough to support Mary and any brood they might have, but not enough to keep Josten Hall—and its occupants—afloat. At least it would have been one less Lockton to worry over.

"And young men looking to make their mark in the world must look the part," Nadine added instructively. "You wouldn't want anyone thinking Josten is cheese-paring or that Harry and Phillip are chawbacons."

"Good Lord, no," Ned agreed mildly.

"Besides, Harry and my Pip are not the only ones to be victimized by Captain Sharp and ill luck," Beatrice put in. "Why, it is being bandied about that soon even Brummell will have to flee the country."

"Who gives a damn about Brummell?" Josten said. "Our concern is the Lockton name."

"Of course," Ned said and then, his gaze lighting on his nephews, "And speaking of which, since they are the authors of the current predicament and all, perhaps either Harry or Pip ought to be the ones flinging themselves on the matrimonial pyre?"

The room fell into stunned silence. Nadine blanched, Josten turned red, Harry's blue eyes popped from his head, and Pip clutched at his cravat as though it were suddenly choking him. Only Ned looked perfectly tranquil. As always.

"No!" Pip managed to gasp.

"No!" Harry squeaked a second later.

"They're too young!" Nadine breathed.

"Just babies!" Beatrice added her voice.

"No family in their right mind would allow them near their daughters," Josten said.

Only Josten's statement brokered any interest from Ned. He raised a brow inquiringly.

"Truth is both the lads were sent down from Eton and everyone knows it. They've managed to garner themselves reputations as regular Bear Garden scapegraces and their antics have seen them excluded from the polite world. Couldn't get them vouchers to Almack's for all the tea in China. Not that I was any better as a lad."

In fact, Beatrice knew he had been quite a bit better, but she wasn't about to say so.

"And I have no doubt they'll be able to repair their reputations and make brilliant alliances. In time. But time is what we do not have. Besides, our troubles weren't *all* the lads' doing," Josten went on gruffly. "The crops failed and, well, who knows where the bloody money went!"

Poor Marcus. He was not much of an economist. It hurt his head to ponder the chicken scratches submitted by the dunners, so he didn't.

Happily, Ned did not argue with Josten's estimation of the boys' chances of procuring a good match. All he did was nod.

Josten hurried on, deciding to take the nod as Ned's agreement. "The Season starts in a few weeks, Ned. You'll want to go to town early, have some new coats made, boots, trousers—yes, I know they aren't allowed at Almack's, but Wellington has worn them and now Harry tells me we all must. And you'll need some cattle, too. Something with dash. Can you still ride with that leg? Well enough to look half-comfortable atop a hot-blooded steed? Young ladies love the look of a man on horseback, don't they, Nadine?"

"Indeed, yes."

"I daresay I can manage to make it down Rotten Row once or twice without toppling off," Ned answered.

"Damn it, Ned. It ain't about whether you can stay astride," Josten said, pacing back and forth.

Beatrice watched him with some misgiving. Whenever Josten was worried, he retreated to a fallback position of autocratic anger. It was most impressive. But in this case he was overdoing it a mite. Ned wasn't arguing.

"It's about how you *look* staying astride," Josten enlightened him. "It's *all* about looks. Society is *all* about looks."

"Hear, hear" murmured Harry appreciatively.

"Shut up, Harry," snapped Josten. He clasped his hands behind his back, rocking back and forth on his heels. "You go to London, Ned. Stay in the town house with the lads."

"No!" Harry and Phillip and Ned all said at once.

"No," Ned repeated. "I am too used to my own quarters."

"Fine. Rent a place. Nadine and Beatrice will doubtless be in town on occasion to squire Mary about, though the girl has stated a preference for being in Brighton most of the Season. I suppose I shall be obliged to make an appearance, too." He said this last without any enthusiasm.

For a man who had once been an Incomparable, Josten had become an inveterate homebody. Not that Nadine minded. She seemed quite content to spend her time in the country. As did Beatrice. Though they all did wish Josten Hall had better heating.

"In the meantime, join my club, be seen in all the most fashionable places, get invited to all those places where susceptible, marriage-minded young ladies might see you, and get one of 'em to fall in love with ya!"

"And for this I need a new coat?"

Again, a disconcerting flicker appeared in Ned's mild gaze but then was gone. If only he had more fire to him, Beatrice thought morosely. He would be quite something.

"Of course! No woman in her right mind is going to allow her daughter near a shabby ex-captain. In order to be introduced to the sort of girl we need you to marry, you must *look* the part of a desirable mate. Like a returned war hero." Marcus's bluster lost its wind, leaving behind exasperation.

"Good God, Neddie, do you not already know this? I shouldn't have let you join the navy. I should have insisted you acquire some town bronze, instead. Society is ruthless, my boy. Filled with machinations and manipulations, where nothing said is meant and everything meant is left to interpretation." His troubled gaze cleared. "It's exhausting."

Josten's concern brought a strange expression to Ned's face. "Don't worry on my behalf, Marcus. I shall fare well enough. But doesn't it all seem very akin to what you were just now denouncing? I mean, does it not seem rather devious? Pretending to be something I am not?"

"Devious? Don't be impertinent. It's not the same thing at all," Josten said, clearly offended. "There is nothing devious in maneuvering yourself into a situation where some rich heiress can find you and fall in love with you. Which will be very hard to do if you can't even get introduced to her."

A slight smile touched Ned's lips. "Assuming I should succeed in finding this lady, why ever should she agree to marry me once she realizes we are, er, potless? How does she profit?"

It was an amazed Nadine who answered. "Why, she'll be marrying a Lockton of Josten Hall. Her brother-in-law will be an *earl*. I recall how thrilled I was when Josten noticed me."

And so she should have been, Beatrice thought. Nadine had come with an enormous dowry but no aristocratic antecedents. In truth, she loved Nadine very well.

But her people, though gentry, were hardly of the same caliber as the Locktons of Josten Hall. Happily, Nadine had never forgotten her good fortune so no one needed to remind her of it. And Marcus . . . Well, he loved her deeply and truly, much as her own dear Paul had loved her.

"An heiress may as well spend her money on us as on anyone else. That's why girls have money, Neddie," Nadine went on as Josten regarded her fondly. "To bring it to their spouses. Why, I brought twenty thousand pounds to the marriage when I wed Josten."

"Exactly," Josten said, nodding. "There are probably scores of wealthy girls who never dreamed of aspiring so high. Still"—he lowered his voice confidingly—"should the choice present itself, I'd prefer a lisping sister-in-law to one who's a cit. But no one walleyed." He paused. "At least not so walleyed you'd notice across a room."

Rather than answering, Ned took a quick bite of apple and chewed vigorously. What had gotten into the boy?

"Now, you do understand what's required of you? You need only to find some girl, woo her, wed her, bed her, and bring her back here."

"Along with her money," Ned said.

"Where else would it go?" Beatrice asked. "You are so strange, Ned. Do you not love us?"

"I do," Ned murmured, looking amazed. "God bless me, I do."

Josten pounced on the admission. "Of course you do. And therefore it is your duty to go to London, buy some new coats, and be a bloody war hero. You'll see, Ned. You'll have your pick of any number of girls."

Chapter Three

Lydia took a sip of wine, gratified that the surface of the red liquid did not shiver with the telltale trembling of her hand. "So the only viable courses open to me are to either marry the wealthiest man I can inveigle into making an offer for me or to continue enjoying my freedom in reduced circumstances. Greatly reduced."

There. She'd managed to sound nonchalant. She didn't feel nonchalant. Her stomach twisted in a knot and her breath seemed to come from somewhere high and shallow in her chest. For the first time since Eleanor had delivered her from the limbo of Sussex back into the brilliant milieu in which she'd been raised, she was uncertain and, yes, afraid. Her world had been built and fueled by seemingly infinite wealth. Except it had been finite. Was, in fact, *fin*.

She'd fled straight from Terwilliger's office—though anyone watching her would have said "strolled"—to her town house, where she was expecting to dine with her friends while dissecting the latest *on dit*. Little had she known she would present herself as the main course.

She gazed about the lovely drawing room while she waited for her friends to digest the information she'd presented. This was her favorite room: light, elegant, and filled with exotic touches. She had selected the tea-colored brocade draperies, the pale, eggshell blue hue on the walls, and the rich Persian carpet underfoot. She and Eleanor had bought the landscape hanging above the mantel at the Academy Showing two years before. Together, too, they had found the porcelain figurine gracing a side table at a street market in Venice when they'd traveled there the winter after her debut. She'd identified it as a Carracci at once.

Her guardian's home had been filled with such artifacts from his travels as a young man. She'd made a habit of studying his collection, honing her eye and discernment during the two years she'd lived in his house in Sussex. There hadn't been much else to do during her exile. And that is how she saw her fourteenth and fifteenth years, as ones of exile. It was a time when, heartbroken with unspeakable grief at her vibrant, loving parents' deaths, she had lost everything and everyone she had ever known.

When she'd been with her parents, traveling from one exotic locale to another, she'd taken for granted the world's brilliance and beauty, its gaiety and sophistication, the conversations and company. Their deaths had put an end to that. In Sussex, she might have learned to appreciate all manner of art and artifact, but things were no substitute for people. For family.

Her gaze moved now to her three companions for this evening's dinner: Eleanor, Duchess of Grenville, her godmother; the very young Mrs. Sarah Marchland, her oldest friend; and, of course, sweet-faced Emily Cod. Sarah's family had owned property in France near one of her parents' residences there. They had played together sometimes as children and become reacquainted the year they both were presented at court in England. Lydia enjoyed many fond social relationships—but these three were her most trusted friends, privy to all her secrets, though she had always had a dearth of those. Until now.

"So which would you choose, my dears? Freedom or wealth?" Lydia asked, determined not to let them know how gravely she'd been affected by Terwilliger's news. She was renowned for her sangfroid. Everyone had remarked on it, praised her for it.

The truth was she hadn't known any other way to react. It was what she had been taught from birth. She might perforce lose her wealth and status, but at least she could preserve her reputation.

"Don't be ridiculous, Lydia. You'll marry, of course," Eleanor said, her deep-set, hooded eyes glinting with irritation. Time might have pared away her once legendary beauty to a refined angularity and silver shot through her smoky hair, but wealth and an unerring sense of style still allowed her to effortlessly command attention. "What good is freedom if you can't afford to do anything with it or go anywhere or know anyone?"

"I shall still know you," Lydia countered mildly.

"Of course," Eleanor said, setting down her own cut-crystal goblet. "But you should hate being a burr, unable to reciprocate invitations, without the wherewithal to pay your own way."

A burr. The contemptuous moniker echoed in the room. Though a cold-blooded assessment, it was an honest one. Lydia appreciated Eleanor's honesty. She had relied on it when she'd come out under her patronage eight years ago, and though the relationship between them had evolved from mentor-student to one of equals, she still valued her counsel.

Eleanor valued their friendship as much as she. The duchess was long on acquaintances and sycophants and short on true friends. For that reason, and for Lydia's sake, she had adopted Sarah and Emily into her very small inner circle. Their inclusion had provoked comment amongst the *ton* and one could recognize why; the arid and attenuated duchess and the rash and round young Mrs. Sarah Marchland were an odd enough pairing. But what common ground could a duchess and a lunatic widow find?

Lydia sometimes wondered that herself.

"You are quite right," Lydia replied. "But I do not see how that is appreciably different than being dependent on one's husband for the same."

"It's not quite the same," Sarah said, picking through an assortment of sweetmeats on the table beside her. Plump, creamy, and plush, with her white-blond hair and light blue eyes, Sarah reminded one of a particularly toothsome blancmange, a mass of sweetness without substance. Loath as Lydia was to admit it, it was not an assessment without grounds. "Husbands are obliged. Friends are not."

"Husbands are only obliged if they are obliging," Emily said from the depth of her favorite armchair. Away from the scrutiny of assessing eyes and in the company of those whom she trusted, Emily's nervousness abated. As did her unfortunate predilection for "borrowing" things.

"Quite right, Emily." Eleanor nodded. "Sarah's husband is willing to look the other way regarding her actions. Not every marriage is so successful." Eleanor spoke without irony. She had buried her duke a decade earlier and, rumor had it, upended a chamber pot over his grave. Discreetly, of course. Eleanor was always discreet.

"Gerald pays handsomely to keep me away from"—Sarah hesitated a moment, then finished—"the farm."

Lydia would have sworn it was not what she'd originally been going to say.

"This is my advice to you, Lydia," Sarah went on. "Marry a rich, accommodating man who promises to be accommodatingly absent."

Like many people, Gerald Marchland had mistakenly assumed Sarah's plump prettiness and guileless blue eyes indicated a docile and indolent nature, when in truth Sarah was and always had been a virago. Even as a child she had delighted in escapades that brokered comment and criticism. The pleasure she took in dining was simply a reflection of an appetite ravenous in other areas as well.

It was well known that Sarah had many . . . admirers. Luckily, Gerald—as stiff as Sarah was lax—disliked Society and stayed well away from London. Sarah swore the situation suited them both. But though Sarah always *seemed* forthcoming, Lydia suspected there was much she did and thought that she kept hidden from Lydia and Eleanor and Emily. Doubtless, because she knew they would not approve.

Lately, Lydia had wondered if Sarah's marriage was as successful as Sarah claimed. Every year, Sarah seemed to grow more restless and careless in her "friendships" and more vocal in her detestation of Gerald.

"I suppose you're right," Lydia said.

"About marrying or what sort of fellow to marry?" Sarah asked, looking quite pleased as she tucked her feet beneath her.

"Both," Lydia replied.

"Of course she's right," Eleanor said.

"What do you think, Emily?" Lydia asked.

Emily was peering into her reticule with a familiar expression of chagrin and Lydia reminded herself to check later for something she might have managed to slip in during the visit to Terwilliger. Stress often preceded Emily's little bouts of larceny—always of items of negligible value. Afterward she was stricken with remorse and often said she didn't even recall taking the things. She would simply die of ignominy should anyone ever catch her in the act of secreting a little something and call her a thief. Not that she ever would be. Whenever she discovered Emily had borrowed something, Lydia wrote a gracious note and sent it along with a very nice gift and, of course, returned the original "misplaced" item.

No one ever took umbrage. It was one of the benefits of being Lady Lydia Eastlake. Rank had its privilege but celebrity had even more.

Emily tugged the reticule drawstring closed and looked up. "Excuse me? I wasn't attending."

"We were discussing whether Lydia ought to get herself a husband," Sarah said, inspecting the gooey center of yet another sweet. "Lydia asked your opinion."

"I don't have one. Don't want one," Emily said.

"Forgive me for pressing you," Sarah said, looking slightly taken aback by Emily's unfamiliar vehemence.

"I believe she was speaking of a husband, Sarah," Eleanor said.

"That's right," Emily agreed. "I don't have one. He's dead."

It had been Emily's husband who'd committed her to the lunatic asylum where Lydia's solicitors had found her. They'd been searching for any additional legal claimants to Lydia's parents' estate and instead found Emily, a distant relation on her mother's side. They had informed Lydia, who forthwith had gone to see the "madwoman."

She hadn't known what to expect, certainly not the small, soft-faced woman who had shyly greeted her. The warden had informed Lydia that after committing Emily for compulsive thieving, her husband had promptly fallen off the face of the Earth—though reports suggested that it had been a ship he'd fallen off while fleeing victims of his fraudulent investment schemes and he'd been ape-drunk at the time. Those same victims had taken every penny Cod had left behind. Ever since, the asylum had been maintaining Emily out of their sense of Christian duty and, Lydia suspected, Emily's usefulness as an unpaid attendant.

Compulsive thievery notwithstanding, Lydia had decided to take Emily home with her. It hadn't been her original intention, but Lydia was wont to act on strong emotion first and justify her choices intellectually later. Emily's situation—her abrupt change in circumstances, her husband's unexpected abandonment, her obvious confusion over how her life had come to such a state, and her loneliness—had brought back to Lydia her own sense of bewilderment and despair the few short years between her parents' deaths and Eleanor's arrival.

She knew what it was to be displaced. She knew about second chances and reprieves from limbo. After Eleanor had extricated her from Sir Grimley's house she had made it her vocation and avocation to enjoy life to the fullest, never to take for granted those things and people she knew and loved.

As no one was paying for Emily's keep, no one objected when Lydia signed the necessary documents to have her released. It proved a fortuitous decision, for not only had she secured for Emily personal freedom but for herself she'd acquired a convenient chaperone. The situation suited both. Lydia accepted Emily's little foibles and Emily did not interfere with Lydia's independence.

"Ah, yes," Emily repeated contentedly. "Dead."

"Emily," Sarah said, her expression growing cunning, "your story suggests to me a solution to Lydia's dilemma. Do you see what I mean, Lydie?"

She did, but the devil that so often played havoc with Lydia's resolve to be serious or modest and that led many to think she was incapable of gravitas, would not be gainsaid. "Well, there's a thought, Sarah. I'll marry some likely chap, convince him to sail with me to Italy, and then shove him off the deck."

Sarah stared at Lydia a second before realizing she was twitting her. "That is not what I meant. I meant that you ought to consider marrying a gentleman in uncertain health."

"An old man?"

Sarah lifted a shoulder. "Uncertain for whatever reason."

"Don't be ridiculous, Sarah," Eleanor said. "Lydie can't marry some pox-ridden fellow for his wallet. Nor can she wed an antique."

"I can't?" Lydia murmured. Not that she would agree to marrying some syphilitic scab, but an aged husband? A *very* aged husband . . . ?

"No," Eleanor said with finality. "Lydia has her reputation to consider. For eight years she has been the beau ideal for every young woman who dreams of independence."

"Oh, fie," Lydia said. "I never set out to be anyone's paragon. If my decision to wed disillusions someone, that is their problem. I refuse to fashion my future to satisfy some romantic notion of me."

She was not being entirely candid. She liked her celebrity. She thrived on center stage; it was where she was most comfortable. She had spent her childhood learning how to please and entertain, to be witty and winsome and pretty and vivacious because that's what people responded to, that's what her parents had delighted in showing off, and that's what she did best: enchant people.

As a child, her reward for being so good at it was to be swept along in the wake of her labile, extravagant parents, taken on all their travels, shown off to princes and princesses, introduced to great men and women. In short, to live a fairy-tale life of opulence and excitement.

The life she had been raised to lead. *This* life. Being Lady Lydia Eastlake was her profession as much as being the prime minister was the Earl of Liverpool's. Besides, who would she be if this were taken from her? In the deepest part of her, she feared she might not like the answer.

"You will simply have to marry a paragon," Eleanor was saying. "Someone as wealthy as you are—were— and with as just much consequence. A gentleman of wealth, breeding, and rank, who will appreciate your independence."

"Easier said than done," Lydia commented dryly, and at Sarah's questioning look elaborated. "As it has lately been pointed out to me, those whom I refused are unlikely to ask again and those who have not asked for my hand are bound to be advised against lending themselves to a similar indignity. I have also been informed that once it is known that I am bankrupt, the mercenary reasons for my interest in them is bound to sit poorly with any proud, wealthy, *suitable* gentleman." She gazed around at her friends.

"Privately we may acknowledge that we wed for fortune and status, but no one wants the fact paraded publicly. We cleave to the notion that someone might actually want us for ourselves." She spoke nonchalantly, but the words struck a tender note in her heart. "And the greater one's status and fortune, the more it seems to matter. Gentlemen do not like to think their suit is being encouraged only because of the size of their purse."

How could one know another well enough to be certain they wanted to wed them? How could one know if someone was worthy of one's respect and admiration, someone in whose company one would always find pleasure and interest? Her parents had fallen in love over the course of years of friendship and, despite what Society had whispered, did not act on that love or declare it until after her uncle's death.

If she was being honest, she would acknowledge that that question had much to do with why she had never accepted any of the marriage proposals that had been made to her. What if she made a mistake, as her mother had in her first marriage? Or what if she wed a man she found out later she did not love, as had Sarah? Or a man whom she despised, like Eleanor? Or a man like Emily's husband?

Yet there was no gainsaying it; Lydia *did* want to marry. She wanted the sort of companionship and affection her parents had known for each other, as well as the intensity of emotion she had oft glimpsed in her father's eye as he watched her mother. She wanted to be regarded with a similar wealth of feeling, undisguised and wholehearted. But she had never felt confident that any of the men who had asked for her hand could provide her with these things. Or she, him. And so the years had slipped by while she waited, never feeling the necessity of having to make a choice, content, if truth be told, to enjoy the independence for which she was known.

That had all changed now. And in some ways it was a relief to finally have to commit to what she had always wanted. Or at least, the possibility of it.

"So what will you do?" Sarah asked.

Lydia canted a brow. "Keep my poverty a secret."

"I agree," Eleanor said at once. "It is imperative you secure an offer before your situation becomes common knowledge."

"Are you advising Lydie to marry under false pretenses?" Sarah asked. She did not sound particularly shocked.

"Good heavens, no," Lydia said. "I would never marry a gentleman without revealing my pockets are to let."

"I should say not," Eleanor agreed. "Any such deception would be discovered well before the marriage could take place, when the papers were drawn up. Even if they weren't, a fellow could have the marriage annulled on the grounds of fraud. Or, if he decided to save face by honoring the marriage, out of spite he could be cheeseparing with her allowance."

"Men can be most spiteful," Sarah agreed, a dark shadow clouding her pale eyes.

"Since avoiding beggary is the reason for her to marry in the first place," Eleanor continued, "such a deception would rather defeat its own purpose, wouldn't it?"

"But"—Sarah sounded thoroughly confused—"if you ain't going to tell them you're poor and you ain't going to lie . . . oh, I *am* beyond muddled!"

Sarah never thought more than one minute ahead of the last. Lydia rose and moved to sit beside her. "I shall inform my beau of my financial straits *after* he proposes and offer to free him of his suit," she explained patiently. "Should he renege on his offer he is obliged to keep my confidence, moving aside to allow another unsuspecting candidate to take his place. It's a matter of honor, don't you see? But if he should let his offer stand, he does so knowing full well my situation and without any reason to begrudge me."

"You think someone will want to marry you after

they discover your pockets are to let?" Sarah asked doubtfully.

"I hope so. If nothing else, I have a fine pedigree. And being the gentleman who secures my hand in marriage should carry some cachet. I am well aware that my name features prominently in the betting books at the various gentlemen's clubs as to when and whom I shall wed," Lydia said, striving to sound a good deal more confident than she felt. "The most valuable thing I own is what Society has given me—prominence. Whether it is enough remains to be seen, but if I play my hand right, by the time the fellow learns of my financial deficits he may decide that I have other qualities to bring to the union." She paused as if considering. "I daresay I can adequately grace a dining table, look ornamental in an open carriage, and am a capable enough hostess that I might prove an asset to a socially ambitious gentleman."

Sarah nodded in understanding.

No one, Lydia noted with a small pang, suggested that the proposed suitor would fall in love with her. It wasn't the way of their world.

"We shall have to start letting it be known that over this last winter Lady Lydia Eastlake has undergone a transformation," Eleanor mused quietly. She had clearly been thinking matters through as Lydia explained the situation to Sarah.

"You can say I have grown lonely," Lydia suggested.

"Piffle," Emily said.

"Emily is right," Eleanor approved. "Loneliness is not an appealing quality. No. We will say you have felt the tug of maternal yearnings. You desire a family."

"Yes," Sarah murmured in an odd voice. "Everyone understands wanting to have children."

Everyone except Eleanor, who was childless, and Emily, who was childless, and Sarah, who though she had two children, never saw them, Lydia thought sardonically.

"Sarah, you must lend me your youngest so I can be seen publicly cooing," Lydia said.

"Can't. His father won't let him leave Hertfordshire," Sarah said shortly.

"Well, *someone* we know must have a baby they are willing to loan me," Lydia said.

"You have an even more Machiavellian mind than I," murmured Eleanor wonderingly. "Sometimes I fear I did you a disservice in befriending you."

"On the contrary. You have greatly benefited me, Eleanor. Without your guidance I should be shivering in a corner right now, paralyzed with fear rather than preparing to go shopping for a new wardrobe, which, you must allow, sounds vastly more fun. I have my reputation as a fashion plate to uphold."

"But . . . how can you afford to do so?" Sarah asked, then flushed. "I mean, you are poor. I will, of course, lend you whatever—"

"No!" Lydia said, flushing, then more quietly, "No, thank you. I shall do what everyone does; I will purchase on credit and expectations. Where those will not serve, I shall sell things no one will realize are gone: paintings, antiquities, and jewels."

"And what if, after all that, no one offers for you?" Emily asked softly.

"Well, then," Lydia said, refusing to think past the

end of the summer, "at least I shall have had one last golden Season."

Eleanor waited until Lydia was taking her leave of Sarah to beckon Emily Cod to her side. "We must do whatever is necessary to ensure Lydia's success. She can be too hasty in her affection and too quick in her judgments."

"Yes. But she often chooses true."

"This is too important to trust to intuition."

Emily agreed. "What do you want me to do?"

"I count on you to help me vet candidates. You hear things, Emily, the rest of us are not privy to."

Emily nodded. People oft forgot that simply because one's eyes were shut did not necessarily mean one was asleep. Ears wide open, she'd heard oftentimes how indiscreet people could be in front of those they considered incidental. She loved Lydia and she would do everything in her power for her.

The whole situation was most distressing. It recalled vividly the circumstances of Emily's own ill-fated marriage and her husband committing her to Brislington Asylum.

Her stomach began to twist and her hands trembled. She didn't want to think of that. She mustn't think of that. She had to think of Lydia and how important it was to all of them that she wed someone who would not be Cod or Eleanor's duke or Sarah's husband. Someone who would let them all live happily together as they had these past three years.

Emily winced at her thought, knowing her motives to be self-serving. But so, too, were Eleanor's and Sarah's. Eleanor because she would have no one without Lydia.

·

And Sarah needed Lydia just as much because no one else would ever think only the best of her, in spite of her actions. Emily knew no one but Lydia would ever overlook her mad, uncontrollable thieving and find value in her.

No, Eleanor did not have to advise her of what was at risk. She was quite aware, far more so than Eleanor, of how important Lydia's choice of husband would prove to them all.

Chapter Four

April, 1816

As luck would have it, the goldsmith Roubalais had gone home for lunch and left his shop in the care of his daughter-in-law Berthe and thus was not there to receive Lydia. In the preceding few weeks, Terwilliger had discreetly handled the liquidation of a great deal of her personal property, but she wasn't sure she could give up the amethyst parure entirely. Accordingly, she'd decided she would simply lend it to Roubalais until such time as she could reacquire it.

Roubalais, once jeweler to the French court, also traded in antiquities, and occasionally, and very discreetly, acted as a pawnbroker for the *beau monde*. It was for the latter purpose Lydia had ventured into the unfamiliar country of Cheapside. The store's unassuming location was responsible for attracting much of the expatriate Frenchman's clientele: gentlemen of the *beau monde* in need of some ready cash and those in the market for a good bargain. Which all men, regardless of their wealth, were to some extent.

Lydia had planned this trip for days, working out every little detail, down to where she would leave her carriage and how many footmen she would have shadow her steps and what she would wear to blend in with her surroundings. But she hadn't reckoned on Roubalais going home to eat his midday meal. How vexing.

Every moment she spent here was a moment more someone could recognize her, and if there was one thing she did not need, it was to have it bandied about that she'd visited a pawnbroker. Not only would it begin the inevitable speculation about her fortune, but a lady never, *ever* visited a pawnbroker. And first and foremost and to the exclusion of all else, Lydia was a lady.

Until today, she thought.

"I suppose I'll have to come back," she muttered.

Roubalais's daughter-in-law shook her head. "No, madam. You mustn't discommode yourself," she said, shedding her voluminous and dirt-streaked smock and flinging it over the back of a chair. "I will go and bring him back at once."

"That won't be necessary."

"But it is no trouble at all and only a few short blocks away. Monsieur Roubalais would never forgive me if he should hear that you visited our shop and I did not fetch him."

"Don't tell him," Lydia suggested. "I was only going to ask for an appraisal of an amethyst and pearl parure. It . . . it belongs to a friend."

The girl was well trained. Her face gave away not a whit of doubt at this prevarication. "But of course! Now, please. You stay. Look about. It will be only a few minutes, I promise."

Before Lydia could protest further, Berthe had hurried out the door, calling over her shoulder, "The baby just settled down before you came in and shouldn't wake while I'm gone."

"Baby?" Lydia echoed, but Berthe had already gone.

A short circuit of the shop proved that a baby did indeed sleep within the emptied bottom drawer of a bombé chest. Lydia had no idea of its age or gender and had no desire to remedy her ignorance. It looked quite content as it was, a drool bubble catching a prism of light, spiderweb-fine lashes sweeping a soft—and faintly sticky-looking—pink cheek, the blanket covering it rising and falling in time with its breathing.

Lydia knelt nearer, studying the little creature. As someone's wife she would be obliged to produce one, if not several, of these. The idea was a touch terrifying. She knew nothing of children, having been the only child in a world of adults.

She hoped when she had children she would grow fond of them. At least, she assumed one would find parenthood more pleasant if one were fond of one's offspring rather than indifferent. Her own parents had been most demonstratively affectionate.

She supposed she would feel the same about her children. If they were pretty and well behaved and bright. And if they were not . . . ? Would she love them then? Would she have been loved had she been a little golem with the manners of a hedgehog?

A sharp, sweet-acrid smell drifted up from the drawer, abruptly ending Lydia's fascination. She shot upright and stepped away, accidentally backing into a ladder behind her. She spun and steadied it, her gaze rising to the top shelf lining the wall. Something colored a gorgeous royal blue glinted from far above. It demanded investigation.

She hesitated. Lydia was well known for her impetuousness, but she allowed herself to be devil-may-care only within the strict parameters of what Society allowed. Charge a stile on horseback? Of course. Tease a prince? Often. But clamber about the dusty shelves of a pawnbroker's shop? It wasn't done.

But . . . why not? No one knew she was here. What harm could come of it? Once more, Lydia's insatiable curiosity joined forces with her impulsiveness to trump caution.

She looked around and spied the smock Berthe Roubalais had left behind. Without further thought, she donned the garment, rolled back the sleeves, and commenced climbing the ladder. It was a good deal more rickety than she'd expected and the notion that this might not be a wise idea occurred to her, but her legs kept moving and before she knew it, she'd made it to the top. On the other side of a moldering cardboard box, a stunning Oriental bowl beckoned.

Her eyes widened with delighted discovery. She recognized this! Certainly it was Chinese. Kangxi? She had to get a better look. . . .

She grasped the edge of a box obstructing the bowl and gave it a cursory tug. The moldering side broke away. Startled, Lydia snatched her hand back, accidentally knocking over a silver candlestick holder and sending it rolling toward the edge. With a gasp, she ducked, but not before the candlestick fell, catching the brim of her hat and knocking it from her head, causing her elegant coiffure to come half undone. The candlestick clattered to the floor.

She held her breath and counted, praying the baby didn't wake. It didn't.

Relieved, she brushed her hair from her face and too late realized her hand was dirty and that she'd just smeared grime across her forehead. "Damn."

She eyed the bowl, still resting above her. It glinted enticingly. She must see if she was right. She stretched to the top of her toes, sliding aside the torn box. It caught up on something and there was no way she could reach around it to the bowl. She dared not attempt to move the crumbling box lest it disintegrate completely. Which meant she would simply have to reposition the ladder—

The bell above the shop's front door jingled jauntily, announcing someone's arrival. And not a moment later, a deep masculine voice said, "Excuse me."

Lydia looked over her shoulder and down toward the door. A tall, broad-shouldered gentleman stood below her, his hat in his hand, the sun glinting off guinea-gold hair.

He was quite simply one of the most handsome men Lydia had ever seen. His face was composed of strong, sculpted features: a high, straight-bridged nose, a wide mouth, and a square, clean-shaven jaw. And was that . . . ? Yes. His chin sported a cleft. She'd always had a weakness for men with clefts in their chin. Her father had had one. He, too, had been a strikingly handsome man.

The gentleman's expression was pleasant but reserved. His bearing was strictly erect but without self-consciousness, the results of training, not of conscious effort.

"Can you help me?" he asked.

Lydia realized that not only was she gawking like a shopgirl at the handsome stranger but that he had, in fact, mistaken her for one. And why not? Her hair had come half-undone, a dusty old smock covered her stylish dress, and there was dirt on her face.

She came to her senses with a start. She couldn't have a gentleman see her like this. *Here.* First and most important, because no one had ever seen Lady Lydia Eastlake in such a grimy state—not that she'd never been in one before, but no stranger had ever caught her in one. And second, because ladies did not engage in vulgar transactions with pawnbrokers. And since being a nonpareil and a lady were amongst the few things she still possessed, she was not going to be disowned of them, too.

There was nothing for it but to pretend she was exactly what he'd mistaken her for. She composed a pleasant, helpful smile and started down the ladder. "Yes, sir. Sorry, sir. Just doing a bit of tidyin' up like," she said, pleased with her Cheapside accent even though the real Berthe Roubalais did not have one. She stepped off the bottom rung onto the floor and dusted her palms off on the smock. "How can I 'elp you?"

The man drew closer, and now that she was back on the ground she could see that his eyes were a soft blue-gray, like spring ice, and banked by thick, sooty lashes. In addition, he was smiling now, making his good looks even more devastating.

Who is he? She knew everyone in Society and she

had never seen him before and she'd wager none of her companions had either. They would have mentioned someone with his extraordinary looks. Yet his manner was that of a gentleman and his coat had clearly been cut by the great Weston.

"I was told that you had some fine walking sticks. I'm interested in seeing them."

"Walking sticks?" she echoed. She had no idea whether Roubalais carried walking sticks. She did know, however, that Littner and Cobb on St. James Street did.

"Yes. Something in silver or ivory, if possible."

"I see." She glanced around as though fearing an eavesdropper and sidled closer, beginning to enjoy her spontaneous stagecraft. "Look 'ere, sir. I'm going to tell you something maybe I oughtn't." She eyed him closely. "'Cause you seem a nice sorta fella, new to town and all."

For a second his surprise flickered in his gray-blue eyes, but his smile remained easy and neutral. "Oh, I am a nice fella," the gentleman avowed. The neutrality in his expression had relaxed into subtle amusement. "And I *am* new to town. But however did you know that?"

Because someone would have told me about a gentleman like you, Lydia thought. She gave him a cheeky smile. "Because your coat is brand-new. Not a seam turned. As are your boots and trousers. And that hat in your 'and ain't never seen a London pea souper."

"How very astute of you. And intriguing."

She tipped her head. She liked the notion of intriguing this gentleman as much as he intrigued her. Tall, lean, and dressed in the height of masculine fashion, he might have been any London gentleman. Except, he did not *look* like a London gentleman. His skin was too tanned and his gaze too frank and his tall figure too straight and . . . formidable.

"What's intriguing?" she asked, knowing she was staring but giving herself permission because she was Berthe the shopgirl and Berthe had never seen the likes of him. True, neither had Lady Lydia Eastlake, but *she* would never stare.

"How your *H* appears and disappears," he said, then clarified, "You said, 'the hat in your 'and.' "

Drat! Heat rushed into her cheeks. It was impossible to say from his tone whether he was twitting her or not.

"I'm trying to improve myself," she said, pulling herself up to her full five foot, four inches. "My uncle says as how one ought to speak like a lady if one is serving ladies."

"Ah!" He nodded. "That explains it. But now, what was this thing you were going to tell me because I am a nice fella new to town?"

"Well . . . truth to tell, we 'aven't"—she paused to correct herself, feeling very clever—"I mean *haven't* the selection of walking sticks that Littner and Cobb over on St. James do."

There. That ought to get rid of him before Berthe and Roubalais returned. . . . Except she realized she didn't want to get rid of him and he didn't seem in any hurry to leave.

"Do they?" he asked. "How kind of you to suggest it, even though it means the loss of a sale for your master."

"He isn't my master," Lydia said without thinking and then quickly amended, "He's my uncle and he sells lots of other sorts of goods, antiquities and jewelry and such, and I assure you he shall not miss the price fetched by one walking stick." She bobbed a curtsy. "Sir."

"That *is* kind of you. Miss," he said. "But before I go, let me first return the favor you've done me by purchasing something from your uncle's shop. What can you show me?"

Show him? She hadn't any idea. She doubted he was in the market for a parure unless there was some lady ... "We have a beautiful parure of amethyst and pearls that *might* be for sale. Perhaps you'd like to look at them for your ... wife?"

"Alas, I am not so blessed," he said. One corner of his mobile mouth twitched. He knew quite well what she'd been about.

She blushed as she was visited by the notion that the reserve she'd noted on first seeing him was, as his posture, a matter of habit, not something he consciously adopted, and that there was more that went on beneath his handsome countenance than his mild expression allowed one to see.

"So no jewelry. Something for myself, I think," he was saying. "Something, well, that you might like."

"Me?"

"Yes," he said, clasping his hands lightly behind his back. "You."

Good heavens. Was he flirting with her? She was caught between being appalled that she was receiving the attentions gentlemen reserved for shopgirls and thrilled that she'd elicited them. She wasn't sure what to make of him. What if he pressed his attention further? How horrifying that would be for both of them, because then she would be forced to reveal herself.

Her distress must have shown, for his gaze softened. *Not spring ice, twilight fog.* "Miss," he said gently. "I am asking for your opinion, not offering you carte blanche."

She blushed deeply. Now she truly felt like a fool. The poor man! Of course he hadn't been flirting with her. A gentleman of his obvious quality wouldn't impose on a girl dependent on his goodwill for her livelihood.

"Of course not," she denied. "I was just wondering what to show you." Now she'd have to think of something. What sort of ridiculous mull had she gotten herself into? Her eye caught on the ladder and she had an idea. "There's a splendid Oriental bowl on the top shelf there that you might be interested in."

"That sounds promising," he said.

"Here. Let me get it for you." She'd just put her foot on the first rung when his hand, broad, long fingered, and masculine, appeared above hers on the ladder rail. She swung around, nearly bumping into him. He was very tall. She had to tip her head to look up into his eyes. This close she could discern a coppery corona around the blue-gray irises.

"This ladder doesn't look too sturdy," he explained.

She backed up, bumping into the ladder, feeling ridiculously callow, stammering and blushing like a fifteen-year-old debutante. Her friends would have laughed themselves ill if they could see her now.

"Kind of you to worry, sir, but I'll be fine," she said, clambering up the rungs past the arm steadying the ladder. Unfortunately, she clambered too quickly.

Her foot slipped and she lost her balance. Before she could even gasp, strong hands had caught her around the waist and plucked her deftly from mid-tumble, swinging her up against a broad, hard chest. For one timeless second she was held gazing into his eyes. Something flickered in their depths. Did he catch his breath or was that her? Her. Because then he was lowering her lightly back to earth and releasing her, his expression showing no more than slight concern.

"Allow me," he said. His voice was entirely calm.

If only the same could be said of her heartbeat. It pattered madly.

Without waiting permission, he moved past her up the ladder. He didn't need to climb nearly as high as she and when he stopped, he had only to stretch out a long arm to secure the bowl and lift it from the shelf.

Who is he?

He returned with it and handed it to her. "This is the bowl?" he asked.

"Yes," she said. She took it from him and her attention shifted. She loved such things.

At first, she'd taken to studying the artifacts in Sir Grimley's house because there'd been little else to do in the big, cavernous manor without any company other than the servants that her guardian employed. But later, she'd developed an honest fascination. Not that very many people knew this. Expertise was not required of a beauty.

Now, her practiced eye moved over the high-footed rim of the bowl, the impressed woven silk pattern under the blue and white glaze and the pinholes in the base. Her own home had many examples of such porcelain.

"Chinese," she murmured. "Kangxi, I believe. One

can tell because of the Islamic influence of the design and the crowding of the figures."

"Ah, you are a connoisseur," he said.

"Merely an enthusiast," she demurred. It was a lovely thing, in perfect condition. "This is a very handsome piece."

"Extraordinary, I'd say." His voice was thoughtful.

She looked up. He was regarding her intently. "You know something about Chinese porcelain?"

"Not really," he admitted. "But I do know quality when I see it. Yes, I believe I have found exactly what I want."

"This is not all that old, less than a hundred years if I am correct, but still quite rare," she said. She could not resist teasing him a bit. "Perhaps you can't afford it."

"I almost certainly cannot." His smile was lopsided and wry.

"Then perhaps you ought to ask the price before you set your heart on it."

"It's too late for that, I'm afraid," he said.

She laughed. "You are too frank, sir. It makes you vulnerable. Someone less honest than I would be tempted to take advantage of such openness."

He sketched a courtly bow. "I am at the mercy of your better self."

"Ah!" She waggled a finger at him. "But you are assuming I have a better self. Perhaps I am entirely mercenary."

"Are you?" he asked and Lydia checked, regarding him in surprise.

He was serious. And he obviously expected her to answer him in kind. She didn't know how to react. Gentlemen of her acquaintance played at conversation. They did not seek honesty from words, only sport.

She felt heat rise in her cheeks as he caught her interest anew, this time with something other than his manners and his looks. Now she wanted to know not only who he was, but what manner of man.

"Miss?"

She was not about to answer a question about whether she was mercenary or not, particularly now, when she'd so recently decided to barter her independence for wealth. "I'm afraid I don't know what my uncle is asking for it," she said instead.

"Ah. Then I'll wait."

At this, Lydia's head snapped around. "No! I mean, my uncle warned me he would be gone for quite some time, hours perhaps, and you can't mean to dally here all afternoon."

"No? But there's so much to explore. So many unanticipated surprises."

Panic touched her. If this man found out she'd masqueraded as a shopgirl, he would think her the worst sort of romp, on par with Caroline Lamb, who for years had made a fool of herself by chasing after Byron. And should he then relate the tale—and men *always* related such tales—oh, no!

Perhaps she should throw herself on his mercy? If she told him all and appealed to him as a gentleman, he would be obliged to keep her confidence. But he would still think her a hoyden. She didn't want him to think she was a hoyden! Oh!

And it was at that moment that Berthe's baby, forgotten and fragrant, wet and hungry, who'd woken when the candlestick hit the floor and had been industriously sucking on his foot for the last fifteen minutes, decided he'd enough of this unproductive occupation and commenced howling.

"What in God's name is that?" the gentleman asked.

"The baby!" Lydia said, clapping a hand to her cheek. She brushed past him, hurrying over to the bombé chest. The baby's face was screwed up in a little red knot, its mouth a circle of outrage.

Without thinking, she reached into the drawer and swept the infant into her arms, blanket and all. "Hush. Hush little . . . little . . . one," she crooned against its damp skull.

It wailed louder.

She stared helplessly at the gorgeous gentleman. He looked as unnerved as she felt.

"Is the baby *yours*?" he asked.

"Good Lord, no!" she burst out. "It's . . . it's my cousin's."

"*It?*" the gentleman echoed.

"The baby," Lydia declared, exasperated. "What should I do?"

Amusement replaced his surprise. "I have no idea. Not only am I without a wife, I am without children."

The baby turned its head and smashed its drool-rimmed mouth against Lydia's chin and began gumming her noisily. Lydia froze, horrified.

"Oh!" Her voice quavered. "Why is it doing that?"

"I think it's hungry," the gentlemen offered seriously.

"Obviously," Lydia replied tartly. "Since it's trying to eat me."

"I don't think so. I think it's, er"—a faint ruddy color rose in his lean cheeks—"seeking its mother's—"

"I know that!" Lydia snapped, an answering heat boiling into her face.

"What is it anyway?" he asked.

She stared at him, confounded, the child's mouth still attached to her chin. "A baby."

"I mean what gender? You keep referring to the baby as 'it.' "

"Oh. How silly of me. It's a"—she took a wild guess—"a boy."

She shifted the baby to the other side, breaking off its fruitless rooting. It shrieked in protest.

"Jostle him," the gentleman suggested. "Gently."

"I thought you didn't have children."

"I have nieces and nephews and their nurse jostled them when they screeched."

"What?" Lydia shouted above the angry yowling.

"Never mind!" the gentleman shouted back. "Jostle him! Gently!"

Lydia did not get the opportunity to try out the suggestion. Berthe burst through the back door of the shop and rushed toward her, arms outstretched, a look in her eyes that was quite alarming.

"My baby!" She snatched the child from Lydia's arms. At once, the little Roubalais quieted, his howls turning into hiccups of infantile relief. The feral light (which Lydia was only now identifying as maternal) faded from Berthe's eyes as she realized just whom she had been about to assault. The color leached from her face. "Oh! Please forgive me—"

"I should think you do ask my pardon, *Cousin*," Lydia broke in. "You have been gone far longer than you originally promised. *Cousin*."

Berthe opened her mouth to speak, but caught sight of the slight shake of Lydia's head and closed it.

"Is my *uncle* done with his lunch, then?" Lydia asked brightly.

"Uncle?" Berthe asked hesitantly.

"Who else?" Lydia manufactured a tight little laugh. "I swear motherhood has played havoc with your wits. I hate to think what will happen with the birth of another. You might mistake me for some *lady*. And what *lady* would appear in a pawnbroker's shop looking like this?" She shot a telling look at her smock and dirty hands. "She'd be the subject of all sorts of untoward comments."

"Oh? Oh!" Berthe said, finally tumbling to Lydia's predicament. "Indeed, yes, Cousin. Motherhood has made me hen-witted. But I was coming to tell you that Father is on his way even as we speak, so you can leave. *Now*. I shall be more than happy to help this gentleman."

Good girl, Lydia thought in relief. Not only was Berthe warning her that Roubalais would be arriving any minute, she was giving her an excuse to intercept him. "Thank you," she breathed gratefully.

She looked at the gentleman. He was regarding her with an odd gentleness, his hands clasped behind his back.

She had little doubt she would see him again. The cut of his coat, the style in which he'd tied his cravat, his deportment, and address all bespoke a man of wealth and taste. She also had no doubt he would *not* recognize her. Take away her fashionable accoutrements and set a lady in a milieu where one does not expect to find her, and few men or women would recognize her as someone they knew. It was the way the world worked. Her world.

She should hurry. Berthe had said so. Yet something kept her. "I hope you can come to terms over your find, sir," she told him.

"Thank you. I will do my utmost to make her mine," he said gravely.

He had the most arresting eyes.

"Best get home before lunch cools," Berthe prompted. "You know how Mother is."

"Yes. Thank you. Good day, sir," she said, and without waiting for his reply she hurried off to intercept Roubalais.

Chapter Five

Ned watched Lady Lydia Eastlake dash out the back door of the shop and smiled.

Thank God the woman was wealthy and had no need to work for her keep because she'd never have made a living on stage. She was a terrible actress. She wore her thoughts on her expressive countenance: first amusement, then enjoyment, then a short-lived fear her accent—a terrible jumble of aristocratic tones and purposely dropped consonants—had given her away, the triumph she'd felt on thinking her explanation had deceived him, fear upon the other girl's return, and finally panicked flight.

It was a pity. She'd been having a grand time playing shopgirl. In fact, he'd been as attracted to her obvious glee in her masquerade as her stunning good looks. There was something about her pleasure that called to him, inveigled him to join. The woman was like champagne, a little intoxicating.

He had known who she was as soon as she'd clambered down off the ladder. He'd have to be a half-wit not to. Every newspaper and magazine carried illustrations of her, and their pages were devoted to descriptions of her and where she was entertained, at what time, and in whose company. Certain playing cards even featured her likeness as the Queen of Diamonds and Sir Thomas Lawrence had recently unveiled his painting of her at the Royal Academy. But most telling of all, there was no possible way two women could have eyes that color.

They really were a remarkable shade, a deep nocturnal purple, like a martin's wing. In other ways, she reminded him of a silky little swallow, too: fluid and elegant and cheeky. She was—

"Sir?"

He looked down. A very small, nervous-looking Frenchman had entered the shop and stood pointing at the bowl Ned still held.

"Ah, yes," Ned said. "How much for this bowl?"

Roubalais suggested a price and Ned paid it, biding his time while the girl wrapped the parcel and giving Lady Lydia ample opportunity to make good her escape. When Berthe finished, she handed him the wrapped package. He considered questioning her about her illustrious client but took pity. It would only put her in the position of either betraying a peer or lying to one.

"Thank you," he said, taking the bowl and tipping his head. Lady Lydia had had plenty of time to flee by now. At any rate, he intended to walk the opposite direction of where her well-known yellow-wheeled carriage was parked, toward Boodle's Club. There was a gentleman there, Childe Smyth, to whom his nephew Harry owed a great deal of money. He frowned, more despairing of the whole situation than annoyed.

It did no good to be annoyed with any of the Locktons. They shared the same family traits: bluff and blustering, softhearted, weak-willed, and unworldly. Wondrously enough, they considered themselves none of these things. Ned considered it an oddly endearing myopia even though he knew this sentiment was just as peculiar. But he'd always been a little staggered by his siblings' unfounded bombast and bravado and they were just as befuddled by his lack of the same qualities.

Once, while in the throes of a good drunk, Ned's god-father, Admiral Nelson, had confided that he considered that rather than Ned being the proverbial cuckoo in the sparrow's nest, a nest of cuckoos had hatched themselves a young hawk. Ned didn't feel like a hawk. Since his return home, he felt more like a mother hen.

Not that he wanted his family to be any different. The truth was, he loved them all very much.

He hadn't always. Like most lads, he'd quite taken them for granted when he'd applied for a situation on Nelson's ship. If anything, he'd been desperate to escape the chaos and confusion, mismanagement and mayhem of Josten Hall. But as the years passed, the gravity of Napoleon's quest for power had turned a schoolboy's lust for adventure into grim duty. The image of Josten Hall and the chaotic family that occupied it had become a lodestone, beckoning him home.

The calm, tranquil boy he'd been no longer existed, though he wore the same smile and had the same manner. His calmness had become stoicism and his tranquil-lity a deep-seated dispassion that had been necessary for him to give the orders he had given, send men where he had sent them, and do what he had done. He never wanted any one of his family to know what he knew, or imagine those things he had seen, or some he had been required to do. And there was no reason they should. He had fought in part to preserve their naïveté, their bombastic, boisterous innocence.

There had been times when only the thought of his family at Josten Hall, just as he remembered them, posturing and blustering and blessedly, wholesomely oblivious, had kept him from despair. There was no question that he would do all within his power for the family, he thought as he approached Boodle's discreet front door. Even marrying an heiress. And why not? He longed for those things for which he'd fought: a home, heirs, security, tradition. It was time he wed a woman of wealth and intelligence, one whom he could admire.

That was his criteria. Had been his criteria until now. Because of a sudden he realized he required—no, not required—he *wanted* more, he thought as he nodded to the doorman at the entrance to Boodle's.

He was no sooner through the door into the foyer when a voice hailed him. "Ned? Captain Ned Lockton?"

He turned to find a slight fellow a few years his junior making his way down the corridor toward him, his movements constrained by the close fit of his pantaloons and the waist-nipping cut of a coat with exaggerated shoulders. A high collar cinched round with an elaborately tied blue cravat obscured the lower half of his face while sandy curls brushed toward his face did a fair job of obscuring the rest.

"Good Lord, Borton, is that you?" Ned asked.

The Honorable George Borton's family, comfortable country gentry, lived ten miles from Josten Hall. Borton had tagged after him when they were lads until Ned had entered the navy. The last time Ned had seen Borton was two years ago, just after his niece, Mary, had turned down his offer of marriage. Apparently, since then Borton had been developing some town bronze. "How fare you, Borton?"

"Flourishing, Ned," Borton said, then noting Ned's appraisal of his ensemble, said, "Hale."

"Delighted to hear it."

"No, not me, me tailor, Captain. Paul Hale. Though your tailor looks to have a done a plumb job, too, sir. Never seen shoulder padding set in so well."

Ned didn't bother telling him his coat had no padding. "Thank you."

"I didn't know you were a member here."

"Josten has submitted my name for consideration."

"Consideration nothing," Borton proclaimed, clapping him on the shoulder. "I'm on the election committee. Here!" He waved a hovering footman over. "Take Captain Lockton's parcel for him and bring us a drink. Port, isn't it? Port it is."

He smiled and clapped Ned on the back again. "Let me show you around. Wonderful library we have, and the most comfortable chairs in all of London. And, lest you need reminding, we, too, have a bow window just like White's.

"Best of all," he continued, "we've got no women. How's your niece, Mary? No, don't tell me. She's not engaged, is she? 'Course not. Would have heard. Where was I? Oh, yes. No women. We are a kingdom of men, an island set above the cacophony of female voices. Should it be your desire, you wouldn't have to set eyes on a female for weeks. How *is* Mary?"

Ned, who had been without female company for the greater part of his adult life, could not help but smile. "It sounds rather like my last commission."

Borton shot him a quick glance and seeing that he was being twitted, smiled. "Forgot that that's hardly an endorsement for you, eh, Captain? So what would be a recommendation? Good food? Congenial company? The most current publications? Why, Brummell himself is a member here, though he's mostly absent of late." He placed his finger alongside his nose and leaned forward. "Dunners." He straightened. "Still there's plenty of sport to be had."

"So I've heard," Ned replied.

Borton's neat features pressed together in consternation. "Forgot about that. Damn foolish thing for your nephew to play against Smyth. Regular Captain Sharp, that one. Nothing untoward, of course. Simply a veteran of more nights of ruinous play than most men twice his age. Heard several of the members tried to talk the lad into quitting the table. No luck."

"I've no doubt of that. Sense is not my family's long suit, I am afraid."

"I feel responsible in part. I should have been watching out for those two. They were like brothers to me until . . . and it weren't their fault Mary . . ." He broke off and colored. "Anyway, knew something like this would happen. Bound to. Never seen such cocksureness as that pair display. And all of it unwarranted."

"Yes. That's very much as I felt upon renewing my acquaintance with them. Still, they are my nephews. Is Smyth here?"

Borton glanced at him. "Haven't seen him."

"Don't worry, Borton. I have only come to repay Harry's debt."

"Oh? Good."

"Tell me what you know of Smyth."

Borton lifted a shoulder. "Other than that he gambles often and deeply, is swimming in lard and likes that state very well, has kept the same mistress for years, and is a terrible snob who ain't got the blood to back up his conceit?"

Ned smiled. "Yes. Other than that."

"Well, one of this spring's choicest bits of tattle is that his grandsire is ailing and has promised to name Smyth his heir *if* Smyth marries before the old fellow turns his toes up. Because the old fella's fortune ain't entailed. And a mighty fortune it is. Though Smyth is wealthy, he would be one of England's *wealthiest* if he wed in time."

"You said he didn't need the money."

"He don't need it to live, but he needs it to live as he'd like," Borton said. "If he could secure that sort of wealth then everyone would have to forget his family was in trade but four generations back. He is accepted, but he is not acclaimed and he wants that very much."

"Good Lord, Borton, you are a virtual font. It makes me wonder what you might know about me," Ned said.

Borton remained unperturbed. "Nothing to your discredit, which in itself ought to make me suspicious."

Ned laughed. "Oh, I have my sins, I assure you."

"Can't imagine what they are. You were always so different from the rest of your family. Me old da used to say that the Locktons were born backward, the youngest having the most sense and the oldest having no . . . Oh. My. I've stepped in it again, haven't I?" Borton flushed.

"Think nothing of it."

"Here. Let me send someone to look around for Smyth." A flick of his fingers brought a footman hurrying over. "See if you can locate Mr. Smyth. I suggest you start in all the rooms with largish mirrors. He's bound to be in front of one."

The footman did not dare smile as he ran to do Borton's bidding, but Ned grinned. "Fond of his reflection, is he?"

"Damn dandy. Don't know why he ain't a member at White's except he'd have too much competition and he might not have been accepted. But now that Brummell looks to be about to sconce the reckoning and head for the Continent, there'll a vacancy in the bow window."

"Perhaps you ought to apply," Ned suggested innocently.

Borton laughed. "Me? Oh, no. True, I enjoy my valet's services, but with the dandies it ain't just about the dress, you know. It's their languor, their *ennui*, and their ability to make something momentous out of the trivial. Last Season two of them almost came to blows at Lady Devonshire's fete over which legume produces the vilest flatulence. No, I'm no dandy. Just well dressed." He preened a bit.

A servant appeared at Borton's elbow, saving Ned from forming a reply. Borton took the glasses from the proffered tray and ushered Ned ahead of him into a large, comfortable-looking room with thick Oriental carpets and tall windows overlooking the street below.

The room was already filled with gentlemen reading newspapers and periodicals or sitting together drinking and talking. Borton spotted a pair of unoccupied chairs near the marble fireplace and led the way toward them, nodding at acquaintances as he went.

"Here we are, Captain. Have a seat. How is that leg of yours, anyway? Wouldn't know you'd had a good piece of it torn out, the way you move. Ain't wooden, is it?"

Ned took the chair Borton indicated and accepted a glass of port. "No. I can vouch for it being all too real. Especially when I ride. Or I should say attempt to ride."

"Well, I should not be too eager to mend."

Ned tipped his head inquiringly.

"However will the ladies know you are a wounded war hero if you do not limp?"

Ned laughed. "I shall have to rely on you to tell them."

At this, Borton put his glass aside and leaned forward, giving Ned a meaningful nod. "Ah. So you *are* thinking of entering the marriage mart, aren't you?"

"Why would you think that?" Ned asked and took a sip of port.

"The new coat had to betray something more than a nascent sartorial interest. Any man who's not a dandy buys a new coat for one of two reasons, to impress a lady or his valet. Since I doubt you have a valet, and I know you are not wed, it can only stand to reason that a lady has attracted your interest."

Ned shook his head, though in truth the mere word *lady* conjured up an image of silky, coffee-colored curls, pale skin, merry violet eyes, and a lively smile that would not disappear.

"Normally I'd advise caution," Borton said. "You're about to launch yourself into far more dangerous waters than you're used to, Captain. Looks, lineage, and wealth such as yours are powerful lures for the predators in these waters, particularly of the mama variety. They would devour a choice morsel such as yourself except . . ."

"Except?" Ned prodded curiously.

"Except you'll be having a great deal of competition this year. Men I never thought to see fall into the parson's mousetrap are preparing to hurl themselves at the altar like lemmings into the sea." He nodded somberly. "The crops are failing, the stock market is falling, soldiers are returning home to no work and bread taxes. Few men have been untouched by the troubled economy. Even amongst those with indemnity, there is a rush to consolidate fortunes and shore up dynasties shaken by these troubled times."

Then, in his mercurial fashion, Borton brightened. His eyes sparkled. "But, then, perhaps I have it wrong and you are interested in persuing a sweeter and more ephemeral association, rather than a permanent and pragmatic one?"

Ned wasn't. He had never had a mistress. Mostly because he'd never had the time but also because there was something in him that resisted the notion of purchased passion. "And here I have always thought those 'ephemeral' relationships were the more pragmatic ones."

Borton chuckled. "Ah, I see. You're either a romantic or a cynic, Ned. I suspected as such."

"Did you?"

"Oh, yes. Heroes only come in those two varieties.

They either care too much, you see, or not at all. Even ones as seemingly imperturbable as yourself. Possibly most especially types such as yourself. So, which is it, Ned: cynic or romantic?"

Ned ignored Borton's question. "For the purposes of discussion, let us say you are correct, Borton, and assume I am looking for a wife. Where would you suggest I start looking?"

Eagerly, Borton rubbed his hands on his knees. "My dear fellow, I am honored you would seek my opinion. Now, let me think. The new crop of debs has not yet sprouted fresh from their court presentations so I've not had the pleasure of looking them over. As to those unwed ladies I do know . . ." He squinted, thinking hard.

"Let me see, let me see. Someone accomplished, beautiful, wealthy"—he darted an apologetic look at Ned—"not that the Locktons have need of wealth, but it is nice if one's wife has a fortune of her own."

Ned did not disagree.

"There's Lady Deborah Gossford—"

"Bad teeth!" a masculine voice proclaimed.

Ned looked around to find a pair of gentlemen standing nearby. The stouter one had thinning ginger hair and an overgrown squash of a nose, the older one, a swarthy, Italianate look.

"True, Elton," Borton allowed, looking over his shoulder. "But nice skin."

"Very," agreed the stout fellow.

"Lord Elton and Prince Carvelli. Captain Lockton, late of His Majesty's navy," Borton introduced the men. "I am trying to recollect this Season's crop of hopefuls."

Ned rose and the prince waved him back into his chair as Borton pulled a chair over for him.

"My sister has excellent teeth," Borton tossed out a little too casually once they were all seated. "And very nice skin."

"She don't want to wed, Borton," Elton said firmly. "She likes her situation with you too well. Might not be able to boss around a husband as easily as she does you."

"No one will have me as long as she's in me house," Borton said dolefully. "She needs to wed. Perhaps, Captain . . ." He broke off abruptly, shaking his head. "No. Can't do it to you, Ned. Like you too much."

"Diane de Mourie is a very pretty young lady," Carvelli said.

"Never do," Elton said. "She's a prude."

"Nothing wrong with prudes," a newcomer declared, approaching them and greeting Borton. "Married one myself. Keeps 'em from interfering with one's nocturnal activities, dontcha know? Prudes never ask what you're doing because then they'd have to pretend to care."

"My congratulations on the efficacy of your union, Toleffer. And my condolences," Borton said, garnering a laugh from the group gathering round them. More introductions were made, more chairs found and pulled close.

"Well, what of Lady Anne Major-Trent?" Elton asked. "Eighty thousand pounds. A figure like Venus—"

"—and the most annoying laugh in the kingdom," Borton said.

"Lady Margery Hicks?" another offered.

"If one could teach her how to dress," someone replied disparagingly, then, "Jenny Pickler is making her bow this year."

"Have you met her mother?"

Ned was barely attending the debate. His thoughts kept returning to Lady Eastlake's ridiculous impersonation. And her purple eyes. And her winsome smile. And the memory of her light, taut body against his chest.

"What about Lady Lydia Eastlake?" he asked.

Chapter Six

Ned might have rolled an unexploded missile into the group's midst. For a moment, no one spoke and everyone stared. Then Borton broke into laughter and the others joined in.

"That is rich! Too, too good, Ned!" Borton laughed and then, abruptly, "Good Lord. He isn't joking. He— Oh, my heavens. I completely forgot."

He took note of the group's confused expressions. "Captain Lockton has never spent a Season in London. He doesn't *know*."

Sounds of understanding rippled through the group.

"Elton, if you would be so kind to fetch The Book," Borton said and sank back, a cat's smile on his face.

The men standing around traded knowing looks while Ned waited, curious. Soon enough, Elton returned carrying a thick ledger that he dropped unceremoniously onto Borton's lap. Licking his index finger, Borton began leafing through the pages, his gaze scanning the years printed on the topmost line. Finally arriving at 1808, he paused and journeyed the tip of his finger down a long column.

"Here," he said, shifting the book so that it faced Ned.

He tapped at an entry two-thirds the way down the page. It read: *Byng wagering Colonel Ross 100 guineas to 10 that the newly arrived violet-eyed toast is not bespoke within in twelve months to this day. April 5, 1808.* The entry was marked paid on the appropriate date.

A little farther down the page, Borton pointed out another record: *Brummell offers Lord Butte 500 guineas to 25 if L.E. does not wed him before next Season. Paid.*

He read aloud a few more entries before moving on to the next year and then the next, reciting a litany of wagers and bets placed on whether or not Lydia Eastlake would marry or become engaged. But as the betting book's years progressed the focus of the bets subtly shifted.

Lord T. 1000 g to H.H.E's 500 should a certain violet-eyed lady dance thrice with the same partner at Almack's Friday next.

General Sneed-Worth Price has 50 g to A. Marly's 5 if Lady L wears a yellow gown to Devonshire's fete.

Brummell 2,000 Col. D 500 should the colonel secure LL's consent to a carriage ride.

There were fewer and fewer bets on how long Lady Eastlake would remain a spinster and more and more on what she would wear, with whom she would dance, and at what hour she would appear at various balls and fetes. Borton found the last entry and tapped it with his finger, raising his gaze to Ned's as he read aloud. " 'Lord A. 10,000 pounds to Lords Glass, Johnston, Barnell, and Fletcher's 5000 if she does not accept his marriage proposal.' Need I tell you who 'she' is?"

"And, Captain," the stout Elton said with a smile, "that wager was lost."

Borton sighed and sank back in his chair. "More men

have dangled after Lydia Eastlake than there have been lures cast in the Thames. Have you met the lady?"

"No," Ned said. "I've merely seen her image and was curious about her."

His companions nodded sanguinely, donning expressions either sentimental or lascivious, depending on their natures.

"Stunning woman."

"A lady of quality."

"The Incomparable."

"Not as downy as she once was." A silky male voice interrupted the murmured accolades. "Though not a mean bit yet."

"Smyth," Borton said in ill-concealed irritation. "There is no chitty-faced wench half as beautiful as Lady Eastlake and you know it well."

Ned rose to his feet and turned. An elegant gentleman in biscuit-colored breeches and dark blue broadcloth jacket lounged against the marble fireplace, idly fingering a Sevres snuffbox. He had handsome, narrow features and artfully tousled dark locks shot through with gray, though Ned supposed him to be close in age to himself. His manner was profoundly languid. His heavy-lidded gaze traveled coolly over Ned and his smile was no more than a thin pleating of flesh at the corners of his mouth.

So this, thought Ned, was a dandy.

"One of the footmen said you were asking after me, Borton," Smyth said.

"That's so, Smyth." Borton rose, too. "Captain Lockton, may I present the Honorable Childe Smyth? Mr. Smyth, Captain Edward Lockton."

"I am glad to meet you, sir," Ned said politely. "I understand you know my nephew Harold, Lord Lockton."

Smyth snapped open the lid of his snuffbox one-handedly, earning admiring murmurs from some of the gentlemen. He dabbed a pinch on the back of his wrist and inhaled it delicately, his thin nostrils pinching closed, before answering. "Ah, yes. Young Harry. I do, indeed."

The circle of gentlemen, intuiting that they'd become *de trop*, faded to the side, leaving Ned with Smyth and Borton, but not so far away that they would miss a choice bit of tattle if they strained their ears.

"I believe you have my nephew's vowels," Ned said. "I would like to make it possible for you to return them to him."

"Good God," Smyth exclaimed with exaggerated surprise, turning to Borton. "Most impressively tactful for a bloody naval captain, ain't he?"

Ned noted Borton fidgeting, anticipating unpleasantness. Borton would be disappointed. It would be a sad day when a few words caused Ned to lose his temper. Far worse had been said of him, and to him, by far better men. Many under his command.

"Not so surprising, surely?" Ned replied. "As a naval captain, one might expect me to make use of the weapon most likely to hit true."

"Weapon? I didn't realize we were engaged in combat," Smyth drawled, looking amused. "I thought we were conversing."

Ned smiled. "But I have been made to understand that in Society all conversations are skirmishes."

Smyth laughed. "Very true, Captain. But tell me, just

what weapon are you most likely to employ in a verbal skirmish?"

"The one least familiar to my adversary," Ned replied.

"As you have done?"

Ned inclined his head while around him the men fell into confused silence and Smyth lifted one sculpted eyebrow. Borton suddenly grinned.

"*Tact,*" Borton burst out like a schoolboy who suddenly thinks of the answer to his tutor's question. "Why, Ned's referring to tact, Smyth! You said it yourself."

Snickers and laughter rippled through the group as they realized Borton was right.

Smyth's eyes narrowed and his mouth tensed before relaxing. "I concede the hit, sir. Well done." The admission was gracious, but no accompanying geniality reached his eyes. "Kind of you to handle this affair with young Harry for your brother," he continued.

Ned let his assumption stand. It served his current purpose to let this dandy think Josten's fortune was intact. No one need know that he was paying Harry's debt out of his captain's share of the prize money from a ship he'd captured in the waning days of the war.

When Ned did not reply, Smyth shrugged, the amusement he'd expected to have at Ned's expense not materializing. "At your convenience, then."

"The funds are available to you now, sir," Ned said.

"Really?" Smyth asked. "Well, this is an unexpected boon. Indeed, this may just be my lucky day. Perhaps you are a talisman, Captain."

"Oh?"

"Yes. My luck has been vile of late, but you've changed

that with a few words. Why, I've half a mind to tow you around as me good luck charm." The words were ludicrous, amusing, and subtly offensive.

Borton flushed.

Ned did not bother replying. Once he left Boodle's, he was unlikely to ever exchange words with Smyth again.

"'Pon my rep," Smyth said when the silence had gone on too long, "I *will* take you with me and you'll want to go, too. For I intend to do you a good turn for the good turn you've done me."

"And what would that be?" Ned asked, growing bored with the fop's affectations.

"I heard you inquire after Lady Lydia Eastlake."

The muscles in Ned's back tensed, as did his biceps. He would take it much amiss if this popinjay said something untoward about the lady. Lydia Eastlake would doubtless laugh at such misplaced chivalry. And that was all it was: the reflexive impulse to protect, engendered in boyhood by a family who always needed protecting from themselves and then further honed during his years as a captain in His Majesty's navy. It wasn't anything more personal. How could it be? He'd not even properly met the lady. He smiled.

Smyth misread his smile. "Ah, as I suspected. Most natural thing in the world," he said with heavy patronization. "She *is* Lady Lydia Eastlake after all. Admired, emulated, and unattainable." He smiled himself. "No. I'm not surprised you are interested in her based on the images you've seen. But I warn you, an image is not always a proper representative of a person."

"What do you mean?" Borton asked, frowning.

"She's a bit unconventional, something of a scape-

grace, truth be told. Oh, not so anyone protests. She is
Lady Lydia, after all." He paused, his brows climbing
inquiringly. "I am sure you've heard . . . you *do* know
about her companion, don't you?"

"Pardon me?"

"Her companion. Mrs. Cod. No one would tolerate
her except that Lady Lydia treats her like a pet, so we
all do. Seeing how Lady Lydia not only sets fashion but
is fashion, it's surprising we don't all trail mad thieves
in our wake. Personally, I'd prefer a dog. Might pee on
the rugs but at least it wouldn't steal the china off one's
hostess's table, eh?"

His remark did not invoke the sniggers he clearly
anticipated and Smyth's eyes studied the group of men
with subtle contempt. Ned barely noted it; he was busy
considering on Smyth's words.

Lydia Eastlake had a thief for a companion? Ned did
not give Smyth's words much credence, but whatever
truth there was in the claim suggested an unexpected
dimension to Lady Lydia's character. Smyth was gazing at him expectantly, clearly waiting for Ned to thank
him for his favor. "I see, Mr. Smyth. Thank you for being
so . . . illuminating."

Smyth looked taken aback. "Oh. Oh, no. *That* ain't
the favor I was going to do you. Consider that bit gratis.
No. I have something much better in mind."

"That won't be necessary."

Smyth ignored him. "I know for a fact Lady Eastlake
will be dining al fresco next Saturday at Lady Pickler's
house. The Pickler is preparing to set her daughter on
Society and if the daughter is anything like the mother,
Society had best beware.

"It will be a dead bore, of course," he drawled. "Lady Pickler is the worst sort of stiff-rumped bully, but she and the Almack harpies are thick as thieves and should you offend by refusing, you might as well sip arsenic because from then on you will be dead to the highest Society.

"Only the cream of the *ton* is tolerated," Smyth went on, and the languid dismissal of his gaze made it clear he doubted any of those standing nearby would be on the guest list. "But say the word and I will secure an invitation *and* the opportunity to meet our legendary Lady Lydia. Why, I'll introduce you myself. We are friendly." He pursed his mouth together in a mocking moue. "Oh, please allow me to do this thing?"

Smyth was welcome to whatever pettiness he plotted, for Ned would not refuse the chance to see Lady Lydia again. He meant to discover if her eyes were really the color of a martin's wing, if she would feel as light on the dance floor as she had in his arms when he'd caught her from tumbling off the ladder, and if her smile was as quick and breathtaking and inviting when she was not posing as someone she wasn't.

"Captain?"

"Yes," Ned said. "Thank you."

"Oh, no, my dear Captain, 'tis I who thank you. You shall have the invitation, I promise." He motioned toward the betting book still lying open on the seat of Borton's vacant chair. "May I take it back to the library? I'd like to enter a wager."

"Of course," Borton said, leaning down and closing the book. He handed it to Smyth, who received it with an enigmatic smile and sauntered off.

"He didn't used to be like that," Borton said, watching him go. "There was a time I rather liked him. But his grandfather's been squeezing him between his thumb and forefinger for years. He feels fiercely his lack of antecedents. Society is growing much more select these days. I believe he took up with the dandies to increase his consequence and now he seeks to impress them."

Borton shook his head worriedly. "You shouldn't have accepted his invitation. He only means to make sport of you to his friends."

"Oh, I know," Ned said.

"Then why ever did you agree?"

Ned smiled. "Why, to meet Lady Eastlake. What else?"

Back in the library, Smyth bent over the betting book. Beside him stood Prince Carvelli. Smyth finished writing and signed his name with a flourish and turned the book for the prince's signature. It read:

> *Childe Smyth 1000 g to Prince C's 100 that a naval captain fresh from battle will be broadsided by Lady L before the Season ends.*

Chapter Seven

"*La Belle Assemblee* has named the newest shade of the Season 'Eastlake *beaux yeux*,'" Eleanor informed Lydia on their ride over to Lady Pickler's in her ducal carriage. She eyed Lydia's newest gown—as it would happen, a purple one—sardonically. Lydia chuckled.

"Come now, Eleanor. I am not so enamored of my own reflection as that. I simply asked for a heliotrope-colored gown."

"Well, you are in marvelous looks," Eleanor declared. "I hope you realize your gown is responsible for adding to my sins."

"How so?"

"Envy. I am loathsomely envious."

"I am certain you will overcome such unworthy sentiments as soon as you remember that circumstance makes it imperative that I show to advantage whilst you show to advantage simply out of habit."

"Blatant flattery," Eleanor declared. "Nonetheless I will accept it as my due."

"Eleanor is right," Emily roused herself from her corner of the carriage to say. "You look most dashing, Lydia."

There were shadows under the older woman's eyes. Lydia suspected Emily was not sleeping well. Not that she ever did, but Lydia's decision to seek a spouse had clearly awoken troublesome memories for Emily. Lydia had reassured the older woman that she would not share in Emily's fate, but though Emily understood this objectively, she explained that what one knows and what one feels are not always the same things.

"Thank you, dear," Lydia said.

"You are certain to attract much admiration," Emily said. "You will have an offer by nightfall, I am convinced."

Emily's determined effort toward optimism made Lydia smile, but it soon faded. If she could just convince herself this husband hunt was a kind of sport, like fox-hunting or searching for June strawberries. But every time she sat down to consider possible candidates, she ended up wondering about the unknown gentleman from Roubalais's.

Over a week had passed since her impromptu masquerade at the pawnbroker's shop. She'd spent them expecting to hear rumors that she had a sister born on the wrong side of the blanket to a French émigré, one currently working at a jeweler's in Cheapside. When this didn't occur, rather than relegating the incident to the past, she found her thoughts returning again and again to the tall, handsome stranger whose solemn mien was belied by the unexpected humor in his blue-gray eyes.

Not that she seriously considered him a potential suitor. That would be absurd on the basis of one brief meeting and under such bizarre circumstances. She wasn't so green. She was a practical, sophisticated woman.

But . . . *had* he wondered about the shopgirl he'd saved from falling? She only had to close her eyes to feel his strong arms and broad chest. Did he feel her imprint against him? No. Of course not. But if he did, did it keep him awake some nights—

"—be careful, Lydia."

Eleanor's voice broke through her reverie like an internal warden. She came out of her musings with a snap. Emily was nestled in the corner of the carriage, her eyes closed fast and Eleanor was regarding her curiously.

"Excuse me?" Lydia managed.

"I commented that the fabric looks delicate, so if you venture into the rose garden, you'd best be careful."

"I will."

Though the dress had cost a small fortune (something a month ago Lydia wouldn't have even known, much less cared about) she was glad she'd ordered it made. Lady Pickler's was the first proper fete of the Season and she needed to be conspicuous and conspicuously attractive. This gown made easy work of that.

Beneath the overskirt of deep rose jaconet flowed a filmy petticoat of the finest shell-pink muslin ending in four rows of pale green embroidery with a lace-edged flounce. The gown's long sleeves were banded with darker green satin à la Duchesse de Berri. A wide sash of the same material nestled just below her bosom, accenting the empire waist, while a diaphanous gauze fichu filling in the low-cut bodice gave a cursory nod to modesty. Perched atop her head she wore a green lacquered bonnet decorated with blackberries and fuchsias.

"You'd best hope it doesn't rain, Lydia," Eleanor continued. "Lady Pickler will still insist on parading us all down to her bottom garden, by which time you shall be shivering so violently, reports next morning will claim you have ague.

"Take my shawl with you." Eleanor held out the Kashmir wrap folded on her lap.

"What? And obscure this dress? I should think not. One must make sacrifices," Lydia replied in an amused voice. Still, she accepted the shawl.

It was unseasonably chill and had been all spring and Emily was sensitive to drafts. Lydia reached across the carriage and gently spread the fine wool over her slumbering companion, then settled back.

"Is she asleep?" Eleanor asked.

"Oh, yes," Lydia answered softly. "Thankfully. She hasn't been sleeping well of late."

Eleanor's gaze stayed for a long while on the sleeping, motherly looking Emily. "I must admit, Lydia, your decision to engage Emily as your companion was a good one."

"Thank you." Lydia appreciated the duchess's admission. She had not initially approved of Lydia's new companion. But Lydia had been unable to deny Emily's polite, hopeless request to remove her from Brislington Asylum. Her appeal had startled Lydia.

In truth, it had frightened her, too. For the first time in her adult life it was borne in on Lydia how much influence she owned and that she could affect things, things both frivolous and important, and that this was not a privilege to be taken lightly. Emily had awoken in Lydia a desire to act.

Yet this sounded nobler than Lydia knew herself to be. It was only part of the answer. Her house was too empty and she needed someone to share it with. Both women saw in each other the family they'd lost.

"I wonder who will be at the Picklers' this year," Eleanor eventually mused as they continued at a leisurely pace.

Lydia glanced out the carriage window. They were approaching the outskirts of St. James, where the Pickler family had years ago decided to straddle rustication and urbanization.

The city was slowly encroaching upon them, however, and what with taxes and debt and offers to purchase portions of their property simply too good to refuse, what had once been a fairly large estate had been whittled down to a fraction of its former size. Not to be gainsaid, Lady Pickler had long ago enclosed the remaining lawns with a high stone wall and proceeded to landscape it as though it were still a hundred acres and not ten. Every year brought a new surprise or horror in the little plot of land—depending on one's sensibilities.

"There will be the usual crowd in attendance, I'm sure: Lord and Lady Alvanley, the Hammond-Croutts, Mrs. Mary Sefton, and Childe Smyth. Brummell was invited, but he has been notably absent from all Society of late," Lydia replied, then went on to name a dozen more in quick succession, finishing by saying, "Very few unexpected names and even fewer unfamiliar ones."

Eleanor's thin brows rose above her deep-set eyes. "Good heavens, Lydie, one would think you knew the guest list."

"I do. My maid is cousin to Lady Pickler's. That same maid is, not coincidentally, currently sporting the very nice blue wool spencer you admired last year."

Eleanor gave her an approving look. "Your ingenuity is impressive."

"I mean to leave nothing to chance this Season, Eleanor."

"Then you will already know that Lady Pickler did not want to invite you to her fete this year," Eleanor replied, watching her carefully.

No. Lydia had not known this. "Why ever not?" she asked. "She's a picksome old tabby, but I have never offended her to my knowledge."

"Her daughter has never debuted before. Lady Pickler knows you'll cast her Jenny in the shade."

"Piffle," Lydia said.

Eleanor ignored this statement as disingenuous, which it was. Lydia had seen the Picklers' Friday-faced daughter. Of course, if Lady Pickler had been her mother, she would have looked like she had a continual migraine, too.

"She didn't dare snub you, of course," Eleanor continued. "She is trapped between fearing you will accept her invitations and outshine her daughter and fearing you won't attend and thus consign her fete to the ranks of the second-rate. I'd feel sorry for her, except that last week she was overheard to comment that she thinks it's absurd that a spinster should have endured as the cynosure of all masculine eyes for as long as you. I believe she feels a new nonpareil is due to ascend. Preferably her Jenny."

"Endured? My heavens, she makes me sound like one of Stonehenge's monoliths," said Lydia. "However do you know this?"

"You are not the only one with a loyal maid who aspires to a fashionable wardrobe."

Lydia chuckled but then murmured, "Oh, bother," as she thought about the difficulty of negotiating a Season filled with worried mamas jockeying for their daughters' futures.

Eleanor patted her hand consolingly. "At least she didn't call you an ape leader."

"Oh, it's not that," Lydia said. "I daresay she's right; I have endured. But I do wish her daughter could make her bow next year, when I will be happily ensconced in my new role as Lord Plentiful's adored and overindulged wife."

"Well, her brat is out now and you will have to plan some way of allaying Lady Pickler's motherly frets," Eleanor, ever practical, stated. "For example, do not be witty. Lady Pickler doesn't understand wit and it makes her uncomfortable. Poor dear has a filthy mind. She is certain anything subtle is indelicate and ought to be kept well away from her babe's innocent ears. Why else do you think Sarah is not with us?"

Lydia, who had been smiling as she watched the street scene outside the carriage, slew about. "What do you mean? I thought she had a previous engagement."

"No. She wasn't asked."

"Not asked?" Lydia echoed with a chill in her voice that few people had heard. Lady Pickler could cavil about her all she liked, but Sarah was another matter. "That's absurd. Have your man turn about at—"

"No, Lydia," Eleanor interrupted with a hand on her wrist. "Sarah knew if you learned of it you would refuse to go and she also knows, apparently better than you, that you can ill afford to offend Lady Pickler this Season."

"Of course I can," Lydia said indignantly. "Of all the nerve. How dare she not invite Sarah after so many years? Tell the driver to stop."

"No. I won't because Sarah *has* been kicking up rough of late and if you are candid with yourself, you will admit it, too."

Lydia's lips pressed together, though she could not bring herself to deny the charge. To anyone else, yes, but not to Eleanor. Because Eleanor was right; Sarah had been acting the hoyden for the past year, paying increasingly little care to her reputation and more to her impulses. Lately she'd been even more distracted and preoccupied. Lydia did not know what to make of the changes in her lifelong friend. She felt in some odd ways abandoned by her, as though Sarah had purposely chosen a path she knew Lydia could not follow.

"I wish Gerald would come to town," she murmured.

"It would only make matters worse. They loathe each other. The problem is that she is still so very young. I sometimes forget how long she's been married. What was she when she wed? Sixteen? And Marchland is my contemporary."

"Yes." Lydia remembered Sarah's initial enthusiasm for the match. Gerald Marchland was wealthy and well connected and if he seemed overly puritanical, Sarah would tease him into lighter moods. And she had at first. But the patterns of forty years were not to be gainsaid and soon those mannerisms he had found winsome, he considered lewd, and Sarah, rather than admiring his sobriety, thought him a bore. They were entirely unsuited. "Is she very unhappy do you think?"

"No," Eleanor said thoughtfully. "If she was, she might

be more inclined to take advice. She actually seems in prime spirits of late and as like to thumb her nose at Society as bend to its rules."

"Perhaps she is simply going through an odd patch and shall pass out of it soon. Or maybe she's breeding again," Lydia suggested thoughtfully. "She certainly looks in glowing health."

"Let us hope not," Eleanor declared. "She has not seen Gerry in three months."

"Who's breeding?" Emily asked in a muzzy voice.

"No one, dear," Eleanor said. "We were simply speculating."

"That would be one good thing about you marrying, Lydie," Emily said. "I should very much like a baby to dandle." Emily's face softened with sentiment. "I never had a baby to dandle."

"Neither have I," Eleanor said, though a good deal more happily. Eleanor had always said she'd no desire to procreate.

"Then we are alike, Eleanor," Emily said. Neither woman seemed to notice anything odd in a former inmate of an insane asylum calling the Duchess of Grenville by her first name. Not that Emily would ever do so in public.

Except for those times she had "misplaced something in her reticule," she was very circumspect. She had, as she had once pointed out, been raised to be a lady, not a madwoman.

"You are much nicer than I, Emily," Eleanor said dryly.

"You don't know how nice you are, Eleanor," Emily protested.

Eleanor sniffed but nonetheless looked pleased.

The coach drew to a halt and the door opened with a flourish as the footman hurried to pull out the velvet-covered steps. They disembarked and Lydia paused, looking up the granite stairs to the entrance of the great house, where the door stood open. Within the entry hall, shadowy figures intermingled and waited.

They were waiting for her.

It was not vanity that made her think this; it was experience. Ever since she'd made her debut, she had been at the center of the public's attention. From birth, she'd been on display. Her parents had well equipped her for the life she was to lead; her manners were exquisite, her deportment gracious. By ten, she knew to speak when spoken to, to be decorative when not, and what words would best please an aged princess or a gruff prime minister.

But on the day her parents were driving up to an acquaintance's villa high in the Swiss Alps and their carriage had overturned on a mountain pass, killing them both, everything had changed.

One week she'd been surrounded by affection, elegance, adventure, and laughter—the next plunged into a world of muted colors, of ticking clocks and hushed corridors. There had been no distraction from her grief. The servants, the governess, the dancing instructor, and the housekeepers were all very kind. Very solicitous. Very . . . separate.

When Eleanor had arrived to sponsor her debut in Society, she'd sobbed with gratitude. And when she'd been presented at court and saw again the familiar expressions of approval and admiration, she'd felt she'd been delivered back into the world of the living.

She'd exerted herself to be the center of excitement and conversation and people, so that she would always be wanted, anticipated, and welcomed. She never made the mistake of taking Society's approval for granted.

And now her future hung in the balance and those social skills that had always come so effortlessly seemed suddenly to have abandoned her. An unnatural tautness settled about the mouth that wore smiles so easily, and an unusual stiffness accompanied her usually graceful step. She briefly closed her eyes, conjuring up a pair of strong phantom arms to enfold her.

And just like that, her balance was restored and her sense of humor came to her aid. She was husband-hunting, not dying. And really, she told herself, it could not begin to approach the difficulty of deciding which modiste would fashion her gown for Spenser's masquerade ball honoring Wellington during this summer of the Glorious Peace. In fact, it was less difficult. She knew exactly what she required in a husband: wealth.

And with that, she took a deep breath, gathered her skirt lightly in her hand, and followed Eleanor up the stairs.

Chapter Eight

"Ah, Lady Grenville, how delightful. And here are you, too, Lady Lydia. Everyone is so kind to come to my little party." Lady Pickler, her keg-shaped body draped in saffron-striped silk, glanced at Emily. "And Mrs. Cod."

First she had the audacity to dismiss Sarah and now Emily? Lydia's back stiffened. "How amusing that you call kindness what everyone else in the *ton* refers to as—"

"—pleasure," Eleanor interjected before she could say "an onerous obligation." The duchess linked her arm through Lydia's, discreetly jabbing a fingernail into her side.

Lady Pickler accepted the praise as her due. "One does what one can to make the Season gay. Not that it isn't a great deal of work. I shall have to retire to my bed for a week come tomorrow. But you all so love my little dinner al fresco. How could I deny you?"

"How could you?" Lydia purred.

On the opposite side of the hall, a group of the *ton*'s most eligible scions spotted their newly arrived party and began making their way over. "Lady Lydia!" they hailed her, trying to navigate through the crowd at the door.

Alas, Lady Pickler had other plans for the bachelors.

"Ah!" she said, taking both Lydia and Eleanor by their elbows and spinning them around. She tugged them forth with the determination of a small barge crossing turbulent waters, Emily trailing in their wake.

"Pardon us. Excuse us. Yes, yes. Oh my. No time to stop," she chirped overbrightly at acquaintances who looked as though they would impede her progress by greeting either Eleanor or Lydia. "Can't stop to chat now. Her Grace is most eager to see what improvements I have made to the park."

Having quickly shunted them through the crush in the house to the relatively empty terrace overlooking the yard, she deposited them with feigned regret at having to return to "greet those other people." She assured them that there were many "wonderful new vistas to explore" and then all but pushed Lydia off the bottom step onto the lawn, flapping her hands playfully as she urged them to "get lost amidst the wilderness!"

"I am sure she would like you lost," Eleanor muttered. "Permanently."

"I don't feel any need to witness the atrocities that woman perpetuates on nature, Lydia," Emily said, puffing a little at having to keep up. "I see a bench over there. If you don't mind, I think I will sit a while."

"But of course, Emily."

Crowds agitated Emily. Lydia suspected the asylum's crowded facilities and the potential for chaos amongst its inmates could account for her distress. She didn't have much time to ponder, however, because the crowds were overflowing the house and spilling out onto the terrace in her wake. It was time to shine.

Like an actress taking her mark, Lydia drew herself up, immersing herself in the role that had become second nature. She greeted those she knew with outstretched hands and smiles and was greeted in kind. For the next half hour she chatted and flirted and told merry stories and listened appreciatively to those stories told by others. She accepted the gentlemen's compliments gracefully and where called for, returned the favor to wives and daughters.

She even managed to prise a smile from Jenny Pickler, who proved completely tongue-tied in the presence of gentlemen. It was a pity, Lydia thought, that she did not smile more often. She was a striking girl with inky hair and straight black brows and remarkable, clear skin. But her expression was so thunderous and unwelcoming, it was hard to appreciate her beauty.

Her sympathies engaged, Lydia lingered to speak to the girl and discovered that the reason Jenny looked so funeral faced was because she aspired to become a bluestocking, one of the earnest—some would say overeducated—ladies whom the *ton* disparaged so vehemently. At least, the *male* element of Society. It was small wonder that Jenny's parents forbade her from associating with the bluestockings, not if they wanted to see their daughter make an acceptable match.

"Why ever did you tell them your intentions?" Lydia asked. "Tell someone your intentions and you are asking to be thwarted."

"What do you mean, Lady Lydia?"

"Don't ask anyone's permission. I never do. Simply follow your head and let the chips fall where they may."

Jenny Pickler frowned, digesting this revolutionary idea.

"Now, mind, that doesn't mean you need to send an announcement to the *Times* about whatever it is you do. A little discretion is always advisable. But should you visit the lending libraries with a maid, or attend lectures with some sympathetic relative—and my dear, for the proper remuneration, there is always a sympathetic relation—by the time anyone notes you've packed your head with knowledge it will be too late. Simply go as you will. No one can keep you from becoming the person you mean to be."

Jenny did not look convinced. "That's easy for you to say. You're Lady Lydia Eastlake. You can do whatever you want with no one to gainsay you." And then, realizing she'd just chided London's reigning toast, she flushed. The surly expression dropped back over her features like a shutter.

"Yes," Lydia murmured, more to herself than Jenny as her thoughts returned to the project at hand. "Well, all things must come to an end."

"What do you mean?" Jenny asked sharply.

Lydia eyed Jenny thoughtfully. She intended to reveal her interest in becoming married anyway and the sooner the better. She could accomplish that mission and do this girl a good turn by letting her be the bearer of the news. At least, it would give her something to talk about.

She mustn't be too obvious, however. "Oh, nothing. It is just that, well, I've been wondering lately if I should consider changing my situation."

"You are going abroad?"

"No, dear."

"Oh, you are thinking of purchasing a new town house?" Jenny asked.

Good heavens, how was the chit to gain bluestocking status when she was so obtuse?

"I'm not referring to my *physical* situation."

"You are converting to Catholicism?" Jenny gasped, her hand flying to cover her mouth.

"No," Lydia said, resisting an impulse to shake the girl. "Though if I follow my current inclination, I will certainly be *converting* my name to another." She spoke with heavy emphasis.

For a second, Jenny stared at her in visible consternation. Then the dust cleared, as it were, and understanding dawned. "Oh. Oh!" Then, realizing the choice bit of gossip that she now possessed, her face brightened to something nearing animation.

"Well, it's been so nice talking to you, Lady Lydia, and I shall certainly take under advisement your suggestion regarding my intellectual pursuits, but I mustn't take any more of your time." She didn't wait for Lydia to agree. She spun around and sped straight to her mother, who'd reappeared by the terrace door.

"I see you've launched your missile into the midst of the fete," Eleanor's droll voice murmured from beside her.

"Is it as obvious as that, Eleanor?" Lydia asked, watching Jenny make her mother's side.

"Oh, yes. I can think of very few things that would inspire Jenny Pickler to actively seek out Lady Pickler, especially since she actually looks eager to do so. Therefore, she is either telling her mother she has received a marriage proposal or she is telling her that you are looking for one." She tilted her head. "Do you think that wise?"

"Definitely. Lady Pickler is one of the *ton*'s biggest gossips. She will spread the word far more effectively than taking an advert out in the *Times* could have done."

With a whisper in her ear and a hand on her arm, Jenny urged her mother a short distance away from the group where Lady Pickler had been holding court. Lydia could follow the conversation simply by watching the changing expressions on Lady Pickler's round face: first annoyance at being dragged away, then impatience, then skepticism, and yes, now amazement, as Jenny repeated Lydia's words verbatim, followed by glee at the choice tidbit she had been handed, and finally horror as she realized Lydia meant to go husband-hunting in the same waters in which her Jenny was currently trolling.

"Well done, Lydia," Eleanor said approvingly. "By breakfast tomorrow, all of London will be speculating whether Jenny is mad or if you really do mean to marry."

Lydia turned. "Thank you. I hope Miss Pickler makes good use—" Her words died on her lips, for as she turned her gaze fell on a tall figure emerging from the house onto the terrace. It was him.

Here.

She spun back around.

"Lydia?" Eleanor asked in concern.

"*Who is that*?" she whispered tightly, though no one was standing near enough to overhear had she spoken in a normal voice.

She stood facing Eleanor. From the expression on the duchess's face she could tell the moment Eleanor spotted "that." Her aplomb wobbled and for a second

the unflappable duchess stood on the precipice of looking impressed. With a visible effort, she regained her
composure.

"I do not know. But only give me a moment and I shall
find out." Before Lydia could protest, she'd motioned
over a footman. "Find out the name of the gentleman
speaking to Lady Pickler. Be discreet but quick."

The footman bowed and hurried off, leaving Eleanor
studying her younger friend.

"Oh, you needn't look at me so, Eleanor," Lydia
said.

"And how is that, Lydia?"

"Superior, smug, and amused."

Eleanor's answer to this was simply to look more superior, smug, and amused. "Tell me, Lydia. From the way
you reacted I would swear you have seen this gentleman
before. How so? Your eyes met across a wooded glen,
perhaps?" she asked sardonically.

No, across a dusty, cluttered store. "Why are you so
certain I have seen him before?" Lydia asked.

"Well, generally when you see someone new you
don't color up like a boiled lobster, duck your head
like a chambermaid caught gawking at the master, and
hiss questions with no proper pronouns. 'Who is *that*?'
indeed."

"I remarked him when I was shopping the other
day."

"And did he remark you?"

"No. Most definitely not."

"Then why are you standing to the side quaking and
tossing glances over your shoulder?"

Begad, she was quaking. Silly. There was no possible

way he would equate the shopgirl with the creature she now presented. She lifted her chin. "I'm not. How odd of you to think so, Eleanor."

Eleanor was not deceived, but she was too good a friend to press Lydia. At least, not here and now.

Lydia glanced at the gentleman. He was not looking at her, Lydia noted with a mix of relief and disappointment. His head was bowed to hear whatever Diane de Mourie was lisping up at him, his expression courteous and interested and . . . oh my, wasn't he glorious?

He stood at least half a head taller than any of the other gentlemen present, but carried the additional height so easily and was so well proportioned that one did not note it until another man passed near him. He'd clasped his hands lightly behind his back, a stance that accentuated the breadth of his shoulders in the blue broadcloth jacket. Encased in biscuit-colored trousers, his long muscular legs owed nothing to artifice. His dark gold hair was clipped short, an easy style with no artfully arranged tumble of locks. He wouldn't see the point in looking purposefully disheveled, she thought on a moment of inspiration.

"Begging your pardon, Your Grace." The footman had returned. "But the gentleman speaking to Lady Pickler is Captain Edward Lockton."

Eleanor's eyes widened at this information and she dropped a coin into the footman's waiting hand. "Thank you."

He pocketed the coin, bowed, and left them.

Lockton. Lydia vaguely recalled some pretty young pup at a ball last year scraping together the courage to ask for a dance. Wasn't he named Lockton?

"What is it, Eleanor?" Lydia demanded. "You know the name, I can see that. Who *is* he?"

"Josten's youngest brother. Josten being Marcus Lockton, Earl of Josten." She gave a light laugh. "I had heard he'd returned from his duty in His Majesty's navy. I should have recognized him. All the Locktons are unrepentantly ravishing."

At Lydia's questioning look she elaborated. "Josten was one of the *ton*'s most eligible bachelors when I made my bow." She smiled in recollection. "I quite favored his company for a while. But I aspired to rule the Polite World and he did not." Her smile faded.

"What happened to him?" Lydia asked. "Why have I never encountered this paragon?"

"Oh, he's still about. He just doesn't fly high or often. He married Nadine Hiddystole, a pretty little widgeon without two ideas to keep each other company."

"And why has this kept him from enjoying Society?" Lydia asked. She lowered her voice. "Is she unacceptable?"

"Heavens, no. Very respectable. No, it's something even more outré than that. Josten prefers the company of his wife to ours." She turned a bright smile on her friend, but Lydia imagined there was something painful beneath this last gay bit of practiced astonishment. "And, dare you believe it? She, his."

Lydia did, indeed. Her parents had been a similarly fond couple—except they were never alone, always at the center of a social whirl that was international. She assumed Josten and his wife must be very dull, sitting in their country house together with naught but themselves for company.

Why, what would one speak of without a constant influx of new people to talk to or gossip about . . . ? The thought was unexpectedly lowering. Was that all she was? A receptacle for gossip and mimer of other people's ideas?

"Not only did he withdraw to rusticate with his new wife, but after he became earl, he insisted his widowed sister, Beatrice Hickston-Tubbs and her brats come live with them," Eleanor went on, adding again in a soft murmur, "And I had higher aspirations."

So Josten was a generous man. All for the good. But the brother wasn't the man. "Yes. But what do you know of *him*, Eleanor. Tell me."

Eleanor looked up, startled out of her musing. "A definite contender," she said in a businesslike voice. "He's a naval captain. Or was. He retired after Napoleon's defeat at Waterloo in spite of the admiralty pressing him to remain. They even promised him a commission, and you know how hard those are to come by now that there are no French or Spanish ships to blow up."

Eleanor lowered her voice. "And speaking of which, the rumor mill says that during his last commission he netted a captain's share worthy of the wounds he suffered."

"Wounds?" He'd been injured? How? Lydia wondered worriedly. Her concern was such that she didn't even notice she hadn't asked the question that was most relevant to her particular situation, that being how much the captain's share had been. "Is he all right?"

"Apparently he survived."

"Tell me of his family," Lydia said.

"Oh, they are very well off," Eleanor said composedly.

"They'd have to be to support the current generation. A litter of dandified greenheads and goosecaps always in some hobble or 'nuther. The kits have discovered gambling and the young heir especially has a penchant for gaming hells and the *tapis verte*. Smyth blistered the boy for a ruinous amount a few weeks back and Josten let him stew damned low in the water trying to raise the ready before sending the captain to settle up. But he did."

Wealthy, well connected, well mannered . . . *Why* wasn't he looking at her? Gentlemen always looked at her, openly, covertly, too forward, too shy, but they always looked. He hadn't even glanced in her direction.

She looked down at her dress. The color was too bland; it made her hair dull. It did not drape properly; it hung. Even the weather refused to cooperate; the diffuse light made her appear sallow. And her bonnet obscured her only really outstanding features—

"Lydia," Eleanor suddenly said. "Now, don't gape, my dear, and try not to stutter, but if you turn around, I believe you are about to be introduced to your paragon."

Chapter Nine

Lydia wasn't gaping . . . well, quite . . . and she had *never* stuttered in her life—but what if he *did* recognize her? No, she reassured herself. That wasn't possible. That disheveled shopgirl and Lady Lydia Eastlake bore no resemblance one to the other. She turned around.

For a second she thought perhaps he did. There was something in his eyes, something quizzical and observant. But . . . no.

"Lady Grenville, how delightful to see you again," Childe Smyth said, bowing to Eleanor before turning to Lydia. "And Lady Lydia, I had hoped to find you here."

Distracted as she was, she still contrived a welcoming smile. She knew others thought little of Smyth, but she had always thought his airs were protective armor and that at his core he was simply a man who'd been taught to question his own value too much. "How are you, Mr. Smyth?" Drat. She sounded breathy.

"Tolerable," he replied. He turned to his companion. "Lady Grenville, may I present Captain Edward Lockton? Captain, Her Grace, Eleanor, the Duchess of Grenville."

"Ma'am, it is a pleasure." The captain bowed, gravely inclining his head just so.

"Thank you, Captain."

"Lady Lydia," Smyth said, and a devil danced in his eyes, "may I make known Captain—"

"Yes, yes, Mr. Smyth, Captain Lockton. I was standing right here," she said with an arch of her brow. She looked up at Lockton, her heart thundering so loudly she was certain he must hear it. "How do you do, Captain?"

She looked straight up into his eyes. They were just as clear and remarkable as she recalled and she could not discern a whit of recognition in them. Her racing heart slowed; she felt an odd little twist in her chest. It must be relief. Not disappointment. Why would she be disappointed? He hadn't recognized her as a dirty little shopgirl. That was hardly a cause for disappointment.

"Very well, Lady Lydia," the captain said. "Thank you."

"As you can see, Lady Lydia does not bend to protocol," Childe Smyth explained. "Protocol accommodates her."

"You are restive of formality, Lady Lydia?" the captain asked curiously.

"Good heavens, Mr. Smyth," Lydia said, with a scolding glance at Smyth. "Only see what you've done. You have given the captain to believe I am an unconventional creature when I am in fact the very definition of conventionality."

"Are you?" the captain asked before Smyth could respond.

"Oh, yes. I may tease propriety at times, but that is all

part of the role. At least, my role. And a very unoriginal one at that, I'm afraid."

"And what role may that be, Lady Lydia?" he asked with such apparent earnestness she almost forgot to be worldly and insouciant. But in many respects she had been worldly long before she had arrived in London and it would take more than a naval captain to make her forget her lines.

"Why, *dandyess*, Captain. I would think that would be obvious." She measured him with her eyes. "Surely you've come across the sort?"

"No, ma'am," he said gravely. "I do not think I have ever met your like before."

A shiver ran through her. Had anyone ever told her being called ma'am could produce a thrill of physical attraction she would have laughed. But it was the way he said it, with such formality and intensity and ... *Good heavens*, she thought. *I am besotted.*

"Mr. Smyth, I see Lady Sefton entering the house. I should very much like to speak to her," Eleanor said. "Would you escort me inside?"

Lydia had forgotten Eleanor. And Smyth. She barely remarked them now. Her whole being seemed attuned to the tall, handsome man attending her with such delicious concentration. She heard Smyth declare it would be his pleasure and then they were retreating across the terrace.

Lydia didn't watch them go but, then, neither did Captain Lockton.

"I assure you that I am hardly rare. But then you've probably been away at sea," she said, continuing their conversation. "Now that you are in London I am sure you will meet many ladies and soon grow so familiar with our habits that we pall."

"I cannot imagine it." He tipped his head. "I can, however, recognize the grounds for such a conjecture."

"Oh?"

"Familiarity can indeed rob a thing of its appeal," he answered. "Take for example mermaids. When I was a lad I was quite besotted with them."

She thought she knew the direction he was taking with his comment and supplied him with his end point. "But you grew tired of imagining what you realized you could never find and left them behind with your childhood." She nodded wisely.

"Oh, no, ma'am," he answered soberly. "I meant that having spent half of my life at sea, I've grown quite inured to their charms."

She started. He'd caught her off guard and she was unused to being caught off guard. Her eyes widened; an answering light danced in his gray-blue eyes. A trill of unrehearsed delight escaped her.

"Oh, seeing mermaids is a mundane experience for you, is it?" she asked through her laughter.

He shook his head ruefully. "If one were only obliged to see them. It's not the seeing that grows tedious. Quite lovely creatures, actually. No, it's their incessant singing that grows tiresome. Always bleating on about some fellow named Jason, lost love, that sort of thing. Mawkish brood."

He leaned a little closer and spoke sotto voce. "You have doubtless heard stories about men being lured to their death by the mermaids?"

She nodded.

"The truth is that most of them died fleeing, afraid they would be stuck listening to piscine sniffles and watery megrims for an eternity."

She was laughing even louder now, the image of terrified sailors hurrying past pathetic lovelorn mermaids too delicious to resist.

He tipped his head, his expression gratified. "You doubt me, Lady Lydia?"

"I think you have told me a Banbury tale, Captain, to remind me that while you have been figuratively at sea, you are not there literally. Your point is well taken."

"But that was not at all my aim," he said, the teasing light fading from his gaze, replaced by something else. "I merely sought to illustrate that those things you take for granted, I find extraordinary. And expect I always shall."

His gaze seemed to her to have grown tender and she was as unused to seeing tenderness in a man's eyes as she was to being caught off guard. Admiration? Amusement? Yes. Even desire. But those looks could be leveled at any inanimate object: a beautiful painting, a political cartoon, a French postcard. Tenderness was far more intimate, reserved for beings, not things.

It brought a flush to her cheeks. Her gaze fell.

"Forgive me," he said, quick to discern the change in her expression. "I've embarrassed you."

"No." She shook her head. "Not at all."

He would think her a poor creature if she could not parry a subtle compliment without growing red cheeks. "I am wondering what other things bore you that would amaze me," she said. "Besides mermaids, that is."

"I shall strive to think of something," he said. Then,

"I have heard Lady Pickler is quite proud of her land-scapes. Perhaps you would care to walk with me and explain what I am seeing?"

"Yes," she said at once and too quickly. What was wrong with her? She should try to muster up at least a soupçon of hesitation. But . . . why? Why be false when in his company being true came so easily?

Finding no answer, she moved down the stairs and onto the lawn. He fell into step at her side, clasping his hands lightly behind his back and measuring his long strides to accommodate hers.

Above them the lowering sky hung breathless, lending a silvery twilight atmosphere to the day and his eyes. Beads of dew hung suspended from leaf tips like crystal pendants left by tiny woodland sylphs and the air shimmered with moistures. The damp from the grass seeped through the thin leather soles of her slippers. She barely noticed.

Mindful of propriety, she stopped on the edge of the lawn. He looked up and his expression betrayed a moment of astonishment. She empathized. Anyone not forewarned about Lady Pickler's landscapes tended to be overwhelmed. In ten acres of artificially rolling land, Lady Pickler had managed to stuff a Roman ruin, a sheep's meadow, a Greek temple, a Japanese pagoda, and a hermit's cave—complete with a hairy little hermit glumly peeling potatoes outside his lair.

"I think he's one of the gardeners when he is not a hermit," Lydia confided, watching the direction of the captain's gaze.

"Good God, I should hope so," the captain exclaimed.

She tipped her head teasingly. "I don't imagine there were any men on your ship whose sole occupation was to peel potatoes and look sullen and unapproachable."

"On the contrary," he replied. "My cook. And he looked far more miserable than that fellow. I shall have to look him up and tell him there is a call for his particular talents in Society."

She laughed again and he looked down into her up-turned face.

Her laughter died as she sank into his mist-wreathed gaze, lost to her surroundings. She became conscious of her lips parting and her chest rising and falling as though she'd been running and she hurried to regain her sang-froid. If she kept staring at him with her mouth slack, he would certainly recognize her as the shopgirl who'd sold him a Chinese bowl.

"Have you been a sailor long, Captain?" she asked, half turning to collect herself.

"Not as long as most men who make a career of the sea," he replied. "I came to it late."

"Oh? How old were you?" She wanted to know everything about him.

"Fourteen."

Her eyes widened. "And that is late?"

"Most midshipmen make their maiden voyage at eleven or twelve. I was obliged to remain at Josten Hall, however, until after my father's death."

She shook her head. "Were you very eager to go?"

"Very."

"And you will return to the sea?"

He shook his head. "I am retired."

"Surely you are young to retire."

"Perhaps." He seemed uninterested in answering her questions, which was very unusual in Lydia's experience. Given scant encouragement, most men loved speaking about themselves. But he seemed more interested in asking her questions than answering them.

Unfortunately, she had nothing all that interesting to impart. What was unusual about her, her wealth and the privilege it garnered her, were not the result of any action or inaction on her part. She had done nothing to deserve her situation. Despite traveling extensively as a child, in many ways her world remained very small, very select, very exclusive, and its concerns very small, very select, very exclusive to its milieu.

But Captain Lockton? The life he had chosen had given him a deeper knowledge of life, far richer and more diverse experiences. He had led men in battle, made decisions that had far-reaching consequences. He had made a difference to the world at large, not just a tiny sliver of it. She liked her life very well, but his was more interesting.

"Tell me of your childhood, Lady Lydia. Were you raised in London?"

"No," she said shortly, then feeling she was being rude added, "My parents traveled a great deal and I with them. Until they died."

"I am sorry." He smiled gently. "Tell me about them."

Tell him about them? She looked at him in surprise. Everyone knew her parents' story, from its scandalous inception to the romantic and tragic end. But then she remembered he had likely been at sea when they'd died.

She didn't know where to begin. The press and Society had always defined them by their unsanctified marriage and the vagabond glamour of their lives as expatriates. But that wasn't what she recalled of them. When she thought of her mother and father, it was not of the scandal or their glamour.

How odd.

"They were wonderfully well suited. My mother was a great beauty and my father a Corinthian of the first order."

"What were they like?"

"Like?" She'd just told him. They were beautiful and gay and . . . beautiful. Hadn't she just said as much?

"Yes. You say they were a handsome pair, but what else? Were they conscientious or impulsive? What did they do for pleasure and what for edification?"

"It was *all* pleasure," she said a little reluctantly, though heaven knew why.

In response, he shook his head. "No. I am sure it was not."

How could he refute her claims as an eyewitness to a life he had never known and people he had never met? She wasn't certain if she felt unnerved or affronted by his certainty. Probably both.

Lydia had always been honest with herself, admitting her failings as well as her strengths. Were her memories of her parents wrong? Or at least, incomplete? What did she know of them other than that they seemed like stars shining in the social firmament, always lighting her way . . . but from a distance, a little chill for all their brilliance?

What partialities, besides a love of gay company,

beauty, and elegance, had they bequeathed her? Surely something . . .

"My father taught me to ride and shoot a pistol before I was ten." She smiled. He'd been proud of her skill, though after her mother found out about it, she'd forbidden further lessons, deeming it unsuitable practice for a young lady. "I think he might have missed having a country house. He was from Wilshire and he liked dogs."

"Ah." His tone was interested. "What else?"

"My mother had no ear for language. She only spoke English. I recall her laughing and saying it was just as well since she was less likely to overhear someone speaking ill of her. But I think . . . I think it made her feel vulnerable and she did not want me to know." And why would that be? Because she did not want anything to threaten the carefully maintained illusion of happiness?

Perhaps it all hadn't been pleasure. . . . A frown flickered across her face. The notion made her uneasy. No one had ever asked her questions like this and her thoughts had never run in this vein before. She'd had enough of her family's history. She wanted to know more about him. "Will you miss the sea now that you've retired?"

"The sea? Yes." He answered in a voice that led her to suspect he was leaving something unsaid. "But Josten Hall overlooks the sea, so I shan't have to pine."

"Josten Hall. This is your family home?"

"Yes. It sits atop the Norfolk cliffs overlooking the sea and is the most beautiful place on earth." He smiled and suddenly looked younger than any man who'd captained a warship ought to. "Do you still maintain your father's home in Wilshire?"

"No. It wasn't an ancestral manse by any means. My grandfather bought the place off a nabob in the seventies. Will you miss your ship?"

He did not answer at once but considered her with a slight, quizzical smile.

"Ma'am, one might think from your questions you would see me gone back to sea. How have I offended?" His voice was light, but she discerned an underlying seriousness.

"No! I am simply seeking to understand you." She flushed at his smile and hurried on. "I mean, why you have given up the sea for the land. Those sailors I know are always pining to return to their ship like a beloved wife."

He finally spoke. "When I was a boy, there was nothing I loved more than to be on a boat bobbing about in the North Sea. When I was accepted as a midshipman on Nelson's command, I was in transports. Going to war was a grand and noble adventure, vastly exciting."

He paused and looked at her carefully again before continuing. "But that was when I was young and when I was serving in another's command. It is quite one matter to obey the order to fire on fleeing men or board a burning vessel, and another to give those orders. Suffice to say, I am glad to be relieved of such duties—" He broke off, shook his head.

Lydia studied him gravely, wanting to reach out and touch his arm, to offer comfort. She could not. He had ordered his men to fight unto the death and he carried the burden of their deaths with him. So much so that he had given up his commission.

"Pray, don't look so stricken, Lady Lydia. This is

hardly suitable conversation on so brief an acquaintance," he said.

He was right. It was entirely too intimate. It was entirely too candid. It was entirely unprecedented. And she didn't want it to end.

"You have only yourself to blame," he said, attempting to lighten the mood. "You have provided too sympathetic an ear and your face betrays none of the alarm, if not distaste, you must be feeling. I applaud your good manners."

"I am neither alarmed nor offended, Captain," she answered. "But I am sorry something you once loved no longer brings you joy. It seems to me there are scant enough things to love that we can afford to lose even one."

She was being too serious, too earnest. She should retreat into a livelier, more flirtatious mien. He would think her somber. But her words felt like a portent and she shivered. *She* could not afford to lose anything more that she loved.

"It is not that I have learned to dislike sailing as much as I have remembered that I love something more. Here." He reached into his pocket and withdrew a simple fob with a locket attached to the end. He flipped the lid open and held it up for her to examine. Inside was a tiny exquisite etching of a handsome manor home set on a prow of land overlooking a suggested sea. "This is Josten Hall."

"It's lovely."

"Yes," he said and snapped the locket shut. "Many of my men carried on their person the likeness of wives or mothers to inspire and comfort them. I have always carried this."

"I see. You have come home," she said quietly. "That is what you remembered you loved."

"Yes," he said. "I am home."

"And now you are prepared to enjoy the family and home you missed while you were fighting Napoleon," she suggested.

"In part."

She tipped her head. "What is the other part?"

"I am also looking for a wife."

Chapter Ten

Lydia stared, unsure she'd heard him right. Gentlemen might say such things to family members or intimates, but they did not make such intentions public, especially not to a viable prospect. But maybe he didn't consider her a viable prospect? Oh! She didn't know what to say, how to react.

"Ah! Oh," she gabbled.

Heaven took pity, for the skies chose that moment to open up and let loose rain, saving her from making more insensible sounds. The captain shrugged out of his coat and held it above her, shielding her.

She blinked up at him, rain tangling in her lashes. Droplets clung to his gold-streaked hair and ran in little rivulets down his cheeks and neck. His cinnamon-colored waistcoat was already darkened on his shoulders and the loose, flowing sleeves of his cambric shirt were damped through, the thin material molding to the big bunching muscles of his biceps as he held the coat over her head. She looked away, flustered by the sight of him.

"Come. You'll get chilled," he said.

Together they dashed back to the terrace, where the

footmen were already raising marquees of oiled canvas over the heads of the guests. Lady Pickler had planned a luncheon al fresco and a luncheon al fresco she would have. They hurried beneath the awning at the foot of the stairs and he lowered his jacket and shrugged back into his coat. What a pity, she thought, to cover such broad shoulders and well-developed arms, and was promptly shocked at herself.

"Thank you. I'll be fine now. My companion has a shawl," she said.

"Allow me to fetch it for you," he said.

Lydia looked about and saw that Emily, too, had fled the rain and found a chair at one of tables just below the stairs under the marquee. Lydia was amused to see that she shared it with an old town tabby, the autocratic dowager Countess of Cavell and her much bedizened spinster daughter, Nessie, invited by virtue of having an eligible son.

"She's sitting at the table over there. She's the comfortable-looking one with red curls."

"I'll be back in a moment," he said and left.

Lydia climbed the stairs, aware of the foolish smile hovering over her lips. At the top, she stopped and looked around, determined not to set her heart or her ambitions too early. She donned a serious mien and scanned the rest of the company, looking for husband candidates, and then nearly laughed at this ineffective attempt at self-deception.

There was simply no one here who could match Captain Lockton. All he needed was to be rich, and Eleanor, who knew everything and everyone, had already confirmed that he was. She sighed, feeling lighthearted and brimming with goodwill. She spotted Jenny Pickler and her amity overflowed.

She would befriend Jenny Pickler and make the girl a toast.

With this generous plan in mind, she headed toward where Jenny stood next to her mother, who stood deep in conversation with one of her more unpleasant cronies. All three women were huddled together, turned away and thus unaware of Lydia's approach.

". . . enough is enough. If she does, I shall not hold my tongue. We indulged her whims far too long. An idiosyncrasy, *she* might term it, and thumbs her nose at us while doing so, knowing no one will dispute her, but forthwith, mark my words, I shall call it what it is: theft."

Lydia stopped short, stunned, then quickly turned and walked away as Lady Pickler and her companion moved slowly toward the stairs leading down from the terrace to the tables below.

Good God. Lady Pickler had been talking about Emily and her intentions were distressingly clear. As soon as Lady Pickler had heard Lydia was in the market for a husband, she must have panicked regarding this competition in her home field. Now she was seeking some excuse to eliminate Lydia not only from her future guest list but from as many guest lists as she could influence.

But she couldn't challenge Lydia's place as the darling of Society without grounds to do so. She suspected Lydia would never be so foolish as to give her that excuse. Lydia might not overstep the bounds of what was acceptable and what was not, but Emily . . . dear heaven, Emily did so on a regular basis.

Lady Pickler saw the means to rid her daughter of a potential rival by discrediting and humiliating Emily. And damn the woman, she could.

Lady Pickler supposed Lydia would not let Emily be humiliated and she was correct, even if Lady Pickler's supposition stemmed not from the observation of Lydia's affection for Emily—affection for a companion being inconceivable to someone like Lady Pickler—but rather from Lady Pickler's belief that Lydia would share by transference any indignity visited on Emily.

Last year, why even last month, Lydia would have damned the woman and the consequences. But now she did not dare alienate Lady Pickler or, more to the point, her friends, the Almack patronesses. A gentleman would not propose to a woman who came already excluded from the upper branches of Society.

There is nothing for it; Emily must not pilfer anything today.

And that meant they must leave without allowing her any opportunity to do so. The sooner the better. Though over the last few years Emily had gained increasingly more control over her compulsion to "take souvenirs," ever since Lydia had informed her of her financial situation, the older woman had been unsettled and restive, symptoms that always presaged a fall from grace.

Certainly, Lydia would be disappointed to leave. But there would be other parties. Other places in which she was bound to meet Captain Lockton. More people than not were willing to turn a blind eye to Emily's unusual habits. She would find Eleanor and then they would collect Emily and make their farewells—

She froze, her eyes widening.

Below her, she saw Emily reach out and slowly inch her hand toward a lace kerchief lying on the tabletop near her. Then, looking around with a bright, innocent expression, Emily flicked it blithely to the ground. Her foot shot out from beneath her hem, covering the lacy scrap, and she began dragging it toward her.

It was a trifling thing, Lydia thought desperately. Just one of a collection of gewgaws and fal-lals cluttering the table. Perhaps it wouldn't be missed. No one had seen Emily's little maneuver.

No one, that is, except Lady Pickler.

Lydia realized it the second she caught sight of the old harridan, righteous glee suffusing her face. Her treble chin fair trembled with her effort not to screech an accusation across the distance separating her from the table Emily shared with the dowager and her daughter. Lydia had no doubt her voice would be loud and carrying when she did confront Emily.

And Emily would die of mortification.

Lydia looked around wildly. She had to find Eleanor. They needed to get Emily out of here as soon as possible, with as little scene as could be managed. She could not bear to think of the effect censorious eyes would have on Emily.

Lady Pickler was advancing with the grim inevitability of a tidal surge. Some intuition must have alerted Emily to her imminent threat, for she reached down and snatched up her prize. Her gaze was wild with dawning horror at what she had done. Springing to her feet, she darted into the crowd, Lady Pickler hard on her heels, and Lydia could do nothing to help her.

"Mrs. Cod." Lady Pickler's voice rang out in stentorian decibels as she plowed forth. Around her, her guests cut off their conversations in midsentence, heads swiveling, sensing a scandal in the making.

"*Mrs. Cod*!"

Her voice only lashed Emily to greater speed. Like a rabbit flushed from its warren, she bolted, at the last minute turning to look back at her pursuer and so running straight into—

Captain Lockton.

A slighter man would have been knocked down, but the tall, muscular captain easily absorbed the impact. Emily stopped with her hands braced against his chest, the telltale kerchief still clutched in her fist between them.

He glanced down at it, up at Lady Pickler, and with a slight smile stepped back and deftly plucked the incriminating handkerchief from Emily's hand. Casually, he tucked it into his cuff. "Why, thank you, Mrs. Cod," he said in a clear, pleasant voice. "I was wondering where I had misplaced my kerchief."

"*Your* kerchief, Captain Lockton?" Lady Pickler asked incredulously upon making his side.

"Yes, ma'am," he answered, donning an expression of chagrin. "I know it seems absurd. I confess it is. But I do love a lace-trimmed handkerchief. Adds a bit of frivolity to all the somber colors we men are obliged to wear."

"That looks very much like Miss Cavell's kerchief," Lady Pickler said, not to be robbed of her prey.

"Does it?" the captain asked mildly. "Well, we can't have this sort of misunderstanding." He edged around his hostess and headed directly to the table where Miss Cavell and her mother sat riveted. He made an elegant leg and rose, smiling brilliantly at Miss Cavell.

He might as well have just hit the poor woman over the head with a club, Lydia thought. For she warranted that from the moment Captain Lockton flashed his dimple at her, Miss Cavell had no idea what she was saying or to what she was agreeing. *Nor* did she care. Likely, Miss Cavell would have concurred her mother had two heads had the captain suggested it.

All he needed to do was brandish the kerchief, sweep it before her bedazzled eyes, return it to his cuff, and say, "This could not be *your* handkerchief, could it, Miss Cavell?"

"Hm? Mine?"

"It's not, is it?"

"No. No, sir. That's not mine."

"Of course it is," Lady Pickler said. "I saw her—"

"Don't be ridiculous, Betty," the Dowager Cavell interrupted querulously, eying the tall, handsome young man smiling so warmly at the daughter who'd not enjoyed such smiles in years. "Why ever would my Nessie be carrying about something that is so plainly a gentleman's accoutrement?" She gazed up at Captain Lockton with unvarnished admiration.

Slowly, Lydia released the breath she'd held, and the muscles that had been rigid with tension, relaxed. She started forward, then stopped. The situation was well in hand. Instead, she fell back a step, watching, her brow furrowing at what she saw because it was so rare.

There were other gentlemen who would have come to Emily's rescue. But they would have done so to promote themselves in the eyes of their peers or to get the best of Lady Pickler, who delighted in malice or even simply to curry favor with Lydia. But there was nothing triumphant or gloating in the glance Captain Lockton gave Lady Pickler. His intention had been to protect Emily, not defeat Lady Pickler. He derived no satisfaction from scoring points against the older woman.

Such pettiness would be alien to him.

He was the consummate gentleman, Lydia thought as she watched Lady Pickler floundering for an appropriate response. He was poised, protective, honorable. Even noble. Was there anything less than admirable about him?

Ultimately, Lady Pickler managed to essay a tight smile and choke down her acrimony. Snapping her fingers angrily at her footman, she barked orders that two more chairs be brought to the table so she and the captain could join the dowager, Miss Cavell and, of course, Mrs. Cod.

She'd been left with no choice. The only alternative was to make herself look foolish and churlish while embarrassing the dowager and her daughter. And the dowager's unmarried son, an earl.

Lydia empathized. She had no choice either. As soon as he'd claimed the silly lace kerchief for his own, she'd fallen headlong in love with Captain Lockton.

Chapter Eleven

Ned did not pay a call on Lady Lydia the next day or any other day the following week. It was not for a lack of impetus and certainly not for a lack of interest. It was because he was a man who valued reason above emotion, who preferred to understand a thing before he acted upon it, and above all, who was not guided by impulse. So he purposely stepped back from his initial fascination with the lovely heiress.

Such a strong and visceral attraction was unusual and he distrusted it. From childhood he'd been predisposed to reflection and thoughtfulness. Years of navigating the stormy emotional seas at Josten Hall and later ones spent on a warship had honed this trait into what was to become the bedrock of his character, extraordinary self-possession and restraint. Not that he was incapable of decisive and immediate action when necessary. In the heat of battle he had often been called upon to make spur-of-the-moment decisions. But he hated doing so, always aware that a rash decision could cost his men's lives.

There were other reasons, too, that kept him from joining the ranks of admirers Borton assured him filled

Lady Lydia's drawing room each day, primarily the depth of the field.

He'd seen the list of failed suitors in Boodle's betting book. He understood quite well that his chances of securing the hand of London's most celebrated beauty were well nigh nil. Obviously, Lady Lydia was either content with her current situation or she was most exacting about the type of man who would convince her to quit her spinsterhood. Ned was not confident he was that man.

The truth of the matter was that having spent half his life at sea, Ned knew precious little about ladies. Those he did know were either his fellow officers' spouses and/or those in his own immediate family. They were not like Lady Lydia. But no one was. And while his mirror confirmed he'd been allotted his share of the Lockton good looks and athletic build, his weeks in London had established that he was no "buck," nor "dandy," nor "Corinthian," nor any of the other species of gentlemen Society adulated. Not that he aspired to be.

He did not understand the fashionable gentleman's manners or affectations, his petty cruelties and outré contrivances, his extravagant ennui and childish quibbles. Yet Lady Lydia seemed to like these dandies—at least, she certainly she seemed to like Childe Smyth. Her greeting had been warm, her manner welcoming.

No, there seemed no sense in pursuing the acquaintance.

Except that he wanted to. And save for the day that he'd run off to join the navy—finally having had enough of the dramatics in his family—he'd done very little that he simply wanted to do, and for himself. Duty drove him; responsibility guided him.

But not when it came to Lady Lydia Eastlake.

Thoughts of her beset his nighttime musings and followed him through the day. He found himself recalling the atrocious accent she'd adopted at Roubalais's and he would smile, wondering how she could honestly believe he would not recognize her as the woman from Roubalais's shop. He kept going over their short conversation in Lady Pickler's garden, finding pleasure in the unexpected honesty of that exchange, a rarity, he had since discovered, amongst the *beau monde*. He was haunted by the image of her looking up at him as the rain began falling, diadems of mist tangling in her hair and shimmering in her long, silky eyelashes.

Yes. He wanted to know her far better. But such a pursuit would be a waste of time and time, Josten kept writing to tell him, was running out. The creditors were getting nasty.

So instead, Ned concentrated on becoming acquainted with other young ladies of the *ton*. They were for the most part nice, agreeable young women in possession of many fine qualities. Dark-haired Jenny Pickler was very pretty and serious-minded, but her mother made any thought of courtship impossible. Besides, Borton had informed him that the Pickler fortune was entailed and thus belonged only to succeeding generations of Picklers. Lady Deborah Gossford was an accomplished pianist whose "bad teeth" proved to be nothing more than a slight overbite that Ned thought charming, but she dreaded water and declared she would not live near the sea. Lady Anne Major-Trent was very pleasant, but he could not think of anything to say to her.

It was simply happenstance that put Ned in front of

Lady Lydia's house the week after the Pickler party and during those hours when ladies generally received visitors. Just as it was simply good manners that had convinced him to present his card at her door. The footman took it and bade him wait while he inquired whether Lady Lydia was at home. A few minutes later Ned was ushered inside.

He took little note of the surroundings, although he did experience an impression of lightness and elegance. He followed the servant down the hall to the first door, amused by his anticipation and eagerness. The footman opened the door and stood aside as Ned entered. He saw her at once.

She sat on a dark gold settee in front of a south-facing window. The sun glazed in her dark brown hair and limned the curve of her cheek, turning her three-quarter profile into a cameo against the settee's dark background. She smiled in delight and he wondered why he had stayed away and knew the answer: She ignited something in him unused and rusty, some part of him that reacted without consideration or hesitation, something that was therefore suspect.

"Captain Lockton," she said, rising.

Now that he was here he felt awkward. Another uncomfortable and alien sensation; he never felt awkward. But his pulse had quickened at the sight of her and his gaze roved hungrily over her features. Yes. Skin as fine as ivory. Yes. Hair as glossy as a seal's pelt. Yes. Eyes the color of brambleberries. Yes. A mouth made for kissing . . . Madness.

"Ma'am." He bowed.

"Won't you be seated, Captain?"

"Thank you." He took a seat opposite her and only then realized they were not alone. Mrs. Cod sat motionless in a chair by the other window, softly snoring in a spot of sunlight. He looked at Lady Lydia, who laid a finger to her lips.

"Perhaps I should leave?" he suggested softly.

"Oh, no," she replied calmly. "That won't be necessary. Mrs. Cod is an inveterate snoozer. Only a loud sound will wake her. We can talk."

Yes, if only he could think of what to say. Oh, there was much he *wanted* to say, questions about her family and her history, what things she considered important, what books she read, what people she admired, all the things that made up the fabric of who she was. . . . But custom demanded he posit only innocuous comments to which she would then frame equally innocuous responses. Though he'd found no trouble making that sort of polite chat with other ladies, he resisted it with her. Because he wanted the sense of intimacy with her he'd tasted at Lady Pickler's luncheon, he realized.

"Another cold day," he finally said.

"Yes," she said, eyes lighting with amusement. "Very cold."

"You have been well since Lady Pickler's party?"

"Yes. Thank you. And you?"

"Good. Good," he muttered. "Kind of you to ask."

The amusement faded from her expression and her gaze dipped to her hands, folded serenely in her lap. "Nothing compared to the kindness you showed my friend, Mrs. Cod. I cannot tell you how grateful I am, Captain Lockton. I am indebted to you—"

"Not at all," he broke in, embarrassed. He did not

want her gratitude. He had done only what decency demanded. "Best to forget the incident."

"I am afraid I cannot do that."

He was surprised. Most people would eagerly accept an offer to void a debt they felt themselves to be under.

"Mrs. Cod means far too much to me to take for granted any act of kindness made on her behalf."

He tilted his head. He'd forgotten his awkwardness now. She was not saying this because it was the appropriate sentiment, he realized. She sincerely loved her thieving companion.

"Mrs. Cod is fortunate in her friend," he said.

Rather than blush and demure, Lydia laughed. "Not so fortunate as I am in her. What other chaperone would so conveniently nap when she knows I wish to hold a private conversation with someone?" Her nod directed him to glance at Mrs. Cod and be damned if the smallest of smiles, so quick he wondered if he'd imagined it, twitched across the plum dame's face. By God, she was feigning the sleep.

And once again Lady Lydia had displayed that bracing, unconventional honesty—

Then the import of Lady Lydia's other words struck him. She'd just told him she wanted to converse privately with him. His gaze swung to her just as a tap on the door preceded the footman's entrance. At a small gesture from Lady Lydia, he brought her a card on his silver tray. She glanced at it and nodded. "Show them in, please, James."

As soon as he left she asked, "Captain, do you know Mrs. Jonas Pendergast and her daughters, Mrs. Samuel Ballard and Mrs. Fitzhugh Hill?"

"No. I have not had that pleasure."

"Then I shall have the happy duty of rectifying that," she said and rose as the footman opened the door and a trio of ladies sailed in, their skirts swishing noisily, their faces alight with animation, and their hands outstretched in the manner of friends greeting one another.

He stood. They saw him.

Their hands dropped and their eyes widened. Their glances darted to Lady Lydia, and he was amazed to see pink stain her cheeks. Had his call embarrassed her? Were the unintelligible sidelong glances signaling some sort of disapproval? Or was there a far more detailed conversation going on, one to which he, as a man, was not privy? If he'd been aware of his relative unfamiliarity with ladies before, he was doubly so now. His quick easiness with Lyd—with Lady Lydia—vanished in front of these newcomers. Oh, he'd no doubt his manners would stand the test of any Society, but the naturalness of their earlier conversation had disappeared, and he regretted that.

The ladies were taking their seats, a flurry of fans and reticules being discarded, dresses rustling, sidelong glances as keen and assessing as a crow's nest watch's surreptitiously taking his measure. Now, Horatio Nelson himself had taken Ned's measure and during those uncomfortable moments when he'd been called upon to account for his actions, he'd stood without a whit of self-doubt. But beneath these three pretty women's gazes he felt himself quaking.

As soon as the introductions had been made and the requisite five minutes of niceties observed, he pardoned himself and retired from their company, though he sus-

pected he did not so much retire as flee, much like a
scow in front of an armada.

But he went back to Lady Lydia's town house the
next day and the one after that and the day after that
and four times the following week. Each time his visits
were bookended by that of other callers and curtailed.
Still, it pleased him to be with her, to watch her interac-
tions with others, to learn the vocabulary of her expressions, how easily her smiles came, how spontaneous her
pleasure and sympathy.

The *beau monde* seemed to Ned both artificial and
small, engorged on extravagance and excess. He would
have thought her eye would grow weak if constantly
bedazzled, her palate be dulled by a constant diet of
the rich and fantastical, and that she would have lost
the ability to be impressed, constantly surrounded as
she was by the exotic and rare. But none of those things
could be said of her. She immersed herself wholeheartedly in the moment, the conversation, and the
experience.

It was fascinating. It was seductive.

The following week he presented himself at her door
knowing full well that he was arriving before visitors
would normally be received. The footman accepted his
card and bade him wait. He stood at the door so long
he'd begun to feel he would be turned away when it suddenly swung open not on the footman, but on a breathless, glowing Lady Lydia, a pert bonnet perched atop her
chocolate-colored curls and a dun-colored pelisse over
her shoulders.

"Ah, Captain Lockton!" she said. "I was just on my
way out. There is a bit of shopping I neglected to finish

this morning and ... well, I believe that's an actual peep of sun overhead, is it not?"

"Yes, ma'am," he said, inclining his head and stepping out of her path. "Forgive me for calling so early."

"Think nothing of it," she said, moving down the steps toward the street.

Ned glanced about. Generally a person's carriage would be waiting outside when they left their house, but Lady Lydia's distinct yellow-wheeled barouche was nowhere to be seen. Perhaps it was being repaired. Still, in that case he would suppose her footman should have arranged for a hired carriage to be waiting.

"May I find you a conveyance, Lady Lydia?" he asked.

"Ah ..." She looked around, obviously a little rattled. "Oh. Yes. Yes. Thank you."

He understood then. She'd decided to go shopping only after receiving his card. He had been too forward, his attention too marked, and she did not want to encourage him any further. He stiffened, surprised by the sharp pain the realization brought. He mustn't allow her to know he understood this, as the knowledge would only embarrass and distress her.

He stepped into the street, raising his arm. Just past the gate leading into the residential circle, a hackney-man waiting for a fare lifted his whip in recognition and started toward them. Ned turned to Lady Lydia, smiling politely.

He would hand her into the carriage and he would not return to her house. He would see her at various functions and that would be enough.

It would be enough.

The carriage rocked to a stop beside them. He pulled open the door before the carriage driver could alight and pulled out the steps. Numbly, Ned extended his arm and she put her hand on his forearm. Even through his jacket and shirtsleeve he could feel the press of each slender finger like a brand. Her clasp tightened and he looked into her upturned face.

She was regarding him quizzically, a little furrow marking the space between her dark brows. He did not know what to say, how to explain himself. He stood disoriented by a sense of loss alien to him, but no less acute for that.

"Captain?" she said, her tone hesitant.

"Yes, ma'am?" he managed.

"I . . . Mrs. Cod is napping and . . . well, I am having friends to dine this evening and I should hate to rob my staff of another pair of hands in James, my footman. . . ." She swallowed, her violet eyes searching his. "Since you were visiting me anyway . . . I mean . . . if you have nothing else . . . no pressing appointment . . ." She trailed off and bit her lower lip, looking mortified.

Understanding unrolled through him like cool water in a parched riverbed; she wanted him to accompany her.

She wasn't trying to discourage his interest. She had raced to dress in her bonnet and pelisse in order that they spend some time together without interruption from visitors. That is why she had been breathless. That is why there had been no coachman waiting. That is why she blushed so deeply.

She swallowed and looked away. "Of course, you have other things to do."

He'd stood silent too long. Her face filled with bright color and her eyes shimmered with mortified tears as she fairly flung herself into the carriage, calling, "James! Please attend me!" and reached out to snatch the door shut.

He caught it before she could, then turned around to say to the advancing footman, "That won't be necessary, James. I shall accompany Lady Lydia. If she allows me, that is?"

The footman looked askance at his mistress. Lady Lydia once more colored up, though this time not so brilliantly, and nodded.

"Thank you," Ned told her softly and only then shut the carriage door before going round to the other side and climbing in.

Chapter Twelve

Halfway to St. James Street, Lady Lydia abruptly asked whether Ned had been to see some fellow named Gunter.

"No. I am unfamiliar with the gentleman," he said.

Her eyes lit with mischief. "No? We mustn't let that stand," she proclaimed. "I cannot in all conscience allow you, as a relative newcomer to London, to continue without a visit. Say you will allow me to introduce you?"

"Of course," he said. He would have agreed to go St. Helena to visit Napoleon to see her look so pleased.

She slid open a small window in the carriage wall behind them and called up to the driver, "Gunter's, please."

She turned back to him, smiling mischievously, and her glance fell on his cuff, from which a pretty bit of handkerchief sprouted. Heat rose up his neck.

Ever since Lady Pickler's luncheon he had been inundated with handkerchiefs. Some came from matrons with marriageable daughters, some from hostesses, and others anonymously. It was all a trifle disconcerting and he wasn't sure what to do with the things.

"A new handkerchief, Captain?" she asked with wide-eyed innocence.

"Hm." On occasion, to lend verisimilitude to the claim he'd made at Lady Pickler's luncheon, he felt obliged to wear one in public, but he felt like a fool doing so. He would feel like an even greater fool trying to explain this to Lady Lydia, who would find it monstrously amusing. Except that as he watched, the impishness left her expression and her face softened with understanding. She caught his eye and gave him a smile of breathtaking loveliness.

"You are very kind, Captain Lockton. And most chivalrous."

He swallowed, unable to look away and incapable of finding a reply to such an overblown compliment. If he discounted it, he discounted her and yet he could not accept such fulsome praise.

She was watching him closely and as if she could read his thoughts, her face lit with merriment. "Poor Captain Lockton," she said. "I know what you're thinking. You don't deserve my commendation."

He glanced at her a little helplessly.

"Because," she went on with feigned gravitas, "you actually *do* like fancy handkerchiefs. And you aren't sporting this one just to give credibility to your claim at Lady Pickler's. In fact, you ought to thank the lady for providing you just the excuse you've been looking for to indulge your taste for fine linen. Indeed, you have been entirely self-serving in this."

She was teasing him, he realized, delighted.

No one, not even in his own family, maybe most especially in his own family, had ever shown such immediate and easy insight into him. It was a little disconcerting.

"Exactly, ma'am. Most perceptive of you," he said with false gravitas.

A short while later the carriage pulled to a stop hard against the rail surrounding the green space in the center of Berkeley Square and parked beneath the tall maples. He noted other carriages loitering nearby, open curricles and barouches, dogcarts and phaetons.

He looked at Lady Lydia askance. She pointed at a stocky, balding fellow in an apron and stained waistcoat dodging through the traffic toward them.

"Ah, Lady Lydia!" the man puffed on making the side of the carriage. "A pleasure to see you, milady. It's been too long. A whole week, if I have me dates right."

"Thank you, Sam," she replied comfortably. "I've brought you a new votary."

The man craned his neck, peering in. "Ah. Good day, sir. Welcome to Gunter's Tea Shop."

"Tea Shop?" Ned echoed. They were parked in the road.

Lady Lydia laughed. "It's over there." She pointed to a shopfront from which a steady stream of men in aprons entered and left, some with trays and others without.

"It's the custom at Gunter's for the waiters to bring the service out to the carriages. I suggest the ices," she confided. "They are sublime."

"And so they are," Sam confirmed proudly. "What might be your pleasure this day, milady?"

She leaned over the side of the carriage, her expression growing serious. "What do you suggest, Sam?"

Clearly this was a well-established routine. The servant donned an equally serious mien, puffing out his lower lip thoughtfully while Lady Lydia waited, looking intensely interested. They might have been discussing vintages from a superior vineyard rather than ices.

"Well, we have a Parmesan crème that is most unique. But in my opinion it's a mite early in the day for something so savory. The ratafia is very nice. And we have the *neige de pistachio*, always popular. And an *ambergris fromages glacé*."

She did not look much impressed and the waiter obviously felt the burden of her disappointment.

"But no," he said dramatically. "Something a little richer, sweet but with sophistication, simple but unexpected. For you, milady, I suggest the burnt cream."

At once, Lady Lydia's face cleared. "That sounds just the thing, Sam."

"And you, sir"—he turned his physic's eye on Ned—"you must try the bayberry ice."

"Then I must," he agreed.

"Five minutes!" the servant vowed and scurried back across the congested street, barely missing being run over by a curricle.

As soon as he'd gone, Lydia laughed. "I fear I have maneuvered you here under a false impression, Captain. But truth be told, I never can pass within a quarter mile of Berkeley Square without stopping for one of Gunter's creations." She settled back. "It is lucky I leave London at the end of the Season or I'd be fat as a pullet. I do love a sweet."

"Perhaps your chef can prepare some ices?" he asked.

"Oh, I don't keep a chef. Only a cook. A single lady

does not have the opportunity to entertain much. I am afraid I am dependent on my friends for my gourmand experiences."

He did not point out that she was having friends to dine that very evening because he doubted there was any such plan. She'd forgotten the ruse. That she had designed one and that he had occasioned it, humbled and flattered him.

"Besides," she went on, "nothing seasons food better than good company."

Though she made this comment lightly, Ned's interest sharpened. Lady Lydia was renowned for her independence and yet she clearly felt herself vulnerable in some ways. Of course, he could be reading too much into a simple phrase. But he did not think so.

"Pardon my ignorance on such matters, but as a captain of a ship, did you not often dine alone?" she asked.

"No," he said. "My officers always joined me."

"That must have proved convivial."

He lifted a shoulder. "During sea crossings and in good weather. But many times we were too tired to converse and we simply fed the body to maintain the soul."

"During battle?" she asked quietly.

"Yes," he said. "But often the lulls between engagements were the most exhausting."

She tipped her head. "I can see how that would be so, how the lulls would be as testing as the actual confrontations. Imagination can be one's most formidable foe."

"Very true, Lady Lydia," he said, once more intrigued by her perceptiveness.

He would have been honored by her interest in him, but he intuited that it was not exceptional. It was her na-

ture to try to comprehend, to seek the heart of a thing—
or a man—and know it. They had met but a few weeks
ago and already she understood more about him than
men who had shared his ship for years.

"Sorry it took some time." The waiter appeared at the
side of the carriage. He had a small tray on which bal-
anced two frosted pewter bowls brimming with iced con-
coctions. "Took a bit to find your spoon, Lady Lydia."

Ned turned to her. "The establishment holds for you
your own spoon?"

She blushed and cleared her throat, but before she
could answer, Sam did. "Ach, yes. And her own bowl, too.
A proper sweet tooth has Lady Lydia," he said proudly.

Ned took his cue from the other gentlemen in the
park and quit the carriage, taking the ice Sam handed
him, tipping him generously, and going round to the
other side of the vehicle. There he leaned against the
rail, one knee bent so that his boot heel notched on
the curb. Now they could converse more freely and he
would not have to turn to gaze at her.

He looked up at Lady Lydia just as she took a spoonful of ice into her mouth. Her eyelids slid closed in luxurious gratification. "Oh, my," she purred in ecstasy.

And just that easily his appreciation pitched from
cerebral to acutely physical. His throat went dry as his
body clenched with abrupt, intense desire. Watching
Lydia Eastlake eat iced crème was as carnal an act as
he'd engaged in for months. He could not tear his gaze
away from her lips, riveted by the way they surrounded
each spoonful of the creamy concoction with languorous
deliberation before she put the spoon fully in her mouth
and then slowly, excruciatingly slowly, withdrew it.

He was no saint, but he had never been at the mercy of physical desire. He thought he knew himself well. But she tested that supposed self-knowledge. His self-possession was formidable, his ability to sublimate heated passion to reason the thing that made him a superior captain. In battle, only reason must be allowed to guide a man, not passion, no matter what the provocation. But this was provocation of a different sort. What he felt at the instant was not respect or admiration; it was pure lust.

Once more, she slipped the silver spoon between her lips, capturing another morsel of the burnt caramel ice and sighed. He swallowed, praying she did not notice the very physical effect she was having on him. The woman made an art of pleasure and damned, but he could not help the images rocketing through his mind's eyes.

"What is it, Captain?" she suddenly asked.

He dragged his gaze from her mouth. He couldn't stand here staring at her like a predator watching a particularly toothsome morsel.

"I've made a glutton of myself, haven't I?" she asked worriedly. "I hope I have not shocked you."

He tried to find an easy answering smile. "Not at all, ma'am," he said. "I was just admiring your ... technique." *God! What an oaf!* Hastily he dug a spoonful of his own ice out of its bowl and shoveled it into his mouth.

"No, no, oh, Captain!" she yelped in dismay. "Don't just gobble it down. This isn't porridge. This is an experience!"

Luckily his sense of humor came to his rescue. "Forgive me. I'm afraid I haven't a connoisseur's palate," he said. "Alas, perhaps I simply do not have your capacity for enjoyment?"

"Oh, no!" She refuted this idea soundly. "I refuse to believe that. Perhaps you have simply forgotten how to enjoy things." She grinned, gaminlike. "Or better, are simply unfamiliar with certain pleasures."

Not nearly as familiar with some as he currently wished himself to be.

"I," she went on with another smile that caused his pulse to thicken, "intend to remedy that."

God save him. He nodded.

"Now, *regarde-moi, s'il te plaît*, while I instruct you in the fine art of enjoying an ice." Very deliberately, she shaved a curl of ice off the top of her dish onto her spoon. She brought it to her lips, closed her eyes, and inhaled, her nostrils flaring delicately.

"Caramel," she said, her eyes still closed. "You can smell the burnt sugar, but it's not pungent. It's like a perfume, promising the sweet to come."

"I see."

"Now taste it, but just a taste, mind, to whet the appetite." She opened her mouth a little. He could just see the pink tip of her tongue dart out to touch the melting ice. Very carefully, she slipped the confection between her lips and then pulled the spoon back. She opened her eyes, tucked her lips together, and surreptitiously swiped them clean with her tongue.

She had no idea what she was doing to him.

"And now," she said instructively, "you allow yourself a full spoonful. Don't swallow it at once, however. Let it melt against your upper palate and fill your mouth with its flavor. Indulge in the sensation of it. Stretch your enjoyment out for as long as possible. Do not think past this spoonful to the next spoonful or behind to the last one. Make this moment, this spoonful, the only one you have known or will ever know."

She put her words to practice and her eyes narrowed blissfully. With difficulty, he managed to maintain his pose of mild affability. He was not given to impulse, but he wanted very much to lean in the carriage, cup the back of her head in his hand, and pull her toward him so he could lick the ice from her lips and then explore the flavor of her open mouth far more thoroughly.

A little desperately, he sought some way to distract himself from her "education."

"Who taught you to enjoy the moment so fully?"

She opened her eyes and regarded him thoughtfully for a moment before answering. "Both my parents, but I suppose my mother most of all."

"How so?"

She gave the spoon a delicate catlike lick. He kept his gaze determinedly fastened on her eyes.

"She impressed upon me how uniquely privileged I was to be able to see so much of the world and meet so many people. She did not want me to take anything for granted."

"Laudable."

"She led by example. But sometimes . . ." She trailed off thoughtfully.

"Yes?" he prompted.

"But sometimes I've wondered whether or not she offered experiences as a substitute for their not being able to provide me with a permanent home. Or maybe it was compensation."

"Why didn't you have a permanent home?" he asked, curious.

Her glance was quick, a touch skeptical. "Because of their marriage."

He gazed at her uncomprehendingly.

She frowned. "You really do not yet know? I thought by now the gossips . . ."

"Pray, know what?"

"My mother was married to my father's older brother." Her gaze met his levelly, assessing, without a modicum of embarrassment. "It was, I am told, a great scandal."

Now he understood. There was an ancient ecumenical ban against marriages between people of affinity, such as a brother's widow. Such marriages were frowned upon in England but more important, they could be declared void by anyone desiring to bring suit. Though marriages of affinity occurred, it was hard to find British clergymen willing to perform the ceremony, especially when the peerage was involved. In Europe, the clergy was more accommodating.

Lady Lydia's parents must have gone there to be wed, then stayed, fearing their return might inspire someone to contest the marriage, a suit that if won would render Lady Lydia illegitimate.

"So you see why I suspect my parents were trying to put a good face on an uncomfortable situation by presenting our nomadic lifestyle as one of choice." She was watching him closely, gauging his reaction.

"Perhaps. Perhaps she simply wanted you to love those things she loved. Did you?"

She flashed a smile. "I did when my parents lived. I

never wanted for anything or anyone. But after they died . . . I discovered—" She broke off, looking away.

"Discovered what?" he asked softly.

Again that hesitant, distracted glance. "I realized the disadvantages of the life we had led. No one knew me well enough to claim me, or to feel obligated or responsible. When my parents died I felt as though I had died, too. Or at least, I felt that I, along with the life I had known, ceased to exist."

Poor child. Poor girl.

"The Crown appointed me a guardian, a pleasant old fellow who had as much interest in a young girl as he did two-headed goats. He moved me to one of his houses in Wilshire. I realized then, when no one came, when no one wrote, that for most of the people we had met and known for a few short weeks in various capitals and manors and palaces, I *had* ceased to exist. And I began to wonder if I had not ceased to exist not just after my parents died, but as soon as we left whatever state, whatever home, whatever country we were currently visiting. Had we been forgotten as soon as we left?"

"I'm sorry."

She lifted her shoulders, almost in apology. "It makes no difference now. I only say it by way of explaining why I didn't follow my mother's footsteps—so many as they were. Despite her best efforts to produce in me a love of a nomadic lifestyle, I resist change now. The older I become the more I treasure what I have. Those people and things I know, I want to continue to know."

He understood. Josten Hall represented a similar permanence and continuity to him.

"I do not want to be forgotten as soon as I leave the room."

It explained much: her flamboyance, her charm, her loyalties.

"But maybe," she added, "my mother had the right of it. Perhaps it makes no sense to cleave too strongly to a thing or a person or even a way of life."

"Surely there are traditions and places and relationships worth maintaining?"

"But to what lengths should one go to hold on to them?" she asked. "Change is inescapable, is it not? How does one know whether a thing is worth the struggle, even the sacrifices, one must make to preserve it?"

He had no facile answer for her. He was willing to enter into a marriage of convenience for the sake of his family, to preserve a manor house and a way of life he had shared for only a scant fourteen years. He'd never questioned whether or not his decision had merit. It was what his family required of him. It was his duty.

The waiter, Sam, appeared at the side of the carriage, come to collect their bowls and spoons. He looked over Lady Lydia's clean bowl approvingly. "Now see here?" he instructed Ned in a friendly manner. "Her ladyship is one who knows how to appreciate a thing to its fullest. A gift that is that few has. A rare 'un, she be."

In the short space of an hour in her company, Ned had experienced fascination, amusement, lust, and finally had been made to evaluate his own choices.

A rare 'un, indeed.

Chapter Thirteen

June, 1816

In the back room of a Lisle Street gaming hell, Childe Smyth held up a snifter of second-rate brandy. He eyed the amber liquid despondently. The color reminded him of his mistress's eyes. He ought to be in her bed now, rather than waiting for one of Josten's brats to finish casting up his accounts in the alley so they could commence dealing the cards. But he had a reputation to maintain and part of that reputation was as a high flier, not as some devoted dog so agog over his mistress he couldn't bear to leave her.

He wasn't. Of course not. But still, he wondered how his mistress kept herself occupied during his absence. He'd never considered himself a jealous man until Kitty. Even after all these years as her protector, he hated it when other men leered at her. Many men took great delight in flaunting their mistresses at Covent Garden and Vauxhall and the opera, but he preferred to keep Kitty to himself. She didn't seem to mind.

In part, that is what had kept him besotted all these years. Not only was Kitty a beauty; she was a comfortable beauty. Satisfied and sensual, she put him in mind of some luxuriant cat that knows a world exists outside the boudoir door but has deemed it not worth the effort to explore. The only time Childe was completely content was in her amiable and attentive company, for those lovely hours finding respite from having to keep up appearances.

Appearances and status were important to Childe. More than important, imperative. His family name was not especially old or illustrious. He was a gentleman, true, and a very wealthy gentleman, but nothing more. His aim was much higher. He longed to stand at the very pinnacle of Society, to be admired and copied and emulated, to know that with a few words he had the power to destroy or elevate—like Brummell.

Childe scowled. It rubbed him raw that someone with far less breeding than himself had reached the pinnacle to which he aspired. But now Brummell was gone, fled in front of his creditors to the Continent and there was a place open for a new king of the *beau monde*. So far he had failed to climb over the other pretenders to seize that throne.

He did not understand why he hadn't succeeded yet. He'd done everything he could think to elevate his status and image. His friendships included Society's most elite members, he adopted their mannerisms and their tastes, he cultivated the right friendships and the right mien, and yet still, social triumph eluded him. Well, he thought, his mood growing even more sour, there was at least one clear path to his goal: wealth.

Not standard wealth. Not well-off wealth. Not plum-in-the-pocket wealth. The sort of wealth that could not be discounted or dismissed, the sort of fortune that could buy a small country. The sort of fortune he was heir to . . . if he should marry before his grandsire died.

At this reminder of his upcoming nuptials to an as-yet-undetermined young lady, he stopped studying the brandy and took a deep swig of it.

It wasn't that he was opposed to marrying. He'd always expected to do his duty and produce a litter of brats to aid in spending his grandfather's fortune. But he resented being pressed to *point non plus* by the old demon's failing health. He had no doubt the hard-fisted whoreson would cut him out of the will with his dying breath if he wasn't leg-shackled by the time said breath was expelled. The only thing the old man hated more than Childe was not being able to force Childe to his will. Well, it looked like he'd finally found a way. . . .

And the old man weren't doing too well of late, either. Damn and blast. He supposed that if he wasn't with Kitty, he might as well be at some dreary cotillion or other, hunting up the future Mrs. Smyth. Someone who would increase his social standing. He just hoped whoever he married did not think he would give Kitty up, for he had no intention of ever doing so.

"Josten's lad still out back counting the cobbles?" an accented voice asked.

Childe glanced up as Prince Carvelli returned from the front of the establishment with three other men, cits with deep pockets.

"Yes," he replied. "His cousin is holding his head and Borton is back there, too, clucking like a broody hen, doubtless cautioning the children about playing with the likes of me. Don't know who designated Borton the boys' nanny."

Carvelli shrugged, his expression sad. "Little good it will do. Lads intent on ruin will find a path leading there."

"Zounds, you sound like deacons, not gentlemen of the green baize road," a hard-eyed young debauchee named Tweed sneered.

"Perhaps we should call it a night?" Carvelli suggested.

"Certainly," Tweed sneered. "If you're too cowhearted to play the deeper game."

Childe disliked the Tweed. He was some baronet's by-blow, a mushroom who thought better of his talents than they deserved, hotheaded and eager to make a name for himself as a Captain Sharp. His two friends, gentler bred and trying hard not to let that be known, clearly lionized him.

Still, he could not let such a whelp call him cowhearted. He shrugged. "Josten can well afford to pay for his cub's education."

He'd play a few hands, then make the rounds of the soirees on the other side of town.

"I'll find us blue ruin. Why don't you lads hunt down the rest of our party?" Tweed said to his chums.

Amidst snickers and grumbles they complied, leaving the room to Childe and Carvelli.

"I do believe that I will excuse myself," the prince said. "Cowhearted as I am."

He was neither cowhearted nor in debt, but clearly he was eager to be gone. Lately, the prince seemed distracted and on edge. One would think *he'd* been given some matrimonial ultimatum.

"You don't have an ailing grandfather back in Italy, do you, Prince?" Childe asked. "One with an unaccountable yearning to dandle your scion on his knee?"

Carvelli started. "No. Why do you ask?"

"I happen to have one myself and was thinking it seemed a pleasant night to find myself a bride. I thought perhaps you, too . . ." He trailed off with an ironic curl to his lip.

"As you might recall, my friend, I already have a wife," Carvelli replied.

"I had in truth forgotten," Childe said. "You rarely speak of her or your family."

"Everything that might be said of her can be summed up in one sentence: She is a saint," Carvelli said and laughed bitterly. "Alas, I am a sinner, a fact both her family and mine and, of course, she herself, remind me of at every opportunity. Is it any wonder I stay in England in order not to give them many?"

"But eventually you'll return to her and raise up a passel of brats. One must fulfill one's duty."

"Saints do not breed," Carvelli said roughly, but then realizing his aplomb had been breached, relaxed into a smile. "I do not foresee my departure anytime soon."

"You ought to get yourself a mistress, my friend," Childe said, thinking once more of Kitty.

Carvelli smiled. "Do you think? Perhaps you are right."

"Without a doubt. Get yourself a mistress and everyone will be the happier for it."

"Perhaps I shall. In fact"—Carvelli clapped him on

the back—"I think I should commence taking appli-
cants for the post at once. If it is a pleasant night to find a
bride, it stands to reason it must be an even more pleasant one in which to find a lover."

And with a gay laugh, and a glitter in his black eyes,
he strode from the room calling for his coat and cane.

Silently, Childe cursed. Now he was stuck with Tweed
and his friends, and Borton and the Lockton unlicked
cubs. At least this last bit provided some amusement.

Oh, how very unhappy the good Captain Lockton
would be if he only knew with whom his nephews were
keeping company. Not that he'd evince any distemper or
utter a word of disapproval. Except at their initial meeting at Boodle's, he'd never heard the fellow make any
comment that was not entirely cordial. Lockton had the
physique of a Corinthian and the looks of a Greek god,
but he did nothing with these qualities. He had no ar-
rogance, no style, no panache or fire.

Not that it mattered what he thought; the ladies of
the *ton* certainly did not find him wanting in any way.
For the past month, they had been pursuing the man
like a pack of hounds after spring's first rabbit. He was
ubiquitous, invited to more fetes and routs than Childe
himself.

Lockton had even found favor with Lady Lydia Eastlake. Her interest wouldn't last, of course. It never did.
Childe fully expected to win his bet off Carvelli. But at
three separate soirees last week Lockton had two dances
with Lady Lydia. It gave one pause. . . .

No. No. It was nothing but an encroaching fancy on
Lady Lydia's part, Childe decided. She was sophisticated, worldly, too fly to the time of day to settle for

a passionless sea captain, no matter how handsome or pleasant or well connected. If the rumors were true—and Childe had no reason to believe otherwise since Lady Lydia's patroness, the Duchess of Grenville, had verified them—the violet-eyed Incomparable was toying with the idea of marrying. It explained much. In the eight Seasons since she'd made her bow, Lady Lydia had never shone more brilliantly than she did this one. And that was brilliant, indeed. Her laughter was like a love charm, her pleasure palpable, her excitement investing the very air around her with champagnelike effervescence.

He mused. Why waste her vivacity on a man who seemed incapable of appreciating fire? Childe thought he knew the answer. These last few Seasons, Lady Lydia had kicked up some larks that had the *ton*'s more staid members raising their eyebrows. Some of them had worthy sons. What better way to reestablish her respectability than by allowing the *entirely* respectable captain to squire her about?

It was just the sort of machination Smyth would expect of someone with Lady Lydia's social acumen—and he respected her for it. Now *she*, he realized, would make him a good wife. She had looks, influence, and a worthy name. More worthy than his own, truth be told, despite the irregularity of her parents' marriage. But that was old news.

She also had a fortune—though this was the least of his concerns. The fortune he would inherit from his grandfather upon marrying was treble that of hers.

She was also, as he'd already noted, sophisticated. She would not object to Kitty. Not once she gave him an

heir and as long as she had freedom to do what she liked
and with whom.

Why, he even *liked* her.

Bangs and thumps disturbed these interesting musings. The door to the hallway burst open and the Phillip
Hickton-Tubbs and Lord Harry Lockton pair stumbled
in, grinning like apes. Both lads were handsome, as all
the Locktons were, though Harry had the appeal of being the heir. If in a few years they managed to develop
some sophistication, they would be plums on the matrimonial tree. That is, if they didn't bankrupt their family
first.

Ah, well, Childe thought, watching the pair attempt
to navigate what he could only conclude they perceived
to be a pitching floor. If the earl wanted to keep making
good the debts of these two, Childe might as well be the
one they owed. At least he gave them time in which to
come up with the ready. Some of his fellow gamesters
demanded their opponents pay their debts within the
day, a demand that necessitated a trip to a banker or
worse, a cent-per-center. There had been a sad affair last
year where a stripling had chosen an even more extreme
measure of ending his indebtedness by shooting himself.
Poor bastard.

"Are you quite all right?" he asked, rising to his feet.

Lord Harry, tall, golden-haired, and noble-looking,
nodded and canted sideways, falling into his chair. Phillip, redheaded and slighter but just as comely, remained
standing, swaying slightly and staring owlishly about the
room. "Where's Twee' . . . I mean, Tweed. Confound it,
feller has to give another feller the chance to recoup his
losses. Only sportin'."

"I am right here," Tweed said, smiling wolfishly from the door. "Did you miss me?" His teeth gleamed like fangs in the lamplight. In each hand he brandished a bottle of gin. "I have simply been making sure we have the means to allay our thirst. And fear not, I shall give you as many hours as you wish in which to reclaim your vowels."

"Tha's most decent of you, Tweed," young Phillip slurred and took his seat.

"Ain't it though?" He had the audacity to wink directly at Childe, as if he considered him to be complicit in the ruin of these children.

It was too much. He didn't care if Tweed declared him cowhearted. He was not a . . . Tweed. He'd had enough stealing from babes for one evening.

"Your deal, Mr. Smyth," Tweed said.

He could make it to the Holland House fete by midnight if he left now. Lady Lydia was bound to be present. And after . . . ? His thoughts turned to Kitty.

"I fold," he said shortly and rose.

Chapter Fourteen

The butler appeared at Ned's shoulder as he critically studied his reflection in the drawing room mirror. Ned was due to arrive shortly at Lord Young's fete and he wasn't yet satisfied he'd pass muster.

The butler cleared his throat.

"What is it?"

"Another handkerchief, sir." He extended a tray upon which rested a silk handkerchief lavishly trimmed with lace.

Ned looked at it blankly. "Who is this one from?"

"Like the others, sir, it was sent anonymously. But if I were to be so bold as to hazard a guess, I would say Helene, Marchioness Dupont."

"Oh?" He did not recall the lady.

"A titian-haired lady with a propensity for wearing turbans with towering ostrich plumes."

"Oh." He *did* recall the lady. "Well, put it with the others in my room, I suppose."

"Yes, sir." The butler bowed and retired with the handkerchief.

He returned to study his attempt at tying his cravat into the fashionable—and deucedly convoluted—knot known as Cupid's Throne. One would imagine a sailor wouldn't find the task too onerous, but thus far he'd been defeated by the endeavor. He wrenched the cravat loose, preparing for one last attempt.

If he couldn't affect this one, he would have to admit to having lost the wager Lady Lydia had made claiming that no gentleman could adequately tie his own cravat. Ned could easily imagine Lydia smiling merrily when he admitted such to her later this evening. "Easily" because the lady was never far from his thoughts.

Ridiculous at his age to be so smitten, but there it was.

Her exotically tilted eyes would sparkle with triumph and she would tip her chin at a subtle degree. He would gladly lose any number of bets to have the pleasure of watching the corners of her lips turn up for just a fraction of a second before blossoming into a full smile. If she was feeling completely at ease, one graceful, long-fingered hand would reach up and brush a curl from her temple, a gesture heartbreakingly *jeune fille* for London's most sophisticated lady and one he found overwhelmingly attractive.

Someday she would reach up and he would find himself clasping her wrist and drawing her into his arms and brushing away that curl away with his lips.

His smile faded. It had been a month since he'd accompanied her to Gunter's. Since then, it had become an unspoken ritual for him to arrive at her door every Monday and Thursday far earlier than etiquette allowed to spirit her away to Gunter's in a hired carriage.

She never suggested they take her famous barouche, and Ned finally thought he knew why. If her barouche were seen, their trips would be remarked and the short, coveted moments they could spend together, alone, would end. She'd be inundated with requests to go on early drives. Indeed, Ned thought in amusement, she might single-handedly change Society's notion of proper visiting hours.

But for now the short, private hours they shared had become the centerpiece of his week.

He often saw her at other functions to which he was invited and she always appeared pleased to meet him there, but she never singled him out for special attention. She treated everyone, man or woman, with the same interest and attention. But he was growing greedy of her time; he wanted more of it. More of her.

He'd left off visiting other single ladies or spending any time that might be remarked upon in their company. There was no sense to it. His . . . affections had been engaged. But the more he desired Lydia, the more urgently he felt the need to explain his family's financial situation.

She might present the world with a facade of urbane and sophisticated insouciance, but he had glimpsed beneath her brilliant disguise to the uncertain romantic beneath. She loved so easily, so naturally, and yet she was uncertain about her ability to inspire love. He was not certain she would like the reasons that initiated his quest for a wealthy bride. And she was uncertain enough of herself that he wondered whether he could convince her that she, not her wealth, had initially attracted him—and continued to do so. That worried him.

He needed to tell her soon about his family's imminent financial collapse.

A sharp rap broke through his reverie. "Come in," he called.

"Lady Josten, Captain," the footman announced, and before he could move aside, Nadine flew into the drawing room with her muslin skirts flapping and tight blond curls bobbing like coiled springs. The footman bowed and hastily withdrew. Ned did not blame him.

"You have to do something, Neddie. You *must*," Nadine cried and promptly collapsed on the settee.

Ned met his sister-in-law's miserable countenance in the mirror and continued tying his cravat. Since Nadine and Beatrice had arrived in town with Mary to enjoy "a little of the real Season," not four days had passed without one of them arriving at his door heralding some crisis or another, a pattern that had resulted in Ned gaining a newfound appreciation for his older brother's shrewdness in remaining stubbornly entrenched in Norfolk.

"What seems to be the problem, Nadine?" he asked.

"It's Harry and Pip."

"Ah."

He was not surprised. Most of the crisis involved either her son, Harry, or Beatrice's Phillip. More often than not, both. A simple visit to the magistrates in the morning generally sufficed to bail them out of whatever hobble they'd landed themselves in.

After retrieving them after the first such incident for "boxing a charley"—the apparently hilarious act of tipping over a night watchman in his box—Ned did not expect he'd have to do again. He'd assumed that spending the evening in a vermin-riddled jail would act as deterrent enough. He had, alas, made this assumption without taking into account the inanity of high-spirited and—he privately thought—not overly bright young men for whom such nocturnal stays acted as a badge of merit.

"*Ah*?" Nadine echoed. "Our world is nigh on shattering and all you can say is 'ah'?"

"What would you have me say, Nadine?" Ned glanced at the clock. He was promised to dine in less than an hour.

"I don't know." She'd given up the tears and segued into exasperation. "Think of something. If Josten finds out he will kill the pair of them this time. I swear he will."

"I doubt that," Ned said. "He's invested far too much time in getting 'em to this point. As nothing suggests potential successors will turn out any better, he seems resigned to seeing the boys reach their majority."

Nadine didn't know how to receive this. She regarded him blankly as his meaning slowly sank in. When it did, she took it seriously. "I don't want any more babies, Neddie." She pinked up. "My figure, you understand . . ."

"I see. Quite." He cleared his throat to keep from smiling. Nadine's figure had once been the fantasy of many a young blade, but those days were long since past. Though still pretty of face, her figure had rounded to a neat little oval.

"Besides, even if Josten doesn't kill Harry, he might kill Phillip and Beatrice will never talk to me again if that happens. I should hate that. And so should Harry. He likes Phillip. And so does Mary like him. And I do, too, for that matter."

Now it was Ned who stared in bemusement, wondering if Nadine could possibly be twitting him. But one look in her face and he saw she wasn't. Again he was reminded of how fond he was of his family. Whatever their faults, a dearth of affection or loyalty was not one of them. His impatience faded. Whether or not she had cause, her concern for her son and nephew was real.

He went to her, sat down at her side, and took her hands in his. "Tell me what this is about."

"It's Harry and Phillip," she repeated. "They are determined to make a splash of themselves in Society and are convinced the only way to do so is to become one of these dandies and ape their habits, both the bad and good, though honestly, Neddie, from what I have seen of them they have no good habits and only bad ones."

She paused only long enough to sniff. "They are unconscionably rude and unspeakably full of themselves. And everyone allows it. Did I tell you that the other night one of the blackguards told Lady Wingbow that her dress was tolerable only from the front and that her train was an offense to the eye and then bade her walk backward out of the room? It's true. *And she did!*"

"Yes, Nadine. But what has that to do with Harry and Phillip?"

"Everything. They were *with* the blackguard! I have it on the account of several people present."

Ned triumphed in keeping his expression bland.

"But it is even worse than that."

"How so?"

"Well, once their father and uncle, my husband, Josten," she added unnecessarily, "told them that you had been so princely as to pay off their debt for them, they were of course overjoyed."

"How heartening," Ned said. "Alas, I can only imagine, as they neglected to inform me of their delight."

"Exactly!" Nadine exclaimed, looking dutifully indignant on his behalf. "They are horribly rude, are they not?"

Ned decided to ignore this query, as instinct told him that while a mother might criticize her son, it would be impolitic for an uncle to do so. "Aside from neglecting to post me a note of thanks, what is it they've done that distresses you so?"

At this gentle question, Nadine ducked her head. Color flooded up her plump neck into her round cheeks. He was startled to realize Nadine was sincerely embarrassed. This was not the feigned melodrama at which she excelled, but honest misery.

It made him angry to see her so put out. He'd a mind to give the lads a taste of the kind of discipline used to punish sailors. Unfortunately, Nadine and Beatrice would never forgive him—though he suspected Josten might secretly be relieved should he overstep the avuncular line.

"Whatever it is, you can tell me, Nadine," he said gently. "I am sure it is not as disastrous as you think."

How much more disastrous could things be? He'd talked to all the private parties—barristers, bankers, stockbrokers, and the money lenders—who now owned some small portion of the Lockton fortune and together now owned nearly all of it. It wasn't just the boys' gambling that had brought the family to this state. Theirs was simply the final step in several generations' long habit of mismanagement, profligate waste, unfounded trust in incompetent brokers, and bad luck.

Ned's private funds had been drained by the myriad financial holes he attempted to plug. It would take years of careful planning and budgeting to drag the family up out of the ditch into which circumstance, carelessness, recklessness, and an overweening sense of noblesse oblige had pitched them.

"Nadine?"

"They . . . they are gambling once more."

He stared. By God, he would have to whip them, after all. Of all the asinine, lout-headed, irresponsible . . .

"You have to stop them. Last night they lost three thousand pounds, Neddie, to some blackguard named Tweed."

"You are sure?"

She took a folded piece of paper from her reticule and handed it to him. It was a page from a scandal sheet. His gaze fell on the betraying article: *Two young gentlemen from North, folk of a certain earl, last night together hazarded three thousand pounds and lost.*

"And, Neddie," she sniffed bravely, but then courage failed her and she wailed, "They are doing it again tonight!"

"What? How do you know this?"

"I heard them discussing it this evening when they thought they were alone. I would have confronted them, but then . . . well, I didn't. I'm no good at confronting people and I shan't be made to feel guilty because I don't pretend to be what I'm not. I do wish Beatrice had been home, but she is chaperoning Mary at the Vedders' musicale. Not that Beatrice would have done any differently, but I should have liked the comfort of her presence when I was obliged to come to you."

She said this last in such a way that Ned felt a villain for his earlier impatience. But, then, reason told him this is exactly what Nadine meant him to feel.

"How long ago did they leave?"

"A few hours."

Ned's brows rose. "It took that long to come to me here?"

Nadine looked at him. "It took that long to dress. My heavens, Neddie, I was in no state to be seen in public. I am the Countess of Josten."

He closed his eyes.

"Are you frightfully angry?"

"No."

She breathed a sigh of relief and smiled. "I *knew* you wouldn't be. You never are. That's why I came to you. You always keep yourself so well in hand. You won't act impulsively. You couldn't. But you must *act*, Neddie. You mustn't just sit around here and hope they come back and all will be well. They won't and it shan't be. I know. I have tried. So, please, *do* something."

He always did. He would again.

"Don't worry, Nadine. I'll take care of it."

She didn't ask him how.

Chapter Fifteen

"Will I pass?" Lydia asked, twirling around before Emily.

The gown had arrived from the modiste that morning. Though certain to excite comment, Lydia still was not sure it was the sort of comment she should welcome. It was a bit bold for a spinster. Even one of Lydia's flamboyance.

For one, there was the color. No gauzy drift of colorless muslin for Lydia. But instead tissue-thin silk in a stunning peacock blue that rustled like the tittle-tattle of gossip—gossip sure to follow her—when she walked. Its puffed sleeves were slashed and inset with shimmering copper-colored satin. The same satin trimmed the bodice and deep flounce embroidered with tourmalines. A tourmaline necklace she'd borrowed from Eleanor hung around her neck and tourmalines hung from her earlobes.

Then there was the cut. The small puffed sleeve sat at the very crest of her shoulders, the neckline plunging in a deep vee, exposing a great deal of pale skin. Perhaps it was a bit more than daring. Perhaps Ned would find it vulgar. Or, she secretly hoped, enticing.

They had spent more time together in the past month than many engaged couples did and he still maintained a strictly respectful proximity. It was beginning to confound her. She'd been kissed before—perhaps too many times, truth be told—and on far less encouragement than she'd given Ned. But the thought of being kissed by Ned made her pulse race. Perhaps, she thought, studying her reflection, tonight that would change.

"You look splendid, Lydia," Emily confirmed. "But you do not need a dress to achieve that."

Lydia laughed and twirled again. "Ah, but you are prejudiced, Emily. You see me with loving eyes."

"It is not *my* affection that lends you such rare looks these days."

Lydia had no secrets from Emily. She knew quite well to whom Emily referred. "Is it so obvious, then?" she asked.

"Yes," Emily said.

"Too obvious?" she asked worriedly.

Emily gave a soft smile. "To whom?"

"Do you think he will feel pursued? Like Byron did by Caro Lamb?"

Emily laughed. "Good heavens, no. I cannot imagine you stalking a gentleman into his home," she said, referring to the infamous visit Caroline Lamb, disguised as a page, had paid on Lord Byron and there attempted to take her own life. Lydia had been as shocked and appalled as the rest of Society by the story.

Caro Lamb should have retained some measure of self-respect, an appreciation of who and what she was. She should have kept something back. But she hadn't. She had loved hysterically and wholly and tragically and then netted the result of her unreasoning passion and now she was accepted only by those willing to dole out a portion of pity or wanting to indulge their curiosity. She was excluded. Alone.

Lydia would hate being alone like that. Again.

Not that it would happen. It wouldn't. Because she would not ever behave in a manner that saw her ostracized from Society. More important, she would marry wisely, a man of standing, someone whose rank matched those of her friends, someone whose wealth enabled a life amongst the *beau monde*.

Someone like Ned.

There was nothing unwise in loving Ned Lockton. It was wise *and* wonderful. Realizing this fact anew, relief swept through her, as it always did when she thought of it, clearing away her unwarranted and mysterious unease.

She nearly twirled again but caught Emily's eye. Her expression had gone from approbation to concern.

"What is it, Emily?"

"Nothing," Emily replied.

"Something is amiss. I can see it in your face. Won't you reconsider and come with me tonight? I should so like your company."

"No, no, dear," Emily said. "I much prefer to stay here. My lumbago, you know. Besides, Eleanor likes to play chaperone in my stead. She rather enjoys showing you off, I think."

"That is not the point, Emily. I should enjoy *your* company."

It was no good, Lydia knew. Ever since Lady Pickler's luncheon, Emily had refused to accompany Lydia to the many private soirees and balls to which she'd been invited. She would plead a headache or fatigue or some other excuse. Lydia knew better. Emily did not dare test her compulsion to take things. She would rather die than put Lydia in an untenable situation.

"Please?"

"No, Lydia. I am far more comfortable staying here and so should you be with my decision."

"Then at least tell me what thought caused you to look so unhappy."

She hesitated. "It's silly."

"I hope so, but I will only be able to reassure you if you confide in me as I always do to you."

Emily gave her a quick smile. "Very well. I was wishing that things could stay as they were and that you weren't obliged to marry. See how silly?"

"But I thought you wanted to dandle my babies?" Lydia said, surprised.

"I do!" Emily exclaimed. "But I don't want you to have to marry."

"Most people find the two situations compatible," Lydia said, attempting a light tone. "One marries; then one has a child."

For a heartbeat, Emily didn't speak. Then she whispered, "Sometimes."

Something in Emily's voice made Lydia glance up sharply. She knew little of the particulars of Emily's marriage to Bernard Cod. Emily seemed far more willing to speak of her years at Brislington than those she'd been married and Lydia had not ever pressed her for more than she'd been willing to impart. All she knew was that Emily's husband had been a banker who'd purportedly cheated his clients and was cruel enough to commit his wife to an asylum and there abandon her.

Had Emily been a mother? If so, what had happened to her child? Had Cod been alive, Lydia would suppose the child would be with him. In cases of separation the father always retained sole custody of his progeny. But Cod was dead.

"Emily?" she prompted gently. "Do you have a child?"

For a long moment Emily was silent, her expression distant with bittersweet recollection. Finally she murmured, "No. She died before she was born. Almost twenty years ago."

Lydia crossed to Emily's side and put an arm around her waist, drawing her gently toward the settee. She sat down and bade Emily do the same and only then said, "I am sorry."

"I am, too." Emily's smile trembled a second until, with an obvious effort, she shook off her melancholy. "But it was a long time ago. Still, you will understand my trepidation. My marriage was not happy."

"I am so sorry you were forced into a marriage you didn't want—"

"I wasn't forced."

Lydia started. Though Emily had never said as much, she had always assumed that the unfailingly gentle woman had been pressured into an unwanted marriage with an abominable man. To hear this was not so surprised her.

Emily glanced at her and smiled ruefully. "It is true that my parents were elderly when I made my debut and most anxious to see me settled in my own home before they died. But they cautioned me against accepting Cod. I thought it was snobbery on their part, because Cod's family wasn't as genteel as my own. If only I had listened." She broke off and started again. "He didn't seem— He was handsome and attentive and self-confident. . . . In short, all the things I was not. I fell in love with him my first Season out and nothing mattered but I be allowed to wed him. My father, unhappy with my choice, had papers drawn up that would guarantee me a yearly annuity and a settlement, but Cod would not sign them. I didn't care. I begged my father to consent. I threatened to elope if he did not." She looked down at her hands again.

"And so we married. You know enough of my history to guess how terribly wrong I was about Cod's character. Within a year of my parents' deaths he had gone through my inheritance on schemes to grow wealthy that never materialized. He became increasingly obsessed with the accumulation of wealth. I learned later that he had begun to defraud his clients."

Her voice quavered and steadied. "He grew bored with me. He grew . . . most critical and dismissive. Then I became pregnant and soon after"—Emily stopped, took a deep breath as one preparing to face something horrible—"I had the accident that resulted in my losing the child. And after that, I . . . lost my way. I began to pilfer little things. I don't know why. I can't explain it. And he sent me to Brislington."

Lydia could not bear the unhappiness in Emily's face. She reached out and clasped her hand. "I am so sorry. You deserve so much better."

Emily squeezed her hand, releasing a long, unsteady

sigh. She closed her eyes for a brief moment and when she opened them, they'd cleared. "You have been so happy as you are, Lydia. I know marriage is your only viable course now. I understand that, but I want you to be cautious. Consider carefully in choosing a husband, and do not be unduly influenced by romantic notions."

Lydia nodded in agreement. Emily spoke wisely, of course, but she could not ignore the "romantic notions" that fluttered in her heart every time she thought of Ned Lockton. But then, she did not have to. Ned had an exemplary character and she was the one with everything to gain from the association—companionship, affection, family, a noble name, and wealth, of course.

"Make certain you are well compensated for marrying. Insist on an allowance in writing and a settlement that can assure your independence when he dies. Captain Lockton seems a very gallant and amiable gentleman, but still, take nothing for granted. Men's hearts are inconstant and the promises they make are unreliable. Only independent wealth can guarantee security, my dear." Emily gave another small sigh and smiled wanly. "But you already know this, don't you?"

Lydia smiled weakly. For the first time, she wondered if she truly did.

Chapter Sixteen

Happily, by the time Eleanor had arrived to pick Lydia up in her carriage and they had made their way through traffic crush in front of Young's house in Cavendish Square and the doorman had hastened down the mansion's marble steps to light their way, and the majordomo had announced her name as a hundred pairs of admiring eyes had turned to where she stood shimmering beneath the glow of a thousand beeswax tapers, Lydia's high spirits had been restored.

She greeted her host and hostess, curtsying and moving on to the crowded floor beyond, eagerly searching for one tall, broad-shouldered figure. He was always easy to spot with his dark gold head of hair and his imposing height. Although in the last weeks she hadn't needed to search him out as he'd always come forward to greet her as soon as she arrived. But tonight he was not immediately apparent.

Her enthusiasm faded, her spirits dampened. So much of her enjoyment of the social whirl now came from knowing that Ned would be wherever she was going, awaiting her with a warm look of admiration, his manner attentive, his comments designed to tease a smile or provoke discussion.

But in the last few days she found her gaze wandering more and more to his mouth, wondering what it would feel like pressed to hers. Or dwelling on his hands, long-fingered and strong, recalling how easily they'd encompassed her waist. Or on his shoulders, remembering how solid and broad and warm they had felt when he had held her in Roubalais's shop.

Ned never hinted that he had recognized her from that encounter. She was glad, of course. She had, after all, been pawning her jewelry. But she could not help but think that had their situations been reversed she would have found something about him familiar. The shape of his mouth, the scent of him, the timbre of his voice . . .

Why the blazes hasn't he kissed me? Or at least told me he *wanted* to kiss me? It plagued her, this itch, this frustration, this sense of burgeoning need. Need? She was not thinking of taking a lover, she reminded herself. She was considering a kiss.

Unfortunately, Ned showed no signs of a similar consideration. He was all that was composed and gentlemanly. Indeed, there was no evidence he had any trouble controlling his ardor. No evidence there was any ardor to control.

Damn.

"Lydia." Eleanor appeared at her side. She looked out of sorts, her usual cool demeanor ruffled. "What ever are you doing standing here staring into space? A lady never waits for a gentleman. Come away before you make yourself even more obvious than you already have."

Lydia flushed, allowing Eleanor to draw her into the crush. The crowd parted as if they were royalty, then closed behind them. At a deliberate pace, Eleanor led the way, pausing here to return a greeting or there to exchange a few words, nodding at an acquaintance and smiling at another, and thus forcing Lydia to do likewise. Introductions were made and news exchanged. Gentlemen requested dances and ladies whispered the latest *on dit*. Admiring glances tracked their progress and hushed words of appreciation heralded their steps.

But Lydia soon grew impatient to return to the front rooms, where Ned would be looking for her. Finally, when the crowds had thinned, Eleanor murmured into her ear, "Stop dragging on my arm like a horse with the bit in its mouth. *He is not here, Lydia.*"

Lydia did not pretend to misunderstand. "He was invited."

"Then he has either been detained or he has decided not to come and do not *dare* ask Lord or Lady Young if they expect him or whether they have heard from him."

"I would *never* be so forward," she proclaimed in an injured voice.

"I wouldn't have thought so, but really, Lydia, you are acting most unlike yourself of late. I swear you are greener this day than you were when you made your bow almost eight years ago," Eleanor replied. "I will not tolerate two of my friends making cakes of themselves, at least not at the same time."

Two? Lydia abruptly stopped. "What do you mean?"

Eleanor glanced around, circumspectly looking for eavesdroppers. Satisfied there were none, but well aware that interested eyes never strayed far from Lydia, she pinned a smile on her face. Only Lydia saw the strain in it. "Sarah. She is with Carvelli."

Prince Carvelli was Sarah's latest in a long list of admirers. Sometimes her flirtations turned into brief affairs, but they only lasted a short while. Lydia was not surprised to hear Sarah was showing off her latest conquest. She was, however, surprised by Eleanor's taut voice.

"She has already had three dances with him and now she has gone in to dine at his side. She is openly affectionate, so much so that their intimacy is bound to invite censure."

"I will speak to her," Lydia said.

"It will do no good. She seems intent on destroying herself."

"I doubt that. Sarah might like to poke and prod at the line, but she has never shown any inclination to step over it," Lydia said soothingly.

"My dear," Eleanor said, "you would be the last to notice the changes in Sarah, being consumed as you are with your own affairs. Which, of course, you ought to be and, indeed, must be."

Eleanor's assessment caught Lydia off guard. True, Ned Lockton occupied her thoughts, but surely not to the extent that she had become oblivious to her friends. . . . *Where is Ned*? She looked around again, craning her neck, but did not see his dark gold head. Had he met with some misfortune? Had something, or someone, else demanded his time? What? *Who*?

"Lydia?"

"Yes?"

"Lydia, are you attending me at all?" Eleanor asked, exasperated.

Childe Smyth strolled up just in time to save Lydia from lying. He'd perfected the expression of the dandy, part boredom and all sardonic amusement. His brows canted up at the bridge of his nose and his lips curled in an attitude that might become a smile but might just as easily be a snicker. "Your Grace. Lady Lydia," he drawled, essaying an elegant bow. "Faith! You have saved my life, m'dears."

"Really? In what way, Mr. Smyth?" Eleanor asked.

"I was about to succumb through sheer ennui. No one has anything to say. I swear all wit and drama sailed off with Byron and Brummell. The 1816 Season shall be remembered as a singularly boring one. Though"—he tapped his nose, his eyes shining—"your good friend, the delightful Mrs. Marchland, seems determined to provide relief, God bless her."

"How so, Mr. Smyth?" Eleanor asked in her most quelling tone.

Lydia knew her friend did not like Childe Smyth. She thought him puffed up and self-congratulatory. But Lydia suspected he did not think quite as much of himself as Eleanor assumed. She discerned a bone-deep unhappiness beneath his brightly malicious gaze.

"When I left the dining table, she was about to move to a new seat"—he paused for effect—"in Prince Carvelli's lap."

"Dear Lord," Eleanor breathed. "Lydia, if you would excuse me?"

She did not wait for Lydia's reply, but hurried off in

the direction of the drawing room, presumably to extract Sarah from impending disaster.

"A fond friend," Smyth said, watching her departure. "Alas, I suppose her intervention will be successful and once more we will all want for a topic of conversation."

"I'm certain we can find some diverting subject," Lydia replied. This was a form of conversation, the exchange of wry innuendo and ironic observation, that she knew well and had excelled at for years. "Come now, Mr. Smyth, you surely have heard some news worth imparting?"

"Let me think," he said, holding out his arm for her. She took it and they began a leisurely stroll. "I have heard about a certain beauty whose name may soon be stricken from Boodle's betting book as having lost the right to bear the title 'the Unattainable.' "

Lydia's heart leaped with excitement. What had led to this speculation? Had Ned been overheard saying something to someone? Or had the gossipmongers seen something in Ned's demeanor? *Or in hers*? She disliked this last explanation, especially after Eleanor's recent scolding. "Oh? And do you give credence to this rumor, Mr. Smyth?"

He smiled. "Oh, yes. Jenny Pickler has made a modest career of reporting a conversation she had with the beauty herself in which the beauty declared her desire to change her marital status. Lady Jenny has, one might say, come into her own armed with this disclosure."

Smyth was speaking in the general. There was no specific speculation. She masked her disappointment.

Childe nodded toward the side of the room, and Lydia indifferently followed the direction of his gaze. She started. She wouldn't have recognized Jenny Pickler in the beautiful, raven-haired and animated young beauty surrounded by a coterie of besotted-looking young men. The girl had clearly arrived.

"Do tell?" she said. "And have any names been forwarded as potential reasons the lady might quit her current circumstances? I am all agog to know."

He glanced at her out of the corner of his eye as they started forward again. "No," he said. "Not yet, though Borton may be on the cusp of entering the name of a former naval captain."

"Really?" She feigned surprise.

"I know. I thought it absurd, too," Smyth said, patting her hand consolingly. "I told Borton that the lady in question would not settle so easily."

Settle? How dare he insinuate that Ned Lockton lacked in some manner. *What* manner?

"You think poorly of this naval captain?" she asked, investing her voice with icy hauteur. "Fancy. I wonder who he can be. For the only naval captains with whom I am acquainted are courageous gentlemen who fought for their king and country. I am sure you would not find anything wanting in any of them."

Smyth shot her an assessing glance but answered easily enough. "Good heavens, no. You misunderstand me. I in no way meant to impugn the good captain's captaining. Lord knows, I could never perform the duty he has. My nature is too volatile. I am too passionate for such employment. I should imagine one would have to have ice water in one's veins to command men to hold under enemy fire." They continued their leisurely stroll.

"Certainly the naval fellow to whom I refer appears

to have the requisite phlegmatic mien and detached nature. I give him credit. Were I to be so frequently in this beauty's company, I would never be able to conceal my ardor. But perhaps the captain is not burdened by intense emotion."

She frowned at his words.

"No. All I meant, Lady Lydia," Childe continued in a suave tone, "is that the lady of whom we are speaking has too high a regard for herself and her station to be content with anything less than the adulation she deserves. Nor should she be." His gaze fixed on her face, his customary cynicism ebbing from his expression, revealing . . . empathy. "Besides, I believe I have tumbled on a reason for the lady's bewildering attachment."

"Oh?" She prayed her voice did not sound as tight as she feared it did. "Pray tell."

"This lady has a reputation for independence and irreverence and on occasion may have sailed a mite close to the mark." He spoke with unexpected gentleness, watching her carefully.

"And how does this explain the company she chooses?"

"What better way to reassure those conservative and cautious families who have an heir looking to wed that one is mindful of one's reputation than by securing the attention of a gentleman with such an immaculate character?"

Though his words themselves were laudatory, the way in which Childe said them made it sound as though having an immaculate reputation was something to be pitied. And she supposed in his circle of friends, it was. *That* couldn't really be what Society thought. That she allowed Ned to squire her around to repair some nonexistent damage to her reputation. It was laughable.

"I sympathize with the lady and I find her choice entirely reasonable," Chide said. "A lady who is both passionate and practical is rare indeed." He smiled warmly at her, but it was a smile in no way suggestive of intimacy.

He meant it, Lydia realized. He really could not conceive that she could be interested in Ned. She wasn't sure how to react. It was so ludicrous.

Did Childe not have eyes? Could he not see the appeal of a tall, manly physique, a handsome vis, subtle wit, humor, gallantry, and unparalleled gentlemanliness? And a fortune, of course. Certainly other ladies had, gauging by the river of handkerchiefs that reportedly flowed into Ned's town house.

Still, she found Childe's concern unexpectedly touching and that had the unhappy effect of forcing her to consider at least some of what he'd said. It was true that Ned was a self-contained man of no discernible excesses. Including an excess of emotion?

But he was a *gentleman*, she reminded herself. He would not impose on a lady by making declarations of affection until he felt they could be returned. *If* he had such emotions . . .

Damn and blast. Did he love her? *Was he capable of strong feelings?* What if he wasn't? What if all he required of her was friendship. A month ago she would have been pleased to count him so, but now that word seemed vapid and pallid, unacceptable in the face of the emotions he aroused in her heart. *Friends*.

Heat spread up her neck into her face, telling tales

she would rather have kept quiet. Childe Smyth studied her with dawning understanding. Pity joined the sympathy in his face.

"Sometimes, Mr. Smyth, the appearance of a thing is not a just representation of its nature." She sounded so confident.

He smiled. "Astute as always, Lady Lydia," he said, bowing slightly. "I am sure you are right."

Poor lass, Childe Smyth thought a while later as he watched Lady Lydia accepting the accolades of her adoring flock. She had actually fallen in love with the stick.

Someone really ought to save her.

Chapter Seventeen

The gaming hell stank of smoke, gin, and the stale reek of nervous sweat. Ned would like to think the latter had been exuded by his nephews as their desperation grew in pace with their losses, but over the last months his faith that the boys might have even that much sense had been extinguished. He eyed them irritably.

They no longer sat at the table, having retreated to the chairs where Ned had directed them, chastened and sullen but just sober enough not to challenge the "suggestion."

Ned did not assume intelligence had motivated their decision to acquiesce to his directive that they take the part of spectators for the rest of the evening. If it had, they wouldn't have been here in the first place, attempting to lose yet another fortune they didn't have. Instead, he chalked up their acquiescence to an instinct for survival because he'd half a mind to drag them down to the docks and throw them to the press gangs. It would do them a world of good. Fortunately for them, he had too much respect for the navy to foist his nephews on it.

Instead, he'd taken a seat of his own in the game. Now he laid his cards facedown on the table and waited for the play of the two other remaining participants, Borton, who'd taken to dogging his nephews' nocturnal vagaries out of some irrational sense of guilt even though his presence never seemed to restrain them in the least, and Tweed, a nasty young cutthroat. A half-dozen observers milled in a semicircle around the table, watching with interest. Tweed had adopted an air of uncertainty that did little to mask his glee. He was certain of his cards and thought by appearing to vacillate he could convince Ned otherwise.

Bon chance, Ned thought. He had played "First Blink" with warships; playing card games with a would-be libertine was no hard task. Borton scowled at the three cards he held, as though force of concentration could change them. From the corner of his eye, Ned caught sight of Pip gesturing to a passing footman by holding up an empty bottle and wiggling it suggestively. Ned turned his head and gazed at the lad. Abruptly, Pip's hand fell and the lad sunk deeper in his chair.

"Well, what of it, Tweed?" Borton finally said. "There's five thousand on the table. Do you have enough to cover the pot if you lose?"

Tweed's face, glistening oil in the candlelight, darkened. A pulse had commenced throbbing in his temple an hour ago and it had not disappeared. "Don't concern yourself with my finances, Borton. I am in."

Borton squinted once more at his cards before puffing out his cheeks and releasing his breath. He set his cards down. "I'm done."

Ned did not bother picking up his cards. Finally they'd come to the end. "In."

In the three-card game they played, the player with

the most tricks won. However, once there were only two people left in the game, a player would need to win all three tricks to take the entire pot. Otherwise it was split evenly between the two last players.

Staring at Ned, Tweed laid down a nine of trump. Ned calmly covered it with the ten, destroying Tweed's chance of winning the entire pot. Tweed did not flinch. He only needed to take a single trick to split the winnings and that still represented a tidy sum.

The room grew quiet with intensity. Still staring at Ned, Tweed played an off-suit ace. Ned trumped it with a three. With a small smile, Tweed played the trump's king and tilted back on his chair. "Ah, well, Lockton. We will have to share."

Ned flipped over his remaining card, the ace of trump.

The tension broke amidst laughs of astonishment. The observers moved in closer, congratulating Ned.

"Well done, Captain!"

"Superior play, sir."

"The evening is yours!"

The front legs of Tweed's chair crashed to the ground. He surged forward, leaning half over the table separating them. "Are you telling me you were dealt three trump cards again? *Again*?"

"On the contrary. I don't recall addressing you at all, Mr. Tweed."

"It's not possible!" Tweed exclaimed, spittle spraying from his lips, his face livid.

Ned was in no mood for this nonsense. "Obviously, it is."

Borton swallowed. The men gathered around them

shifted nervously, backing away. "Now, Tweed," Borton said, "I am sure you did not mean that as it sounded."

"I meant it exactly as it sounded," Tweed declared, surging to his feet.

For a moment Ned considered rising, too. Tweed looked angry enough to try to strike him and he was a fit enough looking fellow, Ned conceded. Earlier in the evening he'd claimed to be a regular at Gentleman Jim's establishment. Looking at the size of his knuckles, Ned could well believe it.

But he took the measure of the man and decided that a pretender such as Tweed would never physically assault a member of the *ton*. Not because he lacked the pluck. He would restrain himself simply because such an act would exclude him from the ranks of gentlemen he so desperately aspired to join.

"Blister me, Uncle!" Harry exclaimed, pushing himself out of his chair with an effort. He swayed, grabbing his cousin's shoulder to right himself. "You ain't going to stand to be insulted like that, are you?"

"At least I'll be standing," Ned answered laconically.

He should have been at the Youngs' hours ago, teasing laughter from Lydia, watching the play of emotions on her expressive face, inhaling the subtle orange blossom scent rising from her glossy brown curls, wondering if her delicately peach-glazed cheeks could be as soft as they looked or her pale shoulders as satiny. . . . Blast Phillip, Harry, and this Tweed. Because of them he'd missed the opportunity to spend the evening in her company.

Had she looked for him? Had she been disappointed? Or had other gentlemen quickly filled the gap left by his absence? *Damn* and blast his nephews. *And* Nadine and Beatrice and Josten for breeding such clunches.

"I have insulted you, Lockton," Tweed was saying, his voice vibrating with anger. "What sort of man are you that you let that stand?"

"A bored one," Ned clipped out as he rose to his feet.

"Challenge the blighter, Uncle! I'll be your second!" Phillip hiccupped from where he slouched.

"Ned can't challenge straight off. It's against the gentlemanly code. Has to wait until tomorrow, Pip," Harry explained in a slurred voice. "I'm sure he'll send round a challenge then, and since I'm the elder I'll be his second."

"You're the future earl of Josten, you can't be risked. I will—"

"Stubble it, Harry," Ned said. "You, too, Pip. No one is going to be my second because there isn't going to be a duel."

Harry's mouth gaped open and Phillip blinked in owlish disappointment. "No duel?" they said as one.

"No." Ned reached down and swept the winnings from the table into his purse, though it grated against every instinct to do so. By winning he'd confirmed in his idiot nephews' minds that one could win. And he hated taking any money off Borton. Added to which, he had no idea what Tweed's situation was. He could only conclude from the fool's willingness to court disaster that it was dire. He disliked being party to the man's downfall. But to leave the winnings here would be a tacit admission that something had been havey-cavey in the game. Damn them all.

"Of course there will be no duel," Borton said angrily. "Why would there be? Ned won fair and square and Tweed is angry about it. No gentleman would take umbrage at a poor loser's ire."

"Did he?" Tweed sneered.

"Good God, man," Borton exploded angrily. "Captain Lockton has been generous enough to let your insult pass and this is the best you can do to thank him? I've half a mind to challenge you meself."

"*Do not you dare*," Ned ground out. All this situation wanted now was Borton getting himself killed over it. "Tweed is ale-blown."

"But, *Uncle*," Harry protested. "The family hon—"

He speared Harry to silence with a glance. "Harry, Pip, I would appreciate your company on my way home. I know you will not disappoint me." He gave a slight bow in the direction of Borton and the other men in the room. "Gentlemen."

He turned and in that moment Tweed, incapable of accepting his good fortune, grabbed Ned's shoulder from behind, attempting to spin him around. But at thirteen stone, Ned did not spin easily. He did stop, however, only a brief tic in the bulge of his jaw indicating he took exception to be so handled.

"You can expect a visit from my second at first light, sir."

Gasps met Tweed's words.

Ned bit back his impatience. "For what?"

Tweed frowned. "What?"

"For what? I assume if you are sending a second it is to issue a challenge and I am curious as to how you intend to justify it. Are you intending to put it out that you challenged me to a duel because you lost? Come, sir, how will that increase your standing amongst your new . . . *friends*?" He raked the young bucks with Tweed with a caustic glance.

As Ned anticipated, the direct question flummoxed Tweed. He scowled thunderously as he hunted for a stinging reply, a sensible one seemingly being out of the running. It took him a few seconds to hit upon one. "*You* offend me, sir. To bloody hell with waiting on the morrow. I challenge you to a duel now."

"And I refuse," Ned replied.

Exclamations and mutters of astonishment met his statement.

"But you can't refuse!" Phillip blurted out. "He challenged you."

"Don't be ridiculous," Ned said shortly, finally losing his temper. "I fight wars. Not boys." He knew he was risking damage to his reputation by refusing. To most members of the *ton*, it would be imperative to answer a challenge such as Tweed had issued. But Ned had seen men kill and be killed for real reasons, for home and family, for the sake of their country or the man standing next to them in battle. Killing or even maiming a man simply because he was stupid was something he could not do.

What the bloody hell was he doing here, anyway? Saving the ungrateful hides of two immature would-be dandies whose idea of sophisticated repartee invariably contained reference to farts and who manifestly lacked any innate ability to learn from previous mistakes. And now, rather than thanking him, they were disappointed because he refused to shed some idiot's blood.

He left without another word, disgusted with his nephews, the evening, the situation, but most of all himself for allowing a sense of duty he was coming to consider misplaced to deprive him of a night in Lydia's company.

Chapter Eighteen

The next day Ned paced up and down in front of the Stanhope Gate that led into Regent's Park and pulled out his pocket watch. He checked the time once again. It was five thirty, half an hour past the usual time Lydia arrived for her daily drive down Rotten Row in her dark blue, lacquered barouche, its bright yellow wheels flashing behind a pair of handsome black horses.

He'd arrived on foot rather than riding the bay gelding Borton had insisted he make use of. Today he'd wanted closer contact with Lydia than simply riding alongside her as her coachman drove up and down the lane. Though he knew he presumed in hoping she would invite him to share her carriage, he had decided to take the chance. His experience of last night had made his path clear to him.

Far from being cowed, Phillip and Harry had been delighted by the melodramatic ending to the evening. They'd spent the coach ride to Josten's town house drunkenly debating the relative merits of guns versus rapiers as dueling weapons. They had not noted that he'd absented himself from their discussion and a good thing, too. Had he spoken, he certainly now would be regretting having lost his temper to an even greater degree.

The only time his knavish nephews' spirits had been dampened was when they'd reached their destination and he'd flung open the carriage door and issued the curt order, "Get out."

The two had blinked at him in confusion, making no effort to move.

"Are you deaf?" he asked. "Get out."

"But . . . but, what about our money?" Harry, either the bolder of the duo or the more simple-witted, had blurted out.

There had been no second request for "their money" and Ned took grim satisfaction in imagining the boy's valet's attempt to remove Ned's boot print from the seat of Harry's pants.

He'd little doubt that within a day or so he would be reproached by Nadine or Beatrice for his unnatural lack of avuncular affection and the outrageous manner with which he'd treated their darlings. He was not looking forward to that meeting. In truth, there was little in London to recommend itself to him. Last night's events had brought home how little he had in common with his so-called peers, the members of the *beau monde*.

Too many were caught up in the minutiae of politesse and social pettiness that he found baffling. They valued things he did not understand and which he had no desire to understand. He found himself impatient with much of Society and vexed by the realization that he did not know his place in it. Perhaps he did not have a place in it.

And yet he had fallen in love with the *haute ton*'s

reigning jewel. He was well aware of the irony of that. It didn't matter, his heart had become a thing separate from his will. And now his heart was demanding more. Somewhere over the last weeks, keeping hush about his family's financial straits had gone from being a strategic evasion to a sin of omission. Love, he'd discovered, abided no ulterior motives, no secrets, no challengers to its reign, not need, not expedience, not pragmatism. So tell her he would. But he mustn't blurt it out. He must approach the situation with delicacy. Never had his choice of words mattered more to him.

Had she missed him at the Youngs' fete? Who had taken her in to dine? With whom had she danced and how often? Had any one claimed more of her time than another? It was a role he'd enjoyed for the last few weeks and he disliked very much the idea that last night another had filled it and might seek to do so again. Was this unknown, phantom rival with her now?

He stopped pacing, amazed. Here he stood, racked by jealousy for a man he didn't even know existed. Worse, there was no understanding between Lydia and him that would entitle him to an opinion about with whom she passed her time.

Except he wanted all of her time. He wanted her. He wanted her with a hunger that grew more ravenous with each moment they spent together.

Being at the mercy of such passion took him aback. He considered himself a gentleman, a Lockton of Josten Hall, an officer of His Majesty's navy, and none of those personas allowed for this cataclysm of emotions—desire and possessiveness and uncertainty and jealousy. Such unworthy feelings would surely shock her. Even more crucial, she did not deserve to be the focus of them. She deserved nothing less than his finest self, a decent, courteous, and respectful man and by God, that is what he would give her.

He stopped pacing, alert to the sound of the approaching jingle of harness braces and the strike of hooves against the cobblestones. A moment later her carriage drove under the gate into the park. His pulse quickened at the sight of Lydia, the sun glinting off a small bonnet perched atop her dark brown curls. He moved off the footpath, crossing to the road to intercept her carriage.

She spotted him at once and her face lit with pleasure. She leaned forward on her seat to tap the coachman, but he was already pulling the barouche to a halt.

"Captain," she hailed him, "you are afoot. Never say you were tossed overboard?"

"No, ma'am," he answered with feigned sobriety. "I embarked on my current voyage without a vessel."

"Ah!" she said. "Luckily for you, I am a patriot. I would never leave a naval hero foundering on dry land."

"Is it so obvious?" he asked, taking hold the near horse's headset to keep him from dancing in place.

"Only to me," she said. "Climb aboard, sir, and let me deliver you to whatever port you are heading."

"In truth, ma'am, I have no specific destination in mind. The day is fine, rare enough this summer, and I thought simply to enjoy a stroll." He patted the horse's neck. "Might I convince you to join me whilst I reacquaint my legs with the notion of walking on solid ground?"

Surprise widened her eyes. Walking was almost unheard of for the *ton*, for if one had the wherewithal for a carriage, one showed it off. But he did not have the wherewithal for a carriage and he needed to acquaint her with that fact, and others of a similar nature.

"I would like that," she answered, adding to her driver, "John, take the carriage to the bridge and wait for me there."

Ned held out his hand. She reached down and took it. Her bones were delicate as tern wings. She alighted at his side, smiling up at him as he reluctantly released her hand and rapped on the carriage's side to alert the driver he could pull away. He gestured for her to precede him.

"Had I known I would be on the strut quite literally, I would have worn a walking dress, not a carriage riding dress," she informed him.

"Is there really a difference?" he asked curiously, falling into step at her side. He was no connoisseur, but he had an attentive eye—especially where she was concerned—and the pale yellow gown seemed to him to be the first stare of fashion.

"Of course there is," she said with feigned incredulity.

"And pray tell me, what is that difference?"

Mischief sparkled in her sidelong glance. "Well, one is for walking," she said gravely, "and the other for riding in carriages."

"Ah. Thank you. All has been made clear," he replied in the tone of one who has had been made privy to a great mystery.

She could not maintain her innocent pose long. Laughter broke from her lips. "You oughtn't encourage me to be facile by playing so readily into my hand," she said.

"Why not?" he asked, leading her along the footpath that eventually found its way to the Serpentine River.

"Because you will encourage me to think myself waggish, and then I shall grow proud and believe myself to be above convention and from there"—she shook her head sadly—"ruin."

"Ruin?" he echoed. "Surely nothing so dire?"

"Well, what worse fate can befall a woman such as myself than to be excluded from Society and unwelcome in homes where once I was granted free access? That is the unhappy result of acting outside the boundary of convention."

His pleasure in her company faded before her words, reminding him as they did that she was a creature of the *beau monde* as much as he was of the sea. Even if she should agree to marry him, could he ask her to leave everything she knew and by her own words, declared herself to love? She was watching him expectantly, clearly puzzled by his silence.

"But, ma'am," he said, "though I am loath to point out the obvious, in the short time I have had the pleasure of knowing you, you have acted in original ways with some frequency."

"It is a narrow line between original and bizarre," she said. "One must rely on one's friends to make sure one does not dare too much, or venture to close to it."

She stopped and he followed suit, turning to look down into her upturned face. The brim of the bonnet cast a crescent of shadow over her face, steeping it in cool tones of blue and green. She searched his face.

"We are *friends*, are we not, Captain?" she asked, touching his sleeve. A frisson of awareness trembled through him. "Friends."

He stared at her, on the cusp of telling her he wanted far more than friendship from her, needing desperately to explain his situation before asking for her hand in marriage. But a public footpath was hardly the place for such a conversation. So instead he smiled and made what pledges were more appropriate to the moment. "I would count myself a most fortunate man if you would consider me such, ma'am."

His answer did not bring the smile he'd hoped. Indeed, for a second he thought he saw chagrin in her expression. But then she turned her head away so quickly he could not be certain, and when she glanced back, her countenance was clear.

They had come to a place in the footpath where it divided. One leg turned toward the gardens that grew north of the Serpentine and the other followed the south bank paralleling Rotten Row with its confluence of carriages, riders, and foot traffic. Assuming Lydia would like to join the late-afternoon mill, he started toward Rotten Row. Instead, she turned north.

He hesitated. Emily was not with her and her driver had gone ahead and she had just been telling him that she cared for her reputation. So, too, did he, and he was therefore obliged to protect it. But they were in full public view and he could have the pleasure of her undivided attention for a short while longer. . . . He followed onto the north path at her side.

"I have heard reports that Lord and Lady Young's fete last night was a success," he said.

"It was a colossal crush," she said. "Five ladies fainted and had to be carried from the house for want of air. In other words, a stunning success."

She had turned her head while they walked, looking straight ahead, her tone conversational and breezy. "I believe that you'd said you were planning to attend . . ." She trailed off, inviting an explanation.

He did not want to tell her that he'd spent his evening in a gaming hell rather than with her, even if he had been there solely to extradite his nephews. He'd stayed, he'd played, and he'd come damn near to giving a thorough thrashing to a man simply because he irritated him. When he'd returned to his rented apartments he'd reeked of stale sweat, stale tobacco, and stale gin. Not his finest moments.

He would not embarrass either Lydia or himself by recounting the sordid tale. "I was, ma'am, but at the last moment an unforeseen obligation claimed my attention."

"Oh." A light apricot color bloomed in her cheeks. She believed she'd been rebuffed.

"I would much rather have been in more congenial company," he told her.

A gratified smile flirted across her full mouth and they fell into companionable silence as they walked. They passed a thicket of evergreens and came out on a grassy knoll overlooking a large field. In the center of the field was a circular boxwood maze.

"The Morrow Maze," she said, nodding in the direction of the tall, thick hedge. "Have you ever been through it?"

"No. I confess I did not know of its existence."

"That's because no one uses it. It's terribly difficult to navigate." She favored him with a knowing nod. "People have been lost in there for days."

"Days?" he repeated skeptically.

"Oh, yes," she replied with certainty. "Rumor has it that one of Prinny's mistresses was lost in there for two whole weeks and when she finally emerged she'd lost so much weight, the prince would no longer have her."

He smiled. The Prince Regent's partiality for plump women was well known. "And have you risked your health by venturing in?"

"A few times when I was a child," she drawled with extravagant nonchalance. "I would not dream of boasting, but I admit that I did not find it much of a puzzle. I have always been something of a navigator," she confided, her eyes brimming with mirth. "But one mustn't look down at those who don't share one's gift." She fluttered her lashes shamelessly, most definitely looking down at him.

"You are not perchance suggesting that *I* lack skills as a navigator?"

"But you are a captain. Some other person handles that responsibility, doesn't he?" she asked innocently.

"I assure you, madam, I am fully capable of navigating my own ship. I daresay a few acres of shrubs wouldn't prove too great a challenge to my skill." He could not believe she'd gammoned him into this conversation. It was absurd. But that was one of her greatest attractions, her whimsy and high spirits and joie de vivre. His family always took whatever he said so earnestly. She invited him to play. Nay, she insisted on it.

"Challenge, Captain?" she said, her eyes widening

when all the while she'd been maneuvering him to just this place. "Are you inferring that *I* have challenged *you* to a contest of some sort?"

"Have you?"

She grinned. "Yes!"

"And I accept." He couldn't do anything else; he was helpless in the face of her enthusiasm. "What specifically is the challenge?"

She pointed at the maze in the bowl below. "See there? You can just make out the top of an ancient tricolored beech tree directly in the middle of the maze. It is standing beside a small fountain in a circular clearing. It is the very heart of the maze."

He nodded. "I see."

"Now, you can enter the maze from one of four directions," she explained. "The south, east, and west entrances each have a different route to the center. Once you make the beech tree, however, you can exit the maze directly by a straight path that leads north out onto a sheep meadow."

She reached down, plucking three blades of grass, and rose. "We'll draw blades to see who goes in from what direction. Shortest takes the west entrance, the middling blade the south, and the longest goes east. North doesn't count, of course. Whoever makes it to the center and touches the beech tree's trunk first wins. Agreed?"

"Agreed," he said. "But first I would like to know what prize we are playing for."

"Is not pride enough?"

"No," he said, surprising her. "Not after all of your crowing, ma'am. Come. Prove to me you are in fact the gamester you pretend to be. Back your hubris with tangible coin and it must be something you value," he warned.

Her extraordinary eyes flashed with surprise. "Captain, I mistook you. When does a sea captain have the time to sharpen his gaming skills?"

His smiled faded a little. "Each time a captain sails his men into harm's way, he is playing roulette with fate, ma'am."

He realized his mistake the moment he spoke and saw the stricken expression on her face. He hadn't meant to say so much, but everything about her invited him to act on instinct and emotion, rather than only after careful consideration.

He smiled, determined to reclaim their former lightness. "But there is an important difference in the gambling I am prepared to do now, Lady Lydia," he said.

The sadness faded from her countenance, too. "What might that be?"

"When I captained my ship, I needed to win. Today, I simply *want* to. Now name your stakes."

She smiled, the light of competition rekindling in her eyes.

"Winner's choice," she declared.

He started. As a woman of the world, Lydia would well understand the implications of such a wager; should he win, she would be honor bound to forfeit *whatever* he demanded. It was either an extraordinarily bold or foolish act. Or a trusting one.

She awaited his answer, her chest rising and falling rapidly, evidence of her agitation. She knew what she ventured. But she met his gaze and hers did not waver.

"You place a great deal of trust in me, ma'am," he said, keeping his voice mild.

"Yes."

"And you are sure?"

"Yes."

"Then I agree, ma'am. Winner's choice."

She released her breath. "Good," she said, "because I am not going to lose. So the question really is, do you trust me, Captain?"

"Aye," he said.

"And that," she said, "may well prove your undoing," She held out the hand still holding the three blades of grass. "Take one."

He chose the east entrance. She picked the west.

"Now," she said, "we must give each other time to make it to our respective positions. Then call out when we are ready to begin."

"You've done this before, haven't you?"

"Played games?" she asked innocently. And with a wicked grin, she took off down the footpath leading toward her maze entrance.

He followed at a more leisurely pace and upon making his starting point called out, "Are you ready, Lady Lydia?"

"Yes!" came her rejoinder, suspiciously south of where he reckoned the west entrance to be ... Why, the little cheat had already entered the maze.

"You may begin!" Her voice *definitely* issued from a different position than her former one.

He didn't bother replying. He strode into the maze and at once was enveloped in a green world of cool shadows and muted silence. The living walls of sheared

boxwood towered eight feet high, dense and impenetra-
ble as solid stone. He held his breath, straining to hear
Lydia, but the greenery absorbed sound, leaving behind
only hush and murk.

No wonder it was not a popular place. Within its walls
there was no possibility of being seen and admired by
one's peers.

He started along the corridor, the pea gravel crunch-
ing underfoot. That Lydia knew this maze better than
she'd let on, he had no doubt. But he was determined to
win the prize. He would navigate this green ocean like
a rocky coast.

He looked up, studying the shadow and light brushing the tops of the boxwood, taking his bearings from
the position of the sun. If he took more western paths
than the others, he ought to eventually find his way to
the center and not double back on himself.

As plans went, it was a perfectly adequate one. It did
not, however, hold up to an empirical test. Within a short
time he was turned around and back where he started.
He made a second attempt, this time choosing a different route. Unfortunately, this choice proved no more
successful than the first with the added onus of getting
him farther in the maze but no farther along toward
finding its center.

He stopped again, looking about at walls that were
as featureless to him as a smooth sea is to a landlubber.
He had only to find one enormous beech tree. How hard
could it be? He ought to be able to see the damn thing.
But the maze corridors were too narrow to allow a view
over their tops and too dense and prickly to climb.

With no choice now, he soldiered on, his only consolation being that he once thought he heard a woman's voice grinding out a very unladylike epitaph and concluded that despite her confidence, Lydia was having a few difficulties of her own. His smile was less than sportsmanlike.

In the end, it was not his skill as a navigator that led him to the beech tree, it was a rabbit, an enormously fat, complaisant rabbit. It emerged from one of the openings Ned had already investigated—or at least he thought he had—and began hopping nonchalantly down the passage, clearly intimate with the maze and oddly indifferent to Ned's presence. Presumably it made its home here, away from the din and dangers of the rest of Hyde Park and, judging by its immense girth, the creature was well acquainted with the sweet grass lawn at its center.

He decided he could do no worse following it than he had stumbling about on his own. Eventually it would either head out of the maze or to the center to dine. He kept well back of it, fearing that if he drew too close, it would scoot into the hedge, the only current deterrent being that it was easier to follow the path than push its mammoth girth through a thicket.

Twenty minutes later he was about to give up, tired of waiting for the rabbit to stop and scratch its ear for the thirty-eighth time—the damn thing must be covered in fleas—when he spotted a patch of light issuing from one side of the maze wall. He strode past the unconcerned rabbit and stopped dead in the middle of an arch that opened right on to a small circular lawn. In the center, a giant beech tree spread its pink and cream and green-veined leaves.

He looked across the clearing to the other side of the

maze and spotted another opening. There was no sign of
Lydia in it. He'd won. Despite her attempt to hoodwink
him, he had made it to . . .

Thirty feet north of the opening, the hedge began to
shake and shed its leaves. He watched in wonder as a
figure on its hands and knees struggled through a narrow gap at the bottom of the hedge pushing a squashed
bonnet ahead of it. Lydia.

With an unladylike grunt she burst free of the shrub-
bery and clambered to her feet, spitting out a long strand
of hair from her mouth and swatting at her gravel-
covered skirts. She was still swatting when she looked
up and spotted him.

She froze.

He smiled.

Her eyes rounded.

His smile turned into a grin. There was no way he was
going to let her win after she'd—

She lifted her ruined skirts and sprinted toward the
tree. He broke into a run. His legs were longer, but his
breeches were damn tight and she'd raised her skirts well
above her knees. They dashed toward the center like
magnets to common steel, her legs flashing, his eating
up the ground. She pushed hard; he pushed harder still.
Ten yards, five, two. She stretched out her arm and—

—he looped an arm around her waist and swung her
in a circle, whisking her fingers from within inches of
the beech's gray skin. She yowled in protest, but he kept
her against his hip, hanging horizontal to the ground. He
reached out his free hand and rapped the beech's trunk
with his knuckles.

"I win," he said.

"That's not fair," she cried.

"Not fair?" he echoed. "As in, say, entering the maze before the start of the contest, or squiggling through rabbit holes instead of following corridors?"

"I don't recall anyone saying anything that prohibited a creative strategy," she said with as much dignity as a woman suspended in the air can muster.

He came to his senses with a jolt, realizing he was still holding her with the negligent ease of long familiarity. Gently, he swung her up more fully into his arms preparatory to returning her feet to the ground and made the mistake of looking into her upraised face. His chest tightened. He wanted nothing more than to kiss her. Instead, he lowered her carefully to her feet and reached up, ostensibly to push aside a low-hanging bough, but in reality grabbing a hard hold of the branch, physically bracing himself against the urge to snatch her up and finally discover the flavor of her mouth.

"Now there's specious reasoning," he said, striving for a normal tone.

Her brown silk curls tumbled in disarray around her shoulders, a leaf caught near her temple. A thin red scratch marked her cheek.

"It is the reasoning of a winner," she countered.

"But you didn't win," he pointed out. He reached out with his free hand and dislodged the stowaway leaf from its berth. She kept her gaze fixed firmly on his, but a faint wash of color flowed up her neck and into her face.

"Only because you used superior physical strength to prevent me from doing so," she said. Her breath came rapid and light. "My little maneuvers did not impede you in any way."

"Is there any possibility I shall get the best of this conversation?"

"It's doubtful."

"Ah, I see. I thought as much," he said. "And may I presume that since you are convinced that I have wronged you, you believe I should concede you the victory?"

"It would be the sporting thing to do," she conceded.

His lips twitched. "Allow me to apologize, Lady Lydia"—her eyes brightened with anticipated victory—"for my lack of sportsmanship. But . . ." He leaned toward her, lowering his head so that they were eye level, his hands still hanging tight to the bough above him. This close, he could see the lighter striations in her amazing irises, the dark indigo and brighter, almost lavender hue. "I still win and you still lose."

She stared, startled, and then abruptly grinned and graciously inclined her head. "Indeed, you have, Captain," she said. "Now what is the winner's portion you would have from me?"

She could have demurred or refused or taken any of a dozen courses to wheedle her way out of the bargain. She instead proved herself honorable, bright, and unfortunately all too obviously innocent of man's baser impulses. Damned innocent. God, he loved her. "Your hand," he whispered.

She blinked, startled, and he grasped that without realizing it he'd spoken aloud his heart's desire. But he had no right, he hadn't told her yet that his pockets were to let, his family stood within a stone's throw of dun territory, and that he had few prospects but many responsibilities. So he held out his free hand, holding as tight to his principles as he did with his other hand to the bough overhead, and gave his words another meaning.

Her brow furrowed as her gaze fell on his hand dividing the space between them. Her gaze rose to his face and her scowl deepened with some emotion he could not name.

"That is it?" she asked. "All you ask is a *handshake*?"

"Why, yes," he replied with admirable aplomb. "What would you have asked for?"

She looked straight up into his eyes. "A kiss, for goodness' sake!"

Chapter Nineteen

Lydia's sorriest fear was confirmed; she was a trollop.

From the moment Ned had looped his arm around her waist and spun her off the ground, even though he was simply manhandling her in order to win the contest, the delicious ease with which he controlled her stoked her imagination with all sorts of wanton thoughts. And they, in turn, took her breath away.

So when he'd stuck out his hand and she realized the prize he meant to have was a sportsmanlike shake, a devil of disappointment and longing let loose the truth.

A deep blush stained her cheeks and her gaze dropped. She could not bring herself to witness his reaction. Ned was the consummate gentleman. At the very least, he would be embarrassed for her—

"Lydia."

She turned and his mouth gently descended on hers. His lips were soft, much softer than she would have imagined, and firm. He angled his head so that his lips parted softly around her top one. She sighed, her eyes drifting, as the pressure increased. He tugged on her lip before releasing it and his mouth glided to her bottom lip to kiss it in the same manner.

She melted toward him and rested her palms on his chest, vaguely aware that except for his lips, he was not touching her at all. But his mouth . . . ! Oh, his mouth made up for the oversight. He lingered in the kiss, moving gently from her top to bottom lip and back again, softly exploring every inch, probing, pulling, and polishing. Her ragged breathing mingled with his and she grew light-headed under the sensual onslaught.

She swooned closer, bracing herself against his chest, her forearms resting against its heavy rise and fall. He was warm and hard, like heated stone, and she was like melted wax, pliant and yielding. The tip of his tongue slipped along the seam of her lips and her knees turned to liquid. Unmoored and incapable of pulling away, she curled a hand around the broad back of his neck and clung, her lips parting to admit his tongue.

A shudder raced through his big body. From far away she heard a feminine sound of surrender and longing, and she realized it was her own. His tongue delved deeply into her mouth, warm and muscular and forcefully masculine.

She heard something snap.

And just that abruptly, the kiss was over.

Ned lifted his head, breaking her hold on his neck and straightening. For a moment he stared past her, his breathing heavy, his nostrils flaring with each exhalation. Whatever his interior vision, it brought him no pleasure. Grave and unsmiling, he looked down at her.

"Lady Lydia—"

"Do *not* apologize," she warned him in a soft, shaky voice.

He looked at her soberly. "But I must," he said. "I

have taken advantage of the remoteness of this place, a child's wager, and a lamentable lack of restraint on my part to impose on you. I promised myself I would comport myself in a manner that honored you and now I have . . ." His jaw bunched and he shook his head slightly, overwhelmed by what he saw as his own objectionable idea.

God. If he thought for one moment that she had purposely maneuvered him into a situation where he would be forced to make her an offer—

"I do *not* consider myself compromised," she blurted out.

"Nor do I," he answered quickly, his expression frustrated and confounded. "You misunderstand me."

"Then pray make yourself understood," she said, substituting ire for mortification.

"Before I can speak of matters you have every right to expect me to address, and which I want above all things to frame, as a gentleman I must make certain things known to you."

"If you feel it necessary," she said stiffly.

He swallowed, looked away, then back at her. He squared his shoulders slightly and broadened his stance, his hands still clasped firmly behind his back, like a captain about to enter close quarters with an enemy vessel. "My circumstances are not felicitous."

Whatever she had expected him to say, it hadn't been that. "Felicitous?"

He nodded. "My name is an old and honorable one, which I have always borne with pride. Josten Hall, my family seat, has been a symbol of my family's nobility and endurance. For a dozen generations, it has elicited admiration and approbation from all who have visited there." He looked at her. "I am telling you this because I am hoping you might understand my attachment to what is just stone and mortar and earth."

"I do," she said. "You once said that you had come home. A home represents solace, does it not? A place from which one draws strength and security? I appreciated them very well. Those are things I depend on my friends to provide if not any one place."

"You would do much to preserve your friendships."

They were all she had left. "Indeed, yes. As would you your family's home."

"Exactly," he agreed quietly, then shook his head at some troubling thought. He took a short, deep breath and went on. "When I arrived home from sea, I was informed that Josten Hall was endangered and unless some remedy was found it would need to be sold."

"Endangered? By whom?"

"By extravagances and poor management, crop failures, a post-war economy, Corn Laws, and the wretched excess of my unfortunate kin," he said calmly.

The import of his words crashed in on her. No. Oh, no. *Oh. No.* How bad was it? Maybe his idea of difficulty meant selling off a few carriages. . . . "Your family is . . . in financial difficulties?" It was unconscionably bold of her, but she had to know.

He smiled ruefully. "My family is flat broke."

She had no warning. One moment she was standing facing him, the next her knees buckled and she was landing in a puff of material on the grass. He leaned over and held out his hand, but she was too intent on getting an answer to her question and ignored it.

"But you *personally* have resources at your command," she said, looking up at him. "The captain's share of all those ships you took, and you would be conservative in your financial dealings. . . ." She trailed off.

His hand dropped and he shifted back into that battle stance. "I am afraid that other than my name, massive financial obligations, and a disastrously profligate family, I have nothing to offer any young lady"—he paused, swallowed—"except myself."

My God, he is as poor as I. She stared up at him thunderstruck, her thoughts whirling like a gyroscope, unable to countenance how in such a few short minutes life had gone from so tantalizing to so terrible.

"I have a duty to do what is in my power to preserve that which generations of my forefathers fought and struggled to make and keep," he said. "Still, I could not—" He broke off abruptly, other than a certain tension in the set of his jaw there was no sign his confession had been painful to make. "I cannot say more until I hear your reaction."

Another realization broke in upon her: He did not know she, too, was "flat broke." And why would he? She had made every effort to keep anyone, including him, from knowing. He must think her outrageously wealthy. . . . Dear God. He had been searching for a rich spouse, the same as she.

No, no, no. Her eyes closed and she started to laugh. She couldn't stop. She buried her face in her hands and tears flowed from her eyes, and she could not tell if she was crying from the tragedy of it or the absurdity.

"Lady Lydia. Lydia," she heard him say, concerned and confused. "Lydia?"

"I'm sorry. Forgive me. I'm fine. I . . ." She pressed her knuckles into her forehead. It had all happened so fast. The kiss, his suggestion that he would like to propose, his disclosure . . .

"Lydia." Ned's voice, taut with anxiety.

She opened her eyes. He hovered over her, his gaze intent but without hurt or even recrimination, only concern. She had to pull herself together. She had to say something.

"Captain," she said from where she still sat at his feet, "I fear we have spent these weeks plotting the same course and with the same destination in mind."

"Forgive me for being obtuse, but I do not take your meaning," he said, his brow furrowing.

"I, too, have been victim of, how did you so succinctly phrase it? 'Extravagances and poor management, crop failures, a post-war economy, Corn Laws, and my *own* wretched excesses.' In other words, Captain"—she smiled weakly—"if your family is living in dun territory, I am the next address over."

"I see."

He handled the news with far greater aplomb than she. *He* didn't fall flat on his bum. His brows drew together before quickly smoothing out again. Hardly surprising; Ned was the ideal of self-possessed gentleman. But this time she did not appreciate his deportment. She hated how easily he accepted the end of their never-to-be relationship. But, then, perhaps his heart was not engaged so much as hers.

She had no doubt he had tender feelings for her. But to what extent? As much say, as Eleanor had for her spaniel—which, granted, was a fair amount, but when the dog began soiling the Oriental carpet Eleanor certainly hadn't resisted moving her to the farm. Or perhaps as much as Sarah seemed to have for Prince Carvelli, over whom she insisted on making such a cake of herself?

There was no sense in speculating. Ned wasn't going to ask her for her hand, not when he had just told her why he wanted it. At least he wouldn't unless he felt himself obligated. And she wouldn't accept it if he did, no matter how much she might be tempted, because when all was said and done, she was no fool.

Such a marriage could be . . . agreeable, even if such a marriage meant a lady must live apart from her friends in unfamiliar surroundings, but only if a lady was certain of her husband's affection and that she had been asked for her hand in marriage despite her poverty, not because a man felt duty bound to do so. But if a gentleman did not love a lady, wholeheartedly, passionately, and devotedly, it would be horrifying for a lady to marry him knowing that by wedding her, a gentleman was forfeiting his honor and turning his back on those he did love. And then she would be truly alone.

She looked up. He was regarding her intently, waiting for her to speak. "Yes, well. You can appreciate the humor of it, can't you? Both of us hunting for a spouse who can extradite us from our financial woes and ending up . . . here." Her bright tone didn't quite last through her final word. No matter.

She tucked her feet beneath her and pushed off the ground. At once, he was beside her, taking her hand in his, the other still behind his back in a courtly attitude as he lifted her to her feet. She bolted upright and backed away, flustered by a surge of potent attraction.

Dear God. She was *worse* than a trollop.

He stepped forward, following her and lowering his head slightly to better read her expression. He would be looking for some sign that she considered there to be an "understanding" between them and being a gentleman—Lord, she was beginning to loathe that term! It allowed a man to conceal so much beneath a facade—he would be quick to see and quicker still to act if he perceived she did. A gentleman did not lead a young lady into supposing an offer would be forthcoming.

She had to make sure he didn't see too much of what she felt in her face. And though she had years of practice keeping a pleasant countenance in place, she did not trust herself now. She had never been in love before.

"Well, Captain," she said conversationally, occupying herself by looking down and brushing uselessly at her ruined skirt. "As disappointed as we both are bound to be, at least some comfort must be taken in the fact that love was never mentioned."

His head snapped back an incremental degree. Her pulse began galloping.

"And thank heaven no one's more passionate sentiments were stirred," she said, trying to sound suave. *Did* he have passionate sentiments for her?

Long seconds passed before he answered. "As you say, ma'am."

But what if they were? What if he proposed? What would she say?

She did not know, she realized in amazement, and hard on its heels came panic. Would she say *yes*? No. *No*. She would not. Dear God, Sarah's madness must be contagious. She could not believe she was entertaining such fantastical notions. He needed a rich wife; she required a rich husband. They weren't two islands, alone and adrift at sea. They had obligations, others who depended on them, and *lives* that precluded their being together. That had been her first thought because it was the obvious thought.

Even if he did love her despite her poverty and asked for her hand, how long would it take before he began to resent his choice and the fact that in marrying her he'd consigned his family to penury? He would never show his resentment, of course, he was a gentleman. But she would always wonder.

To love passionately and wholly and not know whether that love was returned would be terrible. The only thing worse would be to know for a fact it was not. Her thoughts flew unwillingly and unfailingly to Caro Lamb.

She chanced an upward glance. Ned wore a polite and respectful expression, nothing more. She needn't have worried. Either way, she was not going to know. Unaccountably, her throat closed.

"Isn't that a blessing?" she asked in a thin voice.

He inclined his head. "Ma'am."

With each of his deferential replies, her composure became more unraveled. She was at odds with herself. She wanted . . . Oh, damn and blast, she did not know what she wanted! What she did *not* want was to lose his—

"We are still friends, are we not?" Her words tumbled out in a rush. How ironic. Just an hour earlier she had been depressed by the idea that this might be all Ned wanted of her; now the thought of losing his friendship frightened her beyond imagining.

"I beg pardon, Lady Lydia?" His brows drew together, his gaze growing more intense. Or was it just her imagination?

"I wish above all things that we are able to meet again without discomfort or awkwardness and as friends."

"Friends," he repeated in an odd voice.

"Yes. I value our camaraderie and I hope you value it, too."

"Of course."

His gaze flowed over her face, studying her. Lydia could not tell what he was thinking. She did not want to lose him. If she could not have him as a spouse, she must have his friendship.

"We are surely sophisticated enough that we won't allow our amusing mutual misunderstanding about each other's nonexistent wealth to endanger that?" She couldn't stop herself.

He smiled. "But of course."

"Mayhap I could even aid you in your quest?" she suggested, desperate for him to say something, anything more than those terrible, polite monosyllables!

A shift of muscles and sinew, so subtle it was barely discernible, announced the return of tension. "Once more, ma'am, I must beg your pardon. I am clearly out of my depths here."

"I know all the young ladies of the *ton*." The words tumbled out, unscripted and raw. "I am well acquainted with their families. I know their qualities and their faults and their . . . situations and I might be able to help you avoid—" She trailed off, blushing profusely.

He stepped in to save her. "Avoid a situation similar to this one?" he said with complete composure. At his words, she realized how maggoty and distasteful her impulsive offer had been. She also realized how very much it was something she would decidedly *not* like to do. But what could she say? She'd already offered her assistance.

"Yes."

"That is extraordinarily kind of you."

"Yes." She felt ill.

"I accept," he said and then nodded thoughtfully. "And in reply to such a magnanimous offer, I can do no less."

She blinked. "What do you mean?"

He caught both hands behind his back and paced a short ways away and back again and she noted for the first time that in one of his hands he was clutching a handkerchief. Where had it come from? His sleeve no doubt. But who had given him *that* one? Why was he holding it? What did it mean to him?

"I must offer you the same assistance." He smiled at her, but there was a sharpness in his eyes that had never been there before. "Hear me out. I know I have not been long in town, but as a gentleman I am liable to hear things that would never reach your ears. Boodle's is a positive font of information. Please, allow me to be of service. As your friend."

"That isn't necessary."

"I insist. If you are going to be so good as to help me . . . How to say this?" he muttered and then laughed. "Oh, why stand on ceremony? As we are such *good* friends now we can speak plainly with each other, can we not?"

Not. She nodded.

"Excellent!" he said. "So bluntly put, if you are going to hunt me up a bride, I can do no less than find you a groom as well."

She didn't want his help finding a husband any more than she wanted to help him find a bride. "No. It's too much of an imposition, and it seems rather, well"—she cast about anxiously—"rather cynical, doesn't it?"

"Cynical?" His beautiful gray eyes widened. "Good heavens, Lady Lydia. Pray recall our sophistication. There is nothing cynical about expedience. I will, of course, be strictly mute about your finances." She might have thought he was mocking her, but she noticed that his hand had fisted so tight around the handkerchief he held she could see the paleness of his knuckles. "So, we are agreed?"

What could she do? She'd backed herself neatly into an untenable situation. "Agreed."

"Excellent." He moved toward her, looking down into her upturned face, and whatever he saw there caused his smile to lose its odd vulpine edge.

She gazed back mutely, miserable and confused. Uncertainty flickered in his expression and he moved even closer, so close she could feel the slight brush of his breath on her cheeks. He raised his free hand as if to touch her and despite herself, she held her breath, hoping he would.

"Of course, we could just dispense with—"

Whatever Ned had been about to suggest they dispense with was forever lost in a riot of giggling exploding from the hedge a second before a girl broke from the eastern entrance and tumbled into the center, an exceptionally handsome young redheaded lad puffing hard on her heels.

"Jenny, please! You promised! One kiss!" the young man declared.

Jenny Pickler, still laughing, swung about to answer and caught sight of Ned, impeccable as always, and Lydia, her hair down around her shoulders, her skirts ripped and dirtied. Jenny's mouth fell open.

"Lady . . . *Lydia*?"

Lydia, finally, after a hiatus of nearly an hour, found her dignity and recovered her too long absent poise. "Yes, Miss Pickler." She lifted a dark winged brow at the very young and flustered gentleman. "Sir?"

"Ma'am." He bowed deeply.

"Yes. Well. A fine day, is it not?"

"Indeed, Lady Lydia," Jenny stuttered.

She plastered a brilliant, regal smile on her face. "Then good day to you," she said, and with a sense of enormous relief, sailed out of the maze.

Left behind, Ned watched her depart, the swish of her mangled skirts in no way lessening her regality. He withdrew his hand from behind his back and idly unfolded the bloodstained handkerchief pressed tightly to his palm.

"Captain, your hand!" Jenny Pickler gasped. "However did you injure it?'

He glanced around, his gaze finding the girl and her red-faced swain.

"Eh? Oh," he said. "I was attempting to restrain an overwhelming need to express my . . . friendship for a certain person."

"Friendship?" Jenny Pickler echoed, nonplussed by

his odd tone when he used the word and the sight of the jagged tear in Ned's palm.

"Yes. Some would have found a different name for the sentiment—perhaps passion—but a lady I hold in high esteem has informed me that it was not in fact what I was feeling, and I would not argue with her."

"Captain," Jenny Pickler said. "I do not take your meaning."

"No, Miss Pickler," he replied calmly. "Neither does she." His gaze drifted to the shifting youngster behind her. "For God's sake, Pip, straighten your cravat."

And with a bow to Jenny Pickler, he left.

Chapter Twenty

Lydia retired early that night, but sleep eluded her. Her thoughts kept tumbling over one another, the phantom prospect of happiness with Ned fighting for precedence against the looming potential for isolation and loneliness. She had never lacked for courage, never refused to acknowledge a thing because she did not want it to be so. One took what one had and made do, or in fact did better than make do, as had she.

Restlessly, she turned where she lay. What was she supposed to do? What had she hoped would happen? She still didn't know. The news that Ned's family's pockets were to let had deeply shaken her. She had taken his wealth for granted, then fallen in love with him. How could she do otherwise? He was everything she admired, everything she respected. His nobility was one of genuine character, not manners; the things he had seen and done had importance and merit. His masculinity was unaffected and forceful. He was everything she wanted ... except rich.

She sat up and jerked her blanket tightly around herself and huddled with her chin on her knees, glowering out at the darkness with futile resentment. Was she supposed to have told Ned it didn't matter to her that he had no money and then hoped that he felt the same? It would have been a lie. Wouldn't it?

Even if he did return her love and proposed marriage, what was she supposed to have done then? Leave everything she knew behind? Her friends, her position in Society, her lifestyle? Abandon the retinue of retainers and craftsmen and artisans that relied on her? While her concern for them might be based on reasoning that was somewhat spurious, it also had some basis in fact.

She didn't *know* any other way to live. Her brief years in Wilshire had been telling. The isolation and loneliness there had driven home that with her parents' deaths she had lost everyone who cared about her and all her connections to the world. Which is why Emily's plight had resonated so deeply with her. It only made sense that after Eleanor had brought her to London, she had gone about collecting a sort of makeshift family with a fervor that would have been amusing had it not been pitiful.

She sank to her side on her bed, curling in on herself. If she married with no thought to wealth or status, she would be forced to rely on her husband to provide the emotional connections she needed, the sense of closeness, of being more than important to someone, of being necessary. Of being *loved*. What if Ned could not provide that? What if he was, as Childe suggested, incapable of the sort of passion she wanted him to feel for her?

What if he could? Her breath caught with elation over the possibility before cold reason extinguished it. How could she take that chance? *What chance*? He hadn't asked for her hand. He had obligations and responsibilities as pressing as her own. Her speculations were all moot. Ned needed a rich wife and she required a rich husband and that was the end of it.

Some time later, not long after Lydia had finally fallen into a fitful sleep, a light, insistent tapping awoke her. She shifted up onto her elbows, looking about groggily. The night was still black outside her bedroom windows and her room was steeped in shadows. Not yet dawn.

"Lady Lydia?" She heard the whisper of her maid's voice as the door opened a crack.

"Come in," Lydia said, sitting up.

The door swung silently open and the last remaining maid in Lydia's once-large staff entered, fully clad, the only sign she hadn't been awake all night the untidy braid coiled around her head. She held a single lit taper in her hand.

"What is it, Peach?"

"Mrs. Marchland, milady. She is downstairs and insists on seeing you. She is waiting in the morning room."

Sarah? Here? Lydia swung her legs over the side of the bed and the maid hurried over, sweeping a dressing gown from the foot of the bed, holding it open for Lydia to don.

"Is she all right?" Lydia asked, thrusting her arms into the sleeves. "What time is it?"

"It is half past five, milady, and Mrs. Marchland seems agitated, but otherwise in good health."

Hurriedly, Lydia twisted her hair into a knot at the back of her neck and hastened from her room, alarmed. Something dire must have happened for Sarah to come to her at such an hour.

"That will be all, Peach," she said upon reaching the door to the morning room.

The maid bobbed a curtsy and vanished as Lydia pushed open the door to the morning room. Sarah stood inside, her hands knit at her waist, her face anxious and her eyes brilliant. She was dressed for travel.

"What is it, Sarah?" Lydia exclaimed. "What has happened?"

Sarah rushed forward, her hands outstretched to clasp Lydia's. Briefly, Sarah embraced her before drawing her over to the settee in front of the cold hearth. Sarah sat down and faced her. "I am leaving Marchland to go to the Continent with Carvelli this morning," she said without preamble.

Lydia blinked at her, not certain she had heard aright. Sarah couldn't mean it.

"I know, my dear," Sarah said, nodding as if Lydia had spoken. "I have quite shocked you and you are thinking how to best dissuade me from eloping. Pray, spare yourself the effort. I will not be deterred."

"Sarah, you can't," Lydia said.

Sarah smiled ruefully. "Lydie, dearest, I did not come to confer with you. I came to advise you of my plans and"—her voice softened—"say good-bye."

Good-bye. Lydia's heartbeat jumped in her throat. If Sarah did this thing then they would indeed be parted, not only by physical distance but by a far more unbridgeable chasm. Eloping with Carvelli would make Sarah a social pariah. None of their mutual friends would meet her. No one would acknowledge her. No one would have her in their homes. Sarah would be relegated to the ranks of the demireps and lightskirts. This was madness.

"Sarah, you aren't thinking properly. You are not yourself."

"But I am, Lydia," Sarah said. "Never more so than now. Carvelli makes me happy and I make him happy."

"Happiness," Lydia repeated incredulously. She could not believe this was the same woman who only a few months ago had advised her to marry someone accommodating who promised to be accommodatingly absent. "Sarah, how many times have gentlemen 'made you happy'? And how long did that happiness last?"

Sarah flushed and Lydia's heart twisted at her own harshness, but this was no time to spare Sarah's feelings.

"Think of what you are giving up," she persisted.

Sarah's gaze met hers. "I have, Lydie. I know you will not be convinced, but I have thought of nothing else for a week."

"A week?" Lydia echoed.

"Don't sneer, Lydia. A week is a long time for me," Sarah said with unexpected dignity. "Despite your pose of insouciance, I well know you are wont to worry at a thing, and turn it over and examine it from all sides, pondering and fretting it to death." This time Lydia flushed as she recalled the earlier hours of the night. "A week for you is nothing, but for me it demonstrates the deepest introspection."

Here, at last, in a roguish smile Lydia glimpsed a peek of the Sarah she loved so well. Then it was gone. "I love Carvelli and he loves me and we wish to live together as man and wife."

"But you *aren't* man and wife, Sarah," Lydia protested. "You *have* a husband and Carvelli *has* a wife. And if that does not influence you, let me remind you that you also have two children."

Sarah paled. "*Gerald* has children. He refuses to allow me to see them. He says my influence would be detrimental to their moral character."

Lydia had known Gerald kept the children with him, but she had always assumed the choice was mutual. She had never suspected Gerald of purposefully keeping Sarah apart from her children, but one look into her friend's tense and strained face and she did not now doubt it. The tragedy and unfairness of it astounded her. Sarah, of course, had no recourse to fight Gerald's decision. None. Children were their father's responsibility and property.

"So I do not have children, Lydia. But if I am very fortunate," she said wistfully, "I shall bear Carvelli a child someday. He desires that I should above all things."

Lydia pulled her hands from Sarah's. "And should he wish, Gerald could take that child, too." It was the law.

At this, Sarah's mouth closed in a stubborn line. "He wouldn't. He doesn't care enough to want to hurt me and there would be no other reason to take our child."

"Listen to yourself, Sarah," Lydia begged. "You are trying to spin some girlish romance out of a simple, sordid tale. Think past next month or even next year, when the idyll has played itself out and Carvelli returns to Italy. Where will you go then?"

Sarah's face remained mulishly closed.

"Gerald will put you aside," Lydia said. "He must. You will be exiled to some cold, dreary house far from the Society you have always known and enjoyed and

there you will stay, separated from family and friends."
The picture she painted appalled her, doubly so as it so
closely resembled a scene she had imagined for herself,
should she throw everything over to marry Ned. *Had* he
asked her to marry him. Which he had not.

But she had no time to think on that now; Sarah must
be convinced to abandon her plan.

When Sarah finally spoke, she did so without the
anger or affront Lydia expected. She looked suddenly
tired, far older than her twenty-four years and jaded in
a manner Lydia had never before discerned. "I did not
come here for your approval, Lydia. I never thought to
have it. And I realize the potential consequences of my
action far better than you assume. I would be practical if
I could, Lydia, but I cannot. If I do not go with Carvelli,
I shall regret it every day of my life." She held up her
hand as Lydia opened her mouth to speak, forestalling
her. "Doubtless all you say is correct, my dear, but it is a
price I am willing to pay. So . . ." Her gaze flickered away
from Lydia and back again. "Can you not find it in your
heart to wish me well despite your disapproval?"

Lydia flung her arms around Sarah's shoulders and
embraced her tightly. "Dear heaven, Sarah. Of course,
I want what is best for you. That is why I am trying to
convince you to forgo this madness."

"Then, Lydia, don't want what is *best* for me," Sarah
murmured, returning Lydia's embrace. "Want my
happiness."

"The two are not exclusive of each other."

"For me they are," Sarah replied softly.

Lydia had never heard her so subdued or thoughtful.
She clasped Sarah by the shoulders and held her away,

gazing intently into her face. "This is not any path to happiness," she persisted.

"Perhaps not, but it is *a* path and I have been standing still casting about without direction for so long I never thought to find one." She stood up. "Now wish me well."

Lydia rose to her feet beside her, a hand on her forearm. "Sarah," she said. "How can I stand by and 'wish,' when my love for you insists that I protest? You are ruining yourself."

"Let her go, Lydia." Emily spoke from the doorway.

Lydia looked around. Emily stood in the hall just outside the cast of candlelight. She was in dishabille, clutching a shawl around her round shoulders, the sleeping cap atop her head slightly askew.

"Emily," Lydia said, anticipating an ally, "add your voice to mine and convince our dear friend not to—"

"You must let her go, Lydia. You must say good-bye to her and you must let her go," Emily broke in, her soft voice carrying a fatalistic weight. "She has decided."

Lydia did not have time to wonder at Emily's misalliance. She turned back to Sarah. "Have you spoken to Eleanor?"

Sarah laughed. "Ad nauseum. She was as relentless in her determination to dissuade me from my plan as you. I would have thought she would understand better given the circumstances of her own marriage."

Sarah's gaze moved past Lydia to where Emily stood like a mournful little dumpling of a ghost. "You understand, don't you, Emily?"

She nodded. "Yes."

Lydia stood by feeling oddly auxiliary and disoriented, her friends suddenly people she did not recognize or understand.

Emily's word brought a fleeting smile to Sarah's face. "I wish you well, Sarah," Emily said, hugging her shawl tighter as if against a sudden chill.

Sarah nodded and turned to Lydia. "And you, Lydia, will you wish me well, too?"

"But I will see you again eventually," Lydia protested. "Won't I?"

"Of course," Sarah said brightly, reaching out and taking hold of both of Lydia's hands. "Just not in the same venues." But Sarah's eyes flickered toward Emily and with a near physical sensation of loss, Lydia realized how naive she sounded, how facile Sarah's reassurance had been.

There would be no meetings. Sarah loved her too well to presume on a relationship that could only harm Lydia's reputation.

"Sarah—"

"Enough, Lydie. Tell me you love me and wish me well," Sarah said firmly.

There was nothing else to do. "I love you, Sarah"— Lydia spoke in a hushed voice—"and I wish you the utmost happiness."

Sarah blinked and cleared her throat, dropping Lydia's hands and manufacturing a bright smile. "There now," she said, turning quickly away to collect her reticule from the settee where she'd left it. "That was not so hard. Good-bye, my dears."

She did not pause, nor did she look back as she hurried through the door, disappearing into the darkness.

Lydia sat down heavily on the settee, staring after her.

"Nothing you could have said would have stopped her, Lydie," Emily said, shuffling into the room.

Ah, Lydia thought with a hollow sort of objectivity, that is how Sarah had sought and won Emily's sympathy. Both women had known tragic marriages. Only Sarah had taken action to escape it, action Emily must surely wish she'd taken, too.

"Will she be happy?" Lydia whispered. "Can she be happy?"

"For a while," Emily answered quietly. "But that's all some people are allotted in this life, m'dear." She darted a glance at Lydia. "And they would rather take their small taste than never sip from the cup at all. It is those who have been given a full portion and waste it who are to be pitied."

Not me, Lydia thought. *I know how fortunate I have been, how the gods have smiled at me. I will not spill my portion and chase after chimerical hopes and dreams.*

But then why was it, she thought unhappily, that Emily was looking at her with that sadness in her eyes?

Chapter Twenty-one

Morning still stood a ways off by the time Ned let himself into his rented town house. His footman lay slouched on the bench by the door fast asleep, Ned's failure to apprise his household of his doings necessitating the poor blighter to stay up all night waiting for him.

Ned hadn't realized how long or far he had traveled until he found himself east of the London docks by St. George's Church, rising like a dark obelisk in the predawn gloom. He had walked away the afternoon and evening and most of the night. He had made his way down to the river to watch the mudlarks scavenging the low tide, their swaying lanterns like fireflies over the shoals. He'd found no respite and finally, determining that he would not find the answer he was seeking on foot, he had headed back to St. James Square.

He nudged the footman awake with his foot and then moved down the corridor, waiting until he heard the young man scramble to his feet before calling back over his shoulder, "Coffee."

"Right away, sir!"

Jerking off his cravat, he tossed it on the back of a chair as he entered the library. He shrugged out of his coat and restlessly paced to the window, looking out unseeingly over the square as if he might find an answer there.

He had captained a ship through five years of war and engaged in three dozen battles. He had sat in on strategy meetings, his opinions well respected by the admiralty. He was known for his cool head, intelligence, and instincts. But where the battle for Lydia's heart was concerned he was at a loss of how to go on. Or even if he should.

She would have been surprised had he told her he loved her with or without her fortune. She would certainly have doubted him and ascribed his declaration to good manners. If he'd read correctly her comments (and judging from her confidence that he would be well content with friendship, he had) she had decided his "passionate sentiments" were modest at best.

A grim smile tensed his lips as he glanced down. To keep from hauling Lydia into his arms and treating her to a too graphic example of those same tepid desires, he'd gripped the damn beech bough so tightly the thing had snapped, gouging his palm. He'd barely noticed it at the time.

His tight smile softened. She had looked so lovely in the maze with her thick brown hair falling around her shoulders, leaves caught in the tendrils, her purple eyes dancing. He thought she might never have been more beautiful than when she cared about it least. She would not have believed that either.

"We are still friends, are we not?"

It had been a small enough thing to ask and an excruciating thing to contemplate, being Lydia's friend and ever more. But he could no more deny her his friendship than he could order his heart not to beat. So he had stayed to keep her company, as would a friend, and listened in amazement as she presented him with a token of her alleged amity by proposing to find him a rich bride.

His shock had been followed by anger that she thought him so insipid he would let her find him a wife. Had his kiss told her nothing? Had she not recognized the restraint he had exercised in order to keep his passion in check? What sort of man did she think he was to kiss her one moment, then to agree to let her find him a mate the next?

But then, when he had been about to respond with harsh and damning words, he'd looked into her dark violet eyes and seen some fleeting shadow of what her voice and manner and expression were trying so desperately to hide. And it was at that moment that he had realized that Lady Lydia Eastlake would never have made so insensitive an offer to begin with unless some emotion had overwhelmed her innate kindness and for that to be overwhelmed, it would have to be a powerful emotion indeed. It inspired him with a fragile hope that she might return his feelings.

But now what?

If he asked for her hand, she would only say no. She had made it quite clear that she required a husband who could keep her in the same manner in which she'd always lived. And even if he could convince her to say yes . . . should he? *Could* she be happy as the wife of an impecunious retired sea captain?

An image appeared in his mind's eye to confound

him further: Lydia shimmering in silk, diamonds glittering around her throat and wrists, her eyes the brightest gems of all as she danced a waltz or traded sallies. Lydia, that is, being admired, imitated, sought after. Had he even the right to ask her to leave her world and intimates for an unknown life with him?

He ran a hand through his hair. And to a lesser degree there still remained the question of his own responsibilities and obligations. Josten Hall, his home, the home of generations of Locktons. What would the Locktons be without Josten Hall?

"Captain?" The footman's voice startled him from his thoughts.

"Come."

The footman backed into the room bearing a tray with the requested coffee. He set it down, lit the lamps, then returned to Ned with an envelope, which he handed to him, bowing slightly.

"Beggin' pardon, sir, but this arrived for you yesterday afternoon after you'd left the house. The messenger waited until midnight for an answer before leaving."

"Yes, thank you," Ned said, picking up the letter and slitting open the seal. "That will be all."

"Yes, sir," he heard the footman say as the door softly clicked shut.

He read the letter, his expression going from weariness to exasperation:

Captain Lockton,
    Out of my respect for you and your family, I
feel obliged to make known to you the intentions
of your nephew, Lord Harold Lockton, who last

*evening challenged Elsworth Tweed to a duel of
honor. Mr. Tweed has accepted the challenge and
the two are set to meet on Primrose Hill at first
light. Phillip Hickston-Tubbs is acting as Lord
Lockton's second. There is frankly no honor to
be had in this affair. I have done what I could to
dissuade both parties from pursuing what can only
end in tragedy, but to no avail.*

   I remain your servant,
   George Borton

Ned crushed the paper in his hand, flung it into the
fire, and snatched up his coat. Shoving his arms through
the sleeves, he glanced at the mantel clock. A quarter
past four. If he rode like the devil he ought to make it.

He swept his cravat from the back of the chair and
headed for the stables.

In the faint light beginning to seep like a wine stain
down its eastern slope, Primrose Hill belied its pretty
name, looking very much a fitting scene for tragedy,
being barren, fog-clotted, and wind-smacked. The turf
was rough and the slopes devoid of trees, resident only
to low shrubs and a few sheep, their home invaded this
morning by the stately progress of a carriage following
several men on horseback.

Ned reined in the winded bay where the road crested,
looking down at the carriage pulling to a halt. His fear
vanished, replaced by crossness. The fools. Should anything happen to either, Nadine and Beatrice would
never recover from the loss.

He kneed his horse forward as Harry, obvious even

at this distance by dint of his gleaming gold hair, dismounted and disappeared on the other side of the parked carriage. Tweed also dismounted and, tossing his coat to one of his companions, stalked off some distance, shaking off the delaying hands of friends better than he probably deserved. By now, Pip had been joined by another young man and they were bent over a box that Pip had taken from the carriage interior. Borton hovered anxiously by the carriage door talking to someone inside.

Ned arrived just as Pip and Tweed's second finished loading the pistols. They looked up anxiously at his approach, and damned if he didn't think both would have been relieved to discover he was a magistrate come to arrest them all.

"Good morning, Pip," he said politely, swinging down out of the saddle and tossing the reins to the coachman standing by. He shed his leather riding gloves, slapping them against his thigh before tucking them into his belt. "You've certainly been industrious of late. First the Morrow Maze and now this."

Phillip gaped fishlike at him. Not a look Ned imagined Jenny Pickler would fancy.

"Good day, Borton," he said, acknowledging Josten's neighbor. "Where's Harry?"

"What are you doing here?" Pip finally managed to gulp out.

"I've come for the duel, of course."

He looked around for Harry, who had not yet reappeared, and glimpsed a hoary old head poking out of the side of the carriage. The surgeon, no doubt.

"Excuse me, gentlemen," Ned said and went round to the carriage's other side. There, as expected, he found Harry bent at the waist, tossing up his accounts on the grass. Harry had a notoriously delicate stomach. Even the mention of blood could upset it.

"'Allo, Harry," he said mildly.

Harry's head shot up, his eyes bulged in his face, and he promptly doubled up and spewed forth more of his supper. He pressed a handkerchief to his lips and straightened, a little shaky but plucky to the end. Wretched sot.

"Damn it, Ned," he said angrily. "Now look what you've done." He pointed at his boots. "I can't duel with me boots covered in vomit. Find me a handkerchief, for the love of God, that I might clean them."

Ned's eyes widened. Harry had always shown him a healthy deference, but this sounded very much like his father's autocratic tones, which indicated, if this was a trait he'd inherited from Josten, great distress.

Ned reached up and yanked his cravat from around his neck and tossed it to Harry, who fell to one knee and began scrubbing assiduously at his boot.

"What are you doing here, Ned?" he asked resentfully.

"Exercising my familial right to be concerned," Ned answered. "I might ask you the same. What are *you* doing here, Harry?"

Harry glanced up. His light blue eyes were dark with emotion. "Defending the family's honor. Something to which you seem indifferent."

Ah. The boy was blaming him for this contretemps.

"I see. And what offense did Tweed offer?"

In answer to his question, Harry turned brick red and his gaze fell. He mumbled something.

"Pardon me. Cannon fire has robbed me of some hearing. What did you say?"

He looked up, eyes flashing. "He said me dog was a hermaphrodite."

It wasn't often Ned was taken by surprise, but Harry had done it. For a second, Ned wasn't even sure the boy wasn't gammoning him, but one look at Harry's petulant face and he realized he was, indeed, serious.

He cleared his throat. "Thick-witted of me, I'm sure, but in that case, wouldn't it be the *dog's* honor you were defending?"

Harry finished cleaning the vomit off his boot and stood up, flinging the soiled cravat to the ground. "The dog was a metaphor Tweed used to offend our family's honor."

"A metaphor?" Ned was more impressed by the fact his nephew knew what a metaphor was than the metaphor itself. Especially since he doubted Tweed was capable of making use of one.

"Yes!" snapped Harry. "I don't even have a dog."

"Oh." Apparently he was wrong.

"And he called the dog *Captain*."

Ned burst out laughing. He couldn't help it, even though Harry was turning from red to purple, his lips so compressed they'd all but disappeared.

"I am glad you find being called a hermaphrodite so amusing," Harry pronounced coldly.

Manfully, Ned choked back his laughter. "Oh, I . . . I am sorry. It's just so ludicrous, Harry. Why ever would you allow yourself to be manipulated so easily and with such scant effort?"

He'd meant to shake the boy into realizing how unworthy this duel was of him. But looking now at his nephew, he realized he'd only managed to insult him.

"You are not part of this, Ned," Harry said stiffly. "And I will appreciate it if you would leave before the duel commences."

"I am afraid I cannot do that, Harry. Your mother would have my head on a platter if I stood by and watched so much as a hair on the head of her blue-eyed boy be harmed."

"Well, there's nothing you can do about it. I am going to shoot—" The words brought on another bout of sickness. "Damn!"

Ned didn't bother staying to argue. He inclined his head and withdrew, leaving Harry to clean up his other boot. His exasperation had begun to give way to a very real anger. He was beginning to think it would do the boy a world of good to piss himself as he stared down the barrel of a dueling pistol. Perhaps then he might not be in such a hurry to let a scab like Tweed maneuver him into such situations.

Tweed. Ned's eyes narrowed. Harry wasn't the target of Tweed's enmity, he was. Tweed only thought to injure him through his nephew, which in Ned's lexicon was a far worse offense than naming him a dog or suggesting that he'd cheated at cards.

Pip and Tweed's second studied him with round-eyed wariness. He ignored both seconds, motioning for Borton to accompany him. Tweed's man fell in line behind them and Pip started after them. Ned turned and stopped him in his tracks with a glance.

"If you value your hide, Pip, you will stay here and keep your cousin occupied on the other side of that carriage for as long as you possibly can," he ground out, his anger finally surfacing. "I suggest you describe the gory details of wounds you have never seen."

"Wha—oh," Pip said, flushing with understanding.

Ned headed to where Tweed stood, one fist resting negligently on his hip, his back arched slightly, and his chest puffed out. " 'Morning, Tweed," he acknowledged the burly man.

"Lockton," he replied, his nostril flaring in a sneer.

Ned smiled. "I anticipate another cold day. Hard to imagine it's nearly July, what with the frost and all."

"So Lockton has decided to withdraw his challenge, eh? Can't say I'm surprised. Though Hickston-Tubbs should have been his emissary—"

"Oh, no," Ned said, quite gently. "Harry ain't withdrawing anything, I'm afraid. Perhaps *you* would like to broker an apology? No. I didn't think so." He sighed and began shrugging out of his coat.

"What are you doing?" Tweed said, startled out of his insolent sneer.

"Preparing for our duel," Ned replied, removing his coat and rolling his shoulders experimentally. He handed it to Tweed's astonished cohort. "Would you mind holding this? It binds a bit across the back."

"I'm not dueling you," Tweed said.

"Well, unless you care to offer your apologies, I'm afraid you have no choice," Ned said calmly. "I am only doing this as a favor to you, mind."

"A favor? To me? What the bloody hell are you talking about, Lockton?"

"Harry," Ned replied, rolling back the sleeves of his shirt. "The lad's not yet twenty-one and it is against the law to challenge anyone who has not yet come of age to a duel. Truth is, he isn't even twenty yet."

"It is against the law to duel at all," one of Tweed's men said.

"Ah, yes," Ned agreed. "But we all know that the law is likely to turn a blind eye to the affairs of gentlemen. However, if a fellow were to prove himself not of that rank, by, say, dueling with a boy, the law would be most demonstrably displeased. A trial, I believe."

Tweed stared at him, hunting for some way to save face.

"Really, how could it be otherwise?" he asked, turning to Tweed's companions. "Why, Eton and Harrow and Rugby would be littered with schoolboys' bodies if we allowed them to settle their grievances with bullets."

Borton laughed and the other men—save Tweed—snickered appreciatively. Fury scalded Tweed's face. Ned had neatly relegated Tweed's affair of honor to a schoolyard squabble.

"So what will it be, Tweed? An apology or shall we start counting out paces?"

"I will *not* apologize."

Ned hadn't thought he would. He needed this to be over before Harry appeared. "Borton, act as my second? Sharply, man."

Borton understood the need for haste. He nodded curtly and gripping Tweed's second by the arm, dragged him off a short distance to discuss particulars.

"Nice horse," he said conversationally, nodding toward Tweed's gelding.

In answer, Tweed made a rough sound and spun around, stalking back to his friends and leaving Ned alone for the moment. He squinted out at the lightening horizon, shaking his head in an unconscious gesture of negation. Every decent principle protested his involvement in this situation.

He didn't know whom he loathed more right now—Tweed for using his vile nephews to even some imaginary score, or those same wretched nephews for falling so willingly into his scheme. Not that it mattered. He was stuck risking his life because some churlish blighter with a grudge had called a nonexistent hound *Captain*.

Be damned. Loyalty, duty, and sacrifice had been creeds by which he'd lived the past fifteen years but always in what he'd adjudged to be a worthy cause. But what if, as now, the cause was *not* worth the sacrifice? Did it not cheapen those things he had fought for—ideals of freedom and liberty and justice—by ranking them with what amounted to no more than name-calling?

And even more compelling, did it not cheapen his love for Lydia to willingly sacrifice it for two gin-soaked young wastrels? Alone, he might be able to stave off his family's imminent financial collapse for a year. If he married a rich bride as his family had asked, he might help avert it for a decade or even two. But eventually, inevitably, it would not be up to him whether Josten Hall and the Locktons endured. It would be up to those jackanapes.

He loved Lydia. He didn't care whether she was rich or poor, a baron's daughter or a French émigré's niece.

He loved Lydia and he would do everything in his power to win her. All his life he had done his duty, fulfilled his responsibilities, and subordinated his desires to others. No more.

And the richest part of his decision was he had no choice. His heart led now, other considerations fading to inconsequence before its imperative. He had to win her, to convince her of the depth and intensity of his feelings. And if he died before he had that opportunity, by God, he would come back and drag these boys to hell with him.

"Captain." Borton's voice startled him from his preoccupation. "We've agreed. Twenty-five paces. Two shots."

"Two? For a dog's name?" Ned asked in disgust.

"Tweed's second pressed for three, Captain. Only the protest of the others kept him from insisting and myself from being drawn into a duel."

Ned clapped Borton's shoulder. "Well done, then."

"I pray you," Borton said nervously, "should you live, do not let Mary know I had any part of this. She would flay me alive!"

Ned smiled. "Done. Now let us finish this before we need deal with Harry."

He took the pistol Borton handed him and strode out to meet Tweed, already waiting with his second. As soon as Ned reached them, the second gave instructions on how the duel was to proceed and then quickly withdrew, leaving Ned and Tweed to pace out their twenty-five steps.

Fog shifted around Ned's calves like powdered snow as he walked. The day dawning promised to be so bleak that there was as yet no discernible horizon, simply a withdrawal of darkness. His breath condensed in the cold air. He finished his paces and turned, his shoulders sideways to Tweed. Even in the chance light he could see the moisture beading on Tweed's face. A horse nickered. Someone coughed.

"Are the gentlemen prepared to fire?" Tweed's man called out.

"Yes."

"Yes."

Ned inhaled deeply, composing a sketch in his mind's eye of glossy brown hair, tip-tilted violet eyes, their corners pleated with delight, a smile surprised from cherry lips—

"Present!"

Both men raised their pistols.

"At your discretion, gentlemen!"

Tweed fired at once.

Ned's muscles bunched in reaction, but he did not flinch. He waited for the advent of pain, some signal that he'd been hit. The body, he had learned through experience, is not always eager to bear bad news to the mind. But there was nothing. His breath came out in a ragged whoosh. He adjusted the sight line of his pistol on Tweed, whose face had grown ashen.

"One, two, three," Borton's voice called out. "Fire."

Ned's arm swung up. He fired. A gasp of outrage and murmurs of disapproval replied to the crack of the discharge.

"Deloped!"

"Unconscionable!"

"Insulting!"

He'd fired into the air, deloping. It was an act that implied a man's opponent was not worth any potential difficulties his death or injury might put one through. Tweed took it as the grave offense honor deemed it to be. He surged forward a step before his second's voice barked out, forestalling him.

"Prepare for a second volley!"

Both men cocked the hammer back on the second barrel of their pistols and awaited the command to present. Only Tweed, fired by passion and anger, did not wait. His pistol jerked up and fired.

There was, after all, not so long a delay between sensation and recognition as Ned recalled. Fire tore through his temple, knocking him back. He staggered a step, aware that blood was streaming down his face.

If disapproval had met his deloping, condemnation erupted at Tweed's premature shot.

Tweed did not move, and Ned gave points for hubris. He quivered where he stood, his emptied pistol hanging by his side, his face, rather than reflecting shock or shame, twisted into an apoplectic knot. By God, Ned thought, growing light-headed with blood loss. He is only sorry I am not dead.

"Take your shot!" Tweed screamed.

Shakily, Ned raised his arm and took a deep breath, trying to steady himself. He sighted down the pistol's barrel. He could end this now, forever, not only for himself but for his nephews. The law would not prosecute.

But he valued life too much to cheapen it for expedience' sake.

He dropped his arm and discharged his pistol into the ground between them.

Tweed surged forward, further enraged, but his men caught him back, intent on spiriting him away before the news of his dishonor found him. In the distance, Ned heard Harry shouting as the ground seemed to swell up to seize hold of him.

Ned's last thought was that he would miss seeing Lydia that evening.

And then darkness swept in.

Chapter Twenty-two

July, 1816

"But, ma'am, how can I advise you on what material to purchase if you refuse to tell me as whom you intend to go to the Spencers' masquerade ball?" Childe Smyth asked Lydia.

He had accompanied her to Miss Walter's modiste shop in Cavendish Square, Miss Walter specializing in the creation of elaborate and gorgeous costumes. Childe had called just as Lydia was leaving for her appointment and insisted his discerning eye would be needed. Childe did have a discerning eye, Lydia granted him that.

"I can't tell you. It is to be a surprise to everyone. Suffice to say we are seeking some rich stuff of gold."

"Lace? Silk? Satin? Muslin? Net?"

"Yes," she said.

"I am foiled," he announced to the showroom at large, where several ladies were examining bolts of cloth and yard goods. They looked around and tittered. He sketched them an elaborate bow. "I shall take myself thither to yon lace and there devise some other way of discovering who you mean to be. Or, failing that, find you a pretty piece of gold openwork."

He gave her a jaunty smile and strolled toward one of the other areas of the modiste's workroom.

He looked most handsome this morning, Lydia thought. His blue-black cutaway frock coat, the top hat perched atop his dark raffish curls, the Nankeen yellow pantaloons tucked into shining Hessian boots all conveyed sartorial sophistication. Elegance even, what with his silver-headed walking stick and the brilliant red watch fob hanging from his striped pale blue and cream waistcoat.

He not only looked the part of the consummate dandy, he played the part, and exceptionally well. He was droll and dry and obliging, not in the least pressing, which was excellent as she did not think she could bear anyone's ardency. She found his company most easy. He valued the same things she did, knew the same people she knew. The only thing he wanted, which she could provide, were her noble bloodlines.

A very fine gentleman, she acknowledged, though some found him a bit too affected. But then, who was she to quibble? She dined out on affectation. In addition to all his fine attributes, he was rich. And he would be his magnificently, supremely wealthy grandfather's heir if he wed before the old Tartar died.

Yes, all things told, it was unutterably depressing that she did not respond more enthusiastically to so perfect a suitor. For without a doubt, that is what Childe Smyth had become these past days. Ever since Lydia had last seen Ned and they had made their devil's bargain to find each other suitable, and rich, mates. One mustn't forget the "rich" part, she thought with a new cynicism, as it was clearly the only consideration she could have in choosing a spouse. She had already found a "suitable mate," or at least one who suited her.

God, how she missed Ned.

A wave of yearning swept through her, turning down the corners of her mouth. She looked away lest someone think something was wrong. . . . But something *was* wrong. She hadn't seen Ned for over two weeks. She didn't know where he was or what he was thinking. None of her friends or acquaintances seemed to know where he was either, or whether he was even still in town.

Early on she'd heard rumors of a duel that had sent her heart pitching in panic. She had sent a fevered note to his town house, demanding news, and had received a polite reply from him assuring her that he was well and advising her not to take any sensationalized accounts of a person's exploits at face value. He followed this advice with anecdotes illustrative of his point, such as how he had once read she bathed in milk to achieve the perfection of her skin and that she owned a dress made entirely of butterfly wings.

She'd laughed out loud with pleasure and relief at his gentle teasing and missed him more, taking heart in how warm and intimate his words had been. But there had been no more. Then, last week, she had heard the first murmurs that the Locktons of Josten Hall were in the basket. A few days later someone told her that Josten was in negotiations to sell off his stable of racehorses.

Perhaps this had something to do with Ned's disappearance. Perhaps he'd gone wife-hunting in Brighton? The thought racked her with anguish. Whatever the reason, wherever he'd gone, his absence left a hollow in her heart that would not fill. One would think she would

have grown used to it by now, but she hadn't. Each day
the pain caused by missing him grew deeper and more
acute.

As did her need to marry and settle her debts.

She'd spoken to Terwilliger only last week and he'd
pressed her for answers about her intentions, citing the
direness of her financial situation. The first whispered
questions about her financial condition, he explained,
had begun and two nights ago a gentleman had asked
Terwilliger if the Eastlake fleet was overdue. Terwilliger
had been most emphatic that she dare not accrue any
more debt lest she was willing to liquidate all.

So, naturally, she thought with biting humor, she had
decided to go shopping. It was her intention to outshine
everyone attending the masquerade ball given in Wellington's honor by the Earl of Spencer next week and
she had conceived the perfect costume. Perfectly ironic.

The tinkling of the shop door caused her to glance
around as a well-rounded young woman in an elaborate
pelisse and ornate bonnet entered. Lydia smiled with
delight as she recognized Sarah. She had heard Sarah
had not yet left for the Continent and she was delighted
she had an opportunity to see her friend once more.

She started across the shop as the other women
abruptly stopped their chattering and froze in place like
statues under Medusa's glare. Slowly, inexorably, and as
one, they turned their backs on Sarah.

Sarah met this snub with a subtle wince, a recoil more
of the spirit than the body. But then she saw Lydia approaching and for an instant her pretty face bloomed
with pleasure and she took a step forward. Lydia moved

down the aisle of tables to intercept her as the pleasure died from Sarah's expression.

She caught Lydia's eye and gave a small, warning shake of her head. Lydia faltered in her progress. Sarah mouthed the word "no," and Lydia stopped, uncertain, realizing that Sarah was trying to keep her from making a mistake.

Society had deemed Sarah unknowable and Society did not allow independent stands on such matters. The penalties they extracted for it were severe and Lydia could not afford Society's censure. Not at the present.

But this was her *friend*, she told herself. Lydia started forward again, determined to speak to her, but suddenly Childe was at her side, taking her elbow and turning her blithely aside. "I have found some passable gold lace for your consideration," he said, his voice smooth and his gaze cautioning.

She hesitated, feeling like the rankest coward. Murmurs rose from the clutch of women lower in rank and prestige than Lydia and, for that matter, Sarah herself. Lydia caught snatches of their conversation.

"—brazen. Wouldn't have her at my table."

"No one would."

"—wager she's regretting it now."

"Not her. Too wanton for regret!"

Her heart pounded with trepidation. But this was *Sarah*. "Thank you, Mr. Smyth. Perhaps in a few minutes? I have spotted a friend with whom I am eager to speak—"

The shop bell jangled again. Lydia spun around. Sarah had left.

"It is for the best, Lady Lydia," Childe said sotto voce. "She understands this, as must you."

"It's ridiculous," Lydia snapped and was promptly ashamed. Her anger was meant for herself. If she had really wanted to speak to Sarah she would have done so, not vacillated. Childe only meant to spare her.

Childe did not appear offended. He shrugged with elaborate ennui. "It is the way of things, my dear. One might comport oneself however one desires as long one remains circumspect."

"I do not agree with the choices Mrs. Marchland has made," Lydia replied, "but I disagree more strongly still with the idea that while one might know the most dissolute people as long as they have been 'circumspect' with regards to their transgressions one must refuse to acknowledge a beloved friend because she has not."

"I agree in principle," Childe said. "But I am far too lazy to work up much affront on the matter and too worldly, as are you, Lady Lydia," he reminded her. "From her most laudable retreat, it is clear Mrs. Marchland knows. *She* is playing the game by the rules. Can we do less?"

Lydia did not answer, but began mechanically picking through some swatches of trim on a table near at hand.

Childe made it sound so sensible. So simple. But it wasn't. It was confused and murky. The *ton*'s rules had never chaffed before because they had never impinged on her liberty before.

Liberty?

The conventions she had flouted in the past had been minor ones, childish tantrums that had fostered a false sense of free will: a low décolletage, a chaperone lax in her attentiveness, friends who were considered worldly, conversation less than demure. But as far as Society was concerned she had always acted within the boundaries of what was acceptable.

She frowned, disliking the path her thoughts took. This was her environs. This was all she had known. Yes, there were things about it that were unpleasant—and the charge of artifice was just. But how much more unpleasant would be a complete lack of artifice, and the resultant dearth of beauty and elegance? If the cost of a certain moral ambiguity currently seemed high, it was a price she had long since deemed worth paying.

But then she thought of Ned and it struck her forcibly that a moral debt was not the only price she'd paid for her place in the *beau monde*. The toll on her heart was still being tallied.

But, she thought defiantly, Ned had accrued a similar debt and done so apparently without the upheaval she was experiencing. He was being mature about it. Damn him. She flung down the ribbon that had been hanging unseen from her hand and turned around, distracted and distraught.

Oh, where *was* he? Why hadn't he attended any of the events and entertainments of the past two weeks? Had he taken his promise of friendship so lightly that he had left without a single note of farewell?

Was he courting someone rich?

"Lady Lydia, please do not look so distressed," Childe said.

She blinked. She had forgotten he was nearby.

"Who knows? Perhaps you shall meet her again in, say, Calais, where Brummell is holding court. Faith,

ma'am, I shouldn't be surprised. All the best people are
being banished these days."

He mistakenly attributed her unhappy expression to
Sarah. Thank heaven. He was the only suitor she had.
Though she never wanted for attention or lacked for
dance partners, no gentleman seemed inclined to seek
more than a dance or a conversation. She understood
why. This past month and more she'd always been in
Ned's company. Her favor toward him was noted by any
other would-be contenders for her hand and they had
withdrawn from the field. Only Childe Smyth seemed
unaware of it. Or he did not care.

And now Ned had disappeared and the Season was
coming toward its end and she was growing desperate.

That could not happen. At least for a short time,
Sarah had her prince. Without her place in Society—
without Ned—Lydia had nothing and no one. She had
known that state before; she would not know it again.
She had already lost Ned. She could not lose anything
more. She *would* not.

She would shine down the sun at the Spencers' masquerade ball.

She must.

She turned to Childe, smiling with all her remembered flirtatiousness at her command. "Why . . . you are
right! We shall all meet in some other clime." She slanted
a wicked glance at him out of the corner of her eye. "I
only hope it is not one as hot as the one we doubtless
deserve."

He laughed.

Charmed.

Chapter Twenty-three

It was another foul night, cold and dank. The newspaper had already deemed 1816 "The Year without a Summer," and so it appeared to be. The skies were constantly churning with dark clouds, the infrequent rents in this clotted layer giving rise to garish and gorgeous sunsets. Scant compensation for the grim days and dark nights. A masquerade ball seemed just the thing to lighten the spirits and chase away the cold and gloom.

"Dear Lord, if we enter before midnight it will be a miracle," Lydia said to Emily, snapping the curtains shut over the windows of the hired hack, Eleanor's ducal carriage having broken an axle that afternoon. Lydia's own famous barouche had succumbed discreetly to the auctioneer's hammer last week.

They had been en route for over two hours, though the distance between Eleanor's home and Spencer House was less than three miles. Lydia's nerves had frayed during the long wait on roads packed with other carriages. "And then we'll be obliged to wait for hours at the top of the stairs to be announced and five minutes later the ball will be over."

The crush of carriages arriving for the masquerade

ball given in Wellington's honor had caused traffic to
back up for a mile in and about the area, not only due
to the hundreds of coaches carrying guests but from the
hundreds upon hundreds of pedestrians choking the
thoroughfares and lining the streets in hopes of glimps-
ing those arriving in their fancy dress, a free spectacle
for a population plagued with economic hardships.

"All for the good," Eleanor replied. "Five minutes
spent trying to find space enough to breathe is quite
enough." She picked up the child's toy broadsword she
carried and swung it warningly.

Eleanor had elected to attend the ball as Joan of Arc,
a role that suited her attenuated form and aesthete's
countenance. She'd clubbed her hair at the nape of her
neck and wore a deceptively simple shift of unadorned
white mull. When Emily had suggested she did not look
very warriorlike, Eleanor had countered that she was
depicting Joan after the Catholic Church got hold of
her, as virgin sacrifice not as a battle maiden. Though
she did carry a small silver broadsword, she claimed it
was not as a concession to the martial aspect of the story
but simply in anticipation of the overheated crowds, to
be used on anyone standing between her and an open
window.

"With this large a guest list, no one will leave until
dawn," Emily reassured Lydia, patting her hand. Emily
had finally succumbed to Lydia's pleas that she quit her
self-imposed exile from Society and join them tonight.
"And even if the time is curtailed, there will not be one
person who does not think of you long after the ball."

Thank heavens for Emily, Lydia thought. She understood the pressure for Lydia to perform well. And that's

what it was, a performance. Before when she had arrived at a fete or ball, it had been with anticipation of pleasure in the company she would see and the conversations they would have. Not tonight. Tonight she felt only a fevered sort of anxiety she would have to mask.

Lydia turned her hand, catching Emily's and giving it a squeeze.

Emily was as close to family as she had, an acquired convenience that had become a valued friend and beloved confidante. If she lost all else, she would still have Emily. She could think of nothing that could alter that, no change in circumstances of rank, wealth, or reputation that would compromise Emily's loyalty. *She should have been so good a friend to Sarah....*

"Thank you, Emily," Lydia said.

Emily blushed, dipping her head and almost dislodging her wig and enormous mobcap. She had dressed as Mother Goose in old-fashioned black bombazine, a simple lace-edged kerchief draped across her plump shoulders, and a white wig with ringlets atop her head. On one hip, she'd affixed a papier-mâché goose that dangled rather haphazardly without the support of her arm. Lydia only hoped it was not hollow, lest she be obliged before they left the party to empty its paper gullet of items Emily might secrete away inside.

"Childe Smyth at least will stay until the last," Eleanor purred from her corner of the carriage.

Yes. Childe would be waiting for her. He had sent her a gift this morning, a fan fashioned of gold lace, the ribs holding it together also gold. It was an expensive trifle, suggesting a warmer regard than mere friendship that nothing else in his manner had indicated. She'd never caught Childe looking at her with the sort of warmth Ned . . . She looked away, her vision abruptly shimmering, and collected herself.

She prayed Ned would be attending the party.

She prayed he would not.

Not that Ned would ever let it be obvious that his interest was no longer keen. He would trade pleasantries with her. They were, after all, such good friends. But she would know that she was no longer the focal point of his attentions. That place would go to another. Younger? Prettier? Definitely more wealthy.

Dear God, she prayed, let him *not* be there!

"His grandfather is purported to be failing fast," Eleanor drawled.

Lydia's head swung around in confusion until she recalled they'd been discussing Childe. The unusual terms of the older Smyth's will were on the lips of the entire *beau monde*.

"Yes," Lydia agreed. "I believe his situation is dire."

"I have heard a rumor," Eleanor went on mildly, watching her closely, "that Mr. Smyth carries on his person at all times a special license to marry from his godfather, the Archbishop of Canterbury, so that when he receives word that his grandfather's last minutes are approaching, he can pop off with some likely female and checkmate the old man on his deathbed." She gave a little sniff. "How convivial for Mr. Smyth that he has a godfather with such power."

"Why doesn't he simply wed and be done with it?" Emily asked as she pushed her slipping mobcap back into place.

Eleanor's gaze slipped to Lydia. "Who can tell? Eiher simple spite or some juvenile resistance to having his life orchestrated by another. Really, I would think a man of Mr. Smyth's age would know better. All of us eventually must submit to the will, either singly or collectively, of others."

"I heard he hadn't wed because his mistress threatened to leave him if he marries," Emily piped in.

Then Emily had heard a great deal more than she. Lydia turned to her, startled. "Mistress?" she asked incredulously. This was the first time she had heard anything of a mistress.

She looked at Eleanor, who knew everything, for answers. Eleanor was glaring at Emily. Emily was looking about the carriage with an expression of feigned innocence.

"Childe Smyth has a *mistress*?" Lydia asked.

Emily nodded. "And has had for, oh, nigh on a decade, I believe."

Lydia's mouth nearly fell open. She turned to her other friend. "Eleanor?"

Eleanor shifted with a touch of impatience. "Of course he keeps a mistress. Many men do. But it is only to Childe's credit that you did not know about her. He is most discreet. Unlike some whom we shall not name."

Her glare failed to embarrass Emily. Having volleyed this bit of verbal cannon fire into their midst, the older woman wriggled back into the corner of the carriage, folding her hands over her round tummy and closing her eyes.

"Who is she?" Lydia asked, more intrigued by the notion that Childe Smyth kept a mistress than offended by it. "What sort of woman would she be?"

"No one knows," Eleanor replied. "No one ever sees her. He keeps her well away from Society in her own house with her own servants. Some say a Spanish lady of noble antecedents, others a French émigré."

"He must care for her very much."

Eleanor waved a hand. "Come now, Lydia. Childe is notoriously fastidious. He would keep a mistress only out of convenience and an assurance against an unpleasant contagion."

Lydia felt the heat rise to her cheeks, but she would not be gainsaid. "If there is no true affection between them, why would she threaten to leave him if he marries?"

Eleanor shrugged. "It is a game, Lydia. She is angling for a new protector. By leaving Childe before he dismisses her, she can present herself as not being cast aside. Emily's unnecessary speculation notwithstanding." She shot a glare in Emily's direction.

"Childe's failure to marry has no more to do with his mistress than yours does with Ned Lockton, barring the fact that you wasted precious time with him that could have been better spent acquainting yourself with other gentlemen." Eleanor had met the news of Ned's poverty with all the outrage Lydia lacked, roundly cursing him for his deception while conveniently ignoring Lydia's own.

"Acquainting myself? Is that what we're calling it?" Lydia asked. "After being so forthright regarding Childe Smyth's personal situation, I think we can do no less with mine. You mean seducing marriage offers."

"Yes."

Her momentary indignation evaporated. Eleanor was right. She had wasted weeks. She had been complacent, so sure of herself. And Ned.

The carriage slowed to a halt again, but this time the driver shouted. Lydia glanced out the window. They'd turned onto the drive leading to Spencer House and now waited in a long line of vehicles inching toward the gate. The fence surrounding the grounds was hung with dark crowds of sightseers calling for the occupants of the carriages to let down their windows and be seen. More than a few did so and were cheered roundly for their efforts.

"For heaven's sake, Lydia, oblige them so we might have some relative quiet," Eleanor said.

Lydia did not know why she hesitated. She had been in this situation many times and had always been flattered by the crowd's attention. But today she was impatient with their demands, hearing in their shouts and bellows not adoration, but insistence, the same sound the mob made at a horse race or an opera house or a theater. She had become a spectator's sport.

"Lydia, please. They shan't be quiet until someone in the carriage shows themselves and that shan't be me."

Dispiritedly, Lydia pulled back the curtain and drew the hood of her gold domino from her head. The crowd burst into cheers, hooting their approval, and Eleanor leaned forward and flicked back the curtain. "That's quite enough," she said.

The carriage passed through the gates and in a short while rolled to a halt, swaying as the tiger jumped from his perch. The boy opened the door and hauled out the stairs, situating himself at the bottom so Eleanor could use his head as a newel post.

"Be careful of your reputation tonight, Lydia," Eleanor cautioned her before disembarking. "One never knows with whom one is conversing at these affairs. have already heard tattle that several of the gentlemen' mistresses will be presenting themselves under the ano nymity of masks and veils. Brazen creatures, but I sup pose that sort of thing is to be expected when you allov people to pretend to be something they are not."

"That's the fun of it," Emily said, glumly patting he goose. Poor Emily. She tried, but she could not hide he fear that her compulsion would once again overwheln her.

"And so it begins," Eleanor murmured, alighting gracefully from the carriage. Emily followed, but Lydia stayed behind in the carriage, reluctant to start the eve ning, to risk seeing Ned, to know the disappointment o not seeing him.

She watched as Eleanor and Emily entered Spencer House through the wide set of double doors, vacillating She was being ridiculous, she knew, hiding in the car riage like this. She had never before been a coward. She would not begin now.

She drew her enveloping domino close and steppec out of the carriage, following Robin Hood and Mariar up the stairs and into the opulent entrance hall.

Eleanor and Emily were already being greeted by the earl and countess, both wearing identical expressions of fixed and polite interest. She took her place at the end of the line of guests, still wearing the black cloak that covered her costume, her hood still covering her hair. And then she was before them, thanking them and curtsying.

"How good of you to come . . . er, Riding Hood, I as-sume?" the earl asked without much interest and they were on to the next in the seemingly endless reception line.

She caught up with her companions in one of the anterooms reserved for the ladies' use, where ranks of liveried servants collected armloads of cloaks and great-coats and mantles, exposing the costumes beneath: all manner of flora, fauna, and famous personages both real and imagined, some wearing masks, as did Lydia, others bare-faced or with feathers and paint applied. Lydia had decided that drama best served her purposes and so re-fused all offers to take off her domino.

After a quick readjustment of Emily's goose, the trio followed the chattering crowds out of the antechamber. Few paid much heed to Lydia's still-cloaked form, be-ing more concerned with last-minute fine-tuning of their own costumes.

They traveled up the grand staircase, its banisters twined with thousands of white roses, petals strewn over the marble steps. At the top, they were once more obliged to stand in line, awaiting their turn to be an-nounced into the ballroom.

Impatiently, Lydia rose on her tiptoes to see inside. Behind her mask, her eyes widened with appreciation. The room had been transformed into a fantastical gar-den bower. Silk bunting of varying rich green shades draped the walls while paler green gossamer billowed lightly over the open windows leading to the terrace be-yond. Long ropes of woven roses, gardenias, and other hothouse flowers hung from the ceiling while the marble columns had been enveloped with mats of mosses, snow-drops, and violets sprouting from the downy growth.

Tables set at irregular distances from one another

lined the interior wall, artfully draped with thick green velvet. Centered on the wall was a larger table groaning under a fountain of punch cunningly emptying into a silver-lined creek that coursed amongst the light dishes provided to sustain the guests until dinner. Hundreds of servants transported trays loaded with wineglasses, performing astonishing acts of dexterity to avoid spilling anything on the jostling masked and costumed mob.

People dressed as swans, peacocks, leopards, and deer formed part of an astonishing menagerie of animals while Othellos and Cleopatras, infamous Medicis and red-cloaked cardinals bent their noble heads in conversations with the fantastical and allegorical. The music from an orchestra comprised of rabbits, hedgehogs, and foxes could barely be heard beneath the din of human voices. But amongst them, Lydia could not find one gold head rising above the rest. Relief warred with disappointment and relief won.

On the threshold of the doorway, Eleanor hesitated, eying Lydia.

"Love you though I do," she said, "I am not yet of an age to willingly let myself be cast in the shade. Go in, my dear. I shall arrive later."

"But—"

"No 'buts.' Emily, what say you and I begin the evening with a game of whist?" Eleanor asked. She and Emily dearly loved their card games. "Lydia does not need us."

"Indeed, I should be most pleased to accompany you," Emily said. "But wouldn't you find the conversation of a friend more convivial?"

"I am currently *with* my friends, Emily," Eleanor replied.

Emily's face pinked with pleasure at the compliment.

Eleanor turned to Lydia and her autocratic expression softened. "We will meet you later, Lydia. Go along, my dear. Bring them to their knees." She paused. "But do *not* let them announce your name. Let them guess a while. Mystery is a powerful stimulant."

Before Lydia could protest, the hall master's aide was bending close to ask how she wished to be announced. She told him and by the time she had done so, Eleanor and Emily had left and she was alone.

She heard the hall master announce, *"Princess Aurelia, daughter of King Midas. In Transitus!"* She peeled back her hood and pulled the tie at her throat, her cloak dropping into the unseen hands of a footman as she stepped out of the doorway into the brilliantly lit ballroom.

Those around her grew hushed, their silence spreading like a reverse whisper through the crowd. And then abruptly someone applauded and then another as voices rose in approval and admiration. She curtsied, drawing the moment out.

It was too bad Miss Walter could not be here to witness the reception of her creation, Lydia thought. She well deserved the accolades. The modiste had fashioned her slip of thin gold tissue embroidered with gold lama in a subtle trellis design and the overgown of the sheerest net of fine gold thread. She had cut the bodice in a daringly low vee and edged the décolletage with amber and gold beads, as she had the puffed sleeves of gold gauze.

Lydia's maid had plaited her hair into a loose coronet at the back of her head, threading the seal-brown locks with thick gold satin ribbons and bright gold wire. Her three-quarters mask was made of thin hammered gold, the shadow it cast on her face disguising the telling color of her eyes. But the most arresting aspect of her costume was not what she did wear, but what she didn't.

She had eschewed jewelry of any sort, instead liberally dusting her shoulders, neck, arms, and bosom with gold dust so that reflected light glinted with her slightest movement. Rather than white gloves she'd had ones made of thin gold lama so that her hands and forearms looked like solid gold. This coupled with the shimmer of gold dust on her bare flesh gave the pronounced effect of being in the throes of an alchemist transition, already more than half the gold statue Midas's daughter was to become.

She appreciated the irony, even if no one else could.

She glided into the room, murmurs following her.

"Who is she?"

"Lady Anne Major-Trent, I'll lay my favorite horse on it."

"I say Aurelia is Jenny Pickler."

"Hair's too light, gown's too low for a girl who's just made her bow."

"Mrs. Dallyworth?"

"Lady Lydia."

"She'd never hide her eyes. She's too famous for 'em."

" 'Spose you're right."

"*Who is she*?"

Why . . . she hadn't been recognized.

The realization washed over her like cold, clear water, unexpected and bracing. No one knew her. No one had any expectations of her. The notion was intriguing. Even stimulating . . .

She had no obligations, no role to play other than one she scripted for herself. She could be mute or musical, a tartar or a tart, stiff-rumped or loose in the haft or anything in between. She could greet strangers as old friends and ignore those that only duty made it necessary to acknowledge and no one would take offense, because no one would know unless she chose to tell them.

A sense of liberation flooded her, alien and intoxicating. A titled lady by whom she had sat at a dinner last week approached, her smile growing uncertain and then fading as she abruptly shifted direction, deciding she did not know "Aurelia." A genial-looking gentleman bowed as she moved past and she heard herself saying in a husky voice, "Mr. Borton! How fares your sister?"

"Very well, Miss, er, Lady, er . . ." He colored up.

"Aurelia will do, Mr. Borton."

How titillating. Wickedly so, perhaps, but delightful nonetheless. No wonder so many mishaps and scandals occurred during masquerade balls. She had been to masquerades before, but she had never before masked her identity and so had never known the heady license provided by going incognito. It sent a shiver of thrill, even fear, through her. What might she discover in this guise, what she might say half-soused with social immunity?

What might she do?

She threaded her way through the throng. Outside it

might be dark and damp, but in here all was brilliance and warmth. The chandeliers overhead blazed, the air was heated by hundreds of bodies. On the dance floor a quadrille was finishing, an opiate spectacle of feather, color, sparkle, and shine, headdresses and wings and crowns glinting and whirling as those around the dancers applauded and shouted encouragement, laughing raucously as Harlequin's greasepaint dissolved in his sweat and Cleopatra's asp headdress drooped in the swelter.

She spied Childe Smyth, an elegant Mephistopheles in scarlet and black, and was about to make her way to his side when a footman appeared and presented him with an envelope. He flicked it open and read, his insouciant expression tightening. Then he balled the note up in his fist and left the room, clearly in a hurry.

She wondered what news had caused him to leave so abruptly, but in a way she was glad he was gone. If she'd joined him, her identity would have been revealed and she had not yet started to have her fun.

Of course, she intended to reveal herself eventually. That was, after all, the *raison d'être* for this enormously expensive costume, to draw attention to herself, to be seen, to be admired, to be desired. But for a short while, she could afford the unknown luxury of anonymity.

She danced half a dozen times, including a waltz with a Spanish grandee and a cotillion with an Eastern fakir, both of whom she knew, neither of whom guessed her identity. By the time the fakir had returned her to the side of the room, the scent of perfume and glue and paint, the press of bodies and the roar of voices and music had become overwhelming. Overheated and breathless, she left the dance floor, ducking behind the gossamer drapes through the massive French doors that led to the courtyard behind.

Outside, torches encircled part of the courtyard where a few footmen stood sentry. Beyond, the gardens stretched into darkness. Lydia looked around, breathing deeply of the cool, moist air. Others had sought relief here, too, in pairs and groups, and while she longed to take off her mask and let the air cool her face, she was still loath to give up her anonymity. She avoided the other revelers, slipping amongst the shadows between the pools of light cast by the torches and disappearing into the gardens beyond. There, with a sigh, she pulled the mask up and lifted her face to the cold night air.

"Princess Aurelia," a deep masculine voice murmured from behind her ear.

With a start, she dropped her mask back into place and spun around. A tall figure stood before her dressed entirely in black: his coat, skin-tight pantaloons, tall shining Hessians, even the lace on the cuffs of his shirt and the shirt itself. A black tricorn covered his head and he wore a black bauta mask in the Venetian style that left the lower half of his face exposed, revealing a square jaw and a firm chin marked with a cleft.

Ned.

Chapter Twenty-four

A shiver raced through Lydia, part trepidation, but more attraction to the seductive aura of danger surrounding him. Would he know her?

"I do not believe we have been introduced, sir," she said in a husky whisper.

"No? Perhaps not," he said, stepping back, sweeping his hat from his head, and making an elegant leg. His bright gold hair gleamed in the chance light. "I am Night."

She tilted her head. "Night? That is all? Nothing more?"

"What more would you have?"

"*Lord* Night? *Prince* Night? *Sir* Night?" she suggested.

He shook his head. "It grieves me to disappoint you, Princess, but alas, I have no title. I am simply as you see me."

Had he recognized her? Did his words have another context? "Did I say I was disappointed? I am not."

He smiled and her heart thundered in response. Foolish, easy heart.

"You are kind, ma'am, to squander your time with

me when you might spend your last hours amongst
those kings and princes, lords and lordlings who are
your equals."

"Squander? What do you mean?"

"I was here when you were announced as Aurelia
In Transitus. I assumed that meant you draw near the
moment when you are turned entirely to gold and from
which there is no turning back. Was I wrong?"

He'd moved closer, far closer than propriety allowed,
angling his head as he bent near, his gray eyes glinting
like pewter in the half-light, his breath a warm caress on
her neck. She couldn't think. Couldn't breathe.

"Was I?" he asked again, his whisper stirring the soft
tendrils of hair at her temple. He did not recognize her,
she was sure of it now. He would never be so forward
with her.

"No," she answered, barely audible.

"How sad," he murmured, slipping behind her as
silently as the night he professed to be. "Will you miss
your humanity, do you suppose?"

"I don't expect I shall be aware of what I have lost,"
she said, standing very, very still because she thought she
felt a caress, as light as a smoke, drift down the side of
her neck.

"How long do you think before the transformation
is complete? A week? A day?" His voice dropped to a
dark purr. "An hour?"

"I don't know."

He stood behind her now, his body looming over her,
shielding her from the night air. She felt a slight movement at her side and glanced down to see his left hand
cross in front of her and encircle her right wrist, the

black of his glove a stark contrast to the gleaming gold foil covering her hand and forearms. He stepped back and tugged so she pirouetted lightly to face him.

"Let us gauge." From behind the mask, his gray eyes held hers as he lifted her hand to his shoulder and there, carefully, placed it. His velvet-clad fingertips caressed the tender flesh high under her arm and glided to the top of her glove. Slowly, with measured purpose, inch by inch, he worked the fabric down, exposing her skin.

She could not believe this was Ned peeling away her glove with such sensual deliberation. Not this dangerous, lithe, and predatory-looking man. His eyes never left hers, blistering in their intensity. His mouth was taut. A little tic jumped at the corner of his jaw.

She could not move. Her heart drummed so thickly she was certain he must hear it. She grew light-headed as with leisurely deliberation he stripped her glove off, exposing her hand. The shed glove rippled to the ground like a banner of liquid gold, and he raised her hand.

"It still looks like a woman's flesh," he mused and brushed his warm lips across her fingertips. She gasped, reflexively jerking back her hand, but he would not let her go. Instead, he opened his mouth against the shallow indentation at the center of her palm and lingered in a carnal kiss.

"It has the warmth and texture of a woman's skin," he murmured against her skin.

A shudder ran through her. He could *not* know who she was. He'd mistaken her for someone, and something, else. He must. He would never treat her with such impropriety. Or desire, a cruel inner voice suggested.

She should announce herself, now, before this had

gone too far for either of them to forget. She meant forgive. She meant—

He carefully bent her hand back at the wrist and opened his mouth against the pulse beating like a trapped thing there. Her knees went liquid. Slowly, he licked a line across the tender flesh. Her legs buckled.

Carelessly, he swept her from her feet and into his arms.

"You have the taste of a woman," he said, gazing down at her. "Beneath the gold. What of . . ."

He didn't finish his statement, instead easing her higher against his chest. His head dipped low and he whispered against her throat, "Do you still own a woman's heart?" He kissed the base of her throat. "Her response?" He nibbled a slow route along her collarbone.

Behind the gold mask her eyelids fluttered shut, her lips parted as though to drink in the carnal brew with which he flooded her senses and her head fell over his arm, her throat arching like an offering. He took her gift, pressing his mouth beneath her chin and drawing his lips in a heated, openmouthed kiss down the length of her neck to the plump, gold-dusted tops of her breasts. A dark, primal sound rumbled deep in his throat as his tongue tasted her.

She did not protest.

It was erotic, unimaginably erotic, and wicked, and her whole body quaked in response. He lifted his head and only then did she realize that both her hands were tangled in his thick hair, holding his head.

Abruptly, he dropped her feet to the ground, keeping one arm around her waist as he reached up to pull the ribbon holding her mask in place. Just in time, she realized his intent and grabbed his wrist, pulling his hand away.

"No!" He had mistaken her for one of the lightskirts Eleanor had spoken about, some man's castoff mistress seeking a new lover. He must have. And certainly she'd given him no reason to suppose otherwise.

He allowed her to lower his hand, though impatience tightened his lips. "Enough of this, my darling. Remove this mask, strip off this hard shell, and be the woman beneath."

"There is nothing beneath this mask but another," she said, knowing he would not understand.

He stilled. "Well, if that is true, there is no hope for this, is there?" he said in an odd voice, and she was caught by the certainty that any moment now he would leave her.

No.

She flung her arms around his neck and reflexively he caught her to him, holding her fiercely.

"Don't go. Don't leave me."

"God," he said hoarsely. "What would you have me do?"

"Love me."

His jaw tensed and the muscles in his arms and shoulders went rigid as he gazed down at her. Once more, he raised his hand to take her mask and once more she prevented him. But this time it was not because she feared revealing herself; rather she feared that the revelation of who she was would return to him his formidable self-control.

"Love me," she whispered.

Her words fell like a scimitar, slicing through the

thin hesitation holding him. "Be damned," he muttered thickly and swung her back up into his arms.

She wrapped her arms around his neck and laid her masked face against his chest. "Love me."

She did not need to speak again. She felt his answer in the tightening of his arms, the thickening beat of his heart, the rise and fall of his broad chest. Wordlessly, he moved with her farther into the dark, deeper into the umber shadows, where vision failed and other senses awoke.

Within a few strides, the light from the sconces had vanished. The moonless sky provided no illumination, only a different shade of black, and the cobbled darkness did no more than hint at tree and vine and shrub. Soon, she could not make out his features anymore.

Sound and sight and touch took precedence here. She knew when they moved from the footpath, because the crunch of shells disappeared and his steps grew muted. The rich, humid scent of loam and living things rose and filtered around her. Delicate cool tendrils and slick leaves brushed her arms as he turned, backing through invisible undergrowth.

She felt the play of muscles across his chest, the size of the arms supporting her, the velvety touch of his gloved hands on her shoulder, the heat rising from him. He stopped and this time when she felt his hand move behind her head, she did not stop him from removing her mask but kept her arms around his neck, an anchor in this seamless nightscape.

Cool air rushed over her heated face, followed by the silken glide of a velvet-clad hand. He read her features like a blind man, fingertips tracing her eyes and cheeks, skating along her nose and finally across lips. She sighed, canting in to his touch. His finger glided to the back of her head. She felt the warm puff of his breath a moment before his mouth closed hungrily over hers.

Gold had made an excellent mask, but night made an even better one. Where gold allowed a certain license, night encouraged licentiousness. Emboldened by its dark entitlement, she learned the urgency of desire. Her mouth opened beneath his and when his tongue entered her mouth, she opened farther, hungry for more. She arched restlessly against him, raking her fingers through his hair, the locks silky and damp.

He dragged her neckline down and cold air kissed her nipple into a hard tight bud as her breast overflowed the constricting bodice. His mouth scorched a trail down her neck, along her shoulder and lower, stopping at the very crest of her breast. She could hear his labored breathing, feel its heated whoosh against her naked skin. A shudder raked his body and she tugged at his head, willing him to more kisses, bolder kisses, kisses on flesh that had never known a man's touch but ached to do so now. He made a dark sound of capitulation and hunger, and then opened his mouth over her and drew her nipple deep into his mouth.

She pulsed with fundamental knowledge, wanting more, her breath drawn in on a gasp of exquisite torment.

And her gasp broke the spell.

He lifted his head and she panted in protest. She wanted and he was not giving. She tried to pull his head down to kiss her again, but he resisted. She searched the darkness above her, but could not make out his expression, only a sense of tension so palpable the very air seemed charged. Somewhere, at some point, his own mask had been lost.

She heard him drag in a shaky breath, felt a light tremble begin in his broad shoulders and travel through his long body. "No. No. This is wrong."

Damn his right and wrong! Her body hummed with need and frustration, like a starved prisoner held within steps of a feast. She shook her head violently.

"You would regret this."

"No."

"Yes. I— Yes, you would. I . . . Forgive me."

Forgive him? It was back, his masterful, pitiless self-control. Why was it so easy for him to assume when every one of her nerves felt raw and abraded by an acid of yearning only his kisses, his touch, could assuage? Yet he would not act and she was supposed to *forgive* him.

Well, she would not. She would not forgive him for unleashing desires that had only teased her before but now clawed at her with agonizing urgency. He must not understand how cruel he was being because he did not share her torment. If he did, he would act.

She heard her breath break on a sob. "You do not even know who I am. How can you say what I would and would not regret?"

He stilled. "Ma'am?"

She was too humiliated to hear the shock in his voice. Too overset to hear the disbelief. She should be thanking him for finding his self-control, but all she could think was that he hadn't wanted her either as Lady Lydia or as a woman of the night.

"Put me down." Her voice quavered.

When he didn't react at once, she pushed at his chest, struggling. "Please. Put me down." There was a note of desperation in her voice and at once he lowered her to the ground. She dropped to her knees, tugging her bodice back into place and then searching the ground at his feet for her mask.

"You do not believe I—" he began to ask in an incredulous tone, but she cut him off ruthlessly. She knew what he was going to say.

"No, I do not believe you would have been so carried away you would have forgotten yourself." *He does not want me.* Her hand closed around the cold metal mask.

He was silent while she scrambled to her feet and cast about, looking for some light in the dark, some glimmer of where she was.

"I am not sure I take your meaning," he said in an odd voice.

She found a subtle glow above the dark treetops and at the same time heard the distant hum of voice and music.

"My meaning is clear. You recalled yourself, sir, in time to keep from tarnishing your honor."

"*My* honor?" He sounded stunned.

She did not wait for a reply. She started forward, a hand outstretched to guide her.

"Let me take you back," he said quietly.

Take her back and risk having Eleanor or Emily see them and give her away? She would rather die. "No. As you are a gentleman I ask you to allow me to keep what dignity I have left by not trying to discover my identity.

You do not know me." He did not argue. "I would as soon keep it that way."

"I will not speak to you," he promised stiffly. "But you must let me at least see you to the footpath. Once there, I promise not to importune you any further."

She wanted to refuse, to tell him he had never importuned her, that clearly she had importuned him. She had invited all his attentions and then begged for more. But he'd refused. Mortification burned in her face and she opened her mouth to refuse, but reason reasserted itself. She might stumble through the shrubs for half an hour and when she finally did find her way clear, her gown and slippers, hair and arms would bear testimony to a story that she did not want known. She'd had enough humiliation for one evening. "Very well."

She felt his hand at her elbow, a touch so different from the one just moments earlier, so impersonal and proper, she wanted to sob. Instead, she walked stiffly a few feet behind him as he used his body and arm to lift branches out of her way and make a path. It took only a short time to find their way back to the terrace. But by then her mask, both her masks, were firmly in place.

True to his word, Ned did not attempt to follow her once they reached the footpath but instead stepped solemnly aside. His face, though no longer hidden behind the bauta mask, revealed nothing. He caught his hands behind his back and bowed sharply. "Ma'am."

She did not reply.

Ned watched Lydia's flight with narrowed eyes. He had promised he would not pursue her and he was a man of his word, but every primal instinct—and there were many primal instincts clamoring to be acted on this evening—urged him to go after her. But he was also a man of rare self-restraint.

He waited ten minutes before entering Spencer House, unaware of the admiring and speculative glances that tracked his progress through the ballroom. Ladies with histories who had written Ned Lockton off as too genteel paid renewed attention to the pantherish stride of the tall, black-clad captain, and young girls who had deemed him perfectly congenial shivered with sentiments not in keeping with congeniality. He barely noticed the snowstorm of lace handkerchiefs that fluttered at his feet as he stalked along the room's perimeter.

He hadn't meant to touch her, to kiss her. He'd only meant to begin again his courtship after a two-week hiatus, during which he'd lain in his bed, feverish and furious. Though Tweed's stray bullet had only scored a shallow furrow in his scalp, the wound had grown septic. He had done what he could to curtail gossip about the duel, and as Tweed had been spirited out of the country by his friends and those remaining behind had not wanted to be associated with so dishonorable an event, it had not proved too difficult.

A letter from Lydia had arrived soon after the duel, just after his fever set in. In her few terse, anxious lines he'd found the wherewithal to hope. But honor demanded that he keep the confidence of those who'd attended the duel, and so he passed a fitful fortnight, wanting to contact her, but unable to do so.

Borton alone was privy to his situation and condition—both of his wound and his heart. He arrived soon after the duel, inquiring after Mary—and really the man would have to address his continued infatuation with Ned's persnickety niece—then roundly cursing Ned's nephews—who never did arrive to offer their concern for his health let alone their thanks. Then, apropos of nothing, he'd announced, "You might as well make a run at Lady Lydia Eastlake" and with those few words revealed that he understood that Lydia occupied his heart and that there was not, and never would be, room for another tenant.

If only Lydia were half so discerning. His eyes, already flinty, grew darker.

All evening the unfamiliar claws of jealousy had raked him as he watched her dance first with one man, then another. All around her, heads turned to watch, not just because of the beauty of her gown but because of the woman it adorned. Whispers followed her, eyes marked her, conversations stilled, drinks were held suspended.

Everything about her had radiated pleasure and excitement. The impression haunted him. Even though a gold mask covered her expression and hid her eyes, she had never seemed more vibrant and alive than she had tonight, shimmering and glittering like a ray of sunlight transferred to a mortal frame. Why?

Was she falling in love? Had she already fallen in love with someone? Who? The Ivanhoe with whom she waltzed? The cardinal? He did not recognize himself in the tense, hot-blooded man that stalked her movements with his eyes.

But when she'd quit the dance floor, he had followed. When she disappeared down the dark footpath, it was not jealousy that spurred him after her, it was concern.

He'd only meant to warn her to have a care for her reputation, but then she'd feigned not to recognize him and he'd fallen in with the game.

But the rules had changed as they played, and the words took on other meanings and before he'd realized it, he was kissing her and from there? Madness, pulsing, yearning madness shot through him like lightning through a touch rod, setting him afire.

His eyes closed briefly on the memory. He had never been tested so harshly. Nothing he could recall had ever been as hard to give up as what he had denied himself the moment he'd set her from him. Only her gasp had recalled him to the place and the circumstances and that he was within minutes of taking her like a doxy.

And Lydia? How could she think he would *not* know her? His hand splayed at his side. The fact that she honestly did not think he recognized her struck him like a blow, stunning him. How could she think he would, *could*, feel such desire for any woman other than her?

He could not allow that misconception to stand.

Chapter Twenty-five

Lydia found Eleanor in an anteroom playing whist with Emily as her partner. She waited until the cards were being collected for a shuffle and Emily had gone for a glass of punch before causally moving forward to stand behind the duchess. She leaned down and spoke to her in the softest of undertones. "Do not ask why, but I would rather no one knew who I am."

Eleanor understood her role at once. She was an old hand at the games of subterfuge played amongst the *ton*. She did not even turn around to look at Lydia, but instead maintained a haughty immobility.

Everyone knew Eleanor and she were great friends. If Eleanor paid her much attention they would conclude that the mysterious Aurelia was in fact Lady Lydia Eastlake. And they would know it for a certainty if they left together.

"I will take a hansom," Lydia continued.

"What of Emily?" Eleanor murmured as she turned toward Lydia with a quizzical expression as if she had just realized she was being addressed. Anyone watching would think they had just met.

"If you could ask her to meet me on the street in five minutes, I would be obliged," Lydia whispered.

Eleanor nodded as she rose from the table. She turned and said loudly in her quelling tone, "Young woman, I do not know ladies who do not mean to be known."

Without another glance, she swept from the room. Lydia headed in the opposite direction.

At the entrance to the ballroom, Eleanor stopped and looked around for Emily. She did not see her at once, but she did see a very strained, very tense-looking captain emerge from the courtyard and stalk toward the billiard room. Her eyes narrowed thoughtfully. She had not missed the leaves tangled in the gold netting around Lydia's hem.

She did not like this. The captain hadn't the blunt to set Lydia up in the fashion she required. He hadn't the wherewithal to move in the same circles as Lydia. Or she herself. Few did.

The girl couldn't have been so foolish as to have—

Her mouth tightened into a hard line. Whether Lydia fancied herself in love or not, whether she'd stepped over the lines of propriety or not, made no difference as long as no one knew.

And no one would.

The crowd outside Spencer House had begun to thin by two o'clock in the morning, those who made a living for themselves having gone home to bed and ceding the ground to gamblers, young bucks with their giggling consorts, aging prostitutes, old fops, and middle-aged swells, all pausing en route to the next game, the next gin parlor, the rout to see what might be seen.

One muscularly built man in his late forties leaned against the gate attempting to convince a very young and pretty soiled dove that he did indeed have the coin to purchase a few hours of her company. The girl eyed him dubiously. He had an air, true, and his accent was high-toned, but he'd clearly shaved himself, judging by the nicks on his jowls, and though made of fancy brocade, the seams of his coat had been turned more than once. He had the blistered nose of a drunk and his smile didn't reach his eyes.

No matter.

"I'll see this crown you speak of first, Mr. Fish," she insisted.

The man's eyes narrowed. "Are you suggesting I lie?" he asked, his lips curling back in a snarl. His unsmiling eyes had turned to narrow slits and become very mean and the girl was about to run when the door to Spencer House opened and light and music spilled out across the lawn like golden coins. Two women emerged, one dressed like Mother Goose and the other like a golden statue in a gold gown that flashed and glinted like fireflies. She wore a gold mask.

Rapt, the girl—still girl enough to be enchanted—forgot all about her companion. "Gar!" she breathed.

The man turned to see what had attracted her attention and saw the two women getting into a carriage.

"You know who that is?" a handsome golden-haired youngster nearby asked the girl. He lifted the bottle he'd been holding and pointed it at carriage. The girl glanced at him and the glance turned into a stare, he was that good-looking.

"Nah," she said saucily. "Who be that, then, m'lord?"

The boy grinned foolishly, clearly unaware she called any potential customer "m'lord."

"That's Lady Lydia Eastlake," he said carefully. "Not only one of the most gorgeous women in London but also one of the richest."

"And how would you be knowin' that, m'lord?" the girl said, sashaying away from the older bloke and toward this much more comely gull.

"Because I saw her leave Lady Grenville's house in Cavendish Square this evening when I was walking through on my way"—he stopped, glanced around, and put a finger against the side of his nose. He leaned forward—"to a gaming establishment."

"Do tell," the girl said. "Share?" She motioned toward his bottle.

The young man looked at it a moment and then at her. He handed it over and she took a swig.

"Then why's she riding in an old cab if she's so rich?" she asked.

This clearly flummoxed the young god. "Don't know," he finally admitted, retrieving his bottle.

By now the carriage bearing the golden lady and her companion had arrived at the gate and was waiting for the footmen to open it. It was so close, the girl could see right inside the cab. The woman the young buck had said was Lady Lydia was turned away from the crowd, talking to Mother Goose, who had removed her mobcap to reveal a pate of tightly curled red-gray hair.

"Whose the other one? The old one?" she asked.

"Lady Lydia's cousin." He bobbed his head, sanguine. "And constant companion. Dotes on her something fierce."

"What's her name?" The girl's by-now-forgotten would-be client demanded.

The lad shrugged at the older man. "Don't know," he said and then brightened. "But rumor has it she found her in an insane asylum."

The man didn't say anything else, he simply turned and walked away, leaving the girl relieved she wouldn't have to test his temper when she turned him down or worse, have him in her bed should he really have had a crown. She cast a flirtatious look at her handsome new beau.

"What's yer name, then, me lord?" she asked, wresting his bottle from him and taking another long draft.

He looked at her in delight. "Harry," he said.

Chapter Twenty-six

In keeping with a life devoted to controlling his family's lives, Childe Smyth's wretched grandfather had refused to die until he had seen his son knighted, his daughter married to a marquis, and his wife in her grave. That would be his third wife—the first two having already made good their escapes. He had achieved all this in spite of being repeatedly told he would not live to see Napoleon routed. The only one who had refused to bow to his demands had been Childe.

In his more frivolous moods, Childe had wondered whether his refusal to wed had actually extended the old man's life beyond what nature intended for him. Without a doubt, the old devil had been living on vitriol and indignation for years. But then, what nature intended or wanted had never much interested Martin Smyth. Nor had anyone else's desires and wants.

But now, finally, it appeared that even Martin Smyth could cheat death for only so long. He was well and truly dying. Not that this made him any more tolerant or less unpleasant or inspired him to reconsider his lifelong need to be obeyed. Not at all. If anything it had reinforced these unlovely traits.

The note that had arrived at the Spencers' masquerade ball last night had been short and to the point. Childe's grandfather was on his deathbed and demanded his only grandson attend him. Childe had left at once, and gone to find the old man sitting bolstered by a pile of pillows, the silk cap on his head falling over his ears, his sunken eyes filmy.

"Is the pimple here yet?" Martin had asked one of a line of doctors and footmen standing in watchful silence.

"Yes, Grandfather," Childe had replied, dragging his feet to the bedside.

"Wed yet?" The words came out in a low croak.

"No, sir."

He flicked his skeletal hand in Childe's direction. "Don't waste time defyin' me, you atrocious boil. You're too fond of being pretty to be poor."

Unfortunately, he was right. Which is why Childe Smyth now stood outside Lady Lydia Eastlake's town house door at one o'clock in the afternoon, seething inside even as he prepared a pretty speech designed to convince Lady Lydia to be his wife.

Kitty would be furious. Or worse, heartbroken.

God, he hoped it was the former. The thought of little Kitty sobbing her heart out was unbearable. But she was not an unreasonable woman. Surely she would understand. It wasn't as if he *wanted* to wed Lady Lydia. He didn't. Oh, he liked her well enough. She had a lively wit and presence and . . . well, she was handsome enough.

But she wasn't Kitty.

She couldn't make his heart beat faster with a casual smile, or hold at bay the cares of the day simply by toasting some cheese to share with him in front of the hearth. She couldn't make him forget who or where he was by putting her pretty little head in his lap and demanding he feed her grapes. She couldn't make him laugh with her purposely exaggerated accent or moan when she rubbed his feet.

But all that meant nothing compared to the status he would achieve by becoming one of the five wealthiest men in London.

Yes, Kitty would simply have to understand. He had his name to consider and that meant obeying the old man's demand. And from the phlegmy sound the old scab had been making when he left him, he'd better be quick about it, too.

He rapped sharply on the door. A maid opened it and curtsied him in. She led him into a surprisingly modest morning room, where she accepted his hat and cane.

"If you'll wait here, sir, I shall see if Lady Lydia is home," she said and left.

Childe looked around with interest. For a woman known for the unique and rich manner in which she accoutred herself, the room was amazingly free of ornamentation. And furnishings, for that matter. A few paintings of unknown antecedents hung on the wall. An unremarkable mantel clock ticked away the hour. Even the carpet underfoot seemed disproportionately small, as though standing in for its big brother.

The maid reappeared, bobbing another curtsy before informing him that Lady Lydia would be down shortly and asking if he would care for a refreshment. He declined and the maid vanished once again.

He didn't have to wait long before Lady Lydia arrived. She did not look well. Her famous pansy purple eyes were shadowed beneath with a similar hue and her skin had the pale translucence of sleeplessness. Even the curve of her cheeks looked to be riding on bones too sharp. She essayed a thin smile.

He bowed. "Lady Lydia, I am sorry I did not have a chance to claim a dance last night. A family matter required my attendance."

"I hope nothing unpleasant?" she said.

He waved his hand languidly, brushing away her concern as she took a seat and folded her hands in her lap.

"Nothing unexpected, simply inconvenient," he said. He did not answer the query in her expression. If they were to wed, she must learn he led a life separate from hers, one in which she would have no part and which she would not be permitted to question. It was a courtesy he intended to extend to her, too.

"I hear tell the Spencers' masquerade was graced by an Aurelia as mysterious as she was fabulous," he said instead. "One making elegant use of a gold-filigreed fan." He smiled and wagged a knowing finger at her.

He'd thought the compliment would please her, that they would begin trading flirtatious banter, but her answering smile was distracted.

"Yes," she said. "It is a pity you were not there. You would have approved of my costume."

This was direct and uninspired, not a bit of coquetry to it. She looked away, touching her fingertips to her temple. This was not going as smoothly as he'd anticipated. His delightfully blithe companion had gone missing, leaving this wan, preoccupied woman who seemed almost impatient with him.

As though her *ennui* were catching, he found he'd lost what little eagerness he'd had for his mission. Perhaps this was for the best. A business arrangement, even between friends, ought to be discussed in a businesslike fashion, sweetened with a few compliments, of course.

"Lady Lydia, I admire you a great deal." This much was true. "I flatter myself to believe that we have over these last weeks become friends." Again, true.

She looked neither interested nor anxious. She looked resigned. "Yes, Mr. Smyth. We are friends."

"Lady Lydia, I would consider myself a most fortunate man—"

"I have no money," she interrupted flatly.

He stared at her until he became aware that his mouth was slightly ajar. He snapped it shut.

"Before you say anything further, I thought you might like to know this. My fortune is gone. I am without assets, means, or expectations." She said this without any obvious distress, only a great deal of weariness. "The Eastlake fleet has been taken by pirates, my stocks are worthless, and most of my personal property has been sold off to finance this last Season. My last golden Season," she finished with an ironical cant to her brow.

His brows drew together in concentration. Lady Lydia Eastlake's sudden interest in wedlock after years of turning down the *ton*'s most eligible bachelors now made sense. He considered the matter and decided it did not affect his situation.

"I don't care, Lady Lydia," he said in his signature drawl. "After I wed, I shall have the wherewithal to buy ten fleets."

"Oh."

He began pacing up and down in front of her, head down, picking his way carefully. "You have been most direct with me and in a way that forestalled me from making a proposal that would have rendered me obligated. I appreciate that honesty and I mean to return it to you." He paused but still did not look at her.

"If I wed before my grandfather dies, I will inherit a great fortune. If I fail to wed before his death, his fortune shall be given to several universities. One in Edinburgh." He lifted his upper lip in a delicate sneer. "Which would be a great waste of a fortune, don't you think?"

He cleared his throat and struck a stance. "Lady Lydia, I have come to believe that you and I would suit very well. You come from a noble family, have *éclat*, wit, and address and you are sophisticated."

For the first time, a hint of amusement lightened her dark eyes. "You have not mentioned my great beauty."

He'd forgotten it. To him only one woman's beauty was worth comment. "That goes without saying. You are most beautiful."

"Thank you."

He was a little nonplussed by her lack of appreciation, truth be told, but plowed ahead even though he knew he did so with far less suaveness than he was used to conducting himself. "I, too, am imbued with all these qualities—except the noble family, though my antecedents are gentlemen."

"Indeed." She nodded.

"Therefore, Lady Lydia"—he cleared his throat—"it seems to me it would make perfect sense for such compatible people as ourselves to join together in matrimony."

"It would seem to make sense," she murmured. "Perfect sense."

He nodded, abruptly feeling a little glum. "Indeed it does, and seeing as that is so"—he took a deep breath—"Lady Lydia, will you do me the honor of accepting my hand in marriage?"

She did not answer his proposal, instead leaning forward and asking, "You *really* do not care about my lack of wealth? It does not cause you even an instant's hesitation? I mean this, Mr. Smyth: I do not have any money." She waved her hand around the room, inviting his scrutiny.

He looked around, once again noting the paucity of . . . *things*. Ah, yes. This, too, made sense. She'd been selling off her famous collection of *objets d'art*. He hurried to reassure her. "It makes no difference at all. You can keep this house and redecorate. Without consideration to cost."

"I have no other property."

"I don't need land, I need a bride."

"Not a sou in the bank."

"I'll have sous enough for half of London."

"I've even sold the brougham with the yellow wheels."

Well, that was a shame. . . . He sighed. "We'll just have to buy another."

She sank back, looking oddly deflated.

"Will you? Marry me, that is?"

She looked around the room, as though seeking inspiration, and his hopes both rose and fell. "Mr. Smyth," she said, "I am well cognizant of the honor you do me, but I would do you a disservice if I were to claim an affection I do not have."

He lifted a shoulder in a sad little shrug. "As would I. I do not require your love, Lady Lydia, just your hand and I hope, your friendship, which, if given, shall put us leaps and bounds ahead of most married couples."

She was quiet a moment, her head bowed over her folded hands. Twice, he thought she might speak, but both times, her first syllables turned into shaky sighs. He did not press her. He had asked. He could not bring himself to do more.

Finally, she lifted her head. "I know time is of the essence, Mr. Smyth, but I need to think. May I give you an answer tomorrow?"

A day. His grandfather might not be alive. On the other hand, he had a special license already in hand. And what other choice did he have? There were not that many women in London who fit his requirements and, of those, he'd paid court to only Lady Lydia. No lady he would consider wedding would accept an offer made under such circumstances. "If I cannot persuade you to a quicker decision."

"I do not think you can."

"Then, of course." He bowed. "I'll take my leave, hoping your answer will make us both happy."

It was not until he'd accepted his hat and cane from the maid and stepped out the front door that he admitted he didn't know which answer would accomplish that.

Chapter Twenty-seven

Lydia sat for long minutes gazing around a room stripped of nearly all decoration, as had been all the rooms in her town house. The Limoges, crystal bowls, gilt mirrors, auxiliary furnishings, silver candelabras, gold plate, bronze and marble statuary and fine paintings, the enameled snuff boxes, brass andirons, and Persian carpets had all been discreetly sold at auction by Terwilliger's agents.

Stripped of its gilding, one could now see the bare bones of the house, the tall airy windows spaced at regular intervals across the cream-colored walls, the lofty, coved ceiling with its carved plaster medallions, the subtle marquetry in the wooden floor. There was nothing left to distract from either appreciation or criticism of what, at this elemental level, it was.

Childe Smyth had seen only what had been taken, not what was left.

She did not know why she had asked for a day in which to consider his proposal. She would say yes. Of course she would. As he'd said, it made perfect sense. He did not love her, he did not pretend to, but neither did he expect her to love him. He had proposed a marriage of convenience, both parties benefiting equally from the arrangement.

And as he'd said, they were friends. Not great friends, not the sort of friend with whom one might share one's most intimate thoughts and dreams, confess one's weakness and fears, discuss and debate things other than fashion and gossip. Not the sort of friend who made one's heart skip simply by smiling, and whose laughter made one laugh, too. Not the sort of friend whose gray eyes seemed able to see into one's very soul, and whose caress made one weak, whose voice seemed to pluck at some inner chord, and whose mouth inspired unquenchable desire.

Not that sort of friend.

She buried her face in her hands, tears damping her palms, her back shaking in silent sobs. God, what was she to do?

A light rap on the door brought her head up and she dashed away her tears, dabbing at her cheeks with the hem of her gown. "Come in."

Her maid opened the door, her last footman being otherwise occupied. Eleanor did not wait to be announced but swept into the room as she handed the maid her bonnet and pelisse. "That will be all," she told the maid.

Lydia nodded and the maid bobbed a curtsy before retreating and closing the door behind her.

"You look as glum as a cake in a butcher's shop," Eleanor said without preamble. "Whatever is the matter? You should be enjoying last night's triumph. Really, my dear, I didn't know at the time what you were about when you insisted on leaving in so covert a manner, but this morning your strategy has become apparent and, I must say, I applaud you. So clever!" She sat down beside Lydia and patted her hand.

"What do you mean?" Lydia asked.

"The entire *ton* is abuzz with speculation regarding the identity of Aurelia."

"Someone will soon piece it together," Lydia replied without much interest. "Everyone saw me arrive with you."

"Not so," Eleanor said. "Neither Emily nor I showed ourselves in the window. Only you. When we arrived, you wore your domino and stayed back while Emily and I entered. And when you were presented as Aurelia, we were not with you. And leaving before your identity was revealed? Genius. No one is talking of anything besides the golden lady."

She got up and began walking rapidly back and forth, her expression filled with anticipation. "When you do let it slip who you are, Childe Smyth will be falling over himself to ask for your hand." She gave a ladylike snort of derision. "He will have finally found someone worthy to share the stage with him."

"What stage is that?" Lydia asked, unable to keep the bitter note from her voice. Was that all her life would amount to, an act upon a stage?

Eleanor swung around, brows raised. "Why, the world stage, Lydia. How odd you are. Are you feeling all right? If not, for heaven's sake, let my doctor fix you a tisane. You mustn't look like this, like some pitiful ghost, when Childe Smyth comes calling. And he will." Her eyes sparkled. "His grandfather is nearing the end."

"Oh, glad tidings," Lydia said sharply.

Eleanor's head snapped back as if she'd been slapped, astonished Lydia would use such a tone with her. Lydia understood. But she did not apologize. Ned had taught

er the difference between decency and good manners.
Eleanor had gone too far with this gleeful anticipation
f an old man's death.

"You don't even like Childe Smyth, Eleanor," she
aid, "and yet you encourage me to accept his suit."

Eleanor's lips twisted with impatience. "I did not *like*
ny husband and I accepted his suit. That's hardly the
oint."

"What is the point?"

Eleanor sighed and took the chair opposite Lydia,
tripping the gloves from her hands, a sure sign she antici-
ated a lengthy debate and one she did not intend to lose.
Laying them on her lap, she fixed Lydia with a hard gaze.

"The point is, Lydia, that you have only one solution
o your situation: Marry Childe Smyth. You have no
ther options. If you do not accept him, you shall lose all
hose things most valuable to you."

She'd already done that, she thought as Ned's face
lashed through her mind. "And what do you think those
re?"

"Wealth, independence, prestige, and Society."

When Lydia only returned her regard with empty eyes,
Eleanor switched tactic. "Lydia. You surprise me. Why
re you acting as if you did not propose this course of
ction in the first place? You force me to be harsh." She
urned to face Lydia squarely. "You have been raised to
enjoy a certain lifestyle that few people have even imag-
ned. You have never known anything else," she said. "It
s not simply a question of having the wherewithal to
ourchase whatever takes your fancy. Many people can
lo that. It is the position in Society that your wealth has
bequeathed you that is irreplaceable.

"Your wealth has allowed you independence and Society's tolerance of that independence. Because you are the fabulously *wealthy* Lady Lydia Eastlake, all doors are open to you despite your lack of an acceptable chaperone or sponsor. You have entrée to the best Society, the finest arts, luxurious travel, and myriad experiences you would never have known as simply Lady Lydia Eastlake.

"It is not only what you drink but with whom you drink it, not only how you travel but where you travel to, not only that you can afford to purchase a rare Rubens but that you are given access to acquire it. Few people understand the world you were born into, Lydia. Fewer still understand what that does to a person."

"And what exactly is that, Eleanor?" Lydia replied.

"It permeates every aspect of your character. It informs all your actions and choices, with whom you associate, what you do, how you dress, speak, think. It makes you who you are. And without it, you cease to be." She settled back, confident. "*That* is the point. And that is why you must accept Childe's proposal when he offers."

"He already has," Lydia said in a low voice. "He left just before you arrived."

Eleanor's deep-set eyes widened with gratification. "Excellent! Than what are we talking about? Of course it is regrettable the formalities must be done in so havey-cavey a fashion, but we shall contrive to put a good face on it. I will host a reception so grand no one will recall the brevity of your courtship—"

"I haven't accepted him yet."

"What?" Eleanor's brows fell up in twin arcs of asnishment. "Lydia, I understand wanting one's value to e appreciated by not being too eager, but I have word om reliable sources that the grandfather is a half step om death's door. This is no time to play coy."

If only she was. She could not lie to Eleanor. "I am ot sure I will say yes."

"Why not?" Eleanor demanded, astonished.

"Mr. Smyth does not love me."

"All the better," Eleanor said, openly exasperated. He won't interfere with you, then. As long as you be-ave with discretion."

"Unlike Sarah," Lydia could not refrain from saying.

"Yes. Unlike Sarah."

Nothing Eleanor had said struck her as being spurious. Vealth and privilege *had* been her bread and butter, verything she'd known *had* been within the boundaries f the *haute monde*; it *had* defined her.

For a second, Eleanor's eyes hardened with a cold-ess in their hooded depths Lydia had rarely seen. Then t vanished and Eleanor leaned forward, covering both er clasped hands under hers. "You must accept him. I nderstand your concerns. You have lived your adult ife thus far without answering to any one person and t has spoiled you. Yes, Lydia. You are spoiled. But there s no reason to expect your life shall greatly change as myth's wife. Perhaps you'll be required to produce an eir, but even that is unwritten. I, as you well know, did ot. You will marry and carry on exactly as you do now. /ery little, certainly nothing of substance, will change. Nothing needs to change."

No, Lydia thought. *No*. For the first time during this nterview, Eleanor's words struck Lydia as not only

untrue but patently *wrong*. Things always changed
Parents died, babies never drew their first breath
husbands abandoned their wives in insane asylum
friends ruined themselves for love, and Ned woul
marry someone else.

"You will live exactly as you have always lived," E
eanor was saying.

Why, when just a few months ago that had been th
only thing that mattered, did that now seem a sentenc
rather than a reprieve?

"Childe Smyth will make you a fine husband. You sui
each other." Eleanor's voice was growing more insisten
a thread of desperation in it.

She was afraid, Lydia realized, desperately afraid tha
Lydia would turn him down.

"Don't be stupid, Lydia. Don't turn your back o
who and what you are, on everything and everyone yo
know. Don't turn your back on *me*."

"I never would," Lydia protested.

"You will if you don't marry Childe Smyth!" Eleano
burst out and then, with a visible effort, rose, pacing t
the window to collect herself.

There came a knock on the door to which Lydia bad
enter. The maid slipped in carrying a box wrapped wit
string. "Beggin' your pardon, milady, but this come t
the door and the chap what brings it says as he was tol
not to leave until he knows for a fact that it were deliv
ered into your hands."

Lydia nodded tiredly and held out her hands for th
package. "Give him a shilling and thank him."

Eleanor turned, looking over the package. "From
Smyth?"

"I don't know. There's no card." Lydia untied the box and lifted the lid to find a thick nest of tissue paper within. She peeled back the top layer and her heart leaped in her throat. Lying there was a gold lamé glove. Hers.

He knew who I was.

She stared, her thoughts wheeling madly until she realized that it lay atop something more. She picked up the glove, barely aware of Eleanor watching with narrowed eyes.

Underneath was a stunning royal blue and white bowl, the surface crackled with antiquity. The Kangxi bowl she found at Roubalais's shop. He must have recognized her then, too.

Dear heavens.

She swallowed hard, lifting the beautiful thing from its wrapping. A folded piece of paper fell from the tissue. She picked it up, opening it. The thin paper shivered in her hand. There was no salutation.

Eleanor was speaking, but Lydia did not hear what she said. Her eyes were following the bold script, reading.

> *Loath as I am to contradict a lady, I find that I cannot tolerate one more hour knowing you labor under the misconception that I did not or do not "know you." Allow me to make this clear: I have never mistaken you. I never will. No mask you might don, whether cast in gold or comprised of dust, can disguise you from me.*
>
> *In a thousand ways you are revealed to me: The way you illustrate a comment with your fingertips; the manner in which you tilt your head while listen-*

ing to music; the quick intake of breath that precedes your laughter; the quality of your stillness.

I have only to lift my hand to mimic the slope of your shoulder; close my eyes to map the blue-filigreed veins inside your wrist; inhale to recall the fragrance of you. I am an expert on the texture of your skin, a scholar on the changing hues of your eyes, and an authority on the cadence of your breath. And yet I do not need eyes or ears or hands to know you. Shut away, blinded, and deaf, I would still know you. I would still hear you, see you, feel you in my very core.

You may as well accuse the sky of not knowing the moon, for that is how fixed you are in the firmament of my heart. And like the moon, whether you choose to shine or not, here you will remain forever.

So I pray you, Lady Lydia, do not ever say again, I do not know you.
Your most obedient servant,
Captain Edward Lockton

"Lydia? Lydia, whatever does that letter say?" Eleanor asked, coming over to her. "It is from him, isn't it? Lockton." She spat his name, looking down at where Lydia sat, her head bowed in concentration.

"I can guess what this is. Some romantic drivel. Lockton has filled your head with starry-eyed notions, but the facts of the matter are simple ones: He deceived you, abused your trust, and inveigled himself in your . . . good graces and now you are pining for him."

Did Eleanor really not see the hypocrisy of this condemnation? "And what of my behavior toward him, Eleanor?"

"Ach!" Eleanor looked away for a moment as though she could not bear looking at Lydia.

"He cares for me, Eleanor."

"He's a blackguard with the audacity to hound you even though neither of your circumstances are such that you can consider marriage to each other. I don't understand . . . Wait! I do!" she announced, eyes flashing. "You do know what this is? He is setting the groundwork for a future dalliance. Perhaps he has more sense than I credit him with after all."

Lydia's brow creased. "Dalliance?"

"Yes. After you are wed and a decent interval has passed, he hopes to renew your romantic relationship."

No. No. She shook her head. "Not Ned." He was too decent, too honorable. Such Machiavellian intrigues would be as repulsive to him as they were to her. She was not Eleanor or Sarah or Emily. She had seen in her parents' marriage what loyalty and devotion and integrity could make. How ironic when theirs had been a "scandalous marriage."

"You are wrong, Eleanor."

Once again her friend, her very best friend, made a sharp gesture of disgust. "Enough of Ned Lockton. He is a footnote in this affair. You must focus on Childe Smyth."

"No."

"Damn it, Lydia!" Eleanor exploded. "You are not thinking objectively. Stop acting like a child. It may be that Childe Smyth does not make you happy, but he will not make you *un*happy. *He will not break your heart.*

Is that clear enough?" she asked, breathing hard. "He understands your world, its customs and conventions. He understands you. *He knows you.*"

The anger drained from Lydia, leaving only emptiness. She did not want to fight with Eleanor. She supposed she was acting like a child, refusing to accept the inevitable, unappreciative of anything less than her heart's desire. And Childe did know her. At least, he knew who she appeared to be. And really, was there anything more than that?

Yes. There was. Ned had shown her glimpses of that person. Lydia recalled telling him last night that he did not know her and so could not judge what she wanted and did not want. But both the glove and the bowl put a lie to that accusation. He knew her. Because he loved her.

Ned loved her.

There was, after all, little more to be said.

"Lydia, what is it?" Eleanor demanded. "You look strange. Why are you standing up? Where are you going?"

"I . . ." She shook her head. She barely remembered why she stood, why Eleanor had come, why *she* was still here.

Ned loved her.

She swung around, starting for the door.

"I must beg you to pardon me," she said, and without turning around left Eleanor behind.

Lydia, eyes shining and breathless, swept unseeingly past Emily, who stood in the hall outside the drawing room. She'd heard the last part of Lydia's conversation with

Eleanor. She moved slowly. Truth be told, sometimes more slowly then necessary to hear bits of this and that. Especially when she thought she might hear things that affected her. Lydia had never fully understood just how much of a survivalist she was.

"Patent insanity!" she heard Eleanor exclaim as she entered the drawing room.

"Ah, a term I've heard before," Emily said, closing the door.

A little color scored Eleanor's high cheeks. "I was not referring to you, Emily."

"I know," Emily said, taking a seat, something she would never have done had anyone else been there to see, or had Eleanor cared—which Emily knew she did not. As long as no one saw. Just as Lydia did not suspect how much of a survivalist Emily was, she also did not recognize how much of a snob Eleanor was. Not that either of them were bad people; they simply weren't as good as Lydia.

She would like to think it was because they had been tested more severely, but she knew this would be an excuse. Lydia, too, had been tested by adversity. Certainly not physical adversity, but as Emily full well knew, there were other sorts of pain. A loving heart can wither in a barren Wilshire house.

She waited now for Eleanor to say something. A companion did not seat herself before a duchess and Emily knew her place very well and she liked it very, *very* well. That was in fact the challenge: pitting what she wanted against what Lydia deserved. "Please, sit down, Eleanor."

Eleanor hesitated a moment, her gaze flickering to

the doorway and back to Emily, sitting composedly awaiting her. With scant graciousness she sat back down, her back stiff.

"There are far worse places than Brislington Asylum," Emily said in a conversational tone. "The inmates there are never exhibited for public amusement or horror. They are kept to a strict regimen of exercise, meals, rest, and occupation. They are clean and well fed. And yet I was miserable there."

"Of course." Eleanor sniffed. "You did not belong there."

Emily brightened. "Exactly. I did not belong there. Although some might say differently. Lady Pickler, for example, is certain Lydia made a mistake in arranging my release. And she is not the only one."

Eleanor opened her thin lips to make some disparaging remark, but Emily spoke first.

"I understand the concern. I can even empathize to some degree. I do have difficulties controlling my unacceptable impulses." She leaned forward, wincing a little. "There is a bar of soap with a ducal seal impressed on it in my room even as we speak."

Eleanor, well used to missing little things after Emily's visits, did not even blink. "Yes, I recall giving you that gift."

Emily laughed. "You are really kind, Eleanor, and generous." Her laughter faded, and her smile became gently sympathetic. "I would beg you to remember that now, in regards to Lydia, and be as generous to her as she has been to me."

Eleanor's eyes shuttered. "I want only what is best for Lydia."

"You want what is best for you," Emily corrected gently. "I understand that, too. So do I. It's only natural. But we must overcome such selfishness, Eleanor. Lydia does not belong with us any more than I belonged at Brislington."

Eleanor started to protest, but Emily stopped her. "Captain Lockton is offering her a chance for a sort of happiness you and I and Sarah were not fated to know."

"He is offering to take her away from her friends and the Society she was born into!" Eleanor snapped back.

But Emily had already spent many hours fighting this same battle within herself, self-interest against generosity, excuses against uncertainty. She knew all of Eleanor's arguments. And the answers.

"A life very similar, in fact, to the one that her parents chose. I did not have the pleasure of knowing them, but I do know their daughter, her character, and her loving nature, and I can only conclude that theirs was an exceptionally successful and happy union. One that neither regretted. I would hope the same for Lydia and her captain."

"Bah!" Eleanor said dismissively. "It is not the same at all. They were still people of influence. Lockton can only promise Lydia poverty and anonymity."

"They may begin poor," Emily allowed. "But he does not seem the sort of man who would remain that way long if given the proper opportunity. As for anonymity and Society, Lydia deserves to discover who she is when the public, and Society, is not looking. You and I, we already know her caliber and her character.

Her kindness, loyalty, and generosity. I believe Captain Lockton does, too. He *loves* her, Eleanor."

"Love," Eleanor snickered. "How long will his love last? How can he match what I have already given? Years of love and care and guidance. *Years*, Emily.

"And what of you?" the duchess went on. "Do you think they will invite you to live with them when they haven't the wherewithal to keep even themselves in a reasonable fashion? And in what capacity, my friend? As a maid? A nanny?"

"I should like to be a nanny," Emily replied, faraway fondness softening her eyes.

Eleanor made a sound of disgust.

Emily reached out to touch Eleanor's hand. "Eleanor, if Lydia did not love Captain Lockton, I would not be pressing this matter. But Lydia does love him. And he loves her." She met the other woman's gaze. "If you convince her to marry someone else, eventually she will end by becoming one of us: a woman who runs off with her lover to feed her starving heart; or a woman for whom her husband had so little regard he abandons her in an asylum; or a woman so embittered by years of mistreatment she no longer believes in love."

Eleanor drew in a thin hiss of breath, startled and pained.

Emily met her gaze with sad sympathy but no compromise. "Is that what you want for Lydia?" she asked.

Eleanor's gaze fell to her hands clutching each other in her lap. "No," she whispered. "No."

Chapter Twenty-eight

"I'm sorry, old man," Borton said gravely. He stood with his hat in hand, just inside Ned's library door. Having delivered his news, he was preparing to leave. He couldn't leave quickly enough for Ned's sake. It took all Ned's self-possession to simply stand.

"I didn't want you caught off guard when you heard it. I thought it best coming from me," Borton said.

He had come to report that Childe Smyth had proposed to Lady Lydia Eastlake and fully anticipated her consent before the day was through. He had heard Smyth himself, at Boodle's not an hour before. He was being congratulated by his cronies.

"Yes. Thank you."

Ned heard the door open and click shut as Borton left, and he turned toward the window overlooking the garden behind his rented rooms.

Lydia was meant to be his.

He couldn't afford her.

He should never have written.

He was not an impulsive man.

He could not bear the thought that she imagined

he could touch another woman, make love to another woman.

He could not live with the idea that she thought he didn't know her.

He loved her.

She was going to marry Childe Smyth. Wealthy, debonair Childe Smyth.

He loved her.

Bloody hell!

He pounded the wall at head level and let his fist lie there, and he leaned his forehead against it. He heard the door to his library click open again and then shut. Borton with some new bit of torturous information?

"Go away. Please," he said without opening his eyes.

He heard the light rustle of fabric, caught the scent of orange blossoms—he swung around.

Lydia stood inside his library door, enveloped in a hooded cloak. Silently, she untied the knot at her throat and it slipped like a whisper of warning to the floor. Her dusky violet eyes held his, but the lace fichu trembled over her heart.

"You're marrying Smyth." His tone was dead.

"No." She shook her head. As he watched, she reached behind her and with a click, turned the key in the door lock. She dropped it to the floor.

He wasn't aware he moved, how he crossed the room. One minute she was standing, the next she was in his arms and he was kissing her hungrily, ravenously, desperately, and she was clinging to him, her arms locked tight around his neck. He lifted her, lashing her to him with one arm and moving backward until he felt the desk hit the back of his thighs. Then he swung around

is mouth still locked to hers, and leaned over, sweeping
his free arm over the desk, sending the contents flying
across the room.

He seated her on the desk edge and gently eased
back. She anchored herself, holding hard to his shoulders. He followed her down, his tongue moving against
hers as he nudged his leg between her knees. Her thighs
opened eagerly, inciting madness, and he slipped his
hands beneath her, hands filled with the soft mounds of
her bottom, lifting her, pulling her against his hardness.

She purred deep in her throat and his mouth slanted
over hers, feasting on the gorgeous sounds, his tongue
stroking hers in the most erotic of dances, tasting her.
Instinctively, her hips lifted and pulsed in a primal reaction against him. His body tensed to rock-hard readiness
in response, and reason fled in the face of desire as raw
as it was unquenchable.

He tore his mouth away, raising himself up over her on
braced and trembling arms. "Lydia," he said hoarsely.

Her eyes opened and she reached to pull him back
down.

"God, Lydia, there are limits to what I can resist," he
ground out. "What I can bear."

"Are there? I suspect there aren't. I suspect you can
resist anything."

She wasn't making sense. He shook his head, desire
making his thoughts sluggish. "We've got to stop."

"No," she whispered raggedly. "Not this time. Dare
you turn from me now and I swear to you I will never be
here to turn away from again."

She swallowed and his gaze fell on the sight of her
flushed throat like a predator.

"I have tried to convince myself that I am not like Caro Lamb," she whispered, "that I do not love so tempestuously and that reason rules my passion. At least, it always seemed so to me before."

He looked down at her, torn between a desire to comfort her and make love to her. Her dark brown hair spilled across the surface of his desk, her lips slightly swollen from his kisses, her gaze seeking reassurance.

"You are not like Caroline Lamb," he reassured her.

She shivered, her eyes filling with fear, and reached up to stroke his cheek. He closed his eyes, drinking in the carnal pleasure of her voluntary caress. "With you. For you. I may be," she murmured softly. "I love you. Recklessly, stupidly, uncontrollably. Passionately."

"Dear Lord," he breathed.

"I love you," she said, the eyes searching his face filled with qualms, "but I would rather leave here now and never return than be the ridiculous partner in an unequal love, always wanting more until one day you grow tired of being asked for something you cannot give, and leave me."

"Never," he vowed hoarsely. "I will never leave you."

"How can I know that when it is so easy for you to pull away from me, to deny me, to deny this?" Her fingertips skated along his jawline and brushed over his lips.

His pulse hammered in his veins, his muscles burned with the tension of holding himself in check. "What would you have me do, Lydia?" he asked, helplessly nearly overwhelmed by desire. Only the thinnest thread of honor connected him to his resolve to do what was right. "How can I win? You have offered no honorable way for me to win you."

For a long moment she gazed up at him and then a sad, crooked smile touched her lips. Regret darkened her eyes.

"You are right," she said. "I have left you no honorable way to win me. So we shall both lose."

She rose onto her elbows and he lifted himself, his hands braced against the desk on either side of her. "Lydia."

She reached out and gently laid her hand on his chest. He trembled. "Let me go," she said softly.

"Never," he muttered and, seizing her wrist, pulled her roughly up and into his embrace. "Never."

His mouth fell on her in hungry desperation. For a second, she did not react. But then, with a low moan of capitulation, she lashed her arms around his neck and opened her mouth beneath his.

He wrenched off his coat, dropping it to the ground. She tore at his shirt, sending the buttons skittering across the floor. He pushed the silk from her shoulders, tugging down her bodice until her breasts were bared. He broke off their kiss and carried her across the room, lowering her to the leather couch and hissing with pleasure at the feel of her soft breasts crushed beneath his naked flesh, her nipples hardening into pebbles.

His head dipped down to the side of her neck and he traced the elegant line of her throat with his tongue, stopping at her earlobe and nipping it. She shivered and he sucked it gently, moving his hand down to cup the soft, warm mound of her breast. Lord, she was sweet, soft, pliant, and supple. Honey. Brandy. Silk and velvet.

Heated and slickery. Salty and clean. Every texture and flavor of sensuality.

His breath became ragged as he charted a sensuous course down her neck and shoulders, lifting the plump breast to take the nipple in his mouth and suck. She cried out, arching, her hips pumping lightly, instinctively, in a dance as old as time.

He reached down and pulled the panel from the front of his breeches and sprang free, hard and heavy, and then he yanked her skirts to her waist. Lust raked him, desire melted all restraint. He wanted, he *needed* to feel her around him, to take her, have her, join to her.

He clasped one of her knees and raised her leg, hitching it over his hip, her silk stocking sliding against his waist, erotic and sleek. She reached beneath his arms, her hands curling up around his broad shoulders, her fingers digging into his flesh. His reached between them down to the juncture of her thighs. The flesh there was soft and sleek and hot. He stroked the warm folds open and she bucked, her eyes flying wide. He shifted over her, covering her, one big hand holding her thigh high over his waist, keeping her open to him, the other moving, petting, caressing her.

He watched her as he moved his finger gently inside her, watched the progression of expressions on her gorgeous face. Shock. Alarm. Excitement. Hunger. *Need*?

Not yet.

Slowly, her body began to move in incremental answer to each slow thrust of his finger. A thin sheen of sweat glazed her breasts and shoulders. Her hips undulated and he lowered his head, sipping kisses from her half-parted lips, her eyes dazed and fixed as he brought her slowly to crisis.

A whimper broke from her lips and her gaze tangled with his and she gasped, "Ned? Ned?"

He could stand no more. He pulled his hand from between them, gritting his teeth against heeding her cry of protest, knowing the torment of unfulfilled need—he'd lived with it for weeks, months now. He clasped her other thigh and hooked her knee at his waist.

Instinctively, she shifted, locking him tight against her. He felt the muscles in her thighs tense and carefully, with mind-shattering discipline, eased the head of his shaft into her, then waited for her to retreat.

Instead, she moved beneath him, her hands grappling at his shoulders, her hips lifting and falling in unconscious rhythm, drawing him deeper inside right to the portal of her maidenhead. She winced, her eyes widening and darkening and he muttered an oath. She arched against the couch and he buried his face in the lee of her shoulder and neck.

"Be still!" he rasped. *Don't let me hurt her*, he prayed. "Don't move."

"I have to," she sobbed, caught between pain and pleasure. Her legs wrapped tighter about him, destroying his resolve. "Please!"

He thrust into her in one long, searing slide and forced himself to still. Her body closed like a velvet fist around the thickened length of him. He closed his eyes, fighting to remain still. She pushed at his chest, making some space between them. He looked down into bruised and anxious violet eyes. Anxious to trust him.

It had to be good for her. She had to know some

measure of the lust he felt. He had to give her a release. He slipped his arm beneath her and rose to his feet, still buried deep in her body. Her skirts rucked up around her waist, her breasts pushed over the rent neckline. She looked floozy and carnal, her hair wild about her shoulders, her nipples tight, mouth parted, panting and disoriented and needful. She gasped as he lifted her, rising to his knees and pivoting, turning, still buried deep inside her.

He shifted her legs so that she straddled his lap, her knees resting on the cushion on either side. He lay back. She stared down at him, uncertain as he cupped the underside of her breast, massaging the soft flesh, his thumbs playing with the silky, distended nipples. Her back arched and her mouth opened as she drew in a shaky breath, her head falling back, her long brown curls sweeping over his thighs.

He played with her until a moan escaped her lips. Then he caressed her in one long sweep from breast to belly to thigh and then to the soft triangle of mink brown curls between her legs. He found the hard nub between the hot, slick folds and pressed it with his thumb.

She jerked, bracing herself with her hands spread wide on his naked chest. He stroked her again. She looked down, her hair falling like a curtain around them. He clasped her hips in his big hands and, holding her shadowed gaze, slowly lifted her up, her hot, tight core dragging against his sensitive member, sending a quake through the muscles of his chest and arms.

"Ned?" She undulated against him and he ground his teeth.

"Easy, love," he murmured thickly. "I have far less

self-discipline than you think or I shall need if you are to find your finish."

He pushed slowly up into her, seating himself deep within. Her eyelids fluttered. He withdrew again and this time when he pulled her down onto him, he thrust a little harder, his thumb covering her clitoris to make the contact deeper, richer. She cried out. She was so tight. Too tight.

He clenched his teeth, forcing himself to hold back, to let her use his body to find her release. By God, he would last.

Faster and faster she moved on him, her hips rocking in the instinctive rhythm, her hair dancing over his chest. Her eyes fell partially shut, violet lights glittering in their lash-shaded depths, and her lips on little puffs of exertion that were punctuated with throaty whimpers of frustration. And with each movement she made, he withdrew and thrust deeper, faster, harder into her, stroke by stroke building an inferno of pleasure within.

"Please. Anything. Yes. *Please*," she whispered as he crunched up to lick the salty dew from her shoulder and neck.

Then her body was clenching, arching, and she shifted, taking every inch of him deep within her as she worked her hips in a circular movement against his groin. She cried out, tremors racking her, and the sight of her transfixed on the apex of pleasure undid him.

With a growl he rolled her onto her back, lifting her hips and rocking into her in thrust after thrust while her fingers dug into his shoulders and she panted his name which each concussive movement.

"Want me," she whispered.

The words finished him. With a powerful surge he filled her with his seed, holding there, tight within her, chest heaving, arms trembling as he held himself braced above her.

After an eternity, the storm quieted and he could open his eyes again. He reached down and tenderly swept the damp curls from her face.

"Marry me, Lydia. Tell me you will be my wife."

"But—"

He would not let her answer, there was a desperation in his eyes and in his tone she had never heard before. "I don't have the right to ask you. I know what I am asking you to give up. I have no wealth and soon, perhaps, no home. But I swear to you, Lydia, no other man would work harder or more tirelessly for your happiness. I need you, Lydia. I am a selfish bastard, but I need you so very much. Before you all the colors of this world were drab, all the flavors were bland, and every sound was muted. You have made my life . . . brilliant." His gaze raked hers. He reached out and cupped her face between both large hands.

"I love you, Lydia," he whispered. "I could never give you up. Never."

"You will never have to," she promised.

Chapter Twenty-nine

Lydia awoke in Ned's bed to a gentle touch. She smiled without opening her eyes, luxuriating in the sensual feel of chamois soft linen against her bare skin and soft, firm lips brushing her temple.

"Awake, my love," a low masculine voice murmured. "Morning is racing to extract a toll for last night. Your reputation is at stake."

"I don't care about my reputation." She opened her eyes to find Ned already dressed and seated on the side of the bed, gazing tenderly down at her. "Let us elope."

"No," Ned said, quickly enough that she suspected he'd already considered it. He lifted a tress of her hair between his thumb and forefinger and tested the texture. "I do care for your reputation. I would not have it said I took unfair advantage of ladies' well-known penchant for gentlemen in costume to seduce you into a hasty and ill-considered marriage."

"I've never even seen you in your uniform."

"A minor point," he said. "You have an excellent imagination."

"I do, indeed!" she declared, her eyes sparkling wickedly. She laughed and held out her arms. "If I tell you what I am currently imagining, perhaps I can convince you to stay a while—"

His mouth descended hungrily on hers and she arched up, the bedsheet falling to her waist, the light from a single candlelight flickering over her skin. With an obvious effort, he set his hands on her shoulders and broke off their kiss. Then, abruptly changing his mind, he dipped his head and captured her mouth once again in a long, searing kiss, his lips parting before gently pushing her away.

"Please, Lydia, allow me the illusion that I can resist you if I must. And for your sake, I must."

She read the plea in his eyes and stroked his lean cheek. It was rough, but his gaze was inexpressibly tender. "Very well," she finally said. "If you must."

"I'll have a coach waiting for you in the park across the street. My valet will escort you from the side of the house when you are ready." He caught her hand and lifted it to his mouth, pressing a series of kisses on her knuckles. "I would not have you the subject of speculation."

How deeply he cared for this thing called honor that others only paid lip service to, but which he exemplified. As the captain of a ship, his men had depended on his honor. As did his family. As did she now. It was an integral part of him. Without it he would simply be another actor playing the part of gentleman, adopting fashionable manners and attitudes. But Ned *was* a gentleman. At his core. To his very soul. Her gentleman. "Do you forgive me for compromising your honor?" she asked, a little worriedly.

He looked startled. "For what?"

"Compromising you. For . . . finding your limits?" she asked, echoing their words from the night.

He smiled. "You mistake me, Lydia. I care for your reputation only because it is the public face of your character. I am humbled by the trust you bestowed on me by putting your reputation in my care and I will not fail to look after it with all diligence. Now or ever. I love you. How is it a compromise to have everything I ever wanted, needed, or desired here in my arms?"

She settled back, satisfied.

"I am leaving you to go directly to Josten Hall to let my siblings know of their newly lowered expectations," he said. "I would not like them to read of our betrothal in the papers."

"Will your brother be angry?" she asked.

"I don't know," Ned mused. "He never was comfortable with being responsible for so many and so much. I suspect he'll learn easily enough the relief of being unburdened by responsibilities he is ill equipped to handle. He and Nadine were always most comfortable with their own society." Now he took her hands in his and met her eyes. "They are not bad people, Lydia. They are simply nearsighted regarding their importance. As was I when I returned from sea. I believed nothing mattered more than to see the Josten traditions carried on."

"And why is that no longer important?"

"It is still important," he said seriously. "What has changed is my view of my role in that endeavor. I came home without any thought other than to live out my life amongst my family at Josten Hall. I needed and wanted nothing or anyone else. So when Josten suggested I marry someone with wealth enough to initiate my family's financial recovery, it seemed like a small enough thing to ask. I had, after all, been asked to volunteer far more important things—my men's lives."

She watched him carefully. He did not color up this time, uncomfortable with revealing his emotions. He may never share easily those things most deeply held in his heart, but he would with her.

"Besides," he said softly, his gaze tangled with hers, "it was easy to agree to Josten's plans because I did not care. It would be no great sacrifice to promise myself to a woman I barely knew, because I barely knew my heart anymore. I had needed to quiet its demands for so long while I was at war, that it was unused and slumbering.

"War numbs a man's heart, Lydia," he said quietly. "It must or he wouldn't survive. But then I met you and . . . you would not let my poor heart rest. Just by being with you, you insisted I see the world through your eyes, with *your* heart—which is so demandingly vibrant—and you made me discover my own again."

Her gaze fell and he lifted her chin with his finger and leaned in to brush a kiss over her mouth. "You awoke me to pleasure, to beauty, to joy, and to hope again. Within a week of meeting you at Roubalais's, all Josten's hopes of my marrying for convenience was lost."

She was well aware that in marrying her Ned was relinquishing his family's hopes for renewed prosperity. "What of your nephews?"

A sort of rueful resignation filled his handsome face. "My nephews seem determined to ruin themselves. If they have no care for what will one day be theirs—or what would have been theirs—there is nothing I can do to change that. Even if I saved it for them now, they would only lose it themselves later."

"But what will you tell them?"

He smiled. "The truth. No one else will have me now. I am too obviously smitten, too openly besotted. A woman might take exception to being courted by a man whose gaze is constantly, lovingly, adoringly fixed on another."

She smoothed her palm against his rough cheek, thrilled by his words. He turned his face and kissed her palm. "I love you," she whispered.

"There you go again, playing havoc with my resolve," he said hoarsely. "But you must go and the sooner I see my brother, the sooner I can return to your side and we can wed. So, reluctant though I am to ask you to quit my bed, I must do so."

She nodded, determined to prove her intent to co-operate with his plans, which in effect would make her dreams come true, by hurriedly swinging her legs over the side of the bed in order to speed him on his way and thus back to her again.

Lydia awoke for the second time that morning in her own bed. She rolled to her back and stretched her arms overhead in feline luxuriance, feeling well and thoroughly loved. How intoxicating this sensation, how addictive it would be. She hugged the idea close, unraveling the years ahead in her imagination. Years of mornings waking to this feeling, only better because Ned would be by her side.

Ned.

The thought of his beautiful body, the smooth skin

taut over large muscles, the flat belly, the long, powerful legs and arms, set off a pulse of excitement that pooled between her thighs. She blushed, recalling the way he'd played with her body, the path his big hands had taken over her skin, the places he'd found that caused her to catch her breath or arch her back. The way he'd quaked when he'd allowed himself his release, the strain and beauty on his face . . .

She blew out a steadying breath and got up. If just the memory of Ned's lovemaking could make her limbs so weak, what state would she be in after they'd wed? And the week after that? And the next month? Would passion commit her to an invalid's chair?

She laughed and glanced over at the mantel clock. It was ten o'clock in the morning. Six hours since Ned had left and his man had escorted her back to her own house. He would be halfway to Josten Hall by now. Already she was anxious to see him again. If only she could sleep away the hours until his return.

"Lady Lydia?" her maid asked, rapping on the bedroom door. "Ma'am?"

"Come in."

The maid opened the door, looking nervous. "There's a . . . person here insisting that he see you."

"A person?" Lydia repeated. It was too early for callers. "What sort of person? Is he a gentleman?" It couldn't be a merchant here to collect money. She'd paid most all of her debts and the cent-per-center was not owed until the end of the month.

"I can't say, ma'am. He speaks well enough and he is dressed in a gentlemanly fashion, but . . ." She lifted her hands apologetically, unable to convey what about the man gave her pause. "He refuses to give his name, ma'am, but insists he has information of a vital nature that he says you will be most sorry not to hear in time. I didn't know where to put him so he's still in the hall."

In time? Whatever did that mean? Lydia's brows knit together. Did he have news from Ned? She stood up. "Tell him I will be with him shortly," she said, already shedding her nightgown.

It took only a few minutes for her to dress and twist her long hair into a bun and then she was hurrying down the stairs. At the bottom of the steps, she spied a big man she judged to be in his late forties, the buttons of a once-fashionable coat straining to hold the material together over a barrel chest. His boots told a similar tale of having come down in the world, well cut but scuffed and dull. He held a beaver hat in the crook of his arm. He looked up, spotted her, and bowed.

"Lady Lydia," he said and his accent was, indeed, that of a gentleman. She studied him, certain they had never before met. Coarse graying hair sprung over a sunburned balding pate, thick brows lowered over dark, intense eyes. Fleshy swags hung below them and seams bracketed his mouth. Tiny red veins scribbled over a Romanesque nose. "Kind of you to see me, ma'am. I'm sure you'll be interested in what I have to say."

She did not like him. She did not like the feeling he gave her. "We shall see. If you would join me, please?"

She did not wait for him to reply but instead led the way into the morning room. She did not bother sending for refreshments. She did not want him here any longer than necessary. She turned without sitting, obliging him to remain standing, too. Only he didn't.

He looked around and took a seat, placing his top hat on his knee.

Lydia's eyes widened at his forwardness. "Who are you, sir? And why have you insisted on seeing me?"

The man looked up at her from his lengthy survey of the room. "My name is Bernard Cod. I believe you know my wife, Emily."

Emily Cod's hand fell from the doorknob leading into the morning room and she wheeled sideways, an animal readying for flight. But the sound of *his* voice had dealt her a blow more stunning than a club, and her legs buckled. She half fell against the wall and braced herself, closing her eyes, refusing to believe this nightmare could be true.

He was dead. Dead. DEAD.

The matron at Brislington's had told her, had explained that Cod had been lost at sea and that she would have to be transferred to another facility since there was no one to pay for her continued treatment at Brislington. Unless she could contribute.

So she'd contributed. The odd thing had been that she had actually cared whether they sent her to Bedlam or not. By that point in her life, it had been a long time since she had cared about anything, not since Cod had pushed her down the stairs and she'd lost their baby. After that, life had become an endless series of one miserable minute draining into the next.

The only respite from melancholy had been those times when "what if" had caught her off guard and she'd envisioned a baby with auburn curls, tiny fingers, and a rosebud mouth. Then panic crashed in through the door her imagination left open. Her heart would race, her vision blur, and she could not catch her breath, she could not breathe, until something interrupted the terrible escalating hysteria.

Something like stealing.

She had no idea why taking other people's little fribbles should afford relief. She didn't care. She would have done anything to stop that nameless sense of being trapped, cornered, imprisoned in a dark hole and buried alive.

But not long after she'd discovered the relief stealing could give her, Cod discovered her penchant, too. He'd had her committed. And right afterward, he'd gone away. And then she'd heard he'd died.

Dead. He was *dead*, not in the morning room talking to Lydia. She was dreaming. Another nightmare. Because this couldn't be real. It wasn't fair. It had taken so long to piece herself together. It had taken effort and practice and Lydia.

She should go in there, step through the door, and confront her nightmare. But she couldn't. Because she knew he was real and she couldn't bear to look at him. Not after what he'd done to her.

But she could listen to him.

Emily crept back across the hallway and pressed her ear to the door.

Chapter Thirty

"The reports were that you'd died," Lydia said coldly. "You fell overboard off a ship."

This was the vermin that had committed Emily to an insane asylum. She stared down at him, willing him to shrivel under her disgust like a leech dosed with salt. But he was immune to her attitude.

"It wasn't me—it was some Belgian. But it was convenient," he said, spreading his hands wide. "It made it possible for me to take his name and begin a new life.

"You see, people had begun asking uncomfortable questions about my banking practices, in spite of the fact that my initial investors had made a tidy sum. In fact, they all recommended me to their friends." He sounded pleased, even flattered. "Alas, subsequent investors were not so fortunate. If only they had given me more time to convince a third wave of investors to subsidize me, I could have gone on for some time. But they wouldn't and so, well, my demise was best for all."

"Why are you telling me this?" Lydia bit out the words.

"Because I want you to understand why you are going to pay me fifty thousand pounds."

"*What?*"

"I recently returned to England after a . . . misfor-
une abroad. Alas, imagine my disappointment when
realized that my former clients have long memories.
m very much afraid I have already been recognized. In
oite of my new name."

He sighed at the unfairness of it, then continued.
Lately, I have been thinking how well my old investment strategies worked and that it is high time I founded
new bank in a new country, where I will not be recog-
ized. But these things need seed money and that's what
ou shall provide."

"No."

He ignored her as if she hadn't spoken. "I have already
ooked passage on a ship leaving Portsmouth tomorrow
vening. I intend to be on board with the fifty thousand
ounds you will secure for me by four o'clock tomorrow
fternoon. A draft from the Bank of England will do."

"You must be mad." She'd had enough of Bernie Cod.
he turned to ring for the footman. The only one left. He
as a strapping lad and she would take great delight in
iving him instruction to bodily remove this filth.

"I wouldn't be so hasty, if I were you," Cod said, his
oice growing dark.

His tone was such that Lydia hesitated despite
erself.

"I believe you are forgetting about my wife. She *is*
till my wife, you know, my legal responsibility. I must
ay, I was quite amazed to discover that you'd adopted
er as your pet."

"Emily is not a pet. She is my companion," Lydia said,
ut her hand did not tug the bellpull.

"How gratifying to hear how fond you are of he
Otherwise, I would be forced to commit her again. Th
time to Bedlam."

"Emily stays with me," Lydia snapped, but alarm ha
begun to build inside of her.

"As long as I allow it," he agreed. "And I shan't allo
it unless you get me that money."

"You can't do that."

"But I can." He did not sound angry, merely im
patient.

"I shall tell everyone who you are. You will end i
debtor's prison," Lydia declared.

"You know," Cod mused, "I anticipated this reactio
but I still cannot help but be disappointed. I heard yo
were intelligent."

She did not reply, only stood rigid, caught betwee
horror and fury.

"Pray, think, ma'am. My legal problems have no e
fect on my rights as Emily's husband. I can still have he
committed." At her continued silence, he went on. "Th
ton is filled with stories of Emily's bizarre and uncor
trolled light-fingered way. I've asked around. She's quit
notorious. No one is going to oppose her commitmen
If you send for the authorities, I may end up in jail, bu
so will Emily. Of a different sort."

"You cannot be so evil."

"I am not evil. I am a businessman. This is a simpl
transaction and one where you get as good as I." H
sounded so practical, so reasonable. "You give me th
money and I leave. And lest you think I will only im
pose on you again at some future date, consider this.
would be a fool to risk my freedom by returning to En

and now that I realize how long my enemies will hold
grudge. I am no fool and I can hardly commit dear
mily from halfway across the world."

Lydia stared at the man, trying to sort out what to do,
ow to alleviate the threat posed by this man. Ned was
ne and she'd awoken to a nightmare. "I don't have the
oney," she said hoarsely.

"Now *that* is even more than disappointing and it
ily raises my ire, indeed it does." All traces of feigned
quanimity evaporated from his voice. Lydia shivered.
How stupid do you think I am? You are one of the
ealthiest women in the *ton*. Now listen to me, Lady
ydia." His voice grew thick. "I need that money. I owe
oney to people besides the ones here in England.
eople from other countries. Countries with barbarous
actices, if you take my meaning. And these chaps have
r worse punishments for those they catch up with than
ison. Indeed, I'd sooner take my chances in an English
ison than encounter one of them without having the
herewithal to pay them off. Do I make myself clear?'

"Yes. But I am telling you, my fortune is gone. All of

Cod snickered. "Gammon me another, Lady Lydia. I
w the jeweled gown you wore at that masquerade ball,
e gold mask, the gems in your hair. The *ton* is talking
nothing else. And I know it was you. I saw you. I was
the gate when you and Emily drove out."

"It is window-dressing." Lydia's voice rose in desper-
ion. "I spent everything on making myself unforget-
ble. In order to . . ."

She faltered. She had been so careful not to let the
ews of her impoverishment leak. Her friends and Ter-

williger had been the souls of discretion. But if she had
lay her pride on the floor before this monster, she wou
"It was all a ploy to make myself irresistible to a certa
sort of man, a rich man, so he would offer for me."

Cod looked up at that and Lydia held her breath, pra
ing that Cod would believe her. But he wasn't listenin

"Right, then." With a grunt, he rose to his feet, du
ing off his hat. "Have Emily make sure her bags a
packed. On the other hand, there's really no need. Th
only take away everything they bring with them."

"No!" Lydia cried out. She could not risk having Er
ily sent back to an asylum. It would kill her. And s
knew Cod would do it, even if it meant staying in E
gland and going to prison himself. He said he'd rather
in an English prison than meet the men he owed wit
out the wherewithal to pay his debts to them. "No, wa
I can't promise you anything, but I'll try."

"That's all we can ask in life, isn't it, Lady Lydi:
That we try and be prepared for the consequences if v
fail." His tone was once more smooth and conciliator
He reached into his pocket and withdrew a scrap of p
per with writing on it. "Meet me here tomorrow by fo
o'clock."

She stared at his hand, unable to bring herself to dra
nearer to him. He understood and it amused him. With
snicker, he dropped the paper to the floor. He tipped h
head and donned his hat. "Tomorrow, then."

As soon as the door closed behind him, Lydia sar
down to the chair. She bent over and picked up the p
per, noting an address down near the docks.

Four o'clock tomorrow.

She didn't even consider trusting to the courts to so

at if Emily Cod was mad and who would determine
er future. Because she already knew. Husbands, even
criminal ones, held their wives' and children's welfare
hostage in the palm of their hand, or center of their fist,
be sheltered or crushed as they wanted.

Yes, there were laws to protect a woman from being
physically broken too badly, but her person, her prop-
ty, and in most ways her freedom, were her husband's
do with as he saw fit. He could take her children, as
had Sarah's, or her money. He could abandon her, exile
er, or commit her to an asylum with little cause.

The worst of it was that Cod knew he held the
ump card; Emily's peculiarities provided more than
nough reason to have her committed. In truth, there
as enough evidence against her to have her arrested,
convicted, and even transported should someone bring
it. The law could send a boy to Australia for lifting a
andkerchief. It could certainly do as much to a woman
nown to pilfer regularly. Of course, as long as Emily
as with Lydia, she'd been safe. No one would gainsay
ady Lydia Eastlake.

She leaned forward, her forehead falling into her
and, and closed her eyes, trying to think through this
orror.

Ned.

She could send for Ned.

But the rush of comfort thought of him inspired evap-
rated before grim realities. What good could Ned do?

He had no more money than she and far less chance
f finding it in so short a time. Even if she could get a
essage to him at Josten Hall and he could return by
ur o'clock tomorrow afternoon—and she did not

know how that would be humanly possible—nothing [
could do would alter the situation shy of his killing Co
And he would.

He would challenge him to a duel and if Cod refuse
he would kill him outright. Then he would stand trial f
killing Cod. And if Cod did accept, Ned could be hurt
even killed himself. She would not sacrifice Ned to sav
Emily. She couldn't.

She considered taking Emily and running away, b
what good would that do other than buy some time? A
long as Cod was in England, in jail or not, Emily coul
be wrenched from her and sent to Bedlam.

She had friends, powerful friends that she knew sl
might convince to take up Emily's cause should she l
committed. But the laws that deeded a man rights ov
his wife were ones most men would not like trifling wit
The effects of bringing a successful suit against Cod an
his rights to determine Emily's fate would have long
ranging effects that she was not certain her frienc
would want to see come to pass. Even if she did convinc
them, there was no saying they would be successful. An
in the meantime, Emily would languish in Bedlam. Th
thought of that place, the horror stories told about th
treatment of the inmates there, made her shake.

Fifty thousand pounds was an immense sum of mone
Almost impossible to come up with in so short a tim
But there was one man she knew who could do so.

She knew what she must do; she must ask Child
Smyth to loan her the money. She also knew that ther
was scant chance he would make such a loan knowin
she had no way to repay it. Childe had proved himself
pragmatist above all.

She drew a shaky breath. She had one thing Childe
might consider taking in payment: her hand in marriage. And that meant giving up Ned. She closed her
eyes briefly and a tear leaked out the corner and trick-
led down her cheek. What else could she do? She had
not been the friend she should have been to Sarah. She
could not do the same to Emily. Perhaps a month or two
ago she would have railed and cried but ultimately failed
to make such a sacrifice for Emily. But she was not that
person anymore. She had changed. Ned had reawakened
her deepest sense of honor and commitment.

She would never be able to live with herself if she
did. She would know for a fact that all she amounted to
was a pretty, hollow shell without substance or loyalty
or compassion. Ned would hate such a mannequin. *She*
would hate such a mannequin. She was better than that.

She stood up and walked to her small writing desk
and, without sitting down, picked up a pen and hastily
wrote a few terse lines. She tugged the bellpull and while
she waited sealed the note. When the maid entered, she
said, "I want this message delivered to Mr. Childe Smyth
at once. Have the boy await a reply."

Emily Cod heard Lydia's command and knew at once
that Lydia was seeking from Mr. Smyth the means to
ransom her. The older woman knotted her hands together
fretfully, wondering what to do. Lydia might ask for a
loan, but Emily knew Childe Smyth and his situation.
He would demand something in return: Lydia's hand in
marriage. And Lydia would agree.

If Lydia didn't, Cod would send Emily to the asylum. He was vicious enough to do so. He'd been vicious

enough to push her down the stairs when she was pre,
nant because he didn't want to provide for "her brat."

She didn't want to go to Bedlam. The thought of su
a place, endless mutter of the mad, the stench of inco
tinence, the howling and giggling, but worse, the vaca
eyes of those who had entered there not mad, but ov
time had retreated deep within, never to be recalle
again. No. She couldn't.

She thought of all the things she had said to Elea
nor to convince her that Lydia ought to marry Captai
Lockton. But that was yesterday, before Cod. Now . . .

Would it be so bad, after all, if Lydia married Child
Smyth?

They could all settle back into their regular routin
just like Eleanor had been saying. Life could go on muc
as it had since Lydia had taken her out of Brislingto
They could discuss what Lydia would wear to such an
such a party, the latest *on dit*, which operas would wi
acclaim and which would fail. They could go to th
lending library and art museums and shopping arcade
They would plan where to travel during the off seaso
and whose great estate they would visit for huntin
season.

Their lives would once again conform to Society
predictable, opulent rhythms.

And Lydia would be miserable.

Because she loved Captain Lockton.

Emily moved sightlessly up the stairs to her apar
ments. It was a beautiful room, handsomely decorate
and comfortably furnished. Her wardrobe contained
dozen dresses and several gowns. A pearl broach la

nested in an ivory-inlaid ebon box. Both had been gifts from Lydia.

She sat down on the rose-colored satin armchair. Even had Cod not reappeared, Emily's future looked grim if Lydia married Captain Lockton. There might not be room in their much smaller household for a companion. Terwilliger had even said as much. Left to her own devices, Emily doubted she would fare very well.

Lydia had always protected her from the consequences of her petty thievery. True, she'd gained some control over her addiction, but that was only evidence of her contentment. With anxiety, the compulsion grew. Without the safe harbor Lydia provided, she would falter on rocky shores. There was no doubt about it, Emily's interests were best served if Lydia married Childe Smyth. So were Eleanor's. So too even Lydia's.

No, she doubted she could be self-sacrificing enough to try to talk Lydia out of her plan to accept Mr. Smyth's proposal. She had already been forced to sacrifice so much in her life: her dreams, her freedom, her child, her sanity . . .

Emily buried her face in her hands and wept.

Chapter Thirty-one

The trip to Josten Hall had taken Ned sixteen hours by mail coach. While not nearly so hard on his leg as riding astride, the old wound had begun to ache. He'd arrived to discover that Nadine and Beatrice were in Brighton with Mary and Josten was in Portsmouth and not due to arrive until evening. He'd hobbled to his room, there to bathe and change and await his brother. Josten would doubtless rage and roar, he did it well, but in the end Ned did not think marrying Lydia would cause an irreparable break with his family.

Since Josten had been a young man, the weight of inheriting the monstrous, ever-ravenous organism known as Josten Hall had been heavy on his shoulders. He hadn't had a clue how to go about managing the estate, so, lacking guidance, he'd spent his first few years as earl emulating his high-born friends, indulging himself and everyone around him with gifts and presents and toys and in between throwing impressively loud parties.

It was all for show. Josten was a monumentally tenderhearted and sentimental man. Not overly bright, but a born romantic. Which is why he had married Nadine, with whom he had fallen madly and forever in love after one short dance—as, luckily, she had with him—and retired with all haste to the countryside, where the new earl wouldn't have to put on a worldly facade for people he did not really know and in whose company, if truth be told, he felt rather shy. It would be no great sacrifice for either Nadine or him to live modestly. Or Beatrice, either.

But Josten would not like losing Josten Hall, the Lockton ancestral manor. Josten would feel he had failed in his tenure as custodian of the place.

As the hours dragged on, Ned filled them with thoughts of Lydia, remembering her arms stretching up to him, her eyes sparkling with vivid lilac lights, and her smile filling him with the sense of homecoming that Josten Hall no longer could. His heart had been breached, the vessel confiscated, and it was now occupied by a beautiful pirate. It would never belong to another.

He walked through the house gardens to the cliff overlooking the North Sea and finally turned around to study the great old house, no longer seeing it through the eyes of a wounded man seeking sanctuary, a still point in a world that had cruelly changed.

Instead, he now saw so clearly that coming back here and trying to convince himself that things could return to the way they were when he was a lad had never been a feasible goal. There were no still points. Situations changed, children grew, and time traveled on and he would, too, and gladly, because he would be making the journey with Lydia. And all he wished now was to return to her side.

He made his way back to the house and from there to the library and waited impatiently, watching the clock.

The dinner hour rang, then nine, and finally ten o'clock before he heard Josten's booming voice from outside the window on the front drive. "Ned's here? Where is he?"

Ned went into the hall to meet him. A few seconds later, Josten strode into the library looking magnificent and lordly, his air of ownership and *noblesse oblige* never more pronounced. An Irish wolfhound trotted in at his side. The footman started and snapped rigidly to attention, though Josten barely glanced at him.

Why, Ned thought with weary amusement, even footmen held themselves to a higher standard in Josten's presence. He really did have being an earl down to an art.

"Good God, Ned," Josten said when he saw him, "you look fagged to death, mi'lad. What the devil have you been doing? You haven't taken up Will and Harry's nasty habits, have you?" he asked suspiciously.

"No, sir. I have come with news that I am afraid will disappoint you."

At this, Josten, who'd bent over to scratch the head of the great Irish wolfhound, glanced up. Reading the solemnity on Ned's face, he sighed. "Must you?"

"Yes, I am afraid I must."

"Very well, then. Into the library. You may leave us," Josten told the footman. He strode ahead of Ned into the nearby room and flopped down in a leather armchair, his long legs stretched out in front of him. He stared broodingly at his boot tips. "Is it Harry? Have you set him up with the press gangs?"

"What?" Ned asked, startled. "Good God, no."

Josten glanced up, his expression vastly relieved. "You didn't?"

"No. Whatever gave you such an idea?"

"Because I would have," Josten said bluntly. "I had the whole story from Pip. He came down last weekend. He never could keep anything back from his mother, and Beatrice told me and I had the lad in here on the carpet.

"He told me all about Tweed and that card game and how you refused to challenge the blackguard and how Harry, that great oaf, felt the family's honor had been impugned and so Harry challenged the blighter to a duel and you showed up and took his place against this craven Tweed and how my heir managed to get you shot!" He glared up at Ned. "Is that about it?"

"Yes, sir. More or less. But why would this lead you to believe I'd thrown Harry to the press gangs?"

"Because when Nadine searched you out in London to enlist your aid regarding that card game—yes, I had that from Nadine, too. No one in this bloody family is capable of keeping their bottle stopped—you told her you thought your nephews could do with some rigorous discipline of the type found in the navy. I haven't seen Harry since that contretemps and so . . . Well, *I* would have," he repeated gruffly.

"Well, I didn't. I have no idea where your son is. Though the matter I have come to speak to you about does concern him."

Josten blew out his cheeks, a man preparing for bad news. "Yes. Well, out with it, then."

"Lady Lydia Eastlake has done me the great honor of

agreeing to become my wife." Just saying the words aloud filled Ned with a flood of joy, despite the moment.

Josten looked up. His eyes grew round. A broad smile broke over his handsome face and he leaped to his feet, clapping Ned on the back. "Well done, Neddie, m'boy! Well done, indeed! Lady Lydia Eastlake . . ." He rubbed his hands together in pleasure. "I have never met the lady, but her beauty is legendary and her fortune—"

"There is no fortune."

Josten checked. "Er. Say again?"

"There is no fortune."

"But there's *money*."

"No. No money." Ned shook his head. "She is deeper in dun territory than we Locktons. She hasn't a feather to fly."

Josten dropped down in the chair as though taken out at the legs. His head fell back against the seat cushion and he stared at the ceiling. "Well, that is depressing."

As Ned had expected something a great deal more vehement and definitely louder, he took this as an encouraging sign. "I'm terribly sorry."

"Eh?" Josten looked up. "Oh. Yes, well . . . I suppose it couldn't be helped?"

"No. It couldn't be helped. I fell in love with her."

Josten nodded, amazingly unsurprised. "I see. Quite. Love takes the Lockton men that way. A trial really, but nothing to be done for it once it happens except make the chit your bride." For a moment his face reflected remembered passion and delight. "No. Nothing for it once you fall in love. Lasts forever, too, I might as well warn you."

"Yes, sir." Ned hid a smile. "I must say, sir, you are showing far more equanimity than I imagined."

"Don't see as I have any choice. No. I know you, Ned. You're my brother. My blood. I know you like I know myself and there's nothing for it but to accept it."

"What will you do?" Ned asked, feeling a bit dumbfounded by Josten's uncharacteristic composure.

"Do? Sell off all the unentailed land, I suppose. Can't say I'll miss it. Never understood much about acres and bushels and heads and tails and whatever it is the farmers drone on about. Keep the hunting rights, of course," he said as though this were of primary importance, which, Ned supposed, it was to Josten. "And the pack. And a few horses."

"You'll try to keep Josten Hall," Ned said.

Here, at last, grief clouded Josten's gaze. "Keep the place? Doubtful. Things change, Ned. Things come and go. Sometimes in one lifetime, sometimes over the course of many." He smiled. "Did you know that the Locktons originally bought the old pile off the Bortons?"

Ned was surprised. He hadn't known that. He had always assumed the Locktons had built the place, hence the name *Josten* Hall. "No, sir, I didn't."

Josten nodded. "When Bonny Prince Charlie was making a run for the throne, the Bortons had the bad taste to back the Pretender." He leaned forward and said confidentially, "The Bortons never were good gamblers. When the family took a political and extended leave from England, we bought it and rechristened it Josten Hall."

His expression grew calculating. "You know, I

shouldn't be surprised if the Bortons want it back." He paused. "Perhaps as a dowry?"

"You mean a marriage between Mary and George Borton? I thought he'd already asked her and been turned down. Something about his sister," Ned said.

"He did and he was. But that was two years ago, when Mary made her debut. She was quite vain and certain of herself. She ain't so persnickety these days and is liable to be even less so when her allowance has been trimmed to the bone."

"But what of Borton's sister?"

"I have the utmost faith in your niece's ability to drive off any half dozen sisters-in-law. I will say no more." He nodded sententiously. "The trick will be convincing Borton to come up to scratch again. Well, we will see. We will do what we can."

With a slap on his thighs, Josten rose to his feet.

"Thank you, Marcus," Ned said. "You have made this far easier than I anticipated."

"Oh, don't be relaxing yet, m'boy," Josten said with a grim smile. "Nadine and Beatrice will extract whatever toll I have waived. They shall be most put out with you. Shouldn't expect dinner invitations anytime soon."

"I shall contrive to keep my disappointment in hand."

This comment won him a slow, speculative glance from Josten. "You aren't being *ironical*, are you, Neddie?"

"No, sir," Ned denied. There was no sense in perturbing Josten with the idea that he did not know his young brother as well as he assumed. It would only hurt him.

"Didn't think so. We Locktons never are. Now, get some sleep, lad. You look like bloody hell."

*   *   *

ust before three o'clock in the morning, a pounding on
is bedchamber door awoke Ned. He came fully alert
t once, the practice of long years at sea during wartime
oming to his aid, and called out for whoever it was to
nter.

Josten appeared in the doorway, a candlestick in his
and, a nightcap on his head, barefoot and unshaven.

"What is it?" Ned asked, rising bare-chested from the
ed.

"A rider woke the household ten minutes ago. He says
e has a letter addressed to you and has instructions not
o leave until he has delivered it to your hand."

"Where is he now?"

Josten turned and motioned. A travel-stained and
ollow-eyed youngster shuffled in, worrying a knit cap
etween his hands.

"Are you Captain Lockton?" he asked.

Ned nodded curtly and the boy stepped forward, dig-
ing into the leather satchel strapped around his neck
nd producing a thin envelope. He handed it to Ned and
etreated.

Josten turned him by the shoulder and told him, "Go
o the kitchen and have them find you something to eat
nd a place to bed down."

The boy bowed awkwardly and disappeared as Ned
pened the envelope.

Captain Lockton,
    Lady Lydia is planning to marry Childe Smyth
by special license this day next. She does this for
my sake. The need for haste makes it impossible

for me to explain further. Only know she has made
this decision under duress and the gravest of cir-
cumstances. I beg you, do not let her sacrifice her
happiness and yours on my account.
   Emily Cod

The blood drained from Ned's face and he wheeled
around, snatching up the breeches and shirt he'd so recently shed.

"What it is, Ned? What's the matter?" Josten demanded, alarmed. "What can I do to help?"

Ned had already donned his breeches and was shoving his arm through the sleeve of his shirt. "Have the
fastest horse in your stable saddled!"

Josten began bellowing and the servants rushed to do
his bidding. Within a quarter hour, Ned was on horseback, racing toward London.

He rode through the night, stopping only to drink
or switch out horses at the stations along the way. He
galloped, face taut, leg shrieking in protest, lashed by
fear. His heart thundered in time with the hoof strike on
the road. *No. No. No.*

Dawn opened like an artery along the horizon and
bled into the sky and still he kept on, riding like a man
possessed, holding on to one thought: He had to be there
in time to stop her.

Chapter Thirty-two

Childe Smyth did not prove as great a friend as Lydia had hoped and every bit the pragmatist she had expected. He'd met her request that he lend her fifty thousand pounds with a blank stare and then a laugh. When she'd assured him that she was serious, he told her that regrettably he would not be able to make a loan of that size when he knew for a certainty she would never be able to repay it.

He would, however, make certain she had immediate access to such a sum as soon as she became his bride. Indeed, he would make it part of the marriage contract he could have drawn up that very day, in which he would promise to present her with a personal note for fifty thousand pounds directly after the archbishop signed their wedding license.

He needed a wife, he explained gravely, and soon. She needed fifty thousand pounds even sooner. He suggested they come to an arrangement.

And so they had.

All of which Lydia had expected. But expectation hadn't kept her from hoping.

Feeling like a spectator watching the unfolding

events in her life from some balcony seat, she walked down the church aisle toward where Childe's uncle, the Archbishop of Canterbury, waited. Childe moved slowly at her side. Though her face felt numb and her lips stiff her manner remained composed. But inside a voice was screaming. She ignored it. She would not let Cod send Emily back to the asylum.

She would be strong. She would live with her decision. Other women had married for far less important reasons. Other women had been in love with men they could not wed. Other women—

Oh, God. Oh, God. They were before the altar now and the archbishop was saying something and she could not hear him. All she heard was a rushing in her ears and the remembered sound of Ned's voice saying, "I love you. . . ."

The archbishop peered at her closely and she gulped for air. "M'dear?" he prompted.

"Yes." She hoped it was enough. She hoped that it was appropriate. It was all she could manage.

And then more words, Childe Smyth's voice low in the affirmative, the witnesses murmuring behind her. Where was Ned? What would he think? Would he wonder if she'd decided she could not live without wealth? That she'd changed her mind? Oh . . . Oh!

Her head swam but she held on to consciousness. It was best this way. It was the *only* way.

The archbishop pronounced them man and wife.

Chapter Thirty-three

Lydia sat at the ornate dressing table in the bedchamber where Childe had had her things brought. Emily was somewhere else in the house, in some room Childe had assigned her at Lydia's insistence. And she was alone. She heard a sound in the hall and turned her head as Childe appeared in the doorway between the bedroom and dressing room. She turned back around and with a shaking hand put down the pen she had been using to write to Ned.

She closed her eyes. She had thought she would have more time to grow used to the idea, that at least she would be able to finish her business with Cod before Childe—before. She wasn't ready. She would never be ready. Never.

She bit down hard on her lip, her spine stiffening as though in rigor mortis.

"I am sorry," Smyth whispered. His tone was stricken, even anguished, and she opened her eyes to meet his in the mirror.

Lydia's husband was crying. Tears welled in his eyes and his lower lip trembled with his effort to contain himself.

Amazed, she pivoted. "Mr. Smyth? Your grandfathe
Is he . . . ?"

"No. No, the old bastard draws breath yet. It's jus
that . . ." He stopped and came into the room at a foo
dragging pace, approached the high, four-poster be
sitting like a sacrificial altar in the middle of the roon
He sat down on its edge, his hands hanging betwee
his knees, and gave a long, shaky sigh, staring at th
carpet.

"I have never been unfaithful," he said sadly. "Neve
once in all these years."

She didn't know what to think, what he was talkin
about; she only perceived that somehow she'd gaine
a reprieve from her inevitable marital bedding. Relie
however short-lived, set her to trembling. She could no
imagine being intimate with this man, a stranger to he
in so many ways, doing something so profound, so sig
nificant as the act she and Ned had shared. "I beg you
pardon?"

"She will be so hurt," he murmured to himself, slov
tears trickling from the corners of his eyes. "She won'
understand."

"I'm afraid I don't either, Mr. Smyth," she said cau
tiously. "To whom are you referring and what won't sh
understand?"

"Kitty," he said, his face stricken with misery. "M
beautiful little Kitty."

Amazement supplanted confusion. Could he b
referring to a cat? Had she married a madman? Oh
dear. "What of your little kitty, Mr. Smyth?" she aske
carefully.

But he wasn't listening to her. He shook his head vig

orously, his lower lip thrusting out in a resolute pout. "It's no good. I can't bed you."

"Ah!" Her breath came out in a gasp of relief and she fumbled for the support of her table. "*Oh, thank you!*" Tears sprang to her eyes and she swiped them from her cheeks. "And thank your wonderful, glorious feline."

Childe Smyth's dark brows drew together in a vee. "What feline?"

"Kitty."

"Kitty's not a cat. Kitty's my mistress!" he said, clearly astonished.

"Oh. Oh?"

He nodded, his misery slowly returning. "She's been my mistress for eleven years and in all that time I have never been false to her. I have never even been tempted. And she has been just as true to me. All those years . . ." He sniffed. "I was just come to town, down from Eton. I didn't have much. I hadn't inherited my dad's business concerns yet. I was just a green-headed boy with the faint stink of the shop on me." He looked up to see how she took this and his smile grew an edge. "But I will not be looked down on any more than my grandfather. My aunt married a marquis, my father was knighted before he died. And me? I've married Lady Lydia Eastlake. My standing in Society is not only assured but it's now incontestable."

His expression had become pugnacious, but she saw only a young man with the faint stink of shop, hungry for entrée and approbation. "You were telling me about Kitty," she prompted.

His mouth relaxed into a smile. "Yes. Kitty," he said. "She was just sixteen, newly arrived from Spain and the most gorgeous creature I had ever seen. She still is. She could have had her pick of any number of protectors, far wealthier and, needless to say, far more illustrious than I. But she chose me," he said with evident pride. "She loves me."

"And you love her," Lydia suggested

He glanced quickly up at her to see if she was making sport of him, and seeing she was not, he sighed. "Yes. I suppose I do."

"And always will."

"I expect so. So, you see, I'm sorry, but I'm afraid our marriage will have to be one in name only because, for the life of me, I could not live with myself if I were untrue to the truest and dearest of creatures." He gave her an apologetic shrug.

For a second she could only stare at him and then all the pain, all the rage, all the loss and heartbreak and unhappiness of the last twelve hours came boiling up and erupted from her lips. "*Then why the bloody hell did you marry me and not her?*"

He gaped at her.

"You say you love her, you needed a wife, and there is"—she bit off the word—"there *was* no legal or moral reason keeping you from asking for her hand in marriage and yet you did not. By God," Lydia spat, fury such as she'd never known filling her, "if the woman is stupid enough and has so little regard for herself that she would stay with you after this, she deserves whatever unfeeling treatment you give her."

"Don't say that!" Childe shouted, leaping to his feet.

"Why not? It's true."

"I couldn't marry her. She's . . . she's my mistress!"

"Ha! As though no man has ever married his mis-
ess," Lydia said, sweeping aside his excuse. "If you seek
emulate the highest orders, Mr. Smyth, best start by
owing a spine. All great men have one."

"Kitty—"

"Kitty may as well be a cat for all the consideration
u've given her."

"That's a lie!" he shouted, stomping toward her. "I
ve her!"

She flung her head back, impaling him with a fiery
are. "You love your consequence far more. And may
keep you company with all your money, because they
all end up being your only companions."

For a long moment they stared at each other, Lydia's
in high, Childe's face red with indignation and hurt.
nd then, abruptly, all the fight went out of him and be-
re her eyes, he seemed to crumble in on himself. His
ad fell forward and he reached trembling hands up to
s face.

"What am I going to do?"

She looked down at him, her husband, and felt only
ty. He could have married for love and chose not to.
hat a fool. He looked up at her, his eyes red-rimmed
d bleary. "What am I going to do?"

The mantel clock tolled and wearily she looked at
It was three thirty. All the anger drained from her.
hilde's attack of remorse had only been a distraction
om what needed to be done.

Time to go.

"You are going to give me your personal note for fifty
ousand pounds," she said in a hollow voice.

*   *   *

A commotion filled Childe's downstairs hallway. Shou[t]
followed and the sound of running footsteps. He hea[r]
glass breaking and the heavy thud of something fallin[g]

Childe barely noted it. He sat at the dressing tab[le]
his head buried in his arms. What had he done? G[od]
help him, what had he done?

More voices, more thumping. Heavy footsteps surge[d]
up the stairs. Doors slammed open and shut in succe[s]-
sion, growing ever nearer. Childe raised his head. Th[e]
door flew open, shuddering on its hinges.

Ned Lockton stood in the frame, breathing heavil[y]
His coat was open over an unbuttoned shirt, the ta[il]
hanging over his breeches. His boots were mud spa[t]-
tered and his hair disheveled, his jaw dark and unshave[n]
But it was his eyes that arrested. Those light, gentle gr[ay]
eyes. They shone with a bright, lethal kind of madne[ss]
Lockton's stance was wide, as though he stood on [a]
pitching deck.

"Good God, man," Childe said with a humorle[ss]
laugh. "You really must fire your valet."

Lockton was on him in a half-dozen strides, lifti[ng]
him by his lapels out of his chair and shaking him like [a]
dog. "Where is she?"

Childe didn't need to ask whom Lockton mean[t]
"Gone."

With a snarl, Lockton released him, shoving hi[m]
away. "Where?"

Childe tried to muster some sangfroid, some prid[e]
How dare Lockton besiege him in his home. "That[']
none of your business."

With a growl Lockton seized him again. Childe didn[']

care. Nothing this man did to him could compare to what he'd done to himself. Kitty . . . !

"Try to keep her from me," Lockton ground out, "and I will kill you."

He meant it. Childe could see that in his burning eyes, his haunted face, feel it in the fury and anguish pouring out of him. Had he thought this man passionless? A shiver of fear pierced his misery.

"Wait!" he cried as Lockton grabbed hold of his throat. "She needed money. She needed fifty thousand pounds by four o'clock this afternoon. She was to meet Cod at the bottom of the Tower Stairs at the docks."

Lockton dropped him and spun around, heading out the door.

Chapter Thirty-four

Lydia's pelisse was no help against the raw wind blowing in off the Thames, carrying with it the stench of fish and brine. Sewage from the ships anchored farther out in the river sloshed against the bottom steps of the ancient stone stairs leading down from the street to the wharfs. Green weeds undulated in the wash. Overhead gulls keened and wheeled and a lean cat slinked by, eyeing her as an interloper.

She shivered, looking about for Cod. He said he would meet her here at the bottom of the Tower Stairs at four o'clock. It was quarter past that time.

Emily waited with the coachman some little ways down the street above. She hadn't wanted Emily to come, but the older woman had been downstairs in the hall when she'd left, the sad little nosegay of scarlet primrose she'd worn to the wedding wilting on her bodice, her eyes red-rimmed. Lydia had brought her along when it became clear how desperately uncomfortable Emily was in this stranger's house but made her promise to stay in the carriage, purposely keeping her mission a secret. She didn't want Emily to know about Cod.

"Sorry to keep a lady waiting."

Lydia jerked around. Cod was coming along the mold-slick embankment. He made her side and tipped his hat. "Got the money, then?"

"Yes."

"Then let's have it."

Wordlessly she reached into her reticule and withdrew the check Childe had made out to her and handed it to him.

"What's this?"

"A personal check to me from Childe Smyth. I have already made it over to you." She stared at it with anguished eyes. As soon as it was cashed, Childe would have fulfilled his part of the marriage settlement.

He took it with a smirk and raised it to the sky, eying it carefully. His tongue flicked out and wet the corner of his mouth and his gaze fell on her, amused and cruel. "Now, then, that weren't so bad, was it? Likely to hurt even less next time."

She froze. "What do you mean?"

He shrugged. "Just meaning that should I ever run into trouble, it's nice to know I have friends I can count on to help me out."

"You said there wouldn't be a next time," she said. "You promised."

"Did I?" he asked innocently. "What was I thinking?"

"You can't do this."

"Sure I can." He smirked.

And of course he could. He would. He'd lied. There were no men waiting for him in other countries. No one had recognized him here. It had all been part of his pattern, to make her feel confident that if she gave him what

he wanted, he would be gone from her life. From Emily's life. But he wouldn't be gone. Not ever. He would
always be there, a threat hanging over them.

And what would happen should—no, *when*—Childe
finally refused to pay?

She stared at Cod. He *had* committed crimes here.
The reports that had led Lydia to Emily had stated as
much. So she could have Cod arrested. . . . His lips were
twisted in cruel amusement. No. She couldn't because
he would not hesitate to make good his promise to send
Emily to Bedlam if she did.

They were not safe from him. It had all been for nothing. She'd married Childe for nothing. Ned . . .

Darkness crowded the edge of her vision and her
head swam with the implications. She had given up
Ned just to put herself in this vile creature's clutches.
Rage such as she had never felt rushed through her,
making her limbs shake and filling her vision with a
dark mist. She wasn't going to let this happen. She
wasn't going to lose Ned only to be subject to this vermin's blackmail.

"Not going to wish me *au revoir*, then?" he asked and
chuckled.

"Rot in hell," she spat in a voice vibrating with
anger.

His smirk turned to a nasty snarl. "Well, then, I guess
I'll just settle for a kiss good-bye. And you won't protest
now, will you? No, you wouldn't dare."

She backed away from him, reviled. He stalked forward, matching each of her retreating steps until her
back banged into the stone wall behind her. He thrust
his face up close to hers and using the check to lift her

hin, leaned in close. She glared at him. His breath stank
f cheap liquor.

"Just consider it an advance on future proceeds."

Without warning, she snatched the check from his
and and ripped it in half, crumpling the pieces and hurl-
ig them into the Thames before he even realized what
1e'd done. His mouth gaped as he watched the pieces
virl and dance away on the murky water. A sense of
lation filled her. At least she was free of one mistake!

He stared after the ripped check, a string of vile,
pittle-punctuated epitaphs issuing from his mouth.
hen he turned toward her, a vein bulging in his neck.

She would not show this creature any fear. "What's
rong, Mr. Cod?" she sneered. "Don't you know how
o swim?"

"You bloody bitch!" His hand swung up as quick as a
riking snake and his backhanded blow knocked her to
1e ground, hard against the bottom of the stairs leading
p to the street. Lights splinting and rocketing across
er vision, pain exploding in her head. She looked up,
azed, and saw him towering over her, his mouth a red
ash. He gave a snort and stepped toward her again, but
omething caught his eye and she saw him lift his head,
poking behind her. Whatever he saw caused the color
o bleed from his ruddy face.

She slumped against the stone step, biting back
gainst a wave of nausea and looked around. A tall,
road-shouldered figure was coming down the embank-
1ent, his open coat billowing behind him, his shirt half-
nbuttoned over his bare chest. His gold head was bare
nd his face set in dark, savage lines. The wind ruffled
is hair and flickered his collar, and now he was close

enough she could see his eyes gleaming like liquid silve
both hot and cold.

Ned.

This is who the men who'd fought against him saw
she thought muzzily. *This is who led men into battle. Th*
terrible avenging beauty.

He made her side, scooping her up in his arms an
setting her on her feet. "For the love of God, tell me yo
are all right," he said thickly.

She nodded, bracing herself against the oozing ston
wall. His shivering hand raced over her head, shoulder
and arms. And then he turned his head.

Lydia did not see what Cod did. She saw only hi
reaction. He stumbled back a step, then another, the
turned to run. Too late.

Ned surged forward like some infernal machine, hi
long legs eating up the distance between them in second
his boot heels striking the pavement like a hammer on a
anvil. He did not stop, he simply raised his arm and seize
Cod by the neck and with a savage roar, half lifted him
propelling him back and slamming him into the wall.

Cod hung from Ned's one hand while Ned pummele
his face with his other. Blood exploded from Cod's nose
He seized the wrist of the hand pinning him to the wal
digging his nails and twisting, striking out with his boot
to kick savagely at Ned's legs.

If Ned felt any of it, there was no sign. He just kep
backhanding Cod's face, punishing him, battering him
his teeth bared in a feral half snarl as the fight slowl
drained from Cod and the clawing hands grew weak.

"Help! Help!" Cod choked out, and when no help
came sobbed, "For the love of God, he's killing me!"

Only then did Lydia realize Cod was speaking the truth: *Ned was killing him.* The very reason she hadn't gone to Ned in the first place was coming nightmarishly true before her eyes. She would not lose him now to the murder of this vermin!

Lydia pitched herself at the men, grabbing at the steely arm still holding Cod upright and pulling. "No, Ned! No! You mustn't!" she pleaded. "Please, Ned! Stop!"

She pushed her way under his arm and pressed between him and Cod. She flung her arms around his neck and cried against his chest, "Stop, Ned! He's not worth it. Stop!"

She felt him draw a ragged breath. A shudder rippled through his big body and then Cod was free, gasping and choking as he scrambled up the Tower Stairs.

Ned pushed her away from him, starting after Cod just as a shout came from the top of the stairs. Lydia turned to look up toward the street.

Emily stood at the top, her eyes stark in her bloodless face. Cod had grabbed hold of her and as Lydia watched, Emily's mouth opened in a soundless scream and she shoved the burly man back with all the power of her hate and fear.

For a second, Cod teetered on the top step and then his arms were flailing wildly as he sought to regain his balance. Blindly, he reached out but only managed to grab a fistful of Emily's thin jacket. All Emily would need to do to save him was to seize his wrist and jerk him forward to safety.

Time held suspended. Emily stared at his white-knuckled fist, clutching the lapel with its sad nosegay of flowers. Then, with a movement Lydia would never be able to say for a certainty was a conscious act or one of instinctive revulsion, Emily recoiled. With a roar of fury, Cod pitched backward.

Lydia gasped at the sound of his head striking the stone and Ned snatched her away from the bottom of the steps as Bernard Cod tumbled down. Lydia had a brief glimpse of his head twisted at a grotesque angle, eyes bulging, a single red flower still clutched in one hand. Then Ned was pulling her away, turning her from the horrible sight.

He looked down at her. "You have to leave. Now."

"I won't—"

"You will!" he ground out. "You will let me protect you from scandal and the only way I can do that is if you leave now." He pushed her away. "*Go!*"

He was right. With a sob, she stumbled up the Tower Stairs. Emily stood waiting for her. Her face was pale, her expression dazed but also subtly relieved, like that of a woman waking from a nightmare. Which she had. Whether her flinching back had been purposeful or not, whether even Emily could answer that question and whatever the answer might be, Lydia had nothing but sympathy for her friend. Fate could not have provided a more fitting or just end for Cod.

Emily searched her face, her eyes fearful and worried. She needn't be. Lydia didn't say a word, only put her arm around Emily's shoulders and led her away

Chapter Thirty-five

In a semiprivate room of Boodle's club, Ned had commanded the drapes be drawn against the bright sun whose rare appearance this summer he could only view as some form of celestial mockery. He sat sunken into a deep chair, his hands curled around the end of the arms, his chin on his chest. At a table beside him sat a decanter three-quarters filled with brandy. The level had not appreciably changed in the week since he had taken up residence here.

He regretted that. He would certainly have been drunk had he found solace there. He didn't. No amount of spirits could obliterate the blithe phantom that danced and laughed and yearned in his mind's eye. Instead, he was forced to live through each interminable minute and see clearly the long empty progress of those that awaited him.

Lydia was married.

One would think he would have grown used to the idea by now. He hadn't. The realization lived in him like a cancer, eroding his ability to concentrate, to act. In one short day, she had been taken from him as effectively as if she had dropped to the bottom of the ocean. Only this

was worse. Because gone though she was, she was no
absent. If he stayed in London, he was certain to read
about her and . . . Smyth. *See her*.

God help him, he could not.

So, for the first time in his life, Ned Lockton played
craven and hid from what he could not bear. He knew
himself to be a strong man. A durable man. He'd sailed
around the Cape of Good Hope and chased down pirates
And he had done so with cool presence of mind and resolve that had netted him the nickname "Oak-hearted
Ned." But Lydia Eastlake had brought him to his knees.

He steepled his fingertips under his chin, staring
broodingly at a small pile of unopened letters. They
were from her and he could neither bring himself to
read them nor fling them into the fire. So they stayed
taunting and tempting and tormenting him.

Did she explain herself? He didn't want to hear the
explanations because nothing she said could make him
forgive what she'd done.

Did she apologize? Worse.

Or did she grieve over her choice?

Worst of all.

Because if one word she penned betrayed a single
note of suffering he would tear down Smyth's door to
get to her and nothing would be able to stop him: not
honor or morality, no principle or prince, no law of man
or church.

So they piled up by his hand, day after day. A footman most often brought them, laying them quietly on
the table, never commenting on their unread state. He
allowed no one else in his lair, shutting the door against
all and any company.

He would leave soon. Perhaps tomorrow, perhaps the next day. He'd written the company that had previously offered him the captaincy of one of their long-ranging ships and accepted. There was nothing left in England for him but pain.

A commotion broke out somewhere in the club's front rooms. Someone's horse won a race or some politician's latest bribe was revealed, he thought without interest. He poured a single finger of brandy and set it down untouched, tilting his head. The shouts outside did not have a celebratory quality. They sounded outraged, dumbfounded, incensed.

He sat forward, preparing to go out and meet whatever threatened his sanctuary, however temporary. A thief or some jug-bitten would-be Gentleman Jackson, eager to prove himself.

"The sooner you would simply tell me where he is, the sooner I will be gone!" he heard a woman declare in autocratic tones.

A woman? *The* woman.

Her.

He rose to his feet, at the door in a trice, and flung it wide. Lydia stood at the end of the hall surrounded by a circle of gentlemen and footmen, milling and barking at her like a pack of little dogs around a particularly vicious lioness. She was magnificent in her disdain, nonchalantly peeling off her gloves as she ignored the commands of the yapping men.

"Are you by chancing looking for me, ma'am?" he asked from the doorway.

At the sound of his voice, her head snapped up and the smile and eagerness that broke over her beautiful face took his breath away. How could he let her go now that he'd seen her again? Did she know what she risked by coming here? And not only to her reputation.

At the expression on his face, however, the joy faded. She took a small breath and raised her chin. "Why, yes, Captain Lockton. I am."

In answer, he stepped aside from the door and bowed deeply, sweeping his hand toward the anteroom in an invitation to enter. Again her chin hitched up and she sailed toward him, the men before her fussing and fuming.

"You must leave here at once, Lady Lydia! At once!"

"Captain Lockton, women are not allowed in this club!"

"Lady Lydia, you cannot be here!"

"Consider your membership, sir, to be revoked!"

Neither Lydia nor he paid the men or their lackeys the slightest heed. Lydia glided past Ned into the room. He turned around, shutting the door behind him.

"Ma'am?" he said, inclining his head.

Whatever she read in his face caused her to blush and her sangfroid to falter.

"Why haven't you answered my letters?" she demanded.

"Forgive me if something you wrote required an answer. I have not yet read them," he said. God, she was beautiful. A pale green bonnet framed her fine-boned face, the tilted eyes luminous in the dim light of the cloistered room. Her lips were paler than he recalled, her skin more fragile looking. Was Smyth treating her well? He didn't even dare ask.

"You didn't read them?" she repeated.

"No, ma'am."

"Why not?" she demanded, coming closer to him.

He did not know how he could reply. *Because the pain is already nigh unbearable?* And how would that admission help either of them?

So instead he simply bowed his head and said, "Forgive my rudeness, Mrs. Smyth."

Her eyes widened in what looked like surprise. "I hope you are not addressing me, sir, because that title belongs to another."

He frowned, uncertain of what she meant, only certain that he must be misinterpreting it. "Excuse me, ma'am, but I do not take your meaning."

"Had you read my letters," she said, a little storm brewing in the deep purple eyes, "you would already know my meaning, Captain. I am not Mrs. Smyth. I am Lady Lydia Eastlake. My marriage to Mr. Smyth has been annulled."

A strong man, indeed. But she'd already taken him out at the knees once and now she did so again. His breath came out in a whoosh, as though he'd taken a blow. "How?" he demanded, eyes riveted on hers. "*How?*"

"Before we wed by special license, Mr. Smyth signed a contract in front of witnesses in which he promised to deliver to me the sum of fifty thousand pounds by four o'clock Wednesday last. Mr. Smyth did not deliver—at least that is what he told his godfather, the Archbishop of Canterbury, and since no check was ever cashed, the archbishop was obliged to annul the marriage on the grounds of fraud." For the first time a smile touched her face, a gamin smile he found irresistible. "In return for a substantial bequest." She tipped an eyebrow at him.

He could not speak. He didn't trust himself to move. He'd thought all hope dead and now, suddenly, to discover it was not. His heart beat painfully in his chest, his throat closing with emotion.

She frowned and swallowed, a little nervous. "Which Mr. Smyth happens to be able to provide as he has recently come into a great inheritance having followed certain stipulations of his deceased grandfather—God rest his soul—by marrying before the old gentleman died." She glanced at him. "Oh, not me. As you well know, the church does not consider that an annulled marriage was ever a marriage at all. No, Mr. Smyth has married a Miss Kitty La Grasa."

Her face pokered up as she considered. "I wonder how much of the ready Mr. Smyth has laid out for special service from the church this month." She looked at him. "What do you think?"

"Why didn't you come to me?" His words came out in a hoarse whisper. "Why didn't you trust me? When I saw Cod strike you I *died* that I was not there to take the blow, to protect you, to shield you, that you had not given me that right! If he had—" He broke off, unable to go further.

The insouciance fled from Lydia's expression, revealing her pain. "There was no time. I did not dare. I was afraid you would kill him."

He shook his head.

"I wrote. I explained. I told you when the annulment proceeded. I told you when it was signed. I sent word by messenger, by letter, by emissary. And this"—she made a quick sweeping gesture around the room—"bastion of male solidarity refuses to admit ladies under any circumstances." Her lips pressed together primly. "Until today, and they had no choice lest they wished to physically assault a lady."

And he had not given her the benefit of reading her words. He had not trusted her. For long minutes they stood regarding each other, Ned raked by guilt over the wrong he'd done her, and Lydia waiting for some sign, some indication of his feelings. But Ned was ever good at concealing his emotions and suddenly, abruptly, she'd had enough.

"For the love of God, Ned," she finally burst out. "Why am I always fated to be the pursuer? Why am I always so rashly exhibiting love that you so carefully conceal? What must I do to persuade *you* to work at attaining *me*?"

His eyes widened.

Her ire was rising as she spoke, her indignation fanning the color in her cheeks, the brilliance in her eyes. "First the maze, then the Spencers' masquerade, then I come to your town house, and now, now this! I am worse than Caro Lamb, by God, I am. And I will not have it any longer. I have pride, *too*, Captain Lockton, and I am *done* with you and your much vaunted honor—"

And then he was before her, sweeping her up into his arms and kicking open the anteroom door and striding down the hallowed, women-free halls of Boodle's, past the gape-mouthed members and the laughing attendants. She gasped and clung to his neck as he kicked open another door and they were outside and he was striding down St. James.

Horses reared as their drivers checked in astonishment, passersby bumped into one another as they ogled and strained to see, shopkeepers and their clients ran out their doors, and street urchins fell in line behind them, laughing and hooting. And in the fashionable bow window of White's, the dandies spontaneously stood and applauded.

Down St. James he strode, Lydia locked tight in his embrace, heading for the office of the Archbishop of London, whose mother, perchance, happened to have the maiden name of Lockton. He only paused once to look down at her, and nothing was concealed in his expression.

"I love you, ma'am," he said. "And you shall never be done with me."

It was noon in Little Firkin, Scotland. Not a traditional witching hour—midnight being considered more conducive to mayhem and maledictions—but as the townsfolk were always fast asleep by midnight and unwitnessed mayhem was generally acknowledged amongst witchly communities to be a wasted effort, it would have to do.

Besides, every indication suggested that noon was the new midnight. To wit: At exactly twelve o'clock a cock crowed, the bell tower clock struck *thirteen* times, and a weird sound (which later would be identified by a certain skeptic as the Bristol–Fort George train but right now was pretty much universally recognized as the cry of a soul consigned to hell) echoed mournfully through the tiny hamlet.

Otherwise it was a perfectly lovely spring day. The sun glimmered on the river dancing along the town's eastern boundary and shimmered on the snowcapped mountains encircling the small valley that sheltered Little Firkin.

Lovely day or not, what with the clock, the cock, and the eerie moan, the people of Little Firkin—no strangers to portents, portents being their bread and butter, so to speak—stopped what they were doing and paid attention. Those leaning over their back fence for their daily chin-wag hurried to the front yard, while those inside poked their heads out of their front doors. Half a dozen shopkeepers and an equal number of tavern owners—Little Firkians having long ago discovered that living in close proximity with the supernatural was a thirsty business—crowded their windows to see what Something Wicked This Way Came.

On cue, a wind nickered to life in one of the town's few alleys and skittered forth, kicking up a dust devil of leaves and halfpenny candy wrappers as a voice like a strangled cat pealed through the town center.

"Aieeeee!"

Little Firkin rubbed its collective hands together in anticipation. Women with small children shoved their tots behind them, while those with older brats squawked and flapped their arms, shooing them off the street like hens quarantining chicks before a storm. The old geezers in town towed their stools out to get a ringside seat at the anticipated proceedings.

They were not disappointed.

An ancient crone with a face like a withered apple appeared at the end of the town's main thoroughfare midst a swirl of dust, her raggedy multicolored skirts shedding bits of decaying lace along with the crumbs from her morning's biscuit.

"Aieeeee!" The hag's screech broke into a coughing fit that ended only after she expelled a bit of cat hair. She hoisted an oak bole over her head on stringy little arms and cried, "I come to take Little Firkin!"

A collective gasp of consternation and pleasure rose from the onlookers. A witch-off sounded just the thing for a fine spring day, and this promised to be a right doozy of a witch-off.

For half a dozen years, the old crone at center stage, Grammy Beadle, had been trying to lay her witchly claim over Little Firkin. She lived in Beadletown, twenty miles away up in the mountains, and not a town at all but a ramshackle collection of disreputable crofts populated entirely by Beadles—a race of cattle thieves and malingerers.

About ten years ago one of Grammy Beadle's grandchildren, in what was doubtless an attempt to find something other than her family with which to occupy the old hag, had convinced Grammy that she oughtn't hide her light under a bushel and should think of extending her reign of terror—or, more succinctly, reign of annoyance—to the other hamlets in the vicinity. It shouldn't be too hard, this same sanguine grandchild had explained, there not being many witches anymore. And as for the upkeep on Grammy's potential realm, it would involve only a bit of travel now and again to check up on the constituency.

Grammy Beadle liked the idea. Within a year, she was not only the Witch of Beadletown but the Witch of

Ben's Tavern (Ben and his way station, even by Gramm
Beadle's admittedly liberal definitions, not being worth
of hamlet status) and a year after that the Witch of Tha
Pisshole East of Where All Those Damned Beadle
Live.

From there she had turned her malignant gaze sout
toward the metropolis of Little Firkin, population 21
and it was here that her March of Irritation abruptl
stopped. Coming out of the post office at the far end o
town was the person who'd stopped her: a red-haired
very pretty, and very young lady dressed in the height o
Parisian fashion.

Her appearance gave even Grammy pause. Hun
dreds of miles from the nearest city, cloistered by ringin
mountains and raging rivers, marooned in a backwater o
time and place while the rest of the world charged ahea
with industrial fervor, a fashion plate was as unexpecte
as a kootchie dancer at a church social.

A rakishly tilted scrap of straw was perched atop a
ingeniously arranged pile of flame-colored hair, whil
an ostrich feather, dyed to match the periwinkle brai
edging a close-fitting velvet jacket, caressed a softl
rounded cheek. Her skirts molded snugly about a wom
anly derriere before belling out into extravagant yard
of green plaid that brushed the plank sidewalk. Th
open parasol resting on her shoulder dappled her prett
face with sunlight.

Grammy Beadle let out a shriek. "Stop, witch! I com
to take Little Firkin from ye!"

The young lady, about to say something to her com
panion, a slender woman as arresting in her dark hand

omeness as the girl was in her vibrant prettiness, turned
around and faced Grammy.

"I come to take Little Firkin from ye!" the old woman
repeated, hobbling down the center of the street.

"Why bother?" the very young lady asked, the light-
est trace of a Highlands accent in her voice. "I'll just give
it to you."

The old woman's lips compressed. "Oh, no, missy. I'll
not have it said the Witch of Beadletown come by her
dark empire through the pity of a young 'un."

"That's absurd."

"That's the way it be," grumped Grammy Beadle.

The girl cast an imploring glance at her sable-haired
companion. "Just a few minutes?"

"Oh, ballocks," that lady muttered quite clearly. "But
do try to hurry things up a bit, won't you?" And, taking
the girl's parasol, she retreated to a bench outside the
grocer's.

"Ye canna hurry dark magik," Grammy snapped,
reaching into the tattered velvet bag hanging around
her scrawny neck. With an evil cackle, she flung a fistful
of something into the air—something that apparently
had hard bits in it, because she yelped when the wind
blew it back in her face. "Ouch!"

"What was that?" the young lady asked curiously.

"Magik! Magiks made with the feet of a white mouse
born during the full moon."

At this, the young lady's hand flew up to cover her
lips. "You chopped off a baby mouse's feet?" she whispered from behind her fingertips.

Grammy squirmed. "Well, maybe the mouse was still-

born. And maybe it weren't white but it were *very* ligh
gray. But no doubt, 'twere a full moon."

"That's disgusting," the fashion plate said, setting he
hands on her hips. "I am afraid I cannot allow some
one who would chop off baby mice feet, even dead baby
mice, to move into the neighborhood. You will have to
go away."

"No, 'tis *you* who will have to go!"

"I am afraid not."

"I am afraid so—"

"Get *on* with it, will you?" someone shouted.

With a flourish Grammy whipped open her patched
cloak and twirled around. "By the hair of Beelzebub's
chin, by the cloven foot of Bacchus, I expel thee, oh
witch!"

The young lady remained unexpelled, but stood by
politely. Finally, Grammy threw her hands up in frustration. "What are ye doin', you cluck? Spell me!"

"You're done?" the girl asked. "I assumed there was
more to it than that."

Grammy's little sunken face collapsed in on itself
even more. "Of course there's more. I was just giving
you a chance to run away, is all."

Once more, she hefted her stick over her head. "By
Moobkamizer's black heart and Nimbleplast's hor—"

"Who?" the young lady interrupted. "I've never
heard of those two."

Grammy's arms sank and she grinned, revealing a
dimple of such unexpected charm that it went far in
explaining the hitherto unsolved mystery of why there
existed so many Beadles. "That's because they're brand-
new demons."

"Really?" the young lady asked. "How frightfully in-
:sting. Where did you find them?"

'Come to me in my dreams," Grammy said proudly,
then with a sly glance at the townsfolk added, "As
incubus. And I gots more, too. By Shillyman's wart
... and ... Cobbiepouff's whisker, I take what was
s and make it mine. Begone." She spun around. "Be-
e!" She spun around again. "Begone!"

At the end of this last and most violent spin, Grammy
ched sideways, her hand outstretched and her eyes
ling. "I think I'm going to be sick," she said with a
p.

The young lady grabbed the hag's arm, steadying her.
t down."

Gratefully, the old lady plopped down in the middle
he street, holding her side. "Yer turn," she wheezed.

"Come, now. This can wait until you are feeling more
thing—"

"Yer turn!" Grammy insisted.

"Very well," the young lady replied. She took a deep
ath, lifted her hands, palms up to the sky, and pro-
unced in a loud, ringing voice, "Ipse dixit."

Grammy froze like someone who'd taken a spitball
t to the bum. "What? Who's that? What's that?"

"Ipse dixit," the girl repeated. She waved her hands
a circle. "Ipso facto. Ad hoc!"

Anxiously, Grammy patted herself down from head
foot. Upon discovering that everything was in the
ne place it had been that morning, she relaxed. "Yer
gik seems to have left you, missy," she said.

The young lady very discreetly glanced overhead.
ammy Beadle followed her gaze. Directly above them

two dark shadows were making slow, lazy circles in
tranquil blue sky.

"So what?" Grammy said. "A pair of birds."

Nonetheless, she scrambled up and surged forw
on one foot, like a fencer executing a lunge, stabbing
the young lady with her bole. "By the Name of He W
Goes Unnamed and Is Nameless, I take your power a
your towwwwnnnnnn!"

The girl raised a slender finger to her mouth a
nipped the edge of the nail off between her pearly tee
Again, her glance rose to the sky. Grammy's unwill
gaze followed.

The pair of ravens had been joined by a half do
others describing slow pirouettes. A distinctly uneasy
pression crossed Grammy's face. As a witch, Gram
Beadle was extremely conversant with all things of
natural world, and the sudden appearance of a host
silent ravens . . . well, it wasn't natural.

"Dark powers, unite! Heed me, Bacchus, Beel
bub, Moobkamizer, and Nimbleplast, Shillyman, and
and . . ." She trailed off as the young lady, examining
torn nail on her left hand, made a slight indication s
ward with her right.

With a scowl, Grammy looked up.

Twenty ravens?

Furtively, she glanced around, gauging the Lit
Firkians' reactions to the flock of malevolent dea
harbingers. If they had seen the ravens, they apparen
didn't think much of them—except, that was, for the gi
companion, who was leaning forward, frowning up
the sky. The rest of Little Firkin was watching Gramm
and their expressions were frankly disappointed. Eve

ttle pitying. And pity, Grammy Beadle knew, was not a
ood foundation upon which to build a witchly empire.
he'd better get rid of these heebie-jeebies and—

Caw!

The salutary sound sent her gaze overhead. A single
aven was winging its way to join the other—Grammy's
nouth gaped—forty ravens. All silent. Silent as the
omb. Grammy's skin crawled.

Maybe she didn't need to take over the town. Least-
vays, not today.

Still, pride kept her rooted. She'd never live it down
f word got out that a bunch of birds had driven her
ff. Which meant she needed to provide a good reason
or turning tail and running. And what better reason
an—

"Is that all?" Grammy shouted. "Is that the best you
an do? Come on, lass. Give it yer best!"

The young lady's face reflected a second of surprise
efore tightening. "No. That's not all. *Amo!*" she said,
king a step forward.

Gratefully, Grammy commenced quaking.

"Amas!"

Another step. This time Grammy's hand flew to her
hest.

"Amat!"

Grammy staggered back as if impelled by some mon-
trous unseen force. She whimpered for added effect.

The young lady, after a brief look of bewilderment,
ubbed her palms briskly together as if preparing for
ome physical exertion and declared, "Per diem. Non
equitur." Her hand rose toward Grammy Beadle, who
vas now fully engaged in cringing backward.

"E PLURIBUS UNUM!"

With a shriek, Grammy Beadle lifted up her skir displaying a pair of crooked shanks encircled by ir probable red garters, turned tail and shot off down th street, disappearing into a side alley.

The young lady, after a glance overhead at a sky nc completely free of any shadows, ravenlike or otherwi; walked calmly over to her companion. The Little Firk ans gave one another nods of approval and, without single word to their champion and defender, went bac to gossiping, eating, and drinking.

At the same time, a handsome and elegant youn man let a curtain drop back down across the pub wi dow through which he'd been watching.

"What an extraordinary creature. Whatever is sl doing here?" the young gentleman asked, turning h bemused gaze to a man sitting tipped well back in th chair opposite him, a dark, broad-shouldered gentlema with sooty, overlong hair and piercing blue-green eye currently riveted on the scene outside.

Before he could reply, the inn's rotund barkeep a rived at their table bearing two tankards of ale. "That t Amelie Chase," he said. "Our witch."

Also Available From

CONNIE BROCKWAY

Skinny Dipping

Mimi Olsen is crushed to learn that her
family's Minnesota retreat is up for sale.
Unless someone can get the cash to save it,
the house that's served as a peaceful anchor
for generations will go under the hammer.
A free spirit like Mimi has the will—what she
needs is a way. Moving back into Chez
Ducky is a start. But when she meets the man
next door, her life is going to change direction
in ways she never imagined.